PRAISE FOR
Kockroach

"Kockroach is well drawn. . . . Knox has a light comic touch." —*New York Times Book Review* (Editor's Choice)

"The plot has the memorable clarity of fable, but it's the creepy-mythic atmospherics . . . that make this one cook. Surreal, standout debut fiction." —*Kirkus Reviews*

"A dark and grimly funny look at what it means to be human today, grandly told." —*Seattle Post-Intelligencer*

"Roaringly entertaining. . . . Knox's inhuman antihero's tale is told in flawless noir style. . . . A compelling story of greed and power." —*Publishers Weekly* (starred review)

"Literary fiction is not often this wildly fun. . . . Nearly everything about this portrait of the cockroach as a young human is artfully executed and signals the emergence of a promising new novelist." —*Seattle Times*

"Adventurous twist on Kafka's dude-turns-into-a-roach ditty." —*Entertainment Weekly*

"An energetic tour de force that will delight lovers of experimental fiction, Kafka aficionados and fans of all things noir. . . . Inventively hilarious." —*USA Today*

"The book's strengths are in its comic touches."

—*Los Angeles Times*

"Kockroach . . . is one of the oddest innocents ever to creep through American literature. . . . Much of *Kockroach* is classic gangster parody. . . . But there's plenty of rueful, Kafkaesque reflection on what it means to be human too. . . . Pick up this witty, unsettling book."

—*Washington Post Book World*

"Original and entertaining. . . . [Knox has a] gift for creating a vibrant, colorful Runyonesque universe with hard-boiled, poetic dialogue."   —*Sunday Oregonian* (Portland)

"A superb and engrossing story, a streetwise fantasy."

—*Buffalo News*

"Fast-moving. . . . The dialogue is hard-boiled snappy, the plot is creative."   —*Palm Beach Post*

"It works . . . on many levels. And it is funny in the bargain. . . . There is astute writing here . . . and memorable flourishes. . . . Read this fine book."   —*Washington Times*

"[A] postmodern head trip . . . [with] a vintage, gritty noir feel."   —*Orlando Sentinel*

"Kafkaesque Kockroach is nuttily charming."

—*Hartford Courant*

Kockroach

KOCKROACH

TYLER KNOX

HARPER ⬤ PERENNIAL

NEW YORK • LONDON • TORONTO • SYDNEY

HARPER ● PERENNIAL

A hardcover edition of this book was published in 2007 by William Morrow, an imprint of HarperCollins Publishers.

P.S.™ is a trademark of HarperCollins Publishers.

FIRST HARPER PERENNIAL EDITION PUBLISHED 2008.

Illustrations by Will Staehle
Designed by Betty Lew

The Library of Congress has catalogued the hardcover edition as follows:

Knox, Tyler.
    Kockroach: a novel / Tyler Knox. — 1st ed.
        p. cm.
    ISBN-13: 978-0-06-114333-5
    ISBN-10: 0-06-114333-2
        1. Cockroaches—Fiction. I. Title.

PS3562.A75249K63 2007
813'.6—dc22
                                                        2006048138

ISBN: 978-0-06-114334-2 (pbk.)

08 09 10 11 12 WBC/RRD 10 9 8 7 6 5 4 3 2 1

For G.S.

And for Mr. G.,
who introduced him to me

A story, for example, something that could never happen, an adventure. It would have to be beautiful and hard as steel and make people ashamed of their existence.

—JEAN-PAUL SARTRE,
La Nausée

PART ONE

THE SWITCH

1

As Kockroach, an arthropod of the genus *Blatella* and of the species *germanica,* awakens one morning from a typically dreamless sleep, he finds himself transformed into some large, vile creature.

He is lying flip side up atop a sagging pad. Four awkwardly articulated legs sprawl on either side of his extended thorax. His abdomen, which once made up the bulk of his body, lies like a flaccid worm between his legs. In the thin light his new body looks ridiculously narrow and soft, its skin beneath a pelt of hair as pale and shriveled as a molting nymph's.

Maybe that is what has happened, maybe he has simply molted. He reflexively swallows air, expecting his abdomen to expand into its normal proud dimensions and the air to swell his body until the skin stretches taut so it can begin hardening to a comforting chocolate brown, but nothing happens. No matter how much air he swallows, his body remains this pale pathetic thing.

A flash of red rips through the crusts of Kockroach's eyes before disappearing, and suddenly, in the frenzied grip of positive thigmotaxis, he wriggles his legs wildly until he tumbles onto the floor. With his legs beneath him now, he scurries under the wooden frame supporting the pad, squirming back and forth, ignoring the pain in his joints, until he has found a comforting pressure on his chest, his back, his side.

Better, much better. The red light snap-crackles on, hissing and glowing throughout the room, slinking beneath the wooden frame before disappearing just as suddenly. It snap-crackles on and disappears again, on-off, on-off. His fear of the light subsides as the pattern emerges, when something else draws his attention.

A rhythmic rush of air, in and out, an ebb and flow coming from somewhere nearby. He turns his head, trying to find the sound's source before he realizes that a peculiar undulation in his chest matches the rhythm of the rushing air.

Cockroaches don't breathe, per se. Instead, air flows passively into openings called spiracles and slides gently through tracheae that encircle their bodies. There is the occasional squeezing of air from the tracheae, yes, but nothing like this relentless pumping of air in and out, in and out. It is terrifying and deafening and unremitting. It is so loud it must be drawing predators. Kockroach spreads his antennae to check his surroundings and senses nothing. He reaches up a claw to clean the receptors and gasps upon finding no antennae there. The sound arising from his throat is shockingly loud, a great anguished squeal that frightens him into silence.

His shock wanes as quickly as it waxed. He doesn't wonder at how this grossly tragic transformation has happened to him. He doesn't fret about the blinking light or gasping breath, about his pale shriveled skin or missing antennae. Cockroaches don't dwell in the past. Firmly entrenched in the present tense, they are awesome coping machines. When his right leg was pulled off by a playful mouse, he hadn't rolled over and whined, he had scampered away and learned to limp on five legs until he grew a new limb with his next molt. Deal with it, that is the cockroach way. When food is scarce, cockroaches don't complain, first they eat their dead, then they eat their young, then they eat each other.

Kockroach blinks his eyes at the growing brightness in the room. He is tired already. He is used to two bouts of feverish activity in the middle of the night and then a long sleep during the day. The dawn light signals him it is time to retire. Pressed against the edge of the wall, his aching limbs jerk beneath him, his back rises to touch the slats of the wooden frame, and he falls asleep.

When Kockroach awakens again it is dark except for the rhythmic pulse of the hissing red light. He is still wedged beneath the wooden frame. His four legs now ache considerably and a line of pain runs through his back.

From beneath the frame he can just make out the contours of the room, its walls and baseboards veined by inviting little cracks. There is a wooden object in the middle of the room, and beside it, floating above the floor, is a piece of meat, the top of which is obscured by the top of the frame.

Kockroach crawls quickly out from under the wooden frame, stops, crawls quickly again, dashes beneath the meat, heads for a lovely little crack he espied from afar. He dives into it and bangs his head on the wall.

He had forgotten for a moment what had happened to him.

Slowly he brings his face down to the crack that seems now so small. In the recess he sees two antennae floating gracefully back and forth. He reaches to the crack, tries to place his claw in the crevice to touch his fellow arthropod. His digits splay, the claw screams in pain. He articulates the digits, five of them, one by one before his face. What a grotesquely useless configuration. He reaches out one digit and guides it to the crack. Only the slightest bit of soft flesh slips in.

Suddenly, he is overwhelmed by a thousand different sensations that seem strangely more real than his bizarre altered presence in that room. The patter of hundreds of feet, the crush of bodies, the blissful stink of the colony. The feel of his antennae rubbing against the antennae of another, pheromones bringing everything to a fever pitch, being mounted from behind, his hooks grabbing hold. The taste of sugar, starch, the desperate run across a patch of open light. He is slipping back through his life. The shedding of old chitin, the taste of it afterward, the delicious feel of his mother's chest upon his back when he was still the smallest nymph. He slides his digit back and forth along the crack in the wall and falls into a pool of remembrance and emotion, both stunning and unexpected.

But sentimental nostalgia is not a cockroach trait, neither is regret, nor deep unsatisfied longing. He had never felt such sensations before and he fights against their unfathomable power with all his strength. Insectile resolve battles mammalian sentimentality for supremacy over this new body until, with a great shout, Kockroach triumphantly climbs out of the strange emotional swirl and falls back into himself.

He won't let this strange molt ruin him. He will stay true

to the purity of the instincts that have guided him safely through the earlier stages of his life. Whatever has happened, whatever will happen in the future, he will forever remain a cockroach.

He traces his digit up the wall, as if the tip itself is an arthropod making its way to the safety of the ceiling. Halfway to the top his claw alights on a dull white plate with a black switch. Cockroaches instinctively try every crevice, search every nook, climb every tilting pile of dishes. It is in their nature to explore. He flicks the switch.

Light floods the room. Panic. He would flee, but to where? He follows his second instinct to hide against a wall and freeze. He spins and presses himself into the corner and moves not a muscle.

He listens for the sound of a predator and hears nothing.

He presses his head so hard into the corner the vertex of his face throbs.

Still nothing.

With a start, he realizes he is standing and the ache he had been feeling in his legs, the pain in his back, are all slowly receding. This is a body that works best vertically. He will adapt, he is a cockroach.

Balancing precariously on two pale slabs of flesh at the bottom of his lower legs, he takes tiny steps as he turns around, his upper legs moving contrapuntally with his lower legs out of long-ingrained habit. And as he turns he examines the now-lit space in which he finds himself. It is in actuality a small pathetic hotel room, green walls that can barely contain a bed and a bureau and a tiny desk, a single window through which the hissing red neon of the hotel's sign can be spied; it is a sad cramped piece of real estate but to Kockroach it is a palace. And in the center, hanging from the source of light, is the piece of meat.

Kockroach is frightened when he sees it there, shaped as it is like a predator, but it is just hanging, not moving, hanging. He determines it is not a threat and his fear subsides.

Still in the corner, he reaches out his upper appendage, an arm now that he is standing vertically, and with his claw flicks down the black switch on the white plate. Darkness.

He flicks it up. Light.

He flicks it down. Darkness.

So that is how they do it.

Up and down, up and down. After an hour of that he leaves the light on and practices walking.

He falls twice, thrice, six times, struggling to stand again after each fall. He is trying to retain the feel of his cockroach walk, when his legs moved forward three at a time while the other three maintained a steady tripod, allowing for sudden stops and quick switches of directions. This body is not so nimble or steady, the center of gravity is absurdly high, but finally, after much trial and error, he comes up with something that feels organic.

He leans back, his weight to the right as he steps forward with his left leg, his right arm rising reflexively with the step, two digits of his right claw pointing up in the shape of a V, like the pincers of the cockroach claw. Then his weight shifts to the left as his right leg steps, left arm rising, two digits of his left claw shaping the V. Back and forth, rhythmic and steady, it becomes a natural movement as he circles the room, first one way, then the other, covering great gulps of distance with each step, stepping over and back, over and again, until it is mastered.

It isn't long before Kockroach wonders how he ever before crawled on his belly or why.

With his walk in place, Kockroach explores. The bed, the bureau, the small desk covered with bizarre fetishistic objects. He takes in the color, size, the shape of these things, without knowing their purposes or names. There is a door he can't open with all manner of metal running down its side, there is an open door leading to a cozy dark little room with cloths hanging from a rod, and there is another open door leading to another small room, slippery and cold, hard tile covering the floor.

In this room there is a large white seat that seems to fit his new proportions. In his many journeys he had seen seats like this before, in rooms much like this one, and from hiding places in baseboard cracks he had seen creatures sit on these white seats and let out horrible groans that had terrified him. It must be something dangerous, something awful, something truly bestial. Perfect reasons for a cockroach to try it.

He sits and groans, the sound rising, reverberating in the

tiny room, and he feels something, something not entirely unpleasant, causing him to groan ever more loudly. Cockroaches release desiccated pellets which grind as they are forced from the gut through the anus, but this, this is wet and slippery and strangely lovely. And the smell, the smell to a cockroach is ambrosial.

He groans again, louder, lets it out, tries for more, but it is over. There is nothing left. Maybe if he sits on that special seat long enough he can do it again. And again.

But what is that over there? A basin, with a strange panel atop it. He rises from the seat, steps to it. There is a single silver thing sticking out of the basin. He fiddles with it and cold water starts leaking out. He leans over and latches his mandibles around the thing to capture the water until it feels like his gut will burst apart. When he stands straight again what he sees in the panel above the basin sends him backing away with a shriek.

A predator face, staring at him, backing away as he backs away.

He approaches the panel again and stares at it. The face stares back. He tilts his head. The face tilts the same way. He reaches up a claw, points a digit to the face, and the other points a digit back. Kockroach moves his digit closer, closer, and so does the other, until just when their claws are about to touch they reach a barrier.

Twenty minutes later, after realizing that the other is himself and that the face staring back at him is now his own, he examines himself critically. The eyes are tiny and set low, there is a strange protuberance, like a beak, sticking out of the middle of the face, and short bristly hairs cover the bottom half, surrounding a thin wide rictus, the mandibles bizarrely set horizontally and lined with ghastly white teeth. It is horrifyingly ugly, with none of the sharp elegance of a cockroach face. Where are the huge black eyes? Where are the antennae? Where is the smooth lovely frons or the two sets of articulated palpi used to grind and test his food? This face he has now is both hideous and nearly useless.

As he stares in horror, the extent of the disaster that has befallen him slowly becomes manifest. He has become, of all things, a human.

Then he remembers where he saw before a face just like his new face: on the long piece of meat hanging from the ceiling.

He returns to the main room and circles the hanging thing with the exact same face as his own. It is a human, as is Kockroach now, naked, as is Kockroach now. A rope is fitted around the human's narrow prothorax and tied to a fixture overhead. Maybe all humans have the same face, he considers, unlike cockroaches with their infinite differences. The eyes of the human are closed, the hypopharynx is purple and hanging thickly from the mouth. He pushes the hanging human and jumps back, but there is no reaction other than a slow swaying.

Kockroach knows dead and this is it.

A sound erupts from his abdomen. Kockroach spins, scared. The sound comes again and with it he can feel a vibration and suddenly he is certain that it is time to eat.

How can he be so certain?

Because, for a cockroach, it is always time to eat.

Kockroach searches the apartment for food, pulls out drawers, inspects the room with the cloths, the room with the seat. There are the brown lumps in the bowl of the great white seat, but that is feces, he knows, and even cockroaches won't stoop so low as to eat their own feces, though the feces of other species are often a culinary treat.

In the desk he finds a thick black thing with shiny gold edges. He used to eat such things, used to delight in the tasty gobs of pale paste oozing from the back. He tries to gnash the thing in his teeth but his mandibles aren't strong enough. He splits it open and rips out a thin individual leaf with its black markings, stuffs it in his mouth. He chews and chews until it is soft enough to swallow. He leans down, throws it up on the floor, sucks it up and swallows it again. He still is hungry but he doesn't want to eat another leaf.

From the desk he takes a strange rectangular fetish and tries to bite it. Failing to turn it into food, he examines it instead. It is a picture, highly detailed in shades of gray, a picture of humans, a group of them, wearing cloths and shiny coverings on the tips of their legs. He is surprised to recognize variances among the humans. Their faces are not all the same, and somehow he can pick out the facial differences as if the ability is an integral part of this new body. Only one of the faces in the picture is identical to his own. Standing next to the human with the same face as Kockroach is another human, this human covered in white cloths, its face surrounded by masses of light, curly hair, its facial features very soft and very even. This human, and the human with Kockroach's face, have their arms bizarrely intertwined.

Kockroach feels something strange. He looks down. What he had assumed was his wormlike abdomen has swelled and is now sticking straight out. He bats it down but it pops up again and the whole process, the batting down and the popping up, feels good, feels pretty damn terrific. He does it again and again. The abdomen grows even harder, longer, his head swarms as if inundated with pheromones.

He looks back at the picture, at the face with the light, curly hair. So that is a human female and the wormlike thing is not an abdomen. He is relieved that there are human females. And with the relief a new determination appears as if suddenly implanted in his brain.

He raises again the picture to his face. Yes, there are other females in the group, and a nymph, and all the faces are different except for the one that is just like his and just like the face on the hanging human. He turns around and looks at the dead thing. He does not like that they share the same face. Something tells him this is wrong, that he needs to be unique.

His stomach growls.

He slides over to the hanging piece of meat and chews off its face, regurgitates it onto the floor, scoops it up and swallows it.

He eats until he can eat no more. The thing hanging now is faceless, his head just a mass of red chewed meat. Good. Now there is only Kockroach.

He sits on the floor, opens his mouth, and begins to groom himself. He can't reach everywhere, but he cleans what he can with his tongue and teeth. What he can't reach with his mouth he rubs frantically with his legs and arms. It takes an hour.

Suddenly tired, he sees the sky outside his window begin to dawn. Someone must have flicked the switch. He crawls under the bed until he is again surrounded by pressure and falls back asleep.

In the middle of the day Kockroach is startled awake by a banging on the door he couldn't open.

"Hey, Smith, you in there?"

The voice is loud, deep. Kockroach slinks closer to the wall, stays silent and still.

"No one's seen your face since the girl left two, three days ago. You still in there?"

There is more banging, the door shakes but remains closed.

"Smith, hey. You okay? Is something the matter?"

More shaking. Kockroach crouches beneath the bed, ready to scurry away if the door opens.

"Look, Smithy, your week's up tomorrow and we want you out. There's been complaints about a smell. Can you flush the toilet or something, Jesus? People are living here, for Christ's sake. You're out tomorrow or we're gonna have to come in and get you. We need a bust down the door, we're gonna charge you for it. You got that?"

A final bang, a final shake of the door, and then footsteps disappearing.

Kockroach shivers with fear and falls back asleep.

Kockroach knows he must leave. The predator that had been banging in the middle of the day will come back, they always come back he has learned, especially in kitchens in the middle of the night. Here, he knows, there is no good place to hide. But before he leaves he sits again on the white seat and groans loudly and feels the pleasure of the wet thing slipping out of him.

He stares a long time at the picture with the group of humans. The males in the picture are all covered in the same way and Kockroach, missing his chitinous armor, wants to be covered too. He remembers the cloths hanging in the small cozy room.

Using the picture as a guide, he attempts to place the cloths upon his body. He tries the long black tubes on his claws, on his ears, but finds they go best on the tips of his legs. He sticks his legs through the soft white thing with one big hole and three small holes. The center hole between his legs, he assumes, is to allow the wormlike thing between his legs to grow when he is mating. Based on the size of the hole it must grow very big indeed. The soft white thing with one stretchy hole and two smaller holes he puts on his head but finds he can't see and takes it off. Hanging from a hook is a narrow loop with a knot which, from the picture, he can tell goes around his prothorax.

He has an easier time with the larger pieces because he can learn from the picture exactly how they go. The brown cloth to cover his legs, the white cloth to cover his thorax and arms. He spends a long time fiddling with the buttons but finally figures them out. The brown thorax covering goes over the white thorax covering and the narrow piece of cloth slides under the flaps around his prothorax. He discovers that the knot of the narrow piece of cloth slides. He slips it up until it is tight and he likes it, the tighter the better.

On the floor of the little room are two shiny brown things with some sort of pocked design. He caresses one, remembering the feel of his old chitin, before he slips them onto the tips of his legs. There are strings hanging off either side. He pulls hard at the strings and tucks them into the edges of the brown things.

All buttoned up, tightened and taut, feeling much more protected than before, he takes the photograph back to the panel over the basin and stares at his reflection.

Not everything is right.

There are little hairs on his face and none in the picture. He tries to pull them out one by one but it is impossible, they are too short to grip.

All the people in the picture are doing something strange with their mouths. He stares in the mirror and stretches his mouth to show the teeth atop his mandibles. It is a fearsome sight but it must serve some purpose in human culture, maybe a warning. He practices his warning grimace for many minutes.

He will wear it constantly, he tells himself, to keep danger away.

Finally, all the males have something atop their heads. Kockroach searches the room until he finds just such a thing sitting on the bureau. It is brown and stiff, and following the example of the picture, he places it on his head. He goes back to the basin and compares what he sees in the panel with what is in the picture. He turns the thing around. Better. He tilts it. Much better.

"Hey, Smith, you in there?" he says into the panel. His voice is high, almost twittering, but with a deep rumbling undertone that rises like a predator to swallow the high notes. He tries again. "Smith, hey. You okay? Is something the matter?" He keeps speaking, baring his teeth all the while, repeating the sequence of sounds he had heard through the door until his voice matches the voice of the human who had been banging.

He finds a storage pouch in the brown thorax covering for the picture. On the desk he finds something small and brown and shiny, a folder filled with little green papers with human faces on them. He puts this into a different pouch. He considers taking the thick black thing whose leaf he had eaten, but it is too big for the pouches and he hadn't found it very palatable and decides he can do without it.

It is time.

He searches for a way out of the room. He goes first to the window from where the blinking red light slithers. There is a gap in the bottom. He sticks his claws in the gap and pushes the window up. The noise of the outside world attacks him, like a swarm of wasps. He sticks his head out. The red light is right next to him, painfully bright, hissing loudly at him every time it goes on. He wonders who is flicking the switch. He looks down and feels a burst of fear that tells him it is too high to jump. There are humans walking back and forth below him, little humans, a species no bigger than cockroaches. He will be a giant among them. But still he needs to find a way out.

He goes to the door that had been banged on that day. He tries to open it and fails. He fiddles with the hard shiny things along its side and tries again and still fails. He grips the knob on the side of the door and pulls as hard as he can and the door falls apart with a splintering crash.

Kockroach drops the knob, steps over the debris, and strides down the hall, his hat at a jaunty angle, the V's of his claws moving up and down with each step.

"Can you flush the toilet or something, Jesus?" he says as he makes his way down the hall and into the world. "People are living here, for Christ's sake."

2   They call me Mite. You got a problem with that?

Mite, as in Mighty Mite, on account of my size. They meant it as a joke, them bully Thomasson twins from the schoolyard, all gristle and snarl. They hoped the name it would sting, but I took it as a badge of honor and wear it proudly still. Mite. That's what you can call me.

You eating them shrimp?

Boss says I should stroll on over to the hotel, introduce myself, hand over the envelope what you're waiting for. It's all in there, everything I dug up on that son of a bitch Harrington what thought it was a brainy idea to run against the Boss. But I figured, whilst I'm at it, I'd also tell you a little something about the Boss hisself for that blab sheet you're writing for. Do you want to hear the real story, missy, the truth about the millionaire candidate for the U.S. Senate and his soon-to-be bride? The truth according to Mite?

Don't be so quick in saying yes, you might not like what you hear. It's my story and I don't like it one stinking bit.

Am I talking too fast for you? What was you, buried in the society pages afore they tapped you for this exposé? All parties and hemlines and Joes in bad toups trying not to stare at them flush society tits? Hey, what's the difference between a Times Square whore and a society dame? Beats me.

But what I gots here for you is a story what could pull you out of the society racket and put you smack on the front page. A story of the rise and the fall and the resurrection. A story of a man searching for his place in an outsized world and finding nothing but a hole in his heart in which to fall. A story what will murder the Boss's chances for the Senate.

But the Boss's Senate run ain't all I'll be killing. Consider this my suicide note, because after this gets out I'm as good as gone too. But what the hell, I'm in the mood to bump my gums. And I gots my reasons for spilling. Alls I ask is that you write it straight.

So go ahead, missy, and fire up the reel-to-reel. I'm ready to begin.

They call me Mite, as in Mighty Mite, on account of my size.

I was born in Philly, same as the nation, Philadelphia, a city of alleyways and wild dogs. Nights, from the edges of Fairmount Park, you can hear them in the woods, the wild dogs, howling. Once, them Thomasson twins tied a string of wieners around my neck and dragged me into the dark depths of the park. A couple of cutups they was, them Thomasson twins, and when I peed my pants they held their sides and bent over as the laughter, it kicked the snot from their noses. I didn't fight back, didn't bust them boys, big as they was, in the snouts. Instead I ran away, pulling them wieners off my neck as I went—not throwing them away, mind you, in them days meat was meat—but I sure as hell ran. I suppose it was my heritage kicking in. We Pimelias, we're runners.

My father was a runner too, Tommy Pimelia, a running star in high school, what spent his afternoons burning up the cinders on the four-forty track. He was a miler then, but I guess he moved on up to the marathon because he took off long ago and best as I can tell he's still going. I often imagine what he would have been had he hung up them spikes. He might have grown fat, worn cardigans, affected a pipe, he might have called me sonny boy and tiger, had catches with me in the park, brought home toys in big white boxes. But all that hooey was my dream, not his. I was barely old enough to remember him afore he ran away from me. By then he could look at his son standing in the crib, his head still not reaching the top bar, and see him for what he was.

It's not like he was no giant hisself, the son of a bitch.

My mother was like a ghost in my life after my father left, always present and yet not really there. I can see her still, sitting at the kitchen table, thin elbows on the Formica, straggly blond hair falling limply across her face. Her tattered housecoat is belted around her waist. The veins in her ankles pulse slowly. Fluffs of cotton pill off them dirty blue slippers on her feets. She brushes the hair off her eyes and stares out at me from her prison of vast sadness.

"What am I going to do with you, Mickey? What am I going to do?"

"Nothing, Ma."

"Look at you. Let me get you some milk."

"Another glass of milk and I'm going to puke on the floor, Ma."

"Oh Mickey."

I grabs my books, heads to the back door, to the wooden stairwell that leads three flights down to the alley, and then I stop. Back inside I gives my mother a kiss.

A smile flits across her thin lips, it is forced, a gesture purely for my benefit, a feeble attempt to make me feel all is right, and strangely, against all odds, it does. Because in them days I still believed the world was good and that something would come along and save us. What a sap I was, I can't hardly tell. But still, I smiles back at my ma afore taking off for school, leaving her alone at the kitchen table.

My mother at the table, weighed down by her life, a husband long gone, an apartment infested with vermin, an affliction she can't control, a boy what refuses to grow no matter how much milk she pours down his throat.

But hey, life ain't fair, missy. You ever forget that, you're a goner. Life is like a heavyweight on the ropes; no matter how beat you think you got the sucker, it can still reach out with one well-timed hook and send you spinning.

I was nine first time it happened.

My dad now was long gone and I was nine and in school and my ma every day was staffing the register at Klein's Discount Clothes, where she fended off the advances of old man Klein and brought home my wardrobe from the clearance bins. Corduroy pants two sizes too big, stiff canvas shirts, shoes with rubber soles so thick they squeaked. I was like a one-man band when I walked down the school hallway, rub, squeak, scruff, squeak. Throw in Billie Holiday, I could have played at Minton's. But that night, that first night, I was at the kitchen table, doing my homework, surrounded by the piles of sewing my ma took in for the extra money.

She stands at the stove, stirring a pot filled with canned corn—my mother's idea of home cooking was canned corn and a butter sandwich—when suddenly she turns around and I sees something in her eye, or more precisely something not in her eye. Whatever had been there before, the worry, the disappointment, the love, it all has vanished. She is less than a stranger, a wax dummy of my mother filled only with sawdust and the big empty. And she turns around again and again, spinning in ever-tighter circles. I wonders at first if she is playing, but then her body locks in on itself. I'm up in a snap and I grabs hold of her waist as the shaking starts. She hears not my pitiful cries of terror. She is rigid. I struggles to lay her gently on the rough wooden floor, and fails, and her head cracks onto the wood, and she doesn't feel it, she doesn't feel it, not a thing. I hugs her tight and wipes the foam from her mouth as she goes through it, her surface writhing and beneath the surface, scarier still, the big empty.

No comparisons here, missy, nothing to compare it to, had never seen nothing like it before and nothing has been the same since. You want the bright line in my life marking the before and the after, like a Charles Atlas ad at the back of them superhero comic books what I would lift from the drugstore? Well there it is, the bright line, when the big empty entered my life. It slipped inside my mother and latched on and never let go, and neither did I, even as the brown smell of singed corn filled the kitchen, even as the shuddering ebbed and she calmed into a sleep.

She didn't remember what had happened when she awoke on the floor, told me she must have slipped and banged her head, that explained the headache, she said, and I let her tell me just that. But we both knew it was something worse, something simply too huge to talk about. She even later gave it a cute name, Hubert, telling me after I found her passed out on the floor that Hubert had come again to visit, like it was a gentleman caller paying his respects. And bit by bit, as Hubert returned once and then again, she hid herself from the world, left her job at Klein's lest the shame of it hit her there, and started her vigil in the apartment, alone with her sewing, waiting for Hubert to take over again, which he did and did and did and did, growing ever larger, growing ever more ravenous, until he swallowed her whole.

I knows what it is to lose the meaning of things. I knows what it is to watch the world spin around in a tight helpless circle and get eaten by a nothing bigger than everything there ever was.

Pass the sauce, hey, missy?

Them shrimp are tasty little critters. Tiny clots of muscle what slide around the ocean floor and feed on whatever garbage they can scavenge. Sounds familiar, don't it. For alls I know I could be eating a cousin.

What's the matter, you maybe got better things to do than

listening to my sad boyhood song? You'd rather we talk about the president? Why not, everyone else is. Should he stay or should he go? Is he a crook or what?

You wants to know what I think about the president? You wants to know what I think about the special prosecutor, the Senate Select Committee, Ehrlichman and Haldeman and that stoolie Dean? I think this: Who gives a crap? He stays, he goes, it ain't going to change my life a stinking whit.

But this I knows: the Boss, he's been a big supporter from way back, from when the president he was still just an ex–vice president, a two-time loser eyeing the big chair from afar. The Boss has been a big supporter, and not just with a pat on the back. That money theys all talking about now, the hush money, well the Boss, he's been shoveling cash to the big guy from afore the first election. It was the Boss what convinced the president to hang in there all this time, and it was the president what convinced the Boss he ought to run hisself for that vacant Senate seat.

"The party needs people like you," he told the Boss in his deep skulking voice. How you like that apple?

In fact, you know that thing he does, the president I mean, his two arms raised, two fingers of each hand in the air, that thing? He got that thing from the Boss, from the queer way the Boss walks. "I like that," he says when he spied the Boss in the back of some hotel ballroom. "That's good." Next thing we knows the president, he's up on the stage, shoulders hunched, arms raised, doing his imitation of the Boss.

That's what you want, isn't it, the details, the dirt? Oh, I know it ain't nothing personal, you digging the dirt, it's a trait of the profession. Lawyers sue, dentists drill, politicians drill aides named Sue. And reporters want the mud, the slime, want every last drop of excrement, raw and unfiltered. Well hold on tight, that's exactly what I'm giving here. But it's not just the envelope on Harrington you'll be getting, and not just my morsels about the Boss, neither. This ain't your story, this is my story, and I'll tell it like I choose or you won't get word one. You want the meat only, but you're getting the bone and gristle too.

So sit back, missy, and keep the reel-to-reel rolling 'cause it may take us a while.

We was talking about my life in Philly, afore ever I saw New York. Philadelphia, a city of lawyers and whores, of crooners and con men. Like Old Dudley, what found me in the Philadelphia Free Library, Logan Branch, and who was maybe a bit of each.

There I am, in my red jacket and corduroy pants, my thick-soled discount shoes, twelve but looking eight, reading through the fiction section, book after book, because it was safer hiding in the apple barrel with Jim Hawkins, or floating on that raft with Huck and Jim, than it was staying outside in the fresh air where them Thomasson twins could have their way with me. And there was Old Dudley, in his ragged black suit, gray hair pouring out both sides of his head like a torrent of the thoughts that kept his mind a-buzzing. He appeared as nothing so much as a lunatic, leaning over his battered old chessboard, muttering to hisself in strange dead languages as he harvested dandruff from his silver tufts. And every once in a spell he would lift his brow and give me the eye.

I suppose it was inevitable that the two of us would find each other, there in the library. He come over one Saturday afternoon and sat beside me, with the sweet smell of liquor on his breath, and said with that fake bluster of his, "Do you perchance, my boy, want to learn the game of chess?"

It wasn't no mystery what Old Dudley wanted from me, what with how he sat close beside me and squeezed my biceps beneath that red jacket as he taught me how them bishops moved on a slant. What wasn't so clear was what I wanted from him. Maybe I was seeking a substitute for the father who had sprinted off into the horizon, thin black track shoes pounding on the asphalt as he fled. Or maybe I imagined that this man could somehow teach me the mysterious ways of the world. Or maybe I was, even then, searching for a protector of my own, for by that early date I had already intuited the sad truth of my existence. I suppose at some level deep in my skull it was a combination of all of them maybes, and if so, then my instincts was spot on, because almost everything I could have hoped to get from Old Dudley came true. It all came true, with a price to be sure, steep as the crack in the Liberty Bell, but isn't that always the way of it?

And all them maybes, they burst into bloom a few evenings after that first squeeze of my biceps when I left out from the library and, on my way home, stepped into an alley to pee. I thought I was safe in the alley, behind a pair a garbage cans, facing the brick back of a row house, in the dim glow of a bare yellow bulb, I thought I was safe. But in this world, when you're the size I am and you're alone, you are never safe. My knees are still bent slightly, my yard is still out, the stream is still hissing against the brick, when I hears a voice from behind me.

"Well look who it is, the Mighty Mite."

I jam my yard back in my pants, zip up, turn around. Them damn Thomassons.

"Hey, Mite, you hungry?" says the fat one.

"Who cares if he's hungry, let's just hit him," says the fatter one.

"Well if Mite's hungry, he might want a sandwich. Do you, Mite? Do you want a sandwich?"

"Why would we give him a sandwich?"

"A knuckle sandwich, dimwit. With mustard."

"Spicy brown?"

"Sure, that's it."

"Can I get one too?"

"Shut up and hit him."

The fatter one, he grabs the collar of my red jacket and cocks his fist and he is about to feed me my teeth when a figure appears out of the steam from some faulty pipe running through the ground, a silhouette what stands there, legs spread and arms on hips like a hero right out of them comic books. I catch just a glimpse of this heroic silhouette and my breath stops with hope, with hope that it is my daddy, returned from his run, home at last, ready to save my life as he should have from the start, my daddy.

And then the figure strides forward into the light.

Old Dudley, wouldn't you know.

And the fat Thomasson turns around and gapes and the fatter Thomasson drops me to the ground and tries to run, but he can't get away, and neither can the other.

Old Dudley, he grabs both them Thomassons each by their lank hair and smashes their faces one into the other so that their heads resound like two blocks of wood and their noses mash one against the other and the blood first spurts and then streams down their cheeks as they stagger away.

"Well hello there, Master Mickey," says Old Dudley with a rheumy wink as he pulls me up off the concrete. "I doubt those young ruffians will bother you here on in. Children need to be instructed how to properly behave, even towheaded cretins like those two. But now, perchance, if 'tis not too much trouble, maybe you could do a small something for me."

3   **The world,** Kockroach discovers, is marvelously hospitable when your skin is pale and you walk on two legs.

Each morning now, just before dawn, his gut full to bursting, he scurries around corners, through marvelous dank alleyways strewn with aromatic scraps, to a pile of wooden cartons leaning against an old brick wall. He climbs over two cartons, tunnels under a third, arrives at a crate with one edge shattered. Through the shattered timbers lies a comfortably narrow space where he can sleep with pressure on three sides of his body. He carefully takes off his coverings, folds them neatly, grooms himself for an hour or more, and then slips into the narrow space.

At dusk he awakens, grooms himself again, cleans every inch of his coverings with his teeth, places them on his body in the precise order he learned from the picture, and slithers out of his carton, emerging into the night to feed.

Behind almost every building there are containers left out for the great monstrous collectors to devour in the morning, and from these containers Kockroach gorges himself nightly. Soggy breads, rotted fruit, the wilted leaves of great heads of

lettuce, peelings from all sorts of starchy vegetables, por-
ridgy mixtures congealed into delicious balls of gluck.

In his old body it was the starches and sugars for which he
hungered, but this body eats everything and savors, most of
all, the knuckly joints of meat he finds in the containers.
Sometimes, if he is lucky, the meat he scavenges is covered
by a clutch of writhing maggots. He sucks off the maggots,
shakes his head wildly as they slide down his throat, and then
pulls off the red-blooded meat with his teeth.

From puddles, or from snaking green tubes, he washes
down his nocturnal feasts with water.

There is far more in the containers than even he can eat, but
this bounteous buffet is not without its risks. If he makes too
much noise, rattling the containers as he searches, sometimes
humans stick their heads out of windows and shout phrases at
him which he dutifully shouts back. "Get the hell out of there."
"Ain't you got no self-respect?" "Get a job, you bum."

Other times he is forced to share his food with creatures that
fill him with a long-ingrained terror, slippery rats, narrow-
muzzled dogs, raccoons, and, worst of all, cats, with their flat
ugly faces and their quick paws. He remembers these brutal
felines having lazy sport with the young cockroaches that scurried carelessly within the ambit of their gaze. They would flick
out a paw, knock a cockroach on its back, lethargically pierce
its abdomen with a claw. Even though he now stands five times
taller than the largest cat, fear overwhelms him whenever he
sees such a creature. But still he eats. Since when did fear ever
long stop a cockroach from eating.

Once, when he regurgitated his food out of long habit, a

rat rushed between his legs and began to slurp. He has since learned there is no need to regurgitate in this body. His teeth are ugly yet marvelous things, and once he pulps the food in his mouth he can swallow it straightaway.

He should be hugely content in his new life, he is living a cockroach's dream, food and shelter, a nice brown suit and leather wingtips.

But something, something is missing.

Nightly now, after feasting, he makes tentative forays into the world of the humans. He has no longing for friendship, no pathetic need to blend within the jagged contours of human society, but still he feels an urge to insinuate himself among the specimens of this noisome species.

At first his fear and self-consciousness were debilitating. He shied away from anyone who came close, aware that he was being stared at, certain that every human was seeing him for what he truly was. Which of the humans, he wondered as his head swiveled back and forth in alarm, would lurch out and crush him. Which of the humans would dust him with their virulent powder. And no matter where he stood, no matter how far from the street, he threw himself against the nearest wall to avoid the vicious humped things that prowled like hungry yellow cats all hours of the night. But gradually his fears subsided, he felt more comfortable among this bizarre and repulsive species, and he began to explore.

Striding along the sidewalks, weight shifting, arms pumping, the V's of his claws rising and falling in opposition to his step, he follows a human here, a human there, following at a distance, studying their walks, their manners, their words. He halts when they halt, starts again when they start again. He models their behavior. One man stops to tie the strings of his shoes. Kockroach kneels down, as does the man, and quickly learns the order of movement to create two equal loops which keep his shoes from slipping. Another man lifts his hat as a female passes and Kockroach does the same. There is much he doesn't know, but he intends to learn.

The humans he follows seem to be headed toward some great glowing place in the distance, like a day in the middle of the night. He always turns away well before he reaches the glow, his fear of light is deeply ingrained, but each night he moves closer, closer to what he now is certain is the great center of human activity. And each night, as the great center nears, he finds himself surrounded by ever more humans. He even finds the jostling from large crowds pleasant; it reminds him of those times of plenty when his fellow cockroaches climbed each one over the other as they raced for the crumbs of sweet cookies or the stray swollen crust of bread.

As he walks among them, Kockroach listens to the way humans talk among themselves.

"Got a light?" "Looking for a date?" "Who ain't?" "It'll cost you five." "You got it, sweet pea." "Boy, bush, jam-a-lam." "And don't come back, you fresh bastard." "I'm from out of town." "Move along, pal." "Not so fast, big boy." "Girls,

girls, girls." "I like it dark." "That'll cost you more than five, you filthy boy." "Enough with the blatta-blatta-blatta." "Gotta run." "Nothing personal, pal, just beeswax." "I'm hungry, Jerry. Jerry, you hungry?" "Jam-a-lam-a-lam." "Did you hear?" "No." "Yes." "Want to have some fun, honey? You look like you could use it."

Back in his shelter, naked and groomed, pressed against the sides of the crate, he manipulates his hypopharynx to form the sequences of sound he has heard. To get the sounds right, he repeats the phrases to himself, one after another, all the time remembering who said what when and what happened afterward. "Looking for a date?" "Who ain't?" "It'll cost you five."

Each night he learns something new and each day he becomes more ready to enter the great lighted place, the seeming center of all human activity.

Striding behind a human as they move together toward the light, the street growing dangerously bright, the human suddenly stops. Kockroach stops in turn.

There is a table set up on the sidewalk, a cloth over the table, and atop the cloth a myriad of strange objects. The human stands over the table to look and so does Kockroach. There are rows of shiny disks with straps on either side, the purpose of which remains a mystery to Kockroach. There are brown and black folders like the one Kockroach took from the room, though these don't have the green pieces of paper with the faces on them. There are little bottles with a colored fluid inside that smell of stinkbugs and overripe flowers. There are fake black eyes.

"Is this real?" says the human that Kockroach has been following, holding in his hand one of the shiny disks.

"Right off back of truck, and price, you can't get price like this at Macy's."

Kockroach ignores the disks, ignores the bottles and the folders. He reaches down, instead, for the fake black eyes. He has seen humans wearing such things, some clear, some dark like this, and so he knows how they are supposed to fit. Kockroach slips the black rods over his ears and suddenly the world has turned lovely. He looks around at the bleaked landscape, grim and shadowy, and as he does the constant buzz of fear at the back of his prothorax subsides. It is as if he is seeing the world now like he used to see it as a cockroach.

"You like? Ray-Ban. Special shipment. Fell right off truck. I give you nice price."

"I like it dark," says Kockroach.

"Five dollar."

"I'm from out of town," says Kockroach.

"You don't need tell me such ting, I'm not yet blind. Four dollar."

"Move along, pal."

"Hokay. Three-fifty, not penny less."

Kockroach, with the fake eyes still in place, turns and begins to walk toward the lights.

"Hey, you," the man behind the table shouts. "Four dollar you owe me."

Kockroach, still moving, shouts back, "Nothing personal, pal, just beeswax."

"Hey, you. Hey, tief. Stop tief," shouts the man behind the table, and Kockroach can hear the man yelling as he runs toward him.

Kockroach doesn't know why he is being chased, but he knows he must do something. On instinct Kockroach turns around and stands on the very tips of his legs. At the same time he reaches his arms high in the air, V's pointing right at the man. While fearsomely smiling, he jerks his body up and down and lets out a long loud hiss.

The human chasing him stops suddenly, his eyes widen.

Kockroach steps forward on his stilt-like legs.

The human backs away and raises his arms.

Kockroach has fought enough battles when still an arthropod to know that he has won. He turns around again and continues on his way, walking fast now, weaving through the humans.

"You pay later then, hokay," shouts the human. "Five dollar."

"You got it, sweet pea," shouts back Kockroach.

Kockroach keeps walking, fake eyes in place, his world turned comfortably gloomy, ready now to face the brightness and to solve the mystery at the center of human activity.

He is surrounded by lights, great piles of lights, frantically pulsing and glowing lights, shouting lights, shrieking lights, a miasma of lights. Even with his new fake eyes, the noise of the lights is overwhelming and suffuses him with fear. Over here piles of twisting blinking red lights, like the ones outside the room where he changed. Over there a ribbon of lights passing by with the strange mystical symbols he sees everywhere now. Lights, lights, a riotous chorus of lights.

He looks about for the white plate with its black switch which will allow him to silence the lights. It will have to be larger than the one in the room, he knows, it will have to be monstrous, but he finds nothing and the lights keep calling, burning, shouting.

But as he spins around and takes in the entire scene, it is not the shocking volume of the lights that shakes him most deeply. Scattered high in the sky are pictures, like the one in his pouch, only far larger, representing a giant species of which he is not aware. And one picture grabs at his attention like the warning screech of a cat. A huge grimacing face, rising within the deafening expanse of lights, aiming a fierce stare directly at Kockroach, as if the huge creature recognizes Kockroach for exactly what he is. Gripped in the creature's giant claw is a large white fire stick, and pouring out of his fearsome grimace are great circular billows of smoke.

Kockroach has seen humans with the smoldering white sticks which they hold in their mouths or claws and use to spit out smoke, the sickening smell of burning floating about them. He had assumed the sticks were protection against some great predator, but now he knows they are also something else, a tribute to this totem of pure power with his brutal stare and grimace open in fierce warning. Kockroach suddenly has a great craving for a white fire stick of his own.

Cockroaches are not religious creatures. They take what they can as their due and live by a simple morality hardwired into their tiny brains. They never stop to contemplate their place in the great scheme of the universe for they have no doubts about their place in the great scheme of the universe. They are cockroaches. And whatever that sentence implies, they deal with it by surviving. Whenever a cockroach sits back and wonders what it's all about, he gets stepped on.

Cockroaches are not religious creatures, but still Kockroach can't help feeling a kind of awe while staring up at the wonderfully dreadful creature with the great smoking face. Awe is not an arthropod emotion, it is purely human, unfamiliar but not unpleasant, and so Kockroach doesn't fight it as he did the ugly emotional nostalgia that had almost defeated him before. He lets the awe sweep through him and he finds himself, somehow, in the strange, for him, act of prayer, directed toward the fierce creature staring down upon him.

There are no pat words, no liturgical screens placed upon the raw emotions, it is prayer at its purest and most vital, flowing straight from the gut, simple and heartfelt, representing the deepest yearnings of this mortal being. If you could somehow hear this prayer, the sounds would be simple and repetitive. A message of desire that transcends all posits of philosophy to reach a true measure of universality. A sweet, rhythmic song, like plates of chitin scraping one against the other, over and over, into the night. A song whispered reverently by all manner of species, by all manner of men. A song that is heard in every farm field, every suburban lawn, every urban tavern.

A lovely plaintive song which, if translated into human language, would contain a single chorus of a single word repeated ad infinitim, emphasized only occasionally by a short yet urgent imperative.

Sex. Sex. Please. Sex.

4 **All right,** I hears you. Enough with Mite's weepy childhood. Let's bring on the big guy, let's bring on the Boss.

I was in the city when first I spied him, this city, the Apple, handing out leaflets with a coupon for a buck off some second-floor peep show sporting a pack of girls what all needed a bath. And all the while I was keeping a wary eye out for Big Johnny Callas and his mauling fists, what personage I'd been told was looking for me hard and was frankly cheesed.

My moms by this time was dead, done in by the affliction what overtook her ever more frequently until her dying it was a gift. Hubert, which maybe started as something the size of an acorn, grew in her until at the end it was all that was left. I stayed with her to the last, and covered her with my tears, but in those final hours it wasn't my momma lying there no more, it was Hubert hisself, begging me to give him a new home.

"Mickey," he said to me in an empty voice no louder than a whisper. "Mickey, I'll take care of you. Don't let me die. Mickey."

And even after they wheeled her away, it was like that son of a bitch was still whispering in my ear.

I stuck it out a little while longer in Philly, but when the rent came due that was it for me. I dug into the cookie jar, her precious collection of bills and coins meticulously hoarded over the years from her work at Klein's and the odd bits of sewing she took in, and what should have been hundreds was nothing, not a thing, gone. But still I found a way, a cocktail of blood and tears and betrayal, to get me and my goods, pack, shack, and stack, on the bus away from Philly, away from Hubert, a bus to New York and my future in the Square.

I'm talking now of Times Square, in the heart of the Fifties, my Times Square, shimmying in all its gaudy glory, where first I made my mark on this world. The Times Square of pinball palaces and shady dance clubs, of the grand old Sheraton-Astor and the fleabag junkie haunts what surrounded it, of the Broadway theaters where never I set foot and the Roxy Burlesque, with its second-rate strippers playing to a third-rate crowd, where certainly I did. I'm talking of knife fights over college girls at the White Rose, of hot dogs at Nedick's, of high-stakes pool at Ames Billiards, of the neon marketplace with its counterfeit suits and chest expanders, its little brown bottles of Spanish Fly. High heels and low brims, angry taunts and pearl-handled switchblades, jazz fiends looking for green, Benzedrine addicts looking for God, humped yellow taxis and Motogram headlines and politicians strutting and whores strumpeting and Satchmo trumpeting. Fleas pulling chariots, three-headed cows, rubberneckers and pickpockets, street-corner preachers, married suburban men looking for orgies and finding them, oh yes, with bad boys in tight tight jeans. Charlie Parker is blowing wild and incomprehensible at Birdland, Dizzy is blowing up them cheeks at the Onyx. The Criterion is showing *The Desperate Hours*, the

Lyric is showing *Killer's Kiss*. The Pepsi-Cola sign, the Canadian Club sign, the Admiral television sign, the Hit Parade cigarette sign with its slogan: "The Tobacco, the Tip, and the Taste!" Is that a blow job or what? Call for Philip Morris. The Warner is showing *Search for Paradise,* and missy, let me tell you, I emerged from that tunnel motherless and broke, with nothing to go back to but loss and nothing to go forward to but a forlorn hope, and I found my paradise, right there, in Times Square.

It was in the middle of that whole damn circus, beneath the Camel cigarette sign just off Forty-fourth Street, whilst I was handing out my leaflets with the sketch of a stripper looking oh so come-hither, that first I spots the Boss.

He wasn't the Boss then, just a Joe on the street, but there was something about him that caught my eye from the start. Maybe it was the way his brown suit twisted in strange ways around his torso, maybe it was the way he wore his dark glasses even in the thick of the night, maybe it was the clawlike fingernails or the smile plastered onto his bearded face, as if his lips was stapled into place. Or maybe it was the way he stared into the night sky as if scanning the very face of God.

I won't say I had the inkling even then of what he would be, my instincts are good, but not that good. First off I figure him for nothing more noble than a dope fiend looking to score. So even as I kept passing out them leaflets, I sidled up to the bizarre man in the brown suit, lifted the brim of my hat, looked away, and whispered my standard offer out the side of my mouth.

"Boy, bush, jam-a-lam-a-lam?"

He says nothing, instead he flinches for an instant afore looking down at me with those dark glasses. When I turns to meet his gaze I feel just then a shiver. I can't see his eyes for the glasses, but it was like I could, like them dark oblong plates of glass was indeed his eyes, dark and piercing and absolutely cruel in their utter blankness, like the big empty, Hubert hisself, was staring back at me.

He raises his head and points two fingers up to the Camel cigarette sign, you know, the one with the cat blowing smoke out his piehole.

"Smoke?" I says. "Smoke is it?"

"Smoke," he says. "Smoke is it. I'm hungry, Jerry. Jerry, you hungry?"

It wasn't just the words what confused me. His voice was strangely high, almost twittering, but with a deep rumbling undertone. To hear him speak was to hear two men who disliked each other talking at once, one munchkin, one gargantuan, two separate voices harmonizing badly. I looked at him as he continued to stare upward and realized, quite suddenly, that he was either a total nutjob or maybe the coolest, hippest cat on the Square, dropping on me a boatload of jazzman jive I hadn't yet cottoned to.

"Smoke it is," I tells him, hoping for the latter of the two possibilities. "You got the spinach?"

He stares down at me again, that blank stare, Hubert. I reach into my pocket and pulls out the thin wad I affected—a fiver wrapped around six ones, which was all I had just then to my name—and swish it back and forth. He aims his blank stare at the bills in my hand as if he had never seen a buck before.

Then he reaches into his jacket pocket, pulls out a wallet thick with cash, and swishes it in a perfect imitation of me.

"All right," I says, stuffing them leaflets into my pants. "Tag along and I'll take you to your dreams, palsy. What'd you say your name was? Jerry?"

"I'm hungry, Jerry. Jerry, you hungry?" he says.

I shakes my head in confusion.

"Enough with the blatta-blatta-blatta," he says.

"Blatta is it? Jerry Blatta?"

"Jerry Blatta?"

"Well, follow along then, Jerry Blatta, and I'll hitch up the reindeers for you."

"And don't come back, you fresh bastard."

I laugh, tap the brim of my hat over my eyes, and start off for Roscoe's place, where I knows he could cop whatever it was he was looking to cop and where I had business of my own. I glanced back once, maybe, to be sure he was following, but as I led him north, up through the Square along Broadway, I couldn't afford to be worrying about my new friend Jerry Blatta keeping up. Instead I had bigger concerns, like keeping my lamps peeled for Big Johnny Callas and those fists of his, thick enough it was like they had their own saps built in.

"Hey, Mite," says Sylvie, one of the girls what hooked for Big Johnny on the Square. "My man, he's looking for you."

I smiled, or maybe it was more like a wince, and hurried on.

"Mite, you scrawny half-pint," comes a voice, soft and mocking. It was a lean, leather-jacketed joint-swinger name of Tab. Tab was one of those Joes what strutted around like he was all man, a girl's best friend, like he could rub the bacon with the best of them, yet he still was always trying to slip my yard out my pants and a fiver out my wallet. "I got something just for you, sweetheart," he says. "It won't protect your skull from Big Johnny, but I promise you'll enjoy it. Hey, stop running."

Running? Who was Tab kidding? I wasn't running, but damn if I wasn't walking fast. See, just then I was in the middle of what you might call a situation.

Big Johnny Callas, with his big fists and blue-black pompadour, was the main man in the Square for that old geezer Abagados. The Abagados gang was a Greek crime outfit what covered the whole of midtown tight as a noose, and it was Big Johnny who did the squeezing on the Square. He was a sweet-dressing man-about-town, wearing flash suits, sawing steaks at Jack Dempsey's, paling around with Joe D. at Toots's place, pumping starlets in high-heeled pumps, and running a string what included Sylvie. He also booked numbers, booked bets, offered optional protection at a mandatory price, and lent out low amounts at a high vig, which was maybe where the trouble between him and me it began.

It had seemed like a good idea at the time, taking the two Bens off Big Johnny to give to Pepe to get in on a load of porno magazines what were coming up from Louisiana to be resold at obscene profits. As Pepe told me with that droopy smile of his, the hottest porno came from New Orleans, what with all the Frenchies there. In them days I was surviving night to night by handing out my leaflets, or selling reefer to hollow-eyed jazzmen looking to buy their inspiration, or sending businessmen with that hunger in their eyes over to one of Big Johnny's sidewalk socialites for a short spurt of entertainment. My hustles was a step up from my first years in the Apple, when I racked balls for quarters and ran out on rainy nights to get some big dick a pack of cigs, but even so I was barely earning enough to keep me in feed and make the rent on my crappy flophouse bed with the toilet down the hall. I was heading nowheres, fast, and Hubert once again knew my name. He had tracked me to the Square, he was stalking me now like a panther stalks its prey. With my porno deal I thought I could rise to a level where he couldn't reach out and swipe me with his paw, but I should have known never to trust a mope like Pepe. Old Dudley had taught me better than that.

So I was hustling up Broadway, trying to avoid Big Johnny, when I caught a flash of pompadour coming the other way. I quickly ducks into a doorway and holds my breath until it passes on by. Strange thing is this guy, Jerry Blatta, he ducks in with me, faster than ever I could have imagined. I just looks at him, he looks back with them dark glasses.

"What are you doing?" I says.

"Looking for a date," he says back.

I give him a once-over. "Keep your mitts off, palsy."

Just then, down the street comes the pompadour, but not on Big Johnny Callas, instead on some silly snot-nosed stick from Jersey. I let out the breath I had been holding.

"Let's go," I says as I head back up Broadway.

"You got it, sweet pea."

Oh man he was hip, was he ever. I had then the first inkling that maybe this strange man in the brown drape and shades had things to teach me. I guess it was the jive patter he slapped on me, that and the way he walked, that bouncy stride, arms pumping, body moving side to side, split-fingered V's rising and falling with each step. He was quite the sight, he was, following me up Broadway, and you couldn't tell for certain whether he was the coolest cat on the Square, strutting like a jazz band throwing out a syncopated rhythm, or some physically disabled vet wounded terribly in the war. Except I had seen him duck into that alley after me quick and smooth as a snake.

Roscoe sold out of a crappy fifth-floor railroad flat on the West Side. We stepped over a junkie curled like a potato bug just inside the front door. The stairwell was dank and filthy, cockroaches scattered like councilmen at a cathouse raid as we climbed. At the right apartment, I knocks on the door. An eye appears in the peep, the door opens.

"Mite," says Roscoe in his soft, slurry voice. "This is a surprise."

Roscoe stands shirtless in the doorway, leaning carelessly on the right jamb, sweat glistening off the smooth flat plates of his chest. A lit cig dangles from his snarl. It was the era when every other Joe looked like they was ready to drop to theys knees and yell for Stella.

"I brought a customer," I says.

Roscoe's heavy-lidded eyes lift over my shoulder to take in the man in brown behind me. The edges of his mouth twitch. "What you having, friend?"

"Smoke," says Blatta.

Roscoe takes a deep drag from his cigarette. "You're in luck. Received myself a shipment of green just this week."

"But first, Roscoe," I says, "we needs to get square."

Roscoe stares down at me through the smoke from his cig. "Take a bite of air, Mite," he says finally. "The man and I are talking business."

"I must have sent thirty tea-heads up here in the last two months. You owe me my cuts. We had a deal."

"I've changed the arrangement. Go outside and play. We'll talk later."

"Roscoe, man. Man. I need it, the money. You know Big Johnny he's breathing down my neck. I gots to give him something. I figure you owe me like a hundred. That was our deal. Big Johnny, he'll crush me I don't pay."

"I've got two words for you, Mite: grey and hound."

"Roscoe, you're dicking me, man."

"Yes, well." He drags at his cig. "It happens, kid. It happens." With his left hand he quickly grabs my nose and gives it a twist.

Just then Roscoe's gaze, it falls to the floor. A fat cockroach was taking its main chance and sprinting across the threshold of his doorway. With his hand still grasping my nose, Roscoe reaches out the toe of his shoe and flicks the cockroach onto its back. The little bugger's legs spun wildly in the air, like it was trying to ride a bike, afore Roscoe, he brings his shoe down and squashes it with a loud snapping crunch that pops out the pale insides.

I hears a strange gasp from behind me.

"Get the picture?" says Roscoe.

I does, absolutely. I had been bullied before, I would be bullied again, I knows the dance. I'm back on the schoolyard with them Thomasson twins, fat and fatter, passing me back and forth as they lay their blows. And there isn't a damn thing I can do about it. I would have run, I would have, my nature demanded it, except it's hard to make a getaway with your snoot in some Joe's hand, so I am standing there, trembling, when it happens.

Blatta behind me suddenly grabs hold of Roscoe's wrist, the one connected to the hand still latched onto my nose. He grabs Roscoe's wrist and pulls it away from my face and then jerks the arm down with a terrible force. The sound of Roscoe's knees hitting the floor comes at the same time as the snap of the bones in his arm.

The howl Roscoe lets out as he sags back on his heels, cradling the flopping remnant of his arm, brings me out of my shock. I steps back and turns. He's standing there, smiling his maniac smile, Jerry Blatta, the Boss, though not yet the Boss, as calm as if what he had just done was as simple as flicking a switch.

"Who the hell are you?" I says.

"Blatta is it?" he says, "Jerry Blatta? Look, Smithy, your week's up tomorrow and we want you out."

I squints up at him, but not for long. Old Dudley had taught me that when things they slide in unexpected directions there is always advantages to be had. Things here had slid in an unexpected direction all right. I glance once more at Blatta and turns back to Roscoe, who is letting out a high-pitched wail and laying now in a puddle of his own drained dew.

"What about my money, you muscle-bound craphead?" I says.

Roscoe, still cradling his arm, keeps on howling even as he struggles to rise, his eyes steady on Blatta.

Blatta steps forward and smacks Roscoe's forehead with the palm of his hand. The son of a bitch sprawls backwards into the doorway.

I leans over, pats Roscoe's pants pockets, feel nothing but a slippery wetness, wipes my hand on his head, then steps over him into the bare apartment that smells now like some gypsy old-age home, all incense and urine. I toss a few cushions, empty a few drawers, scatter a shelfful of strange religious tracts as I remembers the vicious rumor going round that Roscoe was a Buddhist. The search, it doesn't take me long. For all Roscoe's talents, cleverness wasn't one of them.

The cigar box, it is slipped behind the tank of his toilet bowl, a box filled to the brim with sweet bills of many churches and all denominations. I consider carefully counting out the hundred I was owed, but then figure what the hell and takes it all. Six hundred and some dollars it turned out, enough to get me off the hook with Big Johnny Callas, for sure.

But already I wasn't so much worried anymore about Big Johnny Callas.

I stood inside the apartment, with the wad in my hand, and looked through the doorway, beyond the broken, prostrated body of Roscoe, to Jerry Blatta standing there in his dark glasses, smiling at me with that plastered-on smile. And right there I knew, in my heart, with the inbred instinct that has been the key to any success I've ever grabbed hold of in this life, that I had found another one.

For here it is, the sad truth of my existence: I am not enough to make it on my own. I learned it early, I learned it hard, and since I learned it I have always been on the lookout for someone stronger to latch onto. Others have the strength to head out on theys own, to embody the pioneering spirit what stretched America from one ocean to the next. Others, but not me. Because I am not enough. Let others fill their hearts with the lonely struggle to reach great heights, I need someone to carry me.

And I figured, if I played my cards just right, I had found my someone, a jive-talking, jazzy-walking, shady-eyed customer name of Jerry Blatta. Now all I needed was a plan.

I steps over Roscoe, whimpering as he was, still on the floor, and gives him a kick in the side for good measure. "Stiff me again, Siddhartha, why don't you?" Then I grabs at Blatta's sleeve and says, "Let's blow."

"But first, Roscoe, we needs to get square," says Blatta.

"What?" I says. "You want your cut now? Sure." I separate the bills into rough halves and offer Blatta the thicker share. When you're my size, muscle always gets the thicker share. "Here you go, palsy."

He takes the wad of bills I hand him and examines it, as if he were realizing the value of money for the first time, afore stuffing it in his pocket.

"All righty-rooty," I says. "Time to amscray the hell out of here."

"Not so fast, big boy," says Blatta.

I step backwards as Blatta leans over Roscoe. "Nothing personal, pal," he says. "Just beeswax."

Roscoe squirms backwards in fright, like a wounded spider trying to get away.

Blatta ignores him, staring instead at the still-lit cigarette lying on the floor, loosing a thin white string into the air. Blatta picks it up, looks at it queerly, sticks it in his teeth.

"Smoke," he says.

5 **Kockroach doesn't question** where the little man in the green cloths came from. One moment Kockroach was staring up in awe at the giant face breathing smoke into the night sky, and the next moment, as if upon decree from the great fearsome figure itself, the little man had appeared, spoken to him as if they already were familiar, and gestured for him to follow. Kockroach's immediate instinct had been to scurry into a hiding place, but something about this human, its size, its overt familiarity, the color of its cloths, made it seem a less threatening presence than the other humans he had observed. He decided instead to follow along and see what he could learn.

The little human had taken him to a fierce predator human with the smoking white stick, a human who had proceeded to grab onto the beak of the little human and then to kill one of Kockroach's former brothers. For some reason he couldn't fathom, Kockroach was now in the middle of a battle. It was a fight that Kockroach sensed wouldn't be won by a stilt-legged show of aggressiveness. So instead he had grabbed at the predator human and tried to pull his arm off, like the mouse had pulled off Kockroach's leg many molts ago. Kockroach had failed to detach the arm, but the attempt was enough to injure the predator and just that fast the battle was won.

With a quick victory, and with the placing of the white fire stick in his mouth to pay tribute to the great smoking god, Kockroach's confidence swells. He still doesn't doubt that the humans would crush him had they half the chance, but now he knows it won't be so easy for them to do so. And with that realization comes a familiar and innate urge.

Rams butt heads over ewes, mustangs rear at one another for the right to mount mares. All animals fight over territory, battle over mating rights, struggle claw and breath for sheer superiority. It is the natural order of things for the strongest of a colony to impose his strength upon the others. Kockroach looks around himself, sees the little man, the injured predator human, remembers all those he has passed in the street. Maybe he is stronger than other humans. Delicious possibilities begin to open to him.

After the battle, the little human had given Kockroach more of those green pieces of paper with the faces on them. Those pieces of paper remain a great mystery to Kockroach. He has seen them passed back and forth among humans as a sort of token. He doesn't know what they mean or what they are used for, but he can tell they are important to the humans, so when the little man offered him a number of the papers, Kockroach understood immediately what was happening. The little human had given him a form of tribute, a token bespeaking clearly Kockroach's superior status. He likes the feeling. He wants more tokens from more humans, more green pieces of paper. The desire for these papers grows almost as large as the other desire that burns in his blood. Almost.

Now that the little human has given tribute and acknowledged Kockroach's superior status, Kockroach feels far more comfortable following him out of the building and down the street back toward the seeming center of all human activity.

"So, Jerry Blatta," says the little human, "what can Mite get for you? Anything. I owes you, palsy. You did a job on Roscoe, you sure did."

"Smoke," says Kockroach. That word, which the little human had taught him, seems to have magical properties.

"Oh yeah, let's see."

The little human reaches his claw up to Kockroach's face and takes the white smoking stick from between Kockroach's teeth. It is now short and stubby, no longer glowing, no longer loosing its noxious burning smell.

"We need get you more, we do," says the little human, the human called Mite. "What's your brand?"

Blatta points up at the great visage in the sky with the smoke pouring out its fearsome open mouth.

"Camels it is. You got matches?"

"I like it dark," says Kockroach, pulling what seems to be appropriate from his stored inventory of human sounds.

The little human lets out a loud snort, pats Kockroach on the upper arm, disappears into one of the doorways off the street. Kockroach stares after him but doesn't dare follow. He worries for a moment that the little human has left for good. It was a comfort having him close, someone who acknowledged an inferior status to Kockroach and yet was willing to usher him through the bizarre twists and turns of the human world. Kockroach's smile remains even as he searches with his gaze for the little human. Mite. Of all the humans, his is the only name Kockroach knows. Mite. He wants this Mite to stay near, to guide him through the thickets of this strange new territory.

After many minutes, the human returns. The relief Kockroach feels is both surprising and enjoyable. The little human gives him a small packet with silver at the top. Kockroach stares at it without understanding what it is. The little human takes the packet, rips off the top, taps the bottom so that three of the little white sticks appear. Kockroach takes them all. They are long but without the glowing tips. Still he puts them in his teeth. He tries to give the packet back to the little human, but the human refuses.

"My growth's stunted enough, don't you think? But I got you something else," says the little human. "A gift."

The little human shows him a small shiny thing, golden in color, a thin rectangle with a line running through it. Kockroach peers at it without comprehending its purpose. Then, shockingly, the little human opens the top and spins a little wheel.

Flame magically appears.

Kockroach backs away and squeals. The little man steps

toward him, places the fire to the end of the three white sticks. They begin to glow and smoke.

As Kockroach stands on the street with three smoking white sticks in his teeth, the humans passing him stare. He must seem very powerful with the three sticks, strong with magic. But he grows fearful being noticed like that. He tells himself that from now on, to remain as inconspicuous as possible, he will limit himself to one at a time.

Even as Kockroach is teaching himself moderation in his new smoking habit, the little human does something marvelous; he closes the top of the magic rectangle and places it in Kockroach's claw.

Kockroach rubs the magic rectangle with his digits. "Mite," he says in a soft, slurry voice. "This is a surprise."

"We're pals, ain't we, palsy?"

"You got it, sweet pea."

Kockroach opens the magic rectangle. He spins the wheel slowly. Sparks but nothing more. He tries again, harder, and suddenly a flame erupts. Fire: the bane of arthropods throughout all eras, scorcher of the bold, decimator of colonies. With a bright yelp, Kockroach drops the magic rectangle.

The little man picks the rectangle up, closes the top, and gives it back.

Kockroach opens it again, flicks the wheel: fire. He closes the top, opens it again, spins the wheel, repeats the act over and over, over and over. Fire. Fire. Fire.

Cockroaches have existed on earth for more than a quarter of a billion years. Fossil evidence shows hundreds of species of cockroaches living among the ferns and mosses that covered Pangaea during the Paleozoic age, 150 million years before the coming of the dinosaur. From that distant age to this, cockroaches have evolved little. Any 350-million-year-old cockroach that magically appeared on the sparkling linoleum of a New York kitchen would be recognized for exactly what it was and squashed without a second's thought. They were cockroaches then, they remain so today, crawling along in the manner passed down for billions of generations with nary an advance. So it is safe to say that Kockroach's mastery of fire would qualify as the most stupendous leap forward ever in the bland, static, and yet oh-so-persistent history of his species.

"Hey, palsy," says the little human as Kockroach stares into the flame in utter fascination, "you hungry? You want some grub?"

For a cockroach, the question is rhetorical.

6 **Each night after work,** as she poured the cream into her coffee at the Times Square Automat, Celia Singer watched the ebbs and flows of lightness in her cup as if in the swirling shapes a private message about her future was being relayed, the meaning of which was just beyond her grasp. She was everywhere haunted by the vague terror that she was missing the meanings of things. It was an occupational hazard, she supposed, eight hours each night plugging lines, making connections, eight hours behind the huge grid, sockets connected by fraying cords over which endless words were streaming back and forth in a great communal conversation, words of which she caught the hum and rhythm and yet no meaning.

She added sugar and twirled her spoon in the cup. Her second cup. It was well after midnight and still the Automat was alive with comings and goings, with life. Maybe that was why she came here each night and sat by the window with her coffee and a slice of pie and let the night burn down around her, even as Gregory slept alone in their bed at the apartment. She preferred the tortured intimations of others' lives to the dead quiet of her own, and at the Automat there was a regular group of others on which to latch her attention.

Over there, at their usual table by the coffee spout, were the politicians in their shabby suits, loudly arguing about the great issues of the day as they endlessly refilled their coffee cups. Celia admired their passion, it was obvious that their political beliefs were the most important things in their lives, certainly more important to them than their teeth.

And sitting as far from the cashier as they could sit were the college boys in their sweatshirts, slurping their makeshift tomato soups, concocted from ketchup, Worcestershire sauce, butter, and hot water. They split a sandwich bought with three precious nickels from one of the windows and talked with an uncontained excitement about the new jazz record bought by some hipster named Elmer, and the Céline novel being passed around, and the reform school kid on his way in from Denver, and their plans for getting out of the city and hitting the open open road. They were a jittery crew, slapping arms, jabbing fingers in the air, seeming to buzz with a pure current of energy that electrified the night for them but to which Celia was immune.

Far to the side, hunched over his pie, sat Tab, thin and good-looking, with his black leather jacket and ruined complexion, who trolled the shadows of the Square for men willing to buy what their wives could never give them. Tab made bravura come-ons to all the girls in the Automat, including Celia, just to be sure everyone knew that he was only doing what he did for the money, though no one believed him. Celia felt nothing but sympathy for the young boy, and the things he was forced to do to survive, but still, sometimes, in the mornings she would wake up beside Gregory with a start, realizing she had been dreaming of Tab stretching his lean muscular body over hers. Whatever that said about the state of her malformed id, she didn't want to know.

And at a row of tables pushed together near the great decorative pillar in the center of the dining room sat the comics and chorus girls and trombonists from the shows, calling out hearty greetings and swapping jokes. She was jealous of their laughter, jealous of their direct connection to a brighter world, but jealous most of all of the pretty girls and their ability to dance. The very thought of it pressed tears to the back of her eyes, tears that should have dried and died years ago.

Not to forget Sylvie, on a break from the street, sitting alone, staring into her coffee as if it were to blame for what she had become. Celia supposed she should have felt sorry for Sylvie, in the way good girls feel sorry for girls like that, but Celia was no longer a good girl and what she felt instead of pity was a kind of bitter envy. Sylvie had the most magnificent body, long legs and wide hips, pillowy breasts, all of which she showed off with the sweaters and tight wool skirts and gorgeous high heels that Celia would never ever wear. When Sylvie walked through the dining room with her tray, each man in the restaurant watched the shifts of her body with some sad longing in his eyes. That it was as available as the lemon meringue pie behind the little glass doors if you had enough change didn't alter the way they looked at her.

"You're such a pretty girl," her mother had told Celia over and over. "You have the face of an angel. You'll have the family you deserve, a family to make you whole." This was not what she supposed her mother meant, this ragtag assortment of losers and late night hangers-on that surrounded her each night at the Automat, but this was the closest thing she now had to a family. "The boys will come running, they won't let you slip by just because," had said her mother. Except they had, hadn't they, Mom? All but Gregory, who behaved as if he were doing her the greatest favor of her life, reaching down to help the disadvantaged, like they were two models in a March of Dimes poster.

Maybe Gregory actually was doing her the greatest favor and maybe she should be ever so grateful. He was basically decent and fairly upstanding and not bad-looking in a scholarly sort of way. But Gregory had no problem with indecipherable messages, he delighted in relaying to her the meaning of everything. Of course he was a graduate student in Russian history and so he knew just enough about everything to be unbearable. And of course he was a Communist, which meant his earnestness and self-importance were beyond endurance. But it was not like she had so many alternatives. And he seemed so certain of everything, which was comforting in its way because Celia was the most uncertain person she knew. Maybe his certainty was why she had stifled her doubts and let Gregory move into her little walk-up when his lease ran out.

So now she was living in sin. She laughed ruefully at that. Living in sin was what her mother called it when she spoke of the town strumpet or the widow in the next township. Oh, the image it brought to a young girl's mind. Other girls dreamed of marriage, of children, of the family Celia's mother so desperately wanted for her; Celia had dreamed of living in sin. Well, be careful what you wish for. Where was the canopied bed, where were the long lascivious nights, where was the secret passion that kept the world's scorn at bay?

Living in sin, hell, it was more like living in Cleveland.

She turned to look out the window at the passing stream, a scene decidedly roguish. Sometimes she thought she stayed nights at the Automat to be apart from Gregory, and sometimes she stayed nights to feel a part of this. This was the juice in her life, not Gregory, not the job, not her pale hopes for the future, but her little table at the Automat, sitting with this strange dismal family, separated from the carnival of Times Square by a single pane of glass. It was sometimes hard to impress, even upon herself, exactly how pathetic her life had become.

Someone caught her attention in the throng outside the window. A man in brown, a handsome-faced man in sunglasses walking with a strange, jerky step. He had a ragged beard, his suit was on wrong, though how it was on wrong she was uncertain, his nails were long and unkempt, and he had a bizarre smile fixed around the cigarette in his teeth. Her immediate reaction to spotting him outside her window, just a few feet from her, was an irrational but very real fear. And her peculiar fear increased when he stopped right next to her, turned to the window, and stared inside.

She cowardly dropped her gaze to the tabletop before her. At all costs she wanted to avoid this strange man's gaze. "Please, please," she whispered to her coffee and still-uneaten pie, "don't come into the Automat." Celia loved being part of the midnight world, but only so long as she could maintain sufficient distance from its inhabitants. That was her method of approaching all of her life, the rigid defenses of the maimed.

She stirred her coffee, lifted it to her lips, felt its tepid heat upon her teeth. When she put it down again she glanced up to the window. He was gone. Relief and disappointment both all at once and she wondered to herself at why that man had given her such unease.

It was his awkwardness, his hesitance. Celia could tell in some subliminal way that the mass of instinctual acts we take for a physical presence were not, in his case, being done instinctively. Nothing was easy, nothing was natural. That was it, his raw unnaturalness, and who felt more unnatural than Celia? In that way he was a mirror into her own uneasy place in the world and she mustn't have that. She had troubles enough, she didn't need some lunatic in a bad brown suit pointing out to her with utter clarity her own gnawing sense of alienation. So instead of reaching out, one alien to another, she hid in her coffee cup. How brave, Celia, how wondrously courageous. She felt sick, useless. Maybe that was why she didn't want to go home, so that even Gregory wouldn't find her out.

She glanced up and saw the man in the brown suit suddenly inside the restaurant, his right side brushing the wall as he scurried toward the food. It was a shock to see him and she had to fight a strange revulsion. But having castigated herself before, this time she bravely refused to look away.

He reached the glass serving doors and peered inside at all the offerings, the pies, the fruit, the sandwiches, tuna, egg salad, deviled ham, olive loaf, the crocks of baked beans, the bowls of soup, the little dishes of spinach, of macaroni and cheese, of Harvard beets and carrots glazed with brown sugar. His head moved back and forth and his whole posture bent with a desire so obvious it was pitiable. When had he eaten last? He reached out a hand, caressed one of the little glass doors, grabbed hold of the chrome handle, pulled. It didn't open. He pulled harder. It still didn't open. He slid to another door, took hold of the handle. Then to another. He moved from one to the next, looking for a door that would open. He must be hungry and have no money. He shouldn't be in here if he didn't have any money. Why was he here, ruining it for everyone? Why did he insist on making everyone feel so uncomfortable?

She spun her gaze around the Automat. The politicians, the college boys, Sylvie, the comics, no one was noticing the strange man in brown. Even the cashier was more interested in her nails. It was only she whom he was making uncomfortable. Celia felt suddenly ashamed at everything she had been feeling, the revulsion, the anger, even the pity. Who the hell was she to feel any of those things for anyone else when she felt those exact same things for herself?

Almost as an act of penance she was about to stand and make her way toward him, to buy him a sandwich, when she realized he wasn't alone. There was a smaller man in a bright green suit bustling about him. She recognized the suit immediately.

Mite, the tiny young aspiring gangster who spent his evenings at the Automat huddled over a hot tea, eyes desperate and searching, ever vigilant for a mark to hustle. Mite introduced himself to everyone new at the Automat, sat down, told an elaborate series of lies, and then asked to borrow thirty-nine cents. Always thirty-nine cents, as if the sheer specificity of the number made it hard to refuse the entreaty. He was short, thin, nervous, full of hope and despair all at once, and Celia, over-whelmed by the empathic sympathy only one loser can feel for another, had given up the thirty-nine cents more times than she could remember. Now they were close to friends.

She was shocked to see him there, in the Automat, that night. A few weeks ago he had told everyone about the big deal he was about to score. A little import-export, he had said. All he needed was some up-front cash, he had said. It was sad seeing the hunger that marked his face like a stain, a hunger that couldn't be satisfied in that Automat with all the nickels in the world. It was that hunger that had sent him to Big Johnny Callas, who often held court in that very Automat, to borrow the up-front cash at the Greek's brutal rates. And, as could only have been expected, Mite hadn't settled up when he was supposed to. She hadn't seen Mite for a couple of nights, she had heard he was on a bus to somewhere new, Moline, she had heard, or Fresno, away. She'd been glad he had escaped.

But now here he was, stunningly present, accompanying the strange man in brown. And now here he was leading the man by the elbow, bringing the man across the floor, past the politicians, past Tab and the comics, right smack to her table.

"Yo, Celia," said Mite. "This is my new friend, Jerry. You mind if we sits here with you?"

Celia kept her eyes off the strange man, always obedient to her mother's order not to stare whenever a strange or deformed person crossed her path, much as others fought not to stare at her. She would have liked to say no, would have liked nothing better than to be left alone that night to peer at Mite and the stranger from afar, but Mite just then seemed so anxious to please, so desperate almost, that her heart cracked for him.

"What are you still doing here, Mite?" she said. "I heard you were already on a bus out."

"You heard wrong, then, didn't you?"

"Big Johnny has been telling everyone about his plans for you. They're not very pretty."

"Let him talk." His nonchalance died quickly and he peered out at her warily. "What plans exactly?"

"Something to do with the spleen. You know where the spleen is, Mite?"

"Isn't that in New Jersey somewheres?"

"It's behind your liver. Big Johnny says he intends to remove it."

Mite sucked in a breath and then shrugged. "Well, the hell with him, excuse my Polish. He wants that spleen thing he can have it, I gots no need for it no more."

"Mite, you have to go. It's too dangerous for you here. Do you need money, bus fare?"

"Nah, I decided to maybe stick around a bit. It's a free country, ain't it? Believe it or not, things is looking up for me. Thanks to my friend Jerry, things is looking way up. So can my pal park hisself here while I grabs us some grub?"

"Sure, I suppose," she said. "Any friend of yours . . ."

Mite pulled a chair from the table. "Sit down, palsy. I'll take care your dinner. Keep an eye on him, Celia, won't you, whilst I load up? Anything you want?"

"No thank you, Mite. I'm fine."

Mite winked and then was off to the wall of food.

She watched him go before turning to the man in the brown suit, who was still standing.

"Sit, please, Mr. . . ."

He kept standing until she gestured at the seat Mite had pulled out for him and finally he sat.

The strange pull of revulsion she felt when she spied him outside the window, and then by the wall of food, strengthened in proximity. He had a peculiar smell, strong and furry, less the deep neglected tones of normal body odor, more the higher-pitched animal musk that arose with its own not-so-hidden message from the carnivora house at the zoo. His beard was dark, his hair, beneath his hat, long and greasy. There was something disconcertingly real about him, as if the rough edges of existence, normally smoothed by societal conventions or blurred by the plate of glass through which she viewed the world, were still jagged and sharp on him. He sat there in his dark glasses, unmoving, as if he were blind, but at the same time it seemed as if he were staring at her with a brutal intensity. She tried to stare back, to see beyond her own reflection in the dark lenses, but failed to connect with his eyes.

Suddenly he reached into his jacket pocket and pulled out something small and golden. He flicked open the top, spun

the wheel. A small flame erupted. His smile increased its vast
wattage.

Celia tilted her head, unsure of what the stranger was doing. In the way he smiled and held himself, he seemed to be
trying to impress her, as if he were some prehistoric man
showing off to the females of his clan his ability to make fire.
She felt strangely flattered, there was something almost gal-
lant in the gesture. To be polite, she reached into her purse,
took out a cigarette, leaned forward and lit it on the flame, all
the while staring into the dark lenses.

"Thank you," she said. "Your name is Jerry?"

"Blatta is it? Jerry Blatta?"

"That's an interesting name."

He continued to stare.

Self-consciously she leaned back, crossed her arms over
her breasts. "And you're a friend of Mite's?"

"Sure, I suppose. Any friend of yours . . ."

The register of his strange disjointed voice suddenly slipped
higher, as if in imitation of her own, using even her own words.
She began to laugh, she couldn't help herself, the charming
gesture, the flattering imitation, the disconcerting stare.

He drew back as if under attack, and then through his
fixed smile he laughed too, a laugh as high and girlish as her
own.

Mite returned with a tray laden with plates and cups and
glasses. Before his friend Jerry, Mite placed a ham and cheese
sandwich, cut diagonally into two triangles, an apple, a tapered glass filled with tapioca pudding and topped with

whipped cream, a cup of coffee. Ever frugal, for himself Mite brought only a hard roll, two pats of butter, a glass of water, and a cup of tea. Mite sat himself next to Jerry, solicitously close, and edged the plate with the apple, red and shiny, toward his friend.

"Go ahead, Jerry," he said. "You know what they say, an apple a day keeps the coppers at bay."

Celia watched the strange maternalistic display with a curiosity that turned to amazement as this Jerry Blatta devoured the apple in four bites, swallowing skin, core, all, leaving only the tiny stem sticking out from his teeth.

"He's a hungry boy, your friend," says Celia.

"Ain't we all. Look at him close, Celia. He's my ticket."

"Your ticket?"

"Oh yeah."

"To where, Mite?"

"To the pineapple pie, sweetheart, where we all wants to go. Just like Pinnacio. You ever hear of Pinnacio, what worked out of the Square a few years ago?"

Celia shook her head.

"He's a legend now, sure, Pinnacio, but back then he was just an Alvin like me, a skinny hustler what styled hisself a show biz impresario with nothing but a single blue suit and a pretty face to get him through. He had two clients, a sad-sack comic who got the mokes laughing only 'cause he couldn't stop sweating on stage, and a contortionist what had a fatal fondness for chocolate and couldn't no longer touch her toes. Pinnacio used to hoard his nickels so he could sit over his coffee at the Automat and read a *Variety* he'd pluck out of the ashcan and plot the careers of his two loser clients. And then each night he would squeeze his way through the stage doors of every cheap vaudeville and burlesque house in the Square, scoping for the next big thing. You asked anyone then, the next big thing for Pinnacio was going to be the Bowery. You want cream in that, palsy?"

Blatta didn't answer but continued to stare at the cup filled with hot coffee. As Mite and Celia looked on, he stuck his finger into the cup, pulled it out, stared at it as it reddened from the heat.

Mite took hold of his own cup by the handle, pinkie sticking out absurdly, and lifted it to take a sip. Blatta, seeing this, did exactly the same. It is as if he is learning, thought Celia, as if he is a child learning his way in the world, latching onto the worst possible teacher in Mite.

"So one night, Pinnacio's at the Roxy and he sees a girl what looks no older than twelve doing a semistrip, and the geezers in the house theys just loving her show. She's got something, sweet little Suzy does, something a twelve-year-old shouldn't have, which makes sense 'cause this girl she's twenty-two and working a second shift on her back after the theater darks. But on stage she's playing the little-girl thing for all it's worth and the yards in the joint are springing to life like a crop of winter wheat, you get the picture? So Pinnacio, with this Suzy, he sees his ticket."

Jerry Blatta lifted half of the ham and cheese sandwich off the plate and squeezed the half in his fist until the cheese and mustard oozed out. He stuck the mess into his mouth, jamming it all in until his lips could close one upon the other. Celia stared at him, dumbfounded. Blatta stared back with defiant humor, even as he reached for the other half.

"Well Pinnacio," continued Mite, "just the day before, in a *Variety* he hawked from a can, spied something about an opening for a juvenile in some second-rate C movie they was filming in Brooklyn. He strolls right up to little Suzy what wasn't so little and tells her he can get her an audition if she signs a management contract with him. She shrugs her shoulders and signs, figuring this skinny mope didn't have the pull to get the audition in the first place. But the thing was, this audition it was open, he didn't need no pull, and she didn't need no him, but there it was. And in that audition room she gives it the full twelve-year-old-with-a-glimmer-in-the-eye treatment and the director is a perv through and through and so hot to lay his mitts on a twelve-year-old he practically throws hisself at her feet. Now she's in Hollywood, a real star, and Pinnacio, he's riding around with a tan and a Cadillac, living flush in the pineapple pie. All because he found his ticket."

"Is that true, Mite, or just another one of your stories?"

"True, true, you could look it up. Her name is Susan Harrison or Susan Haywood or Susan something, they changed it for her, but it's true, I'll swear to it. And Celia, sweetheart. I have the damnedest feeling that Jerry here, he's my sweet little Suzy. Ain't you just that, palsy?"

Blatta ignored the question, maintaining his stare at Celia as he moved to the pudding. Reaching his hand into the tapered glass, he pulled out a glob of the yellow and white goop, slurped it into his mouth, and then proceeded to lick his hand clean with his long pink tongue. The sight of him licking off the tapioca even as he continued to stare at her affected Celia in the most peculiar way. The raw hunger, the unmasked appetite, the disdain of elementary manners, the size and color of the organ, all of it she found both revolting and thrilling. Watching him lick the gaps between his fingers with his tongue was like having a cat reposition itself over and over on her lap.

"What do you know about him?" said Celia softly.

"Nothing," said Mite.

"Where is he from? Where does he live?"

"No idea."

"So why do you think he can help you?"

"Oh he can, believe you me."

"And why do you think he will?"

" 'Cause, Celia, I can help him too. See, he's something special, but he needs guidance, he needs management, he needs me. With him and me together, there's no telling where it will end."

"Just like Pinnacio."

"You got it."

"Did you know him personally, this Pinnacio?"

"Nah, not really, but I heard, I heard."

"So the whole story is apocryphal."

"A pocketful of what?"

"Posies, Mite. And what about Big Johnny?"

"What about him?"

"Mite, don't play the fool."

"Let me tell you a secret, Celia." He leaned forward, lowered his voice. "I gots the money."

"You have the money?"

"Like I said."

"How?"

"Sweet little Suzy here."

"You have enough?"

"More than enough. I could pay the dirty creep off and still have enough left over to take you and me to '21.' But it's no sure thing paying that creep off is the answer. See, Celia, I gots Jerry on my side now."

Just then Jerry Blatta reached into his jacket and pulled out a fistful of bills. He held his hand out and offered them to her. His face, his smile, had the same expression as when he flicked the lighter.

"Looking for a date?" he said. "Who ain't? It'll cost you five. You got it, sweet pea. Did you hear? No. Yes. Want to have some fun, honey? You look like you could use it."

Celia was taken immediately aback by the offer of money and the strange words. No hidden meanings here, despite the garbled sentences. He was offering to buy her, like one would buy Sylvie. It had never happened before, no one had ever confused her with a whore, and for a moment her emotions teetered.

Suddenly, involuntarily, she laughed.

She laughed and the strange man in brown laughed and Mite, whose jaw had dropped in disbelief and had stared at her with a worried gaze, he laughed too. And as they laughed and the money in Jerry Blatta's hand trembled and the offer hung in the air like a helium-filled balloon, something stirred in Celia, some long-buried dream.

Not to be a whore, no, not that, never that, but at least to be desired in that way. Isn't that part of it, the dream of love, not just a commingling of purposes, or an acquiescence to another's earnestly held political beliefs, but a commingling of desires too? That was the dream that had died in her, killed off by the virus that had lodged in her spine and the thick sole and brace she now wore on her left foot and the limp that scattered desire onto the floor like so many jacks with each pathetic step. Her mother had been wrong, the boys had not come, the dream had fallen into a deep hibernation, and with the dream went her courage to touch anything beyond the muffled voices of other lives seeping from a distant room. But now it stirred again, the dream, roused by the outstretched bills, the carnivora musk, the long pink tongue, the cat turning in her lap, the strange brutal reality of this man, all of it, and the muffled song of her own pale life seemed so ridiculously wan in its presence that she couldn't help but laugh.

The man in brown, this Jerry Blatta, he turned to Mite and let out a strange hissing sound, almost like a warning. There was a moment when he appeared to begin to rise from his seat.

She fought to regain control, let the laughter fade, tried to compose herself, not sure what was going on in Blatta's strange psyche, whether he took the laughter as an insult when that was not her intention, not her intention at all.

And then she imagined the expression on Gregory's face, the shock, when she would tell him that he absolutely had to move out, and she fell again into a hysterical fit that had them all looking, the politicians and the college boys, Sylvie, Tab, the comics and trombonists at the center table, all of them, and she didn't care, she didn't care, she did not care.

7 **Kockroach feels a surge** of excitement roll through him as the female makes her strange high-pitched bray, the same roll of excitement he had felt as a cockroach when the scent of a willing female's pheromones started his antennae to twitching. It must be part of the human mating ritual, that sound she makes, and so he echoes it as closely as he can, all the while holding out to her the green pieces of paper he means for a tribute. He is ready to mate, certain it is going to happen, when, to his shock, he hears the same mating bray from the little human beside him.

He turns to stare and lets out a warning hiss, but the little man continues to make the seductive sound. Normally this would be a time to fight, to rise up on stiff legs and battle for the attentions of the female, and he is about to do just that, to rise and attack with no mercy and destroy utterly the little man beside him, when something stops him.

The woman's braying subsides and she is looking at him, not at the little man named Mite. And Mite is offering up no tribute of his own, just his braying. And suddenly somehow Kockroach realizes that with this female Mite is not a threat, will never be a threat, as if he were of an entirely different species. Kockroach turns back to the woman, makes the braying sound again, and the female joins in.

Kockroach is certain, absolutely, beyond any doubt, that now, finally, he is going to mate.

The female rises from the table and Kockroach rises with her. Will they do it here, right on the table, atop the scattered plates, like two cockroaches, or will they go instead to her lair? Humans, Kockroach has noticed, don't mate in the open, unless they mate in some strange way he has not heretofore recognized. Maybe that claw-to-claw thing he has seen so often in the street.

The female reaches out her claw to him. He reaches out his claw in the same way and she grabs hold. A jolt of power tingles through his arm and down into the worm between his legs.

"It was a pleasure to meet you, Mr. Blatta."

"Enough with the blatta-blatta-blatta."

She makes the braying sound again and lets go of his claw. Is that it, is that all there is to it for humans? If so, what a sad pathetic species.

"I'll see you around, Mite," says the female. "Be careful, please."

"It's them what oughts to be careful now," says Mite.

She turns her attention again to Kockroach. "Take care of my friend Mite, won't you?"

"You got it, sweet pea," says Kockroach, aware through his assimilation of the bizarre but handy human language that she is asking him to protect the little man and that he has agreed.

But why does she have any concern for Mite if she and Mite are not to mate? And why did he agree to her request, as if instinctively? Is that what human males do as part of the mating ritual, promise anything? What kind of species can survive doing that? It is all a puzzle, and the puzzle grows as the female turns and walks away, walks away without him, her hip rising awkwardly with each step, walking away as if one leg had been twisted by some fearsome predator.

He stares at the female walking away, at the strange uneven gait, at the rods of metal attached to her leg, at the strange rocking motion of her tail. He feels the tingling in the worm again and begins to follow, until Mite grabs hold of Kockroach's arm.

"Is that what you want, palsy, you want a little barbecue?" says Mite.

"Girls, girls, girls."

"Well, why didn't you say so? Nothing could be easier. Half the girls in the Square this time of night have gone commercial, one way or another. Put the spinach back in your pocket and I'll get you one, no problem, anyone you want, just not her, all right? You got that, Jerry? Not her. She's a nice girl, Celia is. But I'll gets you someone else. Look over there. That's Sylvie, what with the tits like atom bombs. A bit mismatched too. We calls them Fat Man and Little Boy, we do, but variety, it's the spice of life, ain't it? What do you think of her? Hubba hubba hubba?"

"Hubba hubba hubba?" says Kockroach as he continues to watch the strange swaying of the first female's tail as she leaves through the spinning glass door.

Mite waves his claw in front of Kockroach's face. "Yo, Jerry, you listening? Anyone but her, all right? Not her. Celia ain't interested in that stuff. She's a cripple, for Christ's sake. No, the Norma Snockers what I was talking of, Sylvie, she's over there."

Kockroach slowly swivels his head in the direction of Mite's pointing digit until his gaze lights on a female sitting alone at a table. Her hair is yellow, her long legs are crossed, she has huge mounds deforming the chest of her thorax, mounds which Kockroach finds strangely appealing.

"Hubba hubba hubba?" says Kockroach.

"Attaboy. Wait here, I'll set it up."

Kockroach watches as Mite walks over to the female with the yellow hair. Kockroach turns for a moment to look at the door where he had last seen the first female, the one known as Celia, but she is gone. He turns back quickly enough to see Mite point at him. The second female, the one known as Sylvie, twists her face in a strange contortion and then shakes her head back and forth. Mite offers her a tribute, waving the green pieces of paper, and then clasps his claws together in a symbol of submission, and still she shakes her head back and forth.

Mite makes his way slowly back to Kockroach. With his eyes narrowed, he looks at Kockroach's face and then lets his gaze drop all along his body.

"Hubba hubba hubba?" says Kockroach.

"Sure, palsy. Sure. But first, maybe, let's wait out the night and then we'll sees if we can clean you up a bit."

It is the substance that slinks out of holes in the street, that rises in slippery wisps and foul exhalations, it is colorless and hot and looks like smoke but it is wet to the touch and it now surrounds Kockroach on all sides with its heat and its pressure and the slime it leaves on his strange pale skin and his dark glasses.

At first, sitting next to Mite with only the glasses on and the single white cloth over his lap, Kockroach's nerves were shouting and he felt more defenseless than he had ever felt before, even more than when he was a white nymph and the mouse sprinted into their midst. There are other humans in the room with the hot wet smoke, sitting on the benches, water appearing on their soft round bodies as if by magic, and he was certain, naked before these other humans, he would be discovered, finally, for what he was and squashed. But the pale hot stuff, schvitz Mite called it, surrounded him and turned the walls dim and his never-ending urge to be protected on all sides eased and he now feels strangely comforted.

It is no wonder that he feels at home in the steam bath. Cockroaches developed in the steamy marshes of the tropical forests in the early millennia of earth's natural history, and while the heat tends to sap the energy of humans, Kockroach finds it positively invigorating.

"Schvitz," says Kockroach.

"It's a machiah, ain't it, bubelah," says an old human in the corner.

"Bubelah," says Kockroach,

"Hey, you Jewish?" says Mite.

"Right off back of truck," says Kockroach, with the accent of the man at the table where he found his dark glasses.

Mite laughs and shakes his head.

Through the smear of fog on his glasses, Kockroach examines the other humans in the schvitz. They all have glistening skin and big pink bellies and the same worm between their legs as does he, although his is bigger. What does that mean? he wonders. Is it good or bad? He is about to ask Mite when Mite speaks to him instead, speaking strangely, using only half his mouth to pronounce the words.

"Yo, Jerry. I might got an opportunity for you if you're interested. Something with huge possibilities what could put us both in the money."

"Opportunity?" says Kockroach.

"A little business."

"Beeswax?"

"Yeah, that's it, beeswax. Something rich. I thought up a plan, see. All you gots to do is follow my lead and let it happen. You interested?"

"Bubelah."

"Good. Great. This is gonna turn out, you'll see. All right, let's hit the shower. I suppose that's a word you ain't heard much lately, is it? Shower."

"Shower," says Kockroach.

"Attaboy."

• • •

A torrent of water falls all about him. Kockroach squeals as he runs about the long gray room with metal tubes sticking out from above, trying to avoid the spray because that is what cockroaches do. They like the water, like to crawl through it, fornicate in it, slurp it with their food, but they fear it when it comes from above, and at the first dangerous drops they scurry to a place of safety.

"What, too cold?" says Mite. He twists a knob. "Try this."

Kockroach sees Mite standing under one of the waterspouts, getting drenched, seeming to welcome the streaming fluid, lifting his face up to it as if it were a gift. Kockroach steps tentatively beneath the water and lets it pound on his belly, his shoulders, over his dark glasses, onto his head. He wonders why he had been afraid of it all those many molts.

Mite rubs a shiny white stone all over his body, creating a weird white froth. Other humans do the same thing. Kockroach takes the same white stone. It is slippery, easily bruised like no stone he has ever touched before. He licks it and spits out the bitter taste. He rubs it all over his own body as the other humans do, and the froth covers him head to toe until the water washes it off.

"The thing," says Mite, again using only half his mouth to speak, "is to let me do all the talking. I know these guys, what they're looking for. But there's going to be a time when you got to show your stuff. You'll know it when you see it, and then, baby, slam bam you do your little act."

"Your little act."

"Yeah, the thing what you did with Roscoe."

"Take care of my friend Mite, won't you?"

"Attaboy. We're a team, ain't we, Jerry? A team."

"You got it, sweet pea."

"Sweet pea. I love that sweet pea thing. You kill me, you know that, Jerry? You kill the hell out of me."

Mite brays and rubs the white stone over his hair and Kockroach does the same and as the water rinses off the froth he feels different than he ever felt before, looser, lighter, fresher.

One thing he has learned for sure. Never again will he lick himself clean.

"My friend Mite," says the tall thin human with the dark skin in a room filled with cats. "Always a pleasure. What can I do for you this morning?"

"I need a suit, Clive, with all the trimmings. Shirt, hat, skivvies, everything."

"Lovely. This suit, you're looking discount or executive?"

"Designer, baby."

"Designer? You're buying designer? Have you found God, little brother?"

"Something better. But I need a class look for it to go over."

"Do tell. But I'm sorry, darling. I don't think I have designer in your size."

"It ain't for me, Clive, I'm all set." Mite jerks his thumb at Kockroach. "It's for my pal Jerry here."

The tall man puts a hand on his cheek, turns to Kockroach, gives him a long look. "Oh my. Oh yes. Lucky you, we just received a load, headed for Des Moines, that never found its way over the bridge. Poor Des Moines. And they could use it so. Let us see."

The tall thin man slips a yellow cord out of his pocket and dances around Kockroach as he stretches the cord along Kockroach's arms, his legs, around different parts of his thorax.

"Mr. Average, isn't he?" says the man, nodding with a smile. "Which is good, because that's what they grow in Des Moines. Forty-two jacket, best as I can tell. Seventeen-inch neck with thirty-five-inch sleeves. Waist thirty-four. I have some nice blues for you, or a lovely gray."

"What color you want, Jerry?" says Mite.

"Color?" says Kockroach.

"That's right, palsy. It's your choice."

Kockroach steps forward and reaches toward the tall thin man. His skin fascinates. It is the color of his old chitin. He misses his chitin, the strength and stiffness, the color. Running around with this white skin, he feels lost and frail, like the weakest of nymphs. He wishes his skin were like this man's, dark and rich and full of protection. He reaches up and touches the man's cheek. "Color," he says.

"Oooh," purrs the tall thin man. "Just so happens I have a forty-two in brown pinstripes, double-breasted. You want to see it?"

"Don't want to see it," says Mite. "I just want to buy it."

"No checks, Mite."

"No checks."

"My, you did find something better, didn't you?"

"How long to get it altered?"

"If you have time, I'll do it right now."

"Clive, my man, you are magic."

"Yes, yes I am."

Kockroach is lying back in the chair, a thick white cloth tight around his neck, surrounded by humans, all grooming him. One man in a red vest, having already smeared Kockroach's face with hot white foam, is now scraping his cheeks and chin with a brutal-looking edge of metal. One man is whipping a cloth back and forth across the shiny brown things on the ends of his legs. One female is cutting and scraping and rubbing the hard tips of his claws. Being so close to so many humans is frightening and yet comforting too. Kockroach feels as if the proper order of things has been established, as if these humans have indeed seen him for exactly what he is and, in lieu of squashing him, have exalted him to his rightful place.

But Kockroach knows it is not his inner self that has caused all this to happen. It is the little pieces of green paper Mite has been giving to all he meets: the human behind the counter at the schvitz, the human with the dark skin who gave him the new brown cloths and hat, the human with the brutal edge of metal who cut and greased his hair and now is scraping his cheeks. He is beginning to understand the power of the little green pieces of paper. He can use them to maintain the proper order of things. He can use them to get the humans to serve his needs. He wonders how many there are and how he can get hold of them all.

"You play chess, Jerry?" says Mite, sitting in a chair set against the wall across from Kockroach.

"Chess?"

"It's a great game," says Mite. "The game of kings, which is what you and me, we're going to be. An old geezer learned me the game in Philly. It teaches you how to use your noggin."

"Your noggin," says Kockroach as the man in the vest takes a towel and starts wiping what's left of the white goop off his face.

"That's it, baby. That's how to get ahead in this world. When this is all over, I'm going to teach you how to play. We'll have usselves a game, you and me."

"You and me."

"What do you think here, Mite?" says the man in the vest when all the goop is wiped off Kockroach's face.

"Nice, Charlie," says Mite. "Very nice. He cleans up good, don't he?"

"Yes he does."

"It's like looking at someone new without the beard. You want a look there, palsy?" says Mite. "Spin him around, Charlie."

The man with the vest dusts Kockroach with a sharp white powder, brushes the back of his neck, pulls away the towel, spins around the chair until Kockroach is staring at a man in a chair staring back at him. He moves his shoulders and so does the other man in the chair. It is the thing he saw before, in the small white room, the thing that shows him himself. He hasn't seen his face since the early days of his strange new molt, and never before without the little hairs on his cheek. He examines himself carefully. He reaches into a pocket of his new jacket and pulls out the picture of the humans he took from the room at the time of his molt. He compares what he sees now with the face that is his in the picture.

Yes, this is the way he is meant to look.

"What you got there, palsy?" says Mite. He steps toward the chair, looks down at the picture. "There you are. I didn't know you was married. Boy, she's a looker, ain't she?"

"Hubba hubba hubba," says Kockroach as he stares at the female in the picture. She has light hair, like the female known as Sylvie, but she reminds him of the female known as Celia.

"Where she at now?" asks Mite.

Kockroach shrugs his shoulders.

"She die on you or what?"

"Or what."

"Oh man, women will get you every time, won't they? That's why I stay away from them. I gots a weak heart, the doctors they told my momma that when I was a tyke. But that's what's so good about them girls in the Square. They're always there for you. Even when theys with someone else, grab a cup of joe, a cig, and next thing you know it'll be your turn at the wheel. You ready for some trucking?"

"Ready for some trucking."

"Good. Let's go find Sylvie."

• • •

The female with the yellow hair known as Sylvie holds Kock-roach's claw as she leads him down a hallway. The shiny black leathers strapped to the tips of her legs, with their sharp spikes, clack on the rough wooden floor but he can barely hear the sound beneath the roar in his head. He sniffs the air, her sweet floral scent, shakes his head, the roar grows louder. This is more like it, absolutely. He slows his step to watch the twitch of her tail but the woman pulls him forward. He lurches into her and the roar turns into a tempest.

She stops at a door. He lurches into her once again. He rubs against her as she fits a key into the lock and turns it. She spins around until she is facing him, her arms behind her, her mounds against his own flat chest. She grimaces at him and brays. He places his claws on either side of his forehead and reaches out two digits like two antennae. She tilts her head and brays again.

"You're a crazy one, you are," she says.

"Sweet pea," he says, wagging his digits.

"You're certifiable, you are."

"Sweet pea, sweet pea, sweet pea."

She stares for a moment at his wagging digits and then places her claws at the same positions on her own head, raises two of her digits into antennae. He reaches down to rub his antennae against hers. She rubs back, her braying turning to squeals.

"Sweet pea, sweet pea, sweet pea, sweet pea."

He leans down to bite her. She pushes him away, turns, opens the door, falls into the room.

He lunges in after her.

The mating ritual of the cockroach differs slightly from species to species within the order, but is generally initiated by the female, who raises her wings and secretes powerful pheromones from a special membrane on her back. Sensors in the male antennae pick up the sweet pheromonal scent from as far away as thirty feet and direct the male to the ready female. This release of pheromone can be accompanied by stridulatory singing or hissing by one or both sexes to help bring the partners together. Some cockroach songs comprise as many as six complex pulse trains, a melody more musically advanced, actually, than many Ramones songs.

When a sexually receptive female and male cockroach do finally meet face to face, they begin whipping and lashing each other over and over with their antennae. Antennae fencing serves to excite the varied sensory receptors up and down the antennae, which begin to tingle as the two cockroaches are near overwhelmed by tactile and chemical stimuli. This electrically charged S&M foreplay can last as long as two minutes among certain European species, though it has been observed to be remarkably abbreviated or ignored altogether by the male American cockroach, which often simply charges and thrusts its genitals at the female. Scientists have wondered if this behavior explains the infestations of female American cockroaches in the holds of transatlantic flights landing in Paris.

Foreplay over, the male cockroach displays a peculiar lack of interest by turning his back on the female. It is a feint of course, unalloyed sexual interest is the singular characteristic shared by males of all animal species. With his back turned, the male cockroach curls the tip of his abdomen downward, bends his legs to lower his head and thorax, and raises his wings to a sixty-degree angle, revealing a lobe on his seventh abdominal tergite. This lobe, called an excitator, releases the male's sex pheromone, called seducin. The male's excitator is small and bristly and yet irresistible to the female, like a cone of rocky road or a medical degree.

Overwhelmed by the seducin and fooled by the male's submissive posture, the female steps forward, climbs upon the male's back, wraps her legs around his torso, and begins to nuzzle and lick the excitator.

Suddenly the male pushes backwards, arches his abdomen, and extends his genitals toward those of the female. The longest of the male's genital hooks reaches up and clamps itself onto the abdominal tip of the female. Once this connection is made, two other smaller hooks reach into the slim genital orifice of the female and grab hold, forming an unbreakable bond between male and female.

The female, as if in reaction to the male's sudden brutal move, tries to escape from the male and break off contact. She is able at first to move only sideways, stepping off his back and around and around until, still hooked up, she is facing directly away from him.

In this position, tip to tip, the male's genitals reaching deep inside the female's, the struggle stops and male and female this way remain, for an hour at least, sometimes far longer, one inside the other, together, motionless except for the slow internal humming of their bodies. They stay connected long enough for the male to slowly transfer to the female an oval-shaped packet called a spermatophore, filled to the brim with sperm.

After copulation, it is cockroach tradition for the female to relax with a dose of urates, a supplemental source of nitrogen donated by the male. In some species, the urates are contained in the shell of the spermatophore itself. After the sperm cells are drained, the spermatophore is pushed out of the abdomen and devoured by the female. In other species, after copulation, the male will raise its wings, direct the tip of his abdomen toward his mate, and from special glands secrete a whitish urate-rich ooze, which is swallowed by the female in a feast that can last many minutes. This part of the process can often be seen, late at night, on the tiny televisions in arthropod motels. With no females to swallow this whitish ooze, an excess of urates can accumulate in the male's body, bit by bit in a toxic swell, until the male's own urates eventually poison him, or so young male cockroaches often claim.

The mating ritual completed, the male cockroach parts, quickly, washes his claws of the entire enterprise, and hurries off. Male cockroaches are positively Washingtonian in their determination to avoid foreign entanglements and hold no interest in the newborn nymphs that emerge from the female's egg capsule many days later, except as a quick snack if hunger strikes. Once safely away, the male cockroach feeds and defecates, scratches his belly, lays a few bets on the silverfish, and awaits the next intoxicating whiff of female pheromone.

• • •

Kockroach, feeling more himself than he has since the strange molt, stares at his face in the mirror. He rubs his teeth with a digit of his claw. He twists his ears. Fully dressed now in his cloths, he squeezes his tie tight and places his hat on his head at the jaunty angle. It is time, he knows in his bones, to leave.

Something scurries across the sink. He lifts a glass, turns it over, traps the small brown thing. He leans forward to examine his prize. It is a cockroach. Slowly he lifts the glass. The cockroach remains motionless.

Kockroach reaches down a single digit and gently pets the back of the arthropod. The cockroach seems to lift higher on its legs, responding to the touch.

On the pad where they mated, he sees the female with the yellow hair, Sylvie. She is lying naked, twisted in the white cloths. Her eyes are open and they follow him as he walks about the room. Her grimace is soft and dreamy. As she looks at him, she opens her arms, revealing the mounds on her thorax, two large whitish things, one slightly bigger than the other, both with dark brown tips. Kockroach feels roaring through him the strange desire to fall upon his bent legs and place the dark brown tips in his mouth. But even stronger is the craving to flee. It grows within him like a sickness.

"Gotta run, sweet pea," he says.

"So soon, handsome?"

"Blatta, blatta, blatta."

"You know where I'll be."

"Lucky me," he says.

Before he leaves he takes from his wallet a few green papers, as a tribute. He places them on the small table next to the pad, beside the glass which he filled in the bathroom, its amber fluid reaching almost to the rim, its uric acid rich in nitrogen.

Kockroach finds Mite outside the building, leaning against the wall by the door, tossing a silver disk into the air.

"Took your time, didn't you?" says Mite.

"I'm from out of town."

"Aw hell, it's the same everywhere, ain't it? Except maybe in New Orleans, what with all the Frenchies there."

"Want to have some fun, honey? You look like you could use it."

"I got no time for such distractions," says Mite. "There's business to attend. You ready?"

"Ready."

"Remember what I told you? How to play it?"

"Nothing personal, pal, just beeswax."

"Absolutely."

Kockroach takes out his wallet and from the wallet takes out the green pieces of paper. "This," he says.

"Oh yeah, don't you know it. We're going to be drowning in it, you and me. That's what it's all about."

"What it's all about."

"The pineapple pie."

Kockroach sticks out his long pink tongue and licks his lips.

"You got it, palsy. It's you and me, partners to the end."

"Partners."

"Attaboy." Mite pushes himself off the wall and starts to walk down the street. "All right, partner, it's off to see the wizard."

8

Was a geezer what hung around the Square name of Tony the Tune, on account of he was always humming to hisself. Missing half his teeth, bent back, wild white hair, voice like a frog, hum hum hum, crazy old Tony the Tune. Had enough money from somewheres that each night at the Automat he would buy hisself from the steam table a Salisbury steak, with masheds and broccoli, two rolls with butter, pick up a cup of joe from the big metal urn, a wedge of lemon meringue from the wall. Many was the night I nursed my single cup of tea and stared longingly as the old mope sat alone and hummed some cheery song to hisself whilst he sopped up the gravy with a thickly buttered roll.

"Hey, Tony. I got something coming down this week, but I'm a little short right now. You got thirty-nine cents you could lend me just till Tuesday?"

"Get away from me, you little scalawag," he'd spit at me. "I got no time to waste on the likes of you."

Tony the Tune.

So one night, Tony started coming into the Automat with some beefy-looking pretty-boy blond with dark eyes and arms like legs. Old Tony would shuffle in and the blond would follow behind with his bouncy step. When they sats down at Tony's table, the blond boy's tray would be groaning with sandwiches and fruit and heaping helpings from the steam table while Tony's tray would have a single orange and a cup of water. Whatever money he had coming in, see, was enough to feed the boy but not hisself in addition, see. They'd sit together and Tony would spend the whole meal patting the boy's hand, whispering in his ear, opening his milk cartons, humming some Sousa march, fetching straws and napkins, buying more food if the pile on the tray wasn't enough to fill the boy's gob.

I figured Tony for a queen in love, simple as that, but it was Sylvie what set me straight. Tony styled hisself a boxing aficionado, spent his days picking up towels at the Gramercy Gym on Fourteenth Street, looking to get his mitts on a palooka with a chance. Now any fighter with any kind of promise could find hisself a sharper manager than old Tony the Tune, so Tony was left to scrape the canvas for the sad saps with slow hands and glass jaws what were dead meat afore ever they stepped into a ring. A no-chancer, such was Tony's boy, a colorful pug only so long as the colors they was black and blue.

A few weeks after it started, the boy followed Tony in one night but he wasn't so pretty no more. His left eye was closed on him, his maw was a swollen mess, his nose busted but good. That night it was soup and milk and pudding mixed with cream, all sucked down by the palooka through a straw. It wasn't long afore Tony started again to come in alone, humming his tunes and ordering his Salisbury steak and masheds and broccoli and two rolls with butter. We never again spied the pretty-boy blond who wasn't so pretty no more.

If you asked me then, I would have told you Tony the Tune was the worst kind of fool, starving hisself so some no-chancer could prove exactly what he was. The worst kind of fool, a fool in love with hope. Because Hubert, that sack of nothing what sacked my ma, he seeks out hope, like he seeks out fear, waits for the instant when hope wanes to rise up and seize your soul. My momma, she showed me that. Tony the Tune was Hubert bait without even knowing it. But suddenly, with the coming of Jerry Blatta into my life, I had a whole new understanding of the grumpy old mope. See, even though I knew the dire consequences of relying on hope alone, I couldn't bring myself to reject its blandishments neither. So just like Tony, I brought my hope into the Automat, loaded his tray with food, groomed him for a shot at the title.

I had my doubts about Jerry Blatta to be sure. Like when I put him to bed the night we met, sacking out myself on the floor so he could have the mattress. I woke the next morning to find Blatta buck naked and curled into a ball beneath the bedsprings. What that was all about I never figured. Or when I noticed he put his legs through the armholes of his under-shirt and pulled it up as high as he could. I had to near bite my lip through to stop my laughing at that. He was a queer one, and I had my doubts, but I had no doubt at all about what he had done to Roscoe. And so, when the choice was to save what I needed to pay off Big Johnny or to spring the bills I needed to clean up my Suzy like he needed to be cleaned, I sprang, yes I did. I spent like a fool in love on Jerry Blatta.

Let me tell you something, missy. You want to know who it was what made the Boss all he is today, the sweet-dressing, sweet-talking man-on-the-rise? You're looking at him, yes you are. Kiss me twice and call me Charlie.

So there we was, the two of us, strutting up the Great White Way. Can't you see us? Me in the front like a herald of sorts, and Jerry Blatta behind, drawing attention what with his fancy new double-breasted suit and dark glasses, his sharp cheekbones, his syncopated jazzy jazz walk, the lit cig bobbing in his lips, the cocky air of the newly laid. He was a sight, he was, as Times Square as Georgie M. hisself, who was so Times Square they gave him a statue. Jerry Blatta, bucking for a statue of his own, following behind as I led him north through the Square. And then a few blocks west, past all them restaurants, one next to the other, French and Irish and Spanish and Italian, a whole marketplace of cheap European cuisine, until we reached a Greek joint called the Acropolis, where in the back room the *Nonos*, what ran all the rackets in Times Square, held court.

Whoa, that perked you up in a hurry, hey, missy? A little organized crime never hurt a story, did it?

Abagados. The *Nonos*. Which in Greek means Godfather, or maybe murderous bastard, either one, didn't much matter the way things played out. Was a time the very whisper of his name sent a shiver through the Square. Prostitution, drugs, extortion, loan-sharking, pocket-picking, tit-shaking, cheap booze, cheap cigs, the more than occasional heist, the more than occasional murder. Abagados ruled his midtown empire from a room behind the kitchen of the Acropolis, hiring soldiers like Big Johnny Callas to patrol his streets, and he took a cut out of every crime and caper what went down, from the garment district, through the theater district, into the restaurant district, and beyond. He was a shadowy figure, no pictures in the press, no gossip in the columns, I couldn't have ID'd him if he strolled up and bit my nose, but every step I took as I struggled to slip a score out from under his shadow, I felt the terrible weight of his power.

And word was out on the street that Abagados, no longer content to feast on midtown, was getting ready to expand south and north and east, into territory controlled by the coloreds, the Italians, the Jews, oh my, getting ready to expand and looking to build an army.

"What fug you doing here, Mite? Get hell out afore Yonni, he take off your head."

"Yo, Stavros, it's sweet seeing you too," I says. "Is Nemo around?"

Stavros, tall and thin with a black fedora and an absurd black mustache, jumped off his stool at the bar of the Acropolis and lifted both his long palms at me like a copper stopping traffic.

"I'm no kidding, Mite. Word is Yonni gonna make example you. He tells whole world he reach in you throat and pull out you *arhidis*."

"Yeah, well, whatever the hell that means, let him try."

"But the *Nonos*, he don't want no trouble in restaurant."

"Well then I picked the safest spot in New York, didn't I, Stavros, old pal? I need to see Nemo."

The bar sat in front of a huge mural of a bunch of maidens la-di-daing around a pile of ruins. The main dining room off to the left was near to full with the pretheater crowd sawing on their kebabs or cutting into great squares of moussaka, while waiters doused burning bits of goat cheese with juice squeezed from lemon wedges to enthusiastic shouts of "Oooopa." The band, three men in puffy shirts and red vests, played maudlin Greek melodies with tears rolling down their cheeks.

Stavros takes a step toward me, like he's about to bounce me out of the joint, when he spies the man behind me.

"Who laughing boy?"

"His name's Blatta." I close an eye and thinks for a moment. "Jerzy Blatta."

"He Greek?"

"How the hell should I know? I didn't check his papers. Look, Blatta and me, we needs to see Nemo."

"He no here for you."

"It's important, Stavros. And believe me, it'll be worth his while."

"He no here. Now spam you."

"The word is scram. Spam is what you feeds the touristas here and call it souvlaki. And the answer is no. I came to see Nemo. I'll just check for myself to see if he's around."

As I push by him, Stavros grabs hold of me. Two other boneheads with fedoras at the bar jump off theys stools and reach into theys jackets as if about to recite the Pledge of Allegiance.

"Boys, boys, boys," I says. "Good to see you all. You're looking swell. But you might want to step aside or I'll start to screaming bloody murder, I swears I will. Won't the *Nonos* like that, me screaming like a siren here in his quiet little restaurant? If you think that gut scraper on the violin can screech, wait till you gets a load of me. Ready?"

I takes a deep breath, screws up my face, open my mouth wide, like I'm about to make like some fat lady with horns, when Stavros, he lets loose my arm.

"Wait here," says Stavros to me. "I go see if Nemo, he wants talk to a *malakas* like you."

A few minutes later Stavros returned, followed by a huge round man who squeezed through the doorway from the kitchen and made his way to the bar. The man had no neck, lips like Capone, a cigarette was held daintily in his thick fingers. Fat Nemo.

Nemo was some sort of high underboss—the hierarchy of the Abagados organization was always Dutch to me—and yet seemed a decent sort for a gangster. As he made his tours through the Square, oozing his bulk down the crowded streets with Big Johnny Callas and Stavros behind him, he was all smiles and glad hands, tossing cigarettes and bills to the beggars, caressing the heads of the hookers with his fat fingers, buying rounds at the taverns he stepped into so as to renegotiate the payment schedules. And whenever he passed my way he always had a warm word of greeting. *How is it with you, Mite? Dressing mighty sharp this evening, Mite. Someday, Mite, you and me, we're going to do some business.*

"Mite," says Nemo, leaning now on the bar of the Acropolis, fiddling carelessly with his cigarette, his grin a little less genuine, more pained, than on the street. "A pleasure as always to see your smiling face. I'd invite you back but it is a private party. Let me instead buy you a drink." Nemo gestured to the bartender. "A glass of retsina for my friend Mite. And another for his friend . . ."

"Jerzy," I says. "Jerzy Blatta."

"Aaah, a fellow countryman perhaps? Then please, use one of our imported bottles, none of that swill we mix up in the bathtub."

The bartender, a lean dark man with hair plastered back, replaced the unmarked bottle in his hand with another, foggy on the outside, sweetly pink on the inside, and filled two of them water glasses like they had at the Automat. I took a sip, sharp like turpentine. I nodded at Blatta and he downed his in one swallow. His eyebrows, they danced just above his dark glasses.

"Now, Mite, I need to get back to the party, so please be brief."

"Word on the Square, Nemo, is you boys is soldiering up."

Nemo carefully raised his cigarette to his lips. "The word?"

"That's right."

Nemo stared down at me as he inhaled. "On the Square."

"The word."

"And you think you, you are the very soldier we may be looking for?"

"Absolutely."

Nemo blew the smoke out in a stream above my head.

"Let me be frank, my friend. I have craps bigger than you."

"That just mean you're eating well, Nemo, and I'm glad to hear it. But it's not only me I'm talking about."

Nemo tilted his head.

"My palsy Jerzy."

"Is that so?" Nemo turned his attention to Blatta. "I haven't seen you around before, Jerzy."

"He's new in the Square," I says.

"I'm from out of town," says Blatta.

"You got much experience there, Jerzy? You a fighting man? You single-handedly destroyed a regiment of Japs in the war?"

Blatta didn't say nothing, he just smiled his smile and Nemo's eyes they narrowed.

"Thank you for thinking of me, Mite, but I've no need now of your help. And I particularly have no need for strangers from out of town who as far as I know couldn't slap their way out of a pita."

"But Nemo," I says, "you don't understand."

"I do, Mite," he says, leaning forward now, his great bulk towering uneasily over me. "Believe me, I do. We don't want nobody nobody sent. The cops are pouring all kinds of finger men into the street to snitch for them, all kinds of lowlifes. And you, Mite, are about the lowest life I know. So now you might want to leave before Johnny steps through that door."

His gaze passes over my shoulder and a dark grin appears.

"Too late," he says.

I didn't need to turn around to know what Nemo was grinning at, the hairs what pricked up on the back of my neck told me as clearly as any mirror. It was Johnny Callas, Big Johnny, what with the fists and the temper, bopping into the restaurant, two of his lackeys following tight behind. He'd be in a fancy suit, no hat to mar the thick slick of blue-black hair, his broad shoulders and deep chest bobbing up and down as he pointed first to his left, then to his right, acknowledging associates here, clients there, bobbing and pointing as he made his way to the center of the bar where stood yours truly, facing away from him. And it didn't matter that I was facing away from him, he'd know who I was right off. There wasn't too many guys my size who worked the Square, and none in a suit as green as mine.

"I been looking for you, you little parasite," he says.

"Johnny, I'm sorry. I'm trying—" I says. But before I turns around fully, I slams his fist with my face and flip sprawling onto to my back.

"You little parasite," he says, leaning over me now. He sucks his teeth and slaps me on the face. "I give you the two bills for your deal of a lifetime and what do I get in return? Nothing. And then you score on Roscoe and clean him out and what do you do with that cash? You buy a fancy suit, a good sweat, a fancy shave, you splurge at the Automat and buy a ride from Sylvie. You get all that and what do I get? Nothing. You little parasite. I'm going to take you apart. But before I do, I want my five C's."

"I only owes you two-fifty."

"There's a late fee of fifty and I get a cut out of the Roscoe deal. I get a cut out of everything goes down in my territory, just like I got to give a cut myself, you understand?"

"I don't got the money no more, Johnny."

"You know, Mite, I was hoping you would say that. I haven't kicked the crap out of nobody in almost two whole days and I miss it."

"Not in the restaurant, Johnny. You can't do it in the restaurant."

"The hell I can't," says Big Johnny.

"What about the *Nonos*? The *Nonos*."

"Well he ain't here now to tell me no, is he?" says Big Johnny. "Stavros, get the band to playing a little louder, and the rest of you boys gather round. No one need see what I do to this loser."

There it was, missy, my defining moment. Not just here, in the bar of the Acropolis, but through all the stages of my pathetic life. Whatever strides I made, whatever precautions I took, it all still ended right there, with me on my back and some bully boy about to turn my face into mincemeat. Look closely and you can see the scars, under my eye, across the bridge of my nose, the white line what runs through my lower lip. My face is a road map of violent despair.

Big Johnny grabbed my lapel, jerked me off the floor, cocked his fat fist and gave it a twirl. It was like poetry, the rightness of it, the beating of my life what was coming as surely as I deserved it. That I thought I could ever put one past the bully boys, manage a situation so over my head, stiff a stiff like Big Johnny and get away with it, all of it was proof that I had goodly earned every last stitch they was going to need to sew up my head. Off to the side Hubert was laughing at my foolish hopes. And I gave him a look of surrender, I did. The morose Greek music it grew louder, as if it was my own funeral dirge, and I didn't squirm and wiggle like I would have in the past. I lost myself in the music, relaxed, closed my eyes, opened my heart to the righteous propriety of what was coming. All right, Big Johnny, do your worst, because I deserve every lick of it. All right, Hubert, hope is dead, come and fill me with your sweet wisdom.

I felt a jerk forward and then a lurch and then I fell back hard on the floor. And the blow must have been worse than anything I had been dished before because I didn't feel it, didn't feel it, it must have numbed every nerve in my face because I didn't feel it.

I slowly opened my eyes and I saw why I didn't feel it.

Big Johnny Callas was high in the air, his legs kicking, his arms twirling, held high in the air by my own palsy Jerry Blatta. He held him there, did Blatta, in the air, held him there as if it were an actual comic book hero doing the holding. And then Big Johnny wasn't held aloft no more, he was flying in the air, over the ducking barkeep, against the three rows of bottles up against the wall, smashing the bottles even as his own head smashed against the mural of the la-di-daing maidens, afore his carcass fell with a thud to the floor, alcohol gushing down upon him.

The music stopped. The deep murmur of the restaurant died.

"My God," says Nemo.

"Take care of my friend Mite," says Blatta.

The two mokes who had come in with Big Johnny made their move and in a flash Jerry Blatta had each by his necktie. As the shouts started flying, Blatta lurched forward and lifted both men in the air. Theys hung there, arms and legs swinging wildly, clutching at theys throats and fighting to find theys breaths.

Stavros pulls his big black gun and points it at Blatta's chest.

I jumps to my feet and stands between the gun and Blatta, the two mokes in the air kicking me as they struggle. "Nemo," I says. "Don't let him. Don't."

But afore Nemo could answer, the door to the kitchen, it opens and a skinny old man, bent like a question mark, leaning on a cane, hobbles hisself forward. Smoldering in his teeth is a short cigar, thick as a thumb. The crowd silences and parts for the man as if it were the Red Sea and the old man was Moses.

"What happen here?" the old man croaks in a thick Greek accent. "Who stop music?"

He looks at Blatta without an ounce of shock, or even admiration, in his eyes, as if it was an everyday sight to see a man hang two of his gunsels in the air by their ties.

"And who the hell you?" he says to Blatta.

"There's been complaints about a smell," says Jerry Blatta. "Can you flush the toilet or something, Jesus?"

The old man looks at the two men held in the air and then at the mess on the far side of the bar. He casually leans over the rail to see a dazed and doused Johnny Callas struggle to pull hisself to his feet. The old man stares down his long nose at Big Johnny.

"Yonni, you *skata*. I should a known you was in middle this. He's right. I should a flush you long ago."

"But *Nonos*, sir," says Johnny, "I didn't—"

The old man raises a hand, the middle two digits missing at the knuckles, raises his three-fingered hand, and Johnny shuts his trap.

"Put down," the old man says to Blatta.

Blatta immediately drops the two gorillas, who fall into gasping heaps on either side of him.

"You come back with me," says the old man, eyes still focused on Blatta. "We need talk."

"He's with me, Mr. Abagados," I says quickly. "We're partners. My name's Pimelia. Mickey Pimelia. But they call me Mite, as in Mighty Mite, on account of my size. You might have heard of me? I certainly heard of you, yes I have. I'm very pleased to meet you sir. It's an honor. Really. If there's anything I can do to help you, sir, just let me—"

"Nemo," says Abagados.

Nemo raises an eyebrow. "Shut up, Mite."

Abagados shakes his head wearily. "Both then. And Nemo, my music."

Nemo looks at Stavros, who holsters his gun and yells, "Play, you fools."

The music started up again, gayer than before, and after a moment, the crowd it began again its loud murmur. The old man leaned on his cane, shrugged his shoulders like he had seen everything and was surprised by nothing, turned, and hobbled his way into the kitchen.

And with Big Johnny Callas and Hubert now both routed, Jerry Blatta and me, side by side, we followed the old man, the *Nonos*, followed the old man into our futures.

PART TWO

THE NONOS

9 **Celia Singer** stared down at the thick slab of beef bleeding on her plate.

There were times, when first she came to New York City, still living in the women's residence hotel, watching her meager savings thin, that the mere thought of a steak so thick could have sent her swooning. In those days, and even in the later days when she lived with Gregory and earned barely enough for her nightly dinners at the Automat, the desperately hoped-for New York success consisted, for her, of a myriad of nights at the popular spots, treated to steaks by one after the other of her imagined beaus—not Gregory, who saw meat as the purest manifestation of capitalists as carnivores, devouring their cows before they devoured their proletariat—but others, the faceless others, linking their arms with hers to drink champagne and laugh at the witty conversation that swirled about them like the smoke of their fashionable cigarettes. She hadn't wanted much, she thought, just everything.

And now, against all odds, here she was, in the barroom of the "21" Club, with a steak the size of a small dog on her plate and almost everything she had ever hoped for having come true . . . well, almost everything. Like the steak, for instance.

The steak she had always imagined would be discreetly well grilled, fully cooked without a hint of blood. But strangely, now, she found the cut of meat on the plate before her, raw enough to still twitch, more to her liking.

"So what happened to him?" she said.

"He was taken care of is all," said Mite. "I was just trying to tell you the way some people are, how they'll try anything to make a fool of you. I mean, the one thing you can be sure is that anyone what claims to be CIA ain't CIA."

"Did Blatta do something to him?"

Mite tried to shush her quiet.

"The things I've heard." Her eyes widened, she smiled slyly. "Did Blatta bite off his ear? Did Blatta break his leg?"

"Look, don't use his name, especially in a joint like this. He don't like that, all right?"

"The things I've heard."

"No one's supposed to use his name, even me. Dig in, why don't you?"

"Don't you trust me, Mite?" There was a flirtatious whine in her own voice that she found disturbing, it was the voice of one of those women who talked to their husbands like they talked to their dogs. *Don't you twust me, my sweet wittle wovey-dovey.*

"I trust you, course I does, Celia. It's just not important to the point of the thing. The point was about how careful you gots to be, how everyone's out for his own self and you can't trust a one of them. What, is something wrong with your steak? You want I tell the chef to stick it back in the frypan a few minutes?"

"No, Mite, thank you. It's perfect."

"It looks a little raw to me. I knows you like it done better than that. Let me talk to Peter."

"Please," she said, "don't," but even as she said it he lifted his arm into the air and snapped his fingers.

She shrugged her shoulders, looked away and scanned the crowd. Gray suits and black wingtips, women in pearls, mink stoles, highballs and high-handed greetings, a swirl of meat eaters and greeters three deep at the long wooden bar or floating table to table, as if at a big party celebrating their own glorious selves. Actors and writers, internists to the stars, theater producers and publicity agents and columnists with phones at their tables, moguls and their second wives, politicians and their girlfriends and their aides playing the beard. Not to mention the gangsters and their molls, smiling fiercely, which she supposed included the two of them, though Mite was an unlikely gangster with his small stature and his loud green suits and Celia an even more unlikely moll. Still, they came once a week, Mite and Celia, sitting side by side at the same fine table beneath the shelves of athletic trophies, facing out at the room so that Mite could sit with his back to the wall. "Gots to keep an eye out for trouble," he explained to her.

From their red leather banquette they spied the famous and the faux famous. Was that Richard Rodgers there, in the corner, sitting next to Ed Sullivan, or just two dour lawyers talking shop? Was that Jackie Gleason with a cigar and a girl singer that looked like she was seventeen, or just some fat man from Toledo and the hooker he picked up off the street? Was that, my God, Ernest Hemingway, throwing his head back in great gales of masculine laughter, his big hand gripped around his Papa *Doble*, or just some Madison Avenue stiff with a beard and a loud voice trying very hard to look like Ernest Hemingway, or maybe, strangest possibility of all, Ernest Hemingway trying very hard to look like Ernest Hemingway?

The glamorous crowd in the barroom of "21" was not at all like the ragtag assortment at the Automat, where never there was a complaint of a Salisbury steak being underdone. Occasionally, at the end of a night out, Celia would stop back in at the Automat and have a look around, the scene remarkably unchanged: the never-ending argument at the politicians' table; the college boys discussing Céline; the prostitutes with their weary expressions; the showbiz types with their forced gaiety. Even Tab, the boy hustler, was still around, though no longer looking so young or so innocent. She liked to visit the old place, see the old crowd that had once been like a family to her, she liked to take it all in and feel the bitter gratitude at having escaped its clutches. No longer did she hoard her nickels to have enough for a piece of pie, no longer would she sit dreamily by the window and watch the world stream by beyond the plate glass.

"Is there a problem, Mr. Pimelia?"

"Yeah, Peter, look at this thing." Mite stuck his fork in Celia's steak and lifted it off the plate, blood dripping down. "It's like you herded the cow through the kitchen and the chef sliced it right onto the plate."

"I'm terribly sorry, Mr. Pimelia. I'll have a new sirloin cooked to order. Medium well, madam?"

"Yes, thank you."

"Excellent," he said as he scooped up the plate and handed it off to one of the waiters.

"Did you hear that there, Celia?" said Mite. "You're now a madam."

"To think," said Celia, "finally promoted to management."

"What's that?"

"Nothing, Mite."

"Anything else you need, let me know."

He winked at her, winked as if this kid who had made good could do any sort of magic with a simple gesture, a snap of his fingers, a twitch of his lid. And maybe he could. He had started as a raggedly dressed waif with thrift-shop clothes, but like a hero out of Horatio Alger he had risen. Now his shoes were from Regal, his suits from Bonds, his shirts from Arrow, his watch from State Jewelers, his ties from King of Slims. He was a man of the Square, absolutely, linked so closely and inextricably to the mysterious Jerry Blatta that full-grown men shivered when he came close.

It was strange the way things had shifted and her own reaction to it. Celia liked being seen now with a big man on the Square, no matter his size, liked being given the best tables, the complimentary bottles of wine. She caught herself showing inflated exhibitions of interest in Mite's conversations, tilting her head and lowering her eyes at opportune moments, letting the light catch her teeth as she laughed at his jokes. When she got right to it, Mite was the most important person she knew, and because of that some Darwinian instinct had clutched at her good sense. He is important, it told her, he has power; these acts of flirtation were genetically compelled and, in the presence of his power, she was powerless to halt them.

She placed her elbows on the table, leaned her shoulder toward his, tilted her head just so. "Is that Jimmy Durante?"

"Where?"

"Over there, at the table by the bar."

"Sure it is. You want he should come over, say hello?"

"You can't do that."

"Sures I can. I'll ask Peter next time he comes around."

"How do you know Jimmy Durante?"

Mite shrugged. "He lives at the Astor. We did him a favor once. I'll ask. By the way, how's the day shift working out for you?"

"Fine, thank you. It's nice to wake up with the rest of the world for a change."

"Yeah good. That Barney guy is all right. He was more than willing to do a favor once I tuned him in. He's treating you all right?"

"Like a queen," she said gaily.

The promotion to the day shift had come well ahead of those with far more seniority at the phone company. She had mentioned it once, an offhand comment that she was tired of sleeping all day and working all night, and suddenly her boss, Mr. Rifkin, had put his arm on her shoulder and squeezed and told her she had been doing such a wonderful job that she was being promoted. He did this in front of everyone and the other girls eyed her suspiciously, which secretly thrilled her, better suspicion in their eyes than pity. She wondered at what Mite had done to convince Barney Rifkin to do him the favor, or if maybe he had sent Blatta to make the request. And she also wondered how offhand her own comment had truly been. They were right to be suspicious, the girls stuck on the night shift, struggling still to sleep through the morning with the honk of trucks outside their windows and light streaming through their shades.

She lifted her empty wineglass and a waiter quickly filled it. Another waiter deftly placed a new steak before her, its surface dark and sizzling.

"So tell me, Mite," she said, "how do you break someone's legs?"

"What?"

"I mean, do you just crack them like twigs—" she snapped a piece of celery with her fingers—"or do you use tools? I know they call your friend Jerry a leg-breaker, so I was wondering."

"It's just an expression," said Mite. "It don't mean nothing. You know what I been thinking? I been thinking I oughts to go see an opera."

"Why on earth would you want to do that?"

"You know, culture. You think I'd like opera?"

"No, I don't. So he's never broken anyone's leg?"

"I don't know, maybe. A couple arms I know for sure. He just twists them behind the mope's back like a chicken wing and that's it."

"What's it like to watch him do it? Do you hear the crack?"

"You don't want to know," he said, but he was wrong, she did, every detail, every scent and sound. She was fascinated by his work, even the dark parts, especially the dark parts, the

Jerry Blatta parts. That the strange man in brown, seeming to be totally lost in the world when first she spied him, could end up being the source of all power in the Square amazed her. She hadn't seen him since that night in the Automat, but she constantly sensed his presence through Mite, and, somehow, it felt as if he were coming ever closer. The thought of ending up face to face with Jerry Blatta again secretly thrilled her.

This thing with Mite, this peculiar relationship, was now the richest part of her life. She first went out with him as a favor, reluctantly agreeing because he seemed so anxious to impress her, but now she looked forward to their dinners with a breathless anticipation. Mite was her lone connection to a more dangerous, more awe-inspiring world, and she wouldn't give this connection up, or the gifts Mite tossed to her as if they were nothing more than trifles. The dark blue dress she was wearing tonight, and the pearls, were from him. But she figured it was a square deal. In exchange for the weekly dinners and the gifts, Mite bought a companion, someone he could sit and talk to without the pressure of having to pretend to be other than he was, a kid who had latched onto something and was riding it high, someone to laugh with as Times Square opened up to him like an oyster. And it wasn't like she didn't pay a price for all he lavished on her: thrilling and dangerous this new world might be, but also distressingly barren. Everyone assumed there was something between her and Mite and no one anymore ever wanted to be on the wrong side of Mite. So she was like a vestal virgin without the virgin part, lavished with gifts and yet remaining untouched, as if being prepared for some great destiny.

For a while, she had wondered when Mite would make his move, the inevitable pass, and what she would do about it. At one point, she had decided that she would let him, she would close her eyes and let him, and that way she wouldn't feel like she was a cheat as she swilled his wine at dinner. At another point, she had decided that she wouldn't, that Mite would have to take only what she was willing to offer, her time, her friendship, her smile, and be satisfied or go on his way. But then she realized that Mite wouldn't ever make that pass. She would have been insulted except she could sense it simply wasn't in him, boiling away like it was in the other men she had known.

"Why wouldn't I like opera?" he asked. "The swells all seem to lap it up."

"If you're having trouble sleeping, Mite, buy a pillow."

"What about that guy with the name what writes them plays. I hear he's pretty good."

"With the name?"

"Like a state."

"Tennessee Williams? Yes, he's wonderful. He has something opening up in the Morosco soon, something about a cat stuck up in a tree or something."

"A show about cats? It'll never go over."

"Maybe, but I'd still love to go."

"Okay, I'll get us ducats, then. Front row good?"

"He's a fruit, you know."

"Is he? Well maybe we'll see something else. There's plenty else, isn't there?"

"So why is he not called an arm-breaker, if that's what he does. I just want to get the lingo down."

"Why are you so interested in the Boss all of a sudden?"

"I'm just curious, Mite. Just curious."

"It's an expression, is all. Look, it's just beeswax. We make deals, we expect them kept. We don't go looking for trouble, but when someone starts talking about the CIA being the reason he can't pay what he owes, we can't go to no police, we gots to take care of it ourselves, that's all."

"Do you hear the crack?"

"All you hear are the pleading and the shake in the voice and then the scream, that's all you hear. A lot of screaming."

"It's the same in opera, too." She leaned toward him. "How does it make you feel, all the screaming?"

"Like my suit's too tight."

She pulled back quickly. It was not what she was expecting. She had expected to hear of the blood pounding, the fingers tingling, she had expected to learn something of the thrill in the raw exercise of power. What she felt now was like going down a fast elevator, a deflating sense of disappointment. Disappointment, she realized with a touch of shame, in Mite.

"Did you ever think, Mite?" she said enthusiastically, trying to mend a rent maybe only she felt. "When I first saw you, you looked like a drowned rat. It was raining, ferociously, and you ran into the Automat, your jacket pulled over your head. And then you hit on each table, one after the other, looking for a piece of change."

"I remembers."

"And after a while you finally came over to my table, water still dripping off your hair onto your face, and asked me for your usual thirty-nine cents."

"And you gave it."

"Why thirty-nine cents, Mite? Why not a dime like everyone else, or a quarter? Why thirty-nine cents?"

"Was a Joe I knew when I was still a boy, an old guy what met me in the public library of all places."

"What were you doing in a public library?"

"I was reading, what do you think? I used to be quite the reader, and not just comic books, thick books. *The Count of Monte Cristo*. You ever read that?"

"It's a boys' book."

"Yeah, especially for a boy what's been getting his butt kicked all over the schoolyard. Anyhoo, this old guy he taught me when you're asking from dough always be specific, a set amount it gives comfort to the mopes paying out. He taught me a lot. Everything I done in the Square, it's like I'm following his blueprint."

"He did you a favor."

"I suppose."

"Suppose? Why look at you. Look at all the money you have now, eating in the finest restaurants. Look at the way they treat you, like royalty. You're Pinnacio."

"Pinnacio?"

"The guy you told me about, the manager now in Hollywood. You told me about Pinnacio like he was a talisman, a symbol that everything was possible. I bet the up-and-comers don't talk about Pinnacio anymore. I bet they talk about you."

"Go off."

"You found it, Mite. What did you call it?"

"The pineapple pie?"

"That's it. It always sounded so tasty."

"But still, sometimes I feel the suit is too tight."

"Buy another," she snapped.

"See the thing is, Celia, the thing is," said Mite, who was clearly trying to tell her something, who was obviously struggling to make himself understood, "my mother was trapped. I don't know I ever told you about my mother."

"No," said Celia, not sure she wanted to hear about his mother, there, in the "21" Club, drinking red wine and eating red meat and watching Jimmy Durante tell stories at his table.

"She was . . . she had . . . I never told no one before, but she had these episodes, she called them. Episodes. They was more like the whole world crashing down. She would spin around and her eyes would roll up the back of her head and she'd be shaking and quivering and she'd fall down bang to the floor and there'd be nothing there, nothing there. The first was this big surprise and the second was not such a surprise and after that she just didn't want to go nowhere in case it happened right there, on the street, with everyone watching. So it was like she was trapped by this thing, this affliction of emptiness which I never told no one about but which scared me small. It still does."

"Do you want more wine?"

"Yeah, sure. And now I see those mokes in their suits, wage slaves Old Dudley called them—Old Dudley was the guy what set me on my way—the suckers riding the train in and working on someone else's money and then riding the train back. Better they hang themselves with them ties, he used to say. Except what are they going back to, Celia? The wife, the kids, the family I never knowed because my dad he ran and my mom she had her episodes, the little houses that Levitt he's building for them out on the Island with them picket fences. And you know, it gets me wondering."

"That's not you, Mite."

"Why not? Why the hell not? I could wear gray, not green. I could fold my paper on the train, fold once, fold twice, a little bend and there it is, the baseball scores ready for my perusal. Hey, Don, how'd them Gints do yesterday? I could like opera, maybe, or that queen from Tennessee."

"Mississippi, actually."

"Well, nows I understand. But see there's a whole 'nother layer in the Square that I know nothing about. All them theaters, all them parties at Sardi's, all them books I don't read no more. Look around, these mokes are all part of it, why can't I be too? Sometimes I feel as trapped as my mother she ever was, like I got the same affliction and the emptiness it's pouring down on me like rain."

"Mite, stop. Please."

She didn't want to hear this, his anxieties and doubts, the weepy telling of his childhood traumas. It was selfish, she knew, he was trying so hard, she could tell, but still his confession was more than she could bear. She needed him to be a cartoon, an amiably winning surface of strut and language whose number had hit and who now was taking her along for the ride. And that other stuff, that darker stuff, the Blatta stuff that tightened his collar, for her that was more than just part of his color, his charm. For her that was, somehow, the root of everything. So she didn't want to see the undersized boy tending to his epileptic mother after his father had run away. She didn't want to see the gangster straining against the violence of his trade and yearning for the bland homilies of suburban life. She didn't want to see the man, naked and alone, bewildered by his existential anxieties. For God's sake, did he think he was the only one with the specter of emptiness threatening to swallow him? Didn't he realize that the surface he wanted to discard, that edge of darkness that sickened him, was the only thing protecting her from the same damn specter? So no, she didn't want to hear any of it, not because of what it said about him, but for what it said about her taste for pearls and wine, her new job on the day shift, her growing hunger for animal flesh cooked rare.

"I'm sorry, Celia. I don't want to ruin your dinner. I just thought you'd understand what it meant, and all, feeling trapped."

Like she was slapped. "I don't feel trapped."

"You know what I meant. We all of us are in—"

"Mr. Pimelia, sir?"

The man who appeared at their table was portly and sweating as he stood, literally, hat in hand. She had seen others just like him on other nights, all clothed with either greater or lesser aplomb but all with the same terror in their eyes. This one had a golden ring on one of his fat fingers and the neatly trimmed beard of a man who wasn't used to standing, literally, hat in hand. She was so relieved to see him it was like he was a reprieve from the sentence Mite was about to impose upon them both.

"Aw hell, Cooney," said Mite, who didn't rise to greet

the man but instead glanced at Celia as if the appearance of the man proved his point, and then sawed into his steak, untouched during his awkward revelations. "How'd you get in here?"

"I'm sorry to disturb your dinner, Mr. Pimelia."

"Yeah? So come back when we're done."

"Can we talk?" The man glanced at Celia. "In private?"

"What's to talk about?" said Mite, sticking a piece of meat in his mouth, chewing, continuing to talk all the while. "You're late again. Two weeks this time."

"The closing, Mr. Pimelia, they keep putting it off. Now it's a problem with the deed. The buyer is ready and willing, but they keep putting off the closing."

"And that's supposed to be our problem? You knew the terms. More wine there, Celia?"

"Yes please," she said brightly. Mite poured the last of the bottle into her glass, raised his hand, snapped his fingers.

"Yes, Mr. Pimelia," said Peter, who had appeared quickly and silently, and was now standing just behind the man with the beard. "Is there a problem? This man said he was a friend of yours."

Mite glanced up at the man in the beard and then said, "No, no problem. We're out of wine here, is all. And get Jimmy over by the bar another bottle of whatever it is he's drinking and tell him I gives my regards."

Peter leaned over, snatched the empty bottle from off the table. "Very good, Mr. Pimelia."

The man with the beard watched until the maître d' had left and then began again with his pleading. "I can't make the two-fifty, per, Mr. Pimelia. I just can't. You'll get it all when we close, I swear, with some extra. But just now, I tried to get the five I owe you."

"And this week's too."

"Of course, yes, I tried. And I can't."

"You got a house, don't you?"

"And three kids, Mr. Pimelia, and a wife and a mother-in-law living in a first-floor bedroom."

"Aw, Cooney, we don't want to hear about your mother-in-law, please, we're eating here. Look, you got something to say, you want to make a deal, make it with the big guy."

The man's eyes swam like two fish, left, right, bulging forward. "No please, God, no. That's why I came to you, Mr. Pimelia, to avoid going to him."

"But Cooney, there's nothing I can do. If you can't make the payments or a deal with the big guy, there is nothing I can do."

Mite sawed at his steak and then looked up at Celia. Celia glanced at the man and though she believed she should have felt pity, compassion, horror over what was being done to him and his family, what she felt instead was a familiar tremor of thrill at being part of some force powerful enough to shake a man like that to his core. The affection she felt that instant for Mite grabbed at her heart, and if he had asked her just then for anything, anything, she would have given it gladly and without hesitation.

"What about that ring you're sporting there, Cooney?" said Mite, while still staring at Celia. "The big gold one. How much it worth?"

"I don't know. It has sentimental value."

"We'll call it five."

"It's solid gold, with two diamonds and a ruby, Mr. Pimelia."

"How big are them diamonds?"

"Mr. Pimelia, please God, I don't remem—"

"How big?"

"Half carat each maybe."

Mite raised his eyebrows and smiled, still looking only at Celia. "All right, you're lucky you got me on a night when my mood is sweet and I might just be in the market for a ring. I'll need to resize it, and that will cost me, still I figure it's good for seven-fifty."

"But, but—"

"Take it off."

The man hesitated and then, quickly, he began scrabbling at his finger, trying to yank off the ring. It wouldn't budge past the knuckle. He gave it a twist, tried again, his face strained with the effort.

"I'll tell him you're clear up to this week. But next time don't come back to me like this. Either bring the money or go see him. And Cooney, believe me when I tell you this, it's better you find him than he finds you."

"I understand," said the man, his voice slow and constipated as he struggled with the ring.

"All right, all right, let's have it."

"I'm trying, Mr. Pimelia," the man said, his face twisting grotesquely from the effort. "All the nervousness, my hands are swollen, but I'm trying."

Celia edged a small crock of butter his way.

She was still feeling a quivering thrill at what she had done when she looked up. Her heart leaped when she saw him. He was coming toward them, energetically darting through the crowd, arms outstretched. His bent back, his famous nose, a great gleam in his eye.

"Mickey, you son of a gun," came the celebrated rasp, full of merriment and rhythm, "how you ended up with the swellest dame in the room I'll never know. It's a mystery, it is. Guess my good news. Guess. All right I'll tell you. I made a killing today in the market. Yes indeed. I shot my broker. Mickey, my friend, you look like a million. So how the hell are you?"

10

Kockroach does not dream. The inner mechanisms of his brain won't admit to gorgeous flights of fantasy and it need not trouble itself with working through the unsolved dilemmas of the day because Kockroach's day has no unsolved dilemmas. He does what he needs to get what he wants and moves on. In fact, Kockroach's life has little day in it. He falls peacefully to sleep at the earliest announcement of the early dawn, the dreamless sleep of the innocent, if innocence is remaining true to inner character, and arises only as the promise of night begins whispering in his ear. What song he hears from the onset of night is the song that has serenaded his species awake for a hundred thousand millennia:

"Darkness comes, sweet darkness, so arise, ye scions of the night, and devour."

At the first rap on his door Kockroach scurries from beneath his bed. He has slept his peaceful slumber in the lovely narrow gap between the bedsprings and the floor, but still the covers and sheets of the bed are tossed and twisted with some fierce abandon. For a cockroach, a night without sex is like . . . well, how would one even know? He pushes himself to standing, protects his eyes with the dark glasses, strolls, naked and unabashed, arms rising languidly in his contrapuntal step, to the door, which he opens.

The man in the red jacket studiously keeps his gaze averted as he rolls in the cart with its twin domes, like two great silver breasts. He parks the cart, bows stiffly, and silently backs out of the suite, leaving Kockroach alone.

Kockroach lifts one dome to find a huge bowl of ice topped with thick pink shrimp, cooked but still in their shells, their little legs clutching at the ice. He dips his hand into the red spicy sauce, licks his fingers clean with his long tongue, and then one by one jams the shrimp into his mouth. He masticates with abandon, letting out a strange series of chortles with each snap of the jaw. He has taken a great liking to shrimp, their briny sweetness, like the briny marshes in which his great and noble forebears first evolved. The lovely crunch of their thin shells reminds him of the crunch of chitin eaten after a molt.

Beneath the second dome lies a great rack of lamb, the bones arranged in a crown, pink paper hats on the tip of each rib. Kockroach lifts the rack, each hand grabbing a number of ribs, lifts it above his head, and then, in a savage jerk, rips it apart. He snaps at the tender chunks of meat rolling off each rib, first from one hand, then the other, and back again, ripping the meat with his teeth, mashing it to pulp with his molars, swallowing the sweet roasted muscle before snapping at more. His lips, his cheeks, his body is smeared with the grease of the rack. When the meat is gnawed off he starts on the bones, crushing them in his teeth, sucking out the marrow.

This fascination with meat, with bone and marrow, with the slippery strips of fat that line each stria of rib, is a corruption of his essential cockroach nature by the carnivorous traits of his human body, and yet, yet . . . it feels right, oh so right. It is different, yea, but not a departure, nay, not a departure at all. Instead it is a great evolutionary step forward, a natural progression from the discovery of fire. This is how cockroaches would eat had they the wherewithal to hunt larger prey, to cook their victims over savage fires, to smear the grease of their roasted conquests across their abdomen, their legs, their genital hooks.

He struts around, his back arched, his legs stepping high, holding the final remnants of the ribs in the air as the light reflects off the smears of fat on his body, struts and laughs and revels.

He is in the shower when the man in the red coat arrives to roll out the cart. The shrimp are gone, muscle and shell. All that's left of the rack of lamb are the tiny paper hats, tossed carelessly across the floor.

Kockroach sits back in the stiff, high chair, the white robe cinched around his body, his glasses on, his grimace fixed, the lower part of his face covered with hot white foam. A man scrapes at the foam with a straight razor. A female rubs his nails with a yellow stick. A man is in the corner shining his shoes. Mite sprawls on the couch, his feet on a coffee table, talking.

"The girls are all out, Jerry, all but Sylvie what says it's so painful she can barely walk. Don't know what it is with her lately, but she ain't bringing in what she was, no surprise the way the skin it hangs off of her like a baggy sack of nylons. She's on the sleeve, I think, but everyone knows not to sell to our girls so I don't know where she's getting it. Having her around, it's bad for business, gets the other girls upset and, truth be told, she ain't so appetizing to the buyers. We need do something about her soon."

Kockroach says little when Mite speaks, but it is not out of a paucity of words. He has learned much of the language, picked it up on the run from conversations overheard, from statements barked by his associates, from the movies Mite sometimes takes him to on hot, slow nights. He now knows the names of the parts of his new body, the names of the human things that surround him. He has collected strung-together bits of noise that he sounds out during the gaps in his sleep until they are polished and ready for the world. The sentences he has learned are short, to the point, active, orders aped from the most powerful humans he has come across. And along with the sentences he has learned a trick about speaking with humans: the fewer sounds you make, the more they respect and fear you; the fewer sounds you make, the more you maintain control.

"The protection's been coming in like clockwork, no worry there, not after what you did to Paddy's place and then to Paddy's wife. Once word got out, the others what was holding back all fell in line like tenpins. Oh she's walking again, by the way, case you was worried, Paddy's wife, though she ain't walking so well."

The man with the straight razor cleans off his blade and strops it on a leather strap hanging from his belt.

"Today's collections is on target," says Mite. "Pinkly's late with his hundred, but I talked to his mom and she says he don't come up with it in a day or two she's good for it. I think she's got a stash somewheres underneath a mattress so it pays to let him get behind. Rickland paid, Somerset paid, Bert is out of town but his girl's still around so he'll come through. And you'll love this. Seven twelve came up, which is Toddy's number, son of a bitch. He owed us six plus, but as soon as I heard the number I got to his runner afore he did, so he's up to date."

"Show me," says Kockroach.

"Sure, Jerry, sure. You know I'm always square with you."

Mite reaches into his jacket, pulls out a thick envelope, drops it onto the coffee table with a solid thwack. The female working on Kockroach's nails slips and digs a knife into the cuticle. Kockroach's hand suffers not a twitch as blood wells on his fingertip. The female cleans it off nervously with a white towel.

"I'm sorry, sir," she says. "I'm sorry."

"Who isn't?" says Kockroach.

"I marked out with a paper clip the *Nonos*'s cut, for you to give him the way you like," says Mite.

Kockroach nods.

"The *Nonos* wants to meet everyone at midnight. Nemo made sure for me to tell you not to be late."

Kockroach shrugs.

"That's it, I guess." Mite drops his feet from the table, slaps his thighs and stands. "I'll see you at midnight then. Have yourself a good night, Jerry."

"What about Cooney?" says Kockroach.

Mite freezes for an instant, and from behind his glasses, Kockroach notices.

"I told you he made up three payments a couple weeks ago," says Mite.

"I didn't see the cash."

"He made it up in trade. He gave us this." Mite screws a thick gold ring off his finger. "I had it sized for me and took the spinach out of my cut, but if you want it, Jerry, be my guest."

Mite flips the heavy ring to Kockroach, who examines it carefully, notices how small it is, notices the shiny metal, the square diamonds, the ruby, and then bites into it as he has seen others bite into gold.

"Swell," Kockroach says, tossing it back to Mite. "Keep it for yourself. But what about this week?"

"He's due, yeah," says Mite, examining the ring with evident disappointment, a bite mark ripping now through its face, "but I think we should give him time. He's been jabbering something about the city holding up his deal. I checked out what he's saying and it's on the up. Once the deal closes and he flips the building he'll have plenty to pay what he owes and a premium to boot. He's got a wife and three kids, he needs a break."

"I think so too, sweet pea," says Kockroach, his grimace, half hidden by the foam, growing wider.

Mite nods, turns to leave.

"Hey, Mite," says Kockroach, "how about a game?"

• • •

The attendants have departed. Kockroach, still in his white robe and his dark glasses, sits at a table across from Mite. Between them lies the board with its array of brown and white squares and the little wooden pieces. Together they are performing a human ritual that Mite has taught to Kockroach, a ritual called chess.

"What are you up to, Mite?" says Kockroach as he stares at the board.

"You know me, Boss. I'm never up to nothing."

"Sweet pea."

Kockroach has learned to enjoy the give-and-take over the board. Mite's was the first name he learned in the human world and he relies on Mite for much as he runs the business of running Times Square, but Kockroach is not certain he can trust Mite anymore. If you know what a human wants, you have control. But Kockroach is no longer sure of what Mite wants. At first he assumed that Mite wanted exactly what he himself wanted: money, power, sex, shrimp, sex. But Mite was never about sex, and money, power, and shrimp seem no longer enough for him, and that is the cause of Kockroach's concern. This mistrust has leaked into all their business dealings. The hesitancy Kockroach noticed this very night is merely another example. But Mite, who is suitably deferential to Kockroach in business, is anything but deferential in the ritual. He schemes, he traps, he attacks without mercy. The only time now Kockroach feels Mite is being completely honest with him is during the ritual of the game.

It took Kockroach a long time to gain an understanding of the ritual. Not the pieces and the moves, that was easy. The slopey pieces move entirely on an angle. The piece shaped like the head of a wasp jumps up and over. The moves and rules of this chess were easy, it was the purpose of the ritual that confused him. It seemed to him at the start a type of battling. When Mite first slipped his large female piece into Kockroach's side of the board like a knife and knocked over Kockroach's boss piece with the cross on top, Kockroach felt a spurt of fear. Now what? he wondered. He tensed his whole body, ready for a confrontation, sad at what he'd have to do to the little man. But Mite merely reached out his hand. "Good game, Jerry," he said. "Keep at it and you'll get the hang," and that was it. Everything after the ritual was the same as before. It seemed to have no meaning. Kockroach didn't understand. Time after time Mite toppled Kockroach's boss piece and nothing changed.

Until something did change, and it slammed into Kockroach like a revelation.

In his first games, Kockroach examined the board and made what appeared to be the strongest move. If a square could be occupied he occupied it, if a piece could be killed he killed it. Cockroaches live eternally in the present tense and he performed the ritual like a cockroach, but each game ended with Mite knocking Kockroach's pieces off the board one after the other before swooping in and killing his all-important boss piece.

"Where did you learn this chess?" said Kockroach early in their practice of the ritual.

"From Old Dudley, what taught me the ways of the world,"

said Mite. "I ever tell you about Old Dudley? He said chess was a good thing to cotton to, teaches you how to think ahead."

"Think ahead," said Kockroach. "What's that?"

But slowly, game after game, Kockroach began to understand. Mite moved that little piece there for a reason; if Kockroach killed Mite's little piece, Mite could kill a stronger piece. If Kockroach moved here, Mite would move there. If Mite moved there and Kockroach moved there, then Mite would move there. Kockroach saw deeper into the game, the rituals lengthened, Kockroach came closer and closer to killing Mite's boss piece.

But that wasn't the fantastic change. As Kockroach stared at the board, sequences of moves played out in his head in glorious ribbons of possibility that grew and lengthened and weaved from the now to the then until, like some sort of strong magic, he was no longer playing only in the present, he was playing in the future, too.

"You're getting tougher, Boss," says Mite as their current ritual heads toward its conclusion. "You been taking lessons?"

"From you, Mite. Only you."

"You got me pinned here. You got me pinned there. Looks like I'm in serious trouble."

"Looks like."

"Except watch this." Mite moves his wasp. "Check."

Kockroach stares at the board. The ribbons of possibility that had been reeling through his head suddenly shrivel. His boss piece is under attack. He has one possible move. He makes it.

Mite moves the female piece that had been protecting his boss piece, leaving his boss piece vulnerable. Kockroach is ready to rush in and kill Mite's boss when Mite says, "Checkmate."

Kockroach stares at the board for a moment longer before he topples over his own boss piece.

"Nice game," says Mite, reaching out his hand as he stands. "It won't be long afore you own me."

Kockroach, still staring at the board, ignores Mite's outstretched hand as he says, "I own you already."

"Maybe next time, Boss," says Mite. He pulls back his hand, hitches up his pants, heads to the door. "Maybe, but I doubt it."

Kockroach keeps staring at the board, willing the ribbons of possibility to reappear and flutter in his brain. The purpose of the ritual, he has learned, is not the game itself, not who kills whose boss. The purpose of the game is these ribbons rippling into the future. Through the practice of the ritual, he has leaped out of the arthropod's slavish devotion to the present tense.

And suddenly, a whole new territory has opened up for Kockroach to plunder.

Pressed and pleated, shaved and shined and buffed, tie tightened, belt cinched, shoes double-knotted, jacket double-buttoned to his throat, glasses on, hat on, grin on, cigarette burning like a warning in his teeth, Kockroach saunters out of the elevator and greets the world.

"Good evening, Mr. Blatta."

"Anything we can get you, Mr. Blatta?"

"Should I check your mail, Mr. Blatta?"

Kockroach stops at the main desk, tells the clerk a guest will be coming during the night.

"Very good, Mr. Blatta."

"Your car is here, Mr. Blatta."

"Step away, please, and let Mr. Blatta through."

A path is cleared as if for a tycoon and doors are opened as if for a starlet. Kockroach walks through the crowded lobby, leaving gapes and green tributes in his wake.

Istvan is waiting for him outside, leaning on the hood of the big humped Lincoln, chocolate brown and encrusted with chrome. Istvan is Kockroach's driver, promoted by Kockroach from the pack of lowly gangsters who police the Square. Istvan's huge arms are crossed, his peaked cap is tipped up on his wide blond head, his narrow blue eyes light up with devotion when he sees Kockroach exit the hotel. Istvan jumps away from the hood and reaches for the door.

"Good evening, Mr. Blatta."

Kockroach ducks into the car without breaking stride.

"What's on the agenda tonight, Mr. Blatta?" says Istvan, his accent thicker than his arms.

"Beeswax."

The Murdock Hotel is a desiccated pile of cracked brick wedged between a dusty supply warehouse to the east and a failing shirtwaist factory to the west. The desk clerk, perched on a stool, hunched over something pornographic, glances up to see Kockroach standing before him and jerks back so hard he slams into the boxes behind him, sending mail and keys clattering to the floor.

"Room two-two-four," says Kockroach.

"Right away," says the clerk as he drops to his knees and searches the floor for the key.

Kockroach climbs the steps slowly, sensing their rotting boards, their foul stench. He slams his fist on the damp wall and a slab of plaster dislodges to crash upon and tumble down the steps. He opens the door to Room 224 without a knock and finds Sylvie shivering beneath a blanket on her bed. She startles when she sees him, sits up, teeth chattering. The blanket slips down, baring her sagging, mismatched breasts and the ribs beneath them.

"Get dressed," he says. "We're going out."

"I can't, Jerry. God, I can't. Don't you see how sick I am?"

Kockroach steps forward and sits on the bed. He gently caresses the side of her face. She leans into his touch.

"I don't want to see you like this," he says.

"I miss you too, Jerry. We're never together anymore. Remember when you used to take me out, when I taught you to dance at the Latin Club? Those were times, weren't they? I know I haven't been working enough, but I'm still sick. Even with the medicine you been giving me, I can't do it anymore. I have to get away. I got a sister in Pittsburgh. I was thinking of visiting her, just for a while, to get back my strength."

"You'll be swell. You need to get up, step out. We'll go for a ride."

"I can't get up. I can't move."

Kockroach reaches into his jacket, pulls out a small wax-paper bundle tied with a bright red string, and drops it onto her bed. The faint aroma of vinegar rises from the blanket.

"Medicine," says Kockroach.

"I don't know what's worse," says Sylvie, "the sickness or the cure."

"Get dressed," he says, standing. "I'll be waiting for you outside."

Sylvie stares at the bundle with the red thread for a long moment, as if deciding on something, and then snatches it to her chest.

"And Sylvie," he says, his smile brightening, "put on something sharp."

Istvan drives the Lincoln slowly through Times Square, the phantasm of light and color reflecting off the brown, the chrome, the glass like a scrambled message from a neon god. Kockroach sits jammed into the corner of the backseat, a cigarette in his teeth, one hand clamped on Sylvie's knee. She is in a black dress with sequins, high heels, a fluffy boa wrapped around her neck. Her face is pale, pale as death, but her lips are painted red.

Istvan slows the car and then stops. Kockroach's door opens, a red-haired woman in a tight sweater and bangle earrings leans into the car. "Sylvie," she says, "dragged your skinny ass out of bed, did you?"

Sylvie snuggles up to Kockroach and licks his ear. Without

turning her head, she slips a stare at the woman. "Get back to work, Denise. There might be a sailor still who hasn't filled your mouth."

"Leastways I'm working, baby."

"Since you're in the dough, let me give some advice. Do something about them snaggleteeth."

The red-haired woman smiles.

"Please," says Sylvie, "before you start frightening small children."

"How's beeswax?" says Kockroach.

"Started slow, must be a Bible convention in town, but it's picking up."

"Let me see."

The woman pulls a wad of bills from inside her sweater. Kockroach takes them, sniffs them, jams them into his jacket. "Any trouble?" he asks.

"A tall hat from Texas thought he was so good he should get it for free. Janine whispered your name and he near pissed himself trying to take the wallet out of his pants."

"I'll be back before dawn. Tell Janine I want her to wait for me."

The red-haired woman nods her head at Sylvie. "Why she get to ride tonight?"

Sylvie leans over Kockroach. "'Cause Jerry is tired of your fat ass and wanted a dose of class."

"Dose of clap is more like it."

Kockroach pushes the red-haired woman out the door and slams it shut. Istvan pulls away, down Broadway, as Sylvie leans over and sticks her tongue out at the window.

The great face rising above the car, its mouth open as if in perpetual surprise, blows a ring of smoke.

The brown car slides through empty streets.

"Where are we going?" asks Sylvie.

"I have something to show you."

Sylvie cuddles up. "Some out of the way club? Some exotic gangster hangout?"

"Something like that."

"Anyplace is fine," she says, drowsily leaning her head on his strong left arm. "Surprise me."

"That's the intention," he says. "Feeling better?"

"Much." She yawns.

"Are you too tired to dance?"

"Don't be silly," she says, rubbing his stomach with her left hand. "I'm never too tired to dance with you."

The streets narrow, twist and turn. The car purrs along, turns right, squeezes through an alleyway. It comes out on a wide stretch of asphalt, lined with blocky brick buildings fronted by wooden frames, the frames empty now of the carcasses hanging daily in the mornings. The thick smell of meat, rotting, luscious, hovers over the puddles and the cracked sidewalks, the dim streetlights, the overturned trash bins being scavenged by rats.

A huge dog in an alley, gnawing on the raw haunch of something, bends in respect as the brown car passes.

"Where are we?" says Sylvie, suddenly sitting up.

"Go to the end, Istvan," says Kockroach.

"Is that the club?" says Sylvia.

"The far end."

The car pulls to the end of the street, turns right, then left again, where they reach a wide, uneven strip of cobbles leading to a row of desultory wooden piers, ill lit, swirling with fog, seeming to be in the very process of slowly, agonizingly, collapsing into the Hudson River. Sylvie shrinks from Kockroach when she sees the piers.

On one, a shadow leans on a post, its very posture a signal of defeat. On another, toward the street, are two shadows, one walking fast, head swiveling, the other, well behind, dragging itself toward the light. A car rumbles along the cobblestones, stops at still another pier, a shadow slips in, the car moves off.

"Why'd you bring me here?" says Sylvie, unable to hide the desperation in her voice. "What business do you have here?"

"Do you see the pier straight ahead?"

"What about it, Jerry?"

"It's yours now, sweet pea."

"Go to hell. I'm no pier monkey. It's only dope fiends and toothless scags that need work the piers."

Kockroach loops a finger around her lower lip and pulls it down. There is a large gap between her front teeth and her back molar. "I'd say you're a bit of both."

"It was you that gave me the medicine. It was you that did this to me."

"You were sick, you needed to be working. Like now."

"Not here, not on the piers. Jerry, don't make me do this."

"Every bum needs a job."

"Jerry, please. I'm begging you, no. Don't do this. Let me go to Pittsburgh. My sister lives there. Front me the bus fare, that's all I'm asking. I'll get well. I'll come back better than ever and be the queen of the Square. I was prime once, don't you remember? We had something, didn't we? We had nights. I taught you to dance at the Latin. Don't do this, please, please, I'm begging you, please."

Kockroach leans over and opens Sylvie's door. "Nothing personal, pal, just beeswax."

"Don't, no, God, don't make me, please, please, not the piers. I'll do anything, anything."

He lets her cry on as a wisp of fog floats in the door. He doesn't have to shove her out, he sits there and waits until she cries herself into silence and then climbs out all on her own.

"You did this to me, you stinking cockroach," she yells as she slams the door shut, losing her balance in the effort.

Kockroach watches silently as she staggers over the wide, uneven expanse of cobbles, reaches the pier, collapses against a wooden pole. He remembers that this is the first human with which he ever mated and wonders if that matters. He decides that it doesn't. Kockroach does not read, but if he did he would agree with Shakespeare that "what's past is prologue." And if Kockroach did, in fact, ever have a book in his hand, he would certainly skip past the prologue and get right to the meat of it, which is the desiccated woman gripping desperately the wooden pole, now, turning from a drain on his finances to a productive member of his organization, now. Something needed to be done.

"You'll check on her later, Istvan, make sure she stays all night."

"No problem, Mr. Blatta. Where to?"

"The Acropolis." Kockroach lights a cigarette. "Word is the *Nonos* wants to talk."

11

If you took a midnight stroll in the Square in them days, missy, what would you see? Degenerate womanizers, degenerate joint swingers, degenerate jazz fiends and drug fiends, and hooch hounds. It was a landscape of degeneration, God bless us all. But of all the degenerate degenerates patrolling the Square in them days, the most degenerate of all were them degenerate gamblers, the DGs.

Was a DG what made his life on the Square when first I arrived name of Jimmy Slaps. He had scuffed shoes and a long face and he wore his greasy old raincoat rain or shine, its filthy beige tail trailing after him like an ugly rumor as he cruised the Square looking for a bet, any bet, at any odds. If was a craps game going off in an alleyway south of Forty-fourth, Jimmy Slaps was there. If was a poker game being dealt in some fleabag flophouse, Jimmy Slaps was scratching behind his ear and raising hard on his two pair. His bible was the racing form, his drug of choice was long-shot odds, he jacked off to queens full.

See, the thing about a DG is he believes he's found the answer to Hubert, the very purpose of life, and that the Main Street fools living without the thrill of seeing if the up card matches the two jacks down are the ones what are missing out on the true sweetness of the world. That's why a sure thing don't never interest guys like Jimmy Slaps. You want a sure thing, sell shoes for a living; Jimmy Slaps, he wanted to gamble.

And here's the killer. If to be good at the thing you love to do is to be blessed in this world, then Jimmy Slaps was a limp-dick Mongol in a Chinese whorehouse.

So there was a poker game going down in the Chelsea Hotel off Forty-first, a big-money game organized by two pros from Chicago, and all the DGs on the Square was hot to take part. I'm talking about legends now. There was Shifty Mahoose, there was Kings Dagboy, there was Ices Neat, there was Tony Marrone. Big game, hot game, and naturally Jimmy Slaps wanted—no needed—to buy in. But the buy-in was a grand and Jimmy Slaps just then didn't have enough to fade a game of nickel craps.

Old Jimmy was left out in the cold until Kings Dagboy, never a generous soul to begin with, agreed to cover Jimmy Slaps's buy-in in exchange for nothing more substantial than a signature. It was a puzzling turn of events, more puzzling still when you knew that the Slap in Jimmy Slaps came from the way Jimmy's eyes lit and he tapped the table with his fingertips whenever the card he was looking for came through.

With a tell like that, it wasn't long afore Jimmy Slaps slapped hisself right out of that game, a thousand off the nut to Kings Dagboy. And Kings started immediately putting the squeeze on Jimmy, literally, throwing him in the crapper of that room at the Chelsea, taking Jimmy's head in his meaty hands and squeezing that long face until Jimmy's eyes near popped.

Jimmy begged for time, Kings Dagboy laughed and let loose his fists, busting Jimmy's nose, knocking out two teeth. If Jimmy Slaps was a sad sack afore, now he was a bleeding piece of meat a thousand to the wrong with nowheres to run and no hopes of getting there. That's when Kings made his offer. It was all a setup from the start, see, all a way for Kings to entertain the two pros from Chicago and make a profit on the thou in the process. And with his back against a toilet and Kings Dagboy's fist aiming once again for his face, Jimmy Slaps had no choice but to agree.

When word got out, every DG on the Square wanted in on the action. Kings was making book and within five hours of the deal there was twenty thou on the line one side or the other, with Kings bound to make a couple G's on the vig alone no matter how it all turned out. They set it up in the basement of an old garment factory on Thirty-ninth and the crowd poured in, a festive high-spirited crowd as interested in the show as in the welfare of their bets. Kings's runners was working the crowd, taking bets to the last minute. Entrepreneurial souls was edging through the room with a bottle and a glass selling whiskey pure for a buck a swallow. Long-lost pals was shouting greetings back and forth like at a county fair.

It were a party until Jimmy Slaps hisself appears like magic beside a crate at the back end of the basement. Hoots and cheers and a few more bets taken and then the crowd quiets. Jimmy Slaps, shivering now, steps up on the crate, sweat pouring down his bloodied face, his filthy raincoat swirling about him, a revolver in his shaking right hand.

"This is my last bet, boys," he tells the crowd in a quavering voice. "Life is all snake eyes without faith in something purer than a string of numbers hit. No more will I put my faith in a king-high straight, now I pledge myself to the King of Kings, the only shooter worth a bet. I have promised God I am finished with the life, and I want you all to keep me to it. If I make it through, no matter how I whine or beg, I'm asking you not to take my bets. Will you do that for me, will you, boys?"

The crowd lets out a roar, but not a roar of assent. It is a roar of disdain, a full-throated bellow of heckles and crude remarks, telling old Jimmy Slaps to quit the Bible-punching and get right to it. A crowd of DGs don't want to hear about no change, no redemption, no promises to the great good Lord. All they wants is the bet laid and the race run so they can head to the window and lay another.

Jimmy Slaps smiles right into that roar, smiles as if, by God, he means every word of it, that he is finished with it all, that face to face with death itself, he has found an answer to Hubert and is ready to change. And in the middle of the crowd, selling my whiskey for a buck a shot, I believe him, that he really has found an answer. And I cheers for the son of a bitch, I does, I cheers as loud as my larynx allows.

Until right then, in the middle of the crowd's disapproving roar and my cheers of hope, Jimmy Slaps puts that gun smack to his head and pulls the trigger.

We was royalty, the Boss and me. We ruled the Square, under the kingly benediction of the *Nonos*. We was funny kind of partners; I did what the Boss told me and he, well, he told me what to do. There it was, the delicate nature of our partnership, and it didn't matter that I was the brains behind our rise in the Square, that I soothed the nerves he rankled and kept the money flowing, because he was the muscle and muscle always gets the bigger say. I knew better than to hold any kingly ambitions myself, but as long as he let me tell him what I needed to do, and then I followed his directions like a lapdog, we got along like gangbusters and we was both of us making out. I had climbed as far as ever I could hope to climb, I was the key man under the key man in Times Square and life was ever so grand.

Or was it?

Jimmy Slaps, what did he want in this world? He wanted to gamble, to bet, to feel the probabilities work their smooth impartial magic on his life. But when it became too real, when the hammer was cocked and the barrel faced his temple at a smooth six-to-one, suddenly he didn't want the magic of them odds no more. You see, sometimes everything you're hustling for it comes true and then you wonder if all that time you been hustling for the wrong damn thing.

In the spare moments between collecting the protection moneys and collecting the sharking moneys and collecting from our whores and collecting our cuts from the beer and drugs and smuggled cigs what was sold on our turf, in the spare moments I began to wonder if maybe I'd be in a whole different line if Old Dudley hadn't sidled up to me in that library and started whispering about chess in my ear and that maybe the whole other line might have been the right line for me.

I see you trying to hide your sniggers. What the hell could

Mite ever hope to be except a hustler, a chiseler, a thief? What other could Mite ever expect for hisself except the bowl of crap he fell into in hitching a ride on the back of the Boss. But see, maybe our fates ain't as fixed as you would have it. Maybe it ain't so set in stone, the way our lives they turn out. What better proof of that than old Jimmy Slaps, swearing afore the whole of his peers that his life would change and never would he take another bet.

I thought about going the Jimmy Slaps route, hitting my knees and asking God to save me, I even strolled every now and then up to old St. Pat's and slipped into the cool calming darkness and watched the light twist blue and red through them windows. But in the end, when it came time for the actual praying, I couldn't go through with it.

I mean let's say He is everything them street-corner preachers say He is, let's just say it. Then He is everything, ain't He? The sun, the moon, the scrap piece of trash floating like a beam of light on the shiv of the wind. And if He's everything, then He's nothing too. Which meant when Hubert came a-visiting my mom, filling her with nothing, maybe he was really filling her with God, and hell with that. I couldn't help the feeling that if ever I dropped to my knees and said the words and tried to open my heart, it would never be what I hoped would come rushing in, some guy with a long white beard and a cardigan and a pipe calling me sonny boy and tiger. No, it would be Hubert hisself jumping in my head and making hisself at home and sending me spinning in the air afore I fell on the floor with foam coming out my mouth.

So no, it wasn't never going to be prayer that saved me, no

way, I was onto that scam. But see, by then I had something else in mind.

First time ever I saw her it was storming like an orphan and I was soaked to the bone and I dived into the Automat for a refuge and there she was, seated by the window, stirring her coffee. Flawlessly beautiful, the line of her jaw, the bump of her nose, the pale white skin, eyes the blue of a sky you don't never see in the city, the blue of a sky over an Iowa cornfield, and missy, I had never been to Iowa and still I knew. And when I saw her, all at once my little hustler dreams they faded like a fog beneath the sun and I understood, with the vicious cruelty of a bully boy, exactly what I was and all them things that would never be mine.

And then she stood and walked her crippled walk over to refill her coffee cup and my heart, my twisted black heart, it cracked open with hope. For I knew then that we was two of a kind, this woman and me, two bodies marked with misfortune, two lonely souls looking for comfort in a world what starts out cruel on the schoolyard and goes downhill from there. You could see the goodness in her, how could there not be with her leg in a brace, and her face it glowed with her goodness, just like my mother's face, even in the throes of her episodes, maybe especially then. And the goodness there, along with her affliction, it gave me the courage to hitch up my pants and slide over to her table and sit down uninvited and tell her a story and ask for my thirty-nine cents. And there it began between Celia and me.

By the time of now I'm speaking, we was painting the town once a week, rubbing shoulders with the hoit-toit at "21," chugging wine, chewing steaks so thick you had to cuts each piece twice, longways and then sideways, just to get it in your mouth. Good times we had then, and I could confide in her everything about my life except the one thing what mattered most, the desire what kept me up at night, the desire to take care of her, to protect her, to matter to her, just like it was with me and my ma. And we wanted the exact same things, Celia and me, I could tell, security, peace, a place of our own, a family, with the kids reaching up theys little arms to us.

Silly, ain't it, a guy like me dreaming that hackneyed picket-fence dream, but when you're my size normalcy suddenly ain't so normal.

Yeah there it is, what would save me from Hubert's grasp, the only thing worth the game. Love, dammit, love would save me. I loved Celia Singer, not like the cricket's love some moke with a highball and a hard-on feels for the dancer what's grinding away on his lap, no, missy. My love was purer than that, higher than the meat and kidneys what rule the day on this soiled heap of dust. It was like a hard cold star in the night sky, like the flight of a white pigeon skimming the rooftops as it makes its way home, like the explosion in my heart when my momma let the emptiness flow through her one last time.

Can you feel it, missy? I still can. From the first moment I laid eyes on her, it never stopped glowing.

I could never tell Blatta about what I was hoping for with Celia because Blatta wasn't the type in who to confide your soft intimate yearnings. And I couldn't tell our girls what were working the Square, and I couldn't tell the barkeeps what were paying our protection, and Peter, over at "21," he didn't want to hear it, and my mother she was dead. In fact, there was only one Joe what I could confide all my hopes and dreams to, only one who seemed to understand. And this you'll never guess, this is a beautiful thing, this, because the Joe I was confiding to was the one Joe what could make it all come true.

Fat Nemo drummed the tabletop with his fat fingers. He was dressed to the nines, double-breasted pinstripes, tie tight. When Nemo, with that neck of his, so thick it was like he had no neck, had his tie tight it meant business. I'm setting the scene, all right, just sos you understand how what happened happened. It ain't so easy to see sometimes. Sometimes it's like the smallest breath of air changes everything. Fat Nemo, I knew by then, was the number two in the organization. Sitting beside Nemo was Mr. Abagados, the *Nonos*. The old man appeared to be sleeping, his hands on his cane, his chin falling down to his throat.

"He knows to come?" said Nemo to yours truly.

"I tolds him so myself," I said.

"Then where the hell might he be, Mite?"

"He's having problems."

"Is that so?"

"With a whore."

"Well, that is a surprise, isn't it, problems with a whore."

The back room behind the kitchen of the Acropolis was set for a banquet, a banquet without no food, the long tables arranged in a O, with the *Nonos* and Nemo at the head table and the bottom U filled with men in slouch hats and bulky jackets, all the headmen of the Abagados mob, sitting back, yawning, rubbing their noses.

"What about we order up some grub," said one of the men.

"And a liter of retsina," said another.

"Any moussaka left in the pan?"

"Maybe some bread and feta."

"And the retsina."

"This isn't a party, Cos," said Nemo. "This is business."

"Is that what it is, sweet pea?" said the Boss, barging through the door. "Business?"

"Thank you for joining us, Jerzy."

"I had a thing to deal with."

"We hope it came off all right," said Nemo.

The Boss, he kept smiling as he strided to the head table. When he reached Mr. Abagados, he stuck a hand into his jacket. He pulled out a bundle of cash and dropped it in front of the *Nonos*. With his chin still on his chest, the old man reached out his three-fingered claw and took hold of the stack.

The Boss then he moved along the head table to the other side of Nemo, where he pulled out a chair and sat down as if that were his very spot, right there beside Nemo, number three, which it was. He had risen fast, had the Boss. With my brains and his cold brutality, he had become an essential member of the Abagados outfit, especially as the outfit geared for war. Big Johnny Callas had been letting things slip as he tried to slip hisself into the glitter of Square society, but the Boss and me, we didn't care about no ball stars or starlets. We brought order back into the territory. And when one of the Italian boys from the east started inching into our territory, a savage brain-dead hood name of Rocco Stanzi, Blatta ended that with silent efficiency, leaving two pizza cowboys broken and Rocco slinking like a slug back east, carrying his ass in a duffel. That was the final bit, the little power play what put Blatta at the head table.

"We are being squeezed, gentlemen," said Nemo, "like a ripe tomato. We have every organization in the city looking with envious eyes at all we have done to develop our territory. When we took over the Square it was a place of honest revelry and burlesque, with only a few pitiful operations that barely wet a whistle. Now who doesn't want to own it? The raiding operation run by that greaseball Stanzi was just the most recent attempt at our territory, and not all have turned out so well. At the same time you know it is not enough that we stay still because, in the world in which we live, you stay still you might as well paint red circles on your back. But to where can we expand? To the east is Tartelli. To the south is that madman Zwillman. And to the north we have the most troublesome of all, that *nothos mauvros*, J. Jackie Moonstone and his colored all-stars.

"Everyone wants to expand, everyone is eyeing their neighbors like they eye their neighbors' wives. The fuse is lit. That's why we've spent the last months enlarging our ranks, building our arsenal, sucking up all the surplus war materials we could graft our hands onto and placing it into a secure location known only to the *Nonos* and myself. We are ready, but for what? If we let it get out of control, we are going to end up ripping each other to shreds like wild dogs. And then, with blood on the streets, the last one standing will inherit nothing but indictments.

"So we've come up with a better plan. The *Nonos* has brokered a series of agreements that serves to divide much of the disputed territory. Zwillman gets the South Bronx, Spanish Harlem, and Washington Heights. Tartelli gets the main part of Harlem from river to river. We get south Harlem and the area north of our current territory."

"But that is all Moonstone's turf," said one of the men. "What does he say about it?"

"He is delighted to help out," said Nemo. "He has invited us all to the party."

"Really?"

"No, not really," said Nemo. "We have no choice but to wipe that *nothos mauvros* off the map. Moonstone has bigger numbers than all of us individually, which is why he's the biggest threat, but together we can destroy him. So long as we work together."

"When do we start?"

"When we give the word, not before. Moonstone is a barbarian, anyone tips him off it will be ten times as bad for all of us. But the purpose of this meeting is not to start a war with Moonstone, it is to let you all know that we now have new friends. Do you trust *koproskilo* like Tartelli and Zwillman? Neither do I, but for now they are our friends. It's like Roosevelt making kissy-face with Stalin during the war. We're going to be allies until it is over, save Berlin for later. No actions against them, no incursions, no fights. We're going to be allies until it is over, and then we will turn on them like savages."

"It ain't gonna be so easy making love to stinking Tartelli's boys."

"You don't have to sit on their faces, Cos, you just need to make nice until Moonstone is taken care of. And we all have to take care of that *nothos mauvros* when the time is ripe. Are there any questions? Do you all understand how crucial it is we all follow direction? Do you all understand what is at stake?"

As the meeting was breaking, Nemo, he gave me the signal, a surreptitious flick, so I didn't storm out the joint with most the rest of them, the Boss included, back to the street to take care of business. Instead I stayed at the Acropolis, buying drinks for Stavros and the boys, cracking jokes and rolling dice for quarters to pass the time, as if I had nothing but time to pass. After my third beer I hopped off the bar, hitched up my pants.

"Remember, boys, you never buys the beer, you only rents it."

So what if the joke was as stale as the brew they served in that joint, a cloud of laughter followed me as I headed to the bathroom. I could still hear it as I rounded the corner, slipped through the kitchen, and nodded at the gunsel guarding the back room.

He let me pass.

We was alone, the two of us. Nemo made hisself scarce,

quite the feat for someone the size of Nemo, and so it was just me and Mr. Abagados at the table, sitting across the one from the other. He was still pitched forward, leaning on his cane, still in his posture that seemed to be one of sleep. But now his eyes instead of being closed were open and focused like twin gunsights on me.

"Tell me, Mickey, how goes things with that girl?"

"Good, *Nonos*, things with Celia are going good. You know."

"Does she yet understand how you feel?"

"I don't know, maybe. She gots to suspect, what with all the cash I'm laying out on her. You don't give pearls to your palsies, now do you?"

"But you didn't yet say."

"No, not yet. The time it ain't just ripe. I don't got nothing set up, no place to take her that she'll want to be, and I don't want to be scaring her off untils I does."

"With women is always better to scare than to bore." Abagados, he reached into the outside pocket of his jacket. "Let me show you this."

From out his jacket pocket he pulled his loppy three-fingered hand, closed over something big and round, as big and round as a grenade. Slowly, he turned over his palm and flipped his hand so as to roll the object across the table at me.

I snatched it off the table afore it fell into my lap. "It's a lemon."

"Tell me, of what does it smell?"

I took myself a sniff. "It smells like a lemon."

"No, Mickey, no. Close your eyes, try again. In my village was grove *lemoni*. The owner, he paid children climb top branches and pull down fruit. The smell I still remember. It brings back the child. Roll it in your hands, breathe."

"This come from Greece?"

"California. I bought my own grove in California. Place to retire when my time here is over."

"That's a good racket, I'd bet, letting the sun do all the work and then picking fruit off them trees like they was dollar bills."

"You'd think yes. The foreman he knows *lemoni*, and he is Greek, but he is also thief. I need someone watch him, someone I trust. Someone sharp enough to turn sun into money."

I took the lemon in my hand, rolled it back and forth, lifted it to my nose, let its fragrance, sweet and rich, rise through me like a Louis Armstrong song, like a movie kiss.

"What does it smell like, Mickey?"

"Like a lemon."

"See, that's why I enjoy you. You know how to hold back. You are a man who will go far."

"How far?"

"Think three thousand miles to the west."

Without saying nothing, I took another sniff.

"And not alone, you understand," said the *Nonos*. "Never again alone. This is dangerous time. The wolves are circling. They smell something too. What do they smell?"

"Lemons?"

"Betrayal. And this I found in my life. Two sweetest scents

in all the world, *lemoni* fresh from tree and betrayal. The wolves are circling and I need something from you, my friend. Something of the utmost importance."

When I left the Acropolis that night, I had a lemon in my hand and a knot of fear in my gut, but more than that, dead in my sights I had my main chance. It ain't no easy thing to change the world; how much harder is it to change yourself? Some, they say it can't be done, that early on the bones is thrown and everything after is simply a matter of the odds. An Alvin like me what makes good is still just an Alvin what hit his point. It's easy enough to believe it, to shrug your shoulders and say there is nothing to be done and go on going on. It's easy enough, except I had an example to guide me. Jimmy Slaps, what stood on that crate and proclaimed his change to all the world afore he placed the gun to his head.

And it didn't much matter to me if the change claimed by old Jimmy Slaps, it didn't take, if soon as the chamber it clicked empty he slipped back into his old ways, flashing his newly gapped grin as he threw the dice or peeked at his hole cards. His face it grew longer, his raincoat it grew grimier, the gaps in his smile grew wider, the odds against him grew filthy long.

Last I saw of Jimmy Slaps was in an alleyway off Forty-fourth where he spun the cylinder like you spin the dice and put another gun to his head. Before him in a box lay assorted bills, a fiver, two tenners, a pile of ones, the paltry payoff for which Jimmy Slaps was letting once again the odds work their smooth magic on his life. It hadn't been enough no more to watch the odds work on the cards or the dice or the ponies.

Once he had a taste of the ultimate bet, the yes-or-no play of the revolver, he couldn't think of nothing more. He couldn't stop hisself. Time after time he was betting with his life.

And now, so was I.

When I left the Acropolis that night, I had a lemon in my hand and a knot of fear in my gut. I tossed the lemon in the air and hoped to hell it worked out better for me than it did for good old, dead old, Jimmy Slaps.

12 **Kockroach waits patiently** in the car. He has an inhuman patience, the patience of a fly on the wall, a spider in its web. Istvan taps the steering wheel with his fingers as they wait, but Kockroach moves not a muscle. The car is parked half a block before the restaurant, behind a wide truck that bars much of the car's view of the street, but from the rear seat Kockroach can see the entrance of the Acropolis. He waits, patiently.

"Maybe he went out back," says Istvan.

"No," is all Kockroach says.

"You want I check he's still there?"

"No."

Istvan taps his fingers. Kockroach waits. The door opens and a small man in a green suit and a green fedora steps into the night. There is something in his hand, something small and yellow. The man tosses it into the air.

"What is he holding?" says Kockroach.

"*Lemoni*, Mr. Blatta."

Kockroach watches as Mite turns down the street and walks away, toward the Square, still tossing the lemon up and down. In the past, Kockroach would only have seen a man with a lemon, but that was before he learned the ritual of chess. Now, Kockroach can see the ribbons of possibility float through time, Mite's ribbons, flowing out from the Acropolis, slithering toward some great prize in the time to come.

"What are you up to, Mite?" says Kockroach out loud.

"You want me to follow?" says Istvan.

"No need." It is like the ritual of chess, being played out by the two of them on the streets of the city. And Mite, as usual, is planning a trap. But Kockroach has taken to heart the lessons of the ritual, he has plans of his own now, his own ribbons of possibility reaching out like clawed legs to strike at the future, to battle it and subdue it and turn it to his will.

"To Yonkers then?" says Istvan.

"Yes, to Yonkers."

The Lincoln pulls away from the curb, turns left on Eighth, and begins heading north, toward a place called Yonkers. Kockroach has never stepped foot there, Yonkers, has only heard the name a few times, Yonkers, but already he likes it. Yonkers. Yonkers. It feels in his mouth like the sound of lamb bones crunching between his teeth.

The house is large and white and sits on a leafy street on the crest of a hill a few miles north of Yonkers Raceway. A shallow white picket fence surrounds the front of the property. Outside there are lights blazing, streetlights, security lights, a light on the post that announces the address. Outside is bright, inside is as dark as terror.

"Wait here," says Kockroach before slipping quietly out of the car. He makes a quick circle around the house, spies the weakness with an unerring instinct, crawls through the gap in the basement window, dusts off his suit, straightens his glasses, his tie, his hat, begins his ascent up the stairway.

Since his earliest days in this strange body, Kockroach has learned much about the humans. They are a species, he has discovered, governed by emotion. Some of these emotions he understands, emotions such as greed. Greed is the second strongest of all cockroach emotions. His incessant hunger is merely a manifestation of his boundless greed, for a cockroach always hungers, always, even with its belly full and its uric acid spent. To see something is to want it, a speck of starch, a drop of water, a shed plate of chitin, a cozy hiding place, a female rising on her hind legs, to see something is to want it, need it, got to have it. But a cockroach's greed has boundaries, a cockroach's view is necessarily limited by its height and size, the narrowness of its territory. How much more can a human desire with its better viewpoint, its stronger eyes, its ability to traverse great breadths of territory.

Yes, Kockroach understands greed, and its cousin envy. For why should one human have something when Kockroach himself could have it just as well, be it food, be it a woman, be it money, be it turf, be it power, be it favor in the eyes of the great god of smoke rising high over the Square. Kockroach knows not Abel but understands Cain.

Other emotions Kockroach has yet to fathom. Love is a word he hears in every song and in every one of the movies to which Mite drags him, it is a word he overhears in many human conversations, yet of it he still has no understanding. It has something to do with sex, yes, and sex he understands, sex is the one thing that travels pure from one species to another, but love, he suspects, is something more. It has to do with the mashing of lips, the clenching of bodies without the purpose of procreation, the swelling syrup of thick music when one set of huge eyes on the movie screen stares into another. All he knows for sure is that every human wants it, and so, therefore, does he: greed and envy work their magic beyond the realm of understanding.

Just as he has no understanding of love, he has no understanding of hate. Yes, he can be violent, brutal and swift, but it is all for him a matter of business, a matter of greed. He does what he must to get as much as he can. It is never personal because for Kockroach nothing is personal. Even to see Mite slink out of the Acropolis long after he should, even to assume he is plotting something with the powers inside, even that is not a personal affront. Mite has greed too, of course he does, is he not also a creature of this world? To see him toss that lemon up and down causes no hate to flash across Kockroach's calm. Kockroach doesn't hate, he handles.

Similarly Kockroach fails to understand the way some humans are angry at other humans simply because of the sound of their last names, the shape of their eyes, the color of their skins. To him they are all of the lower orders, all humans, and to differentiate among them because of color or accent or the vowels in their last names is to differentiate among different orders of feces, all tasty, sure, but still.

And pride, embarrassment, vanity, all things that seem to cripple humans have no meaning for a cockroach. Such traits denote a struggle to change, to grow, to fulfill a dream of becoming something different. But cockroaches don't dream of being crickets and singing sweetly into the night, don't dream of being spotted hawks and soaring to great heights, don't dream of being humans and expressing all the world's joy and sorrow in discrete lines of poetry. *I too am not a bit tamed, I too am untranslatable, I sound my barbaric yawp over the roofs of the world*. What human would not have wished to write such a line, what cockroach would even consider it, though for a cockroach it be more apt? Cockroaches embrace their cockroachedness. If they have a charm that is it. They are content with what they are and so are beyond vanity, beyond the possibilities of pride and embarrassment, beyond poetry.

But with all Kockroach still cannot understand of the human matrix of emotion, there is one emotion other than greed that he understands completely. If you could examine the twin strands of a cockroach's emotion, rising like the twining strands of its DNA, you would find fear and greed, greed and fear, fear and greed, always the two, one with the other, yes and no, stop and go. It is greed that drives a cockroach forward, toward the wet slop of goop upon which it desires to feast—a near-uncontrollable desire to obtain, to mount, to devour—but it is fear that stops him cold, that spreads his antennae, that sends him sniffing for predators before he heads once more toward the goop. Fear. It is why cockroaches sleep in the tightest spaces, why cockroaches are silent, why they scurry, why they scurry in darkness.

Kockroach understands fear, and in dealing with the human he has learned that, of all the emotions, it is fear that drives it, fear even more than pride or vanity, hate or greed, even more than the mysterious joys of love. Fear of hunger, fear of pain, fear of dismemberment, fear of insects, fear of a stranger rising unbidden in your very own house, rising step by step, silently, in the darkness, up your stairs while you sleep, rising to your kitchen, opening your refrigerator, devouring your food with great noisy chomps while the light bathes his front, ripping meat off bones, swallowing raw eggs whole, and, though still not sated, wiping the residue off his mouth with the back of his hand before passing the door of your mother-in-law's room and rising ever farther up your stairs, skulking past your three sleeping children, entering your very own bedroom, sitting on the side of your very own bed, where you and your wife sleep the sound sleep of the unsuspecting.

Shaking you awake in the darkness.

Startling you awake with a shake in the darkness.

"What? What?" you ask, as if the darkness itself will hold some answers. And it is the darkness itself that responds, darkness in the shape of a shadow, a shadow with broad shoulders and a fedora cocked on its head, a shadow whose voice is both twittering and deep, the deranged voice of fear itself.

"Cooney," it says. "Cooney. You're late."

Kockroach sits in the back of the car as it speeds through the Bronx toward Manhattan. He examines a spot on the cuff of his shirt, a dark splatter. He rubs at it with his thumb but the splatter has soaked into the fabric.

"Back to the Square?" asks Istvan.

"Yes," says Kockroach, still rubbing futilely at the spot, "but first stop at Kirschner's."

In Manhattan, the brown car double-parks in front of a small storefront, Kirschner's Delicatessen. In New York, all creatures have a favorite deli, even cockroaches, especially cockroaches. The neon beneath the name reads: OPEN ALL NIGHT.

"The usual?" says Istvan.

"Two."

"Hungry tonight, Mr. Blatta?"

Kockroach doesn't respond. It is a foolish question; he is hungry every night. After a few moments, Istvan steps out of the delicatessen with a brown paper bag, nearly translucent with grease on the bottom.

With the car again on its way south, Kockroach opens the bag, takes a deep whiff. The rich oily scent, starchy and sweet, reminds him of his childhood.

Sitting now beside Kockroach in the back of the car is a woman with dark hair piled high. Her heels are spiky, her earrings dangle, her white blouse is tucked into her tight gray skirt: a secretary tarted up for a late night assignation with the boss. The look is catnip for conventioneers. Her thin mouth shifts and wriggles like a nervous worm on a hook. The brown car jerks east between two cabs on Forty-second Street.

"He was going to stiff me, the bastard," she says.

"Never use my name."

"I had to tell him something."

"Lie."

"My momma taught me never to lie. Whoring was okay, but not lying. Is it the truth what I heard about Sylvie?"

"None of your beeswax."

"Okay. Sure. She's been tough to take lately anyway, still thinking she was some kind of queen bee even with her junkie shakes. She's better off on them piers, how skinny she got. I'm tired and hungry and my dogs are barking. What's in the bag?"

"It's not for you."

"C'mon, Jerry. I'm hungry. Just a bite. It smells good."

"I need something from you, sweet pea."

"Of course you do."

She slips off the seat onto her knees, begins to unhook his belt buckle. He pushes her away.

"There is a man in a bar."

"There's always a man in a bar," she says.

"He's tall, thin, his suits are expensive and too tight. You can tell him by the way his hair grows down to his eyebrow. You'll go in. He'll make a move. You'll promise him a freebie and take him to the alley behind the bar."

"Then what?"

"That's it. I'll take over from there."

"Never knew you liked the other side, Jerry."

"I like everything, sweet pea. And you mention my name again, you'll be strolling the piers with Sylvie."

"You wouldn't."

"Here we are. Hair down to his eyebrow. Put on a smile and make nice."

Kockroach waits in the alley behind the bar. He stands stock-still, in the darkest crevice of shadow, well out of the single shaft of light that pierces the darkness. He waits with his in-human patience.

He doesn't imagine what is happening inside the bar, the music, the smoke, the laughter and slapped backs, doesn't imagine the woman sitting on her stool, turning her head, smiling at the tall man in the tight suit, taking a cigarette from her purse, placing it in her fingers, waiting for the man to leave his friends, step over and light it. Kockroach doesn't imagine the repartee, the sexual innuendo, the flitting erotic imaginings that slip through the man's brain as the woman places the lit cigarette in her mobile lips. He has already worked out the moves in advance and so now he simply stands there. The brick of the alley is weeping. A cat scampers around a puddle and jumps atop a metal trash can. The intermittent sound of cars passing by the narrow alley rises and falls in an endless series, the closest Kockroach has ever gotten to the sound of ocean waves. If you ever wondered what a cock-roach was thinking when standing motionless on your kitchen floor, don't. It doesn't move, it doesn't think, it merely waits for the proper stimulus.

A world opens, the sound of trumpets and piano, of talk-ing, of clinking glasses and celebration, then the sound dies with a slam. He hears footsteps, a spark of laughter, a growl.

"Where you going, baby?" A man's voice. "Here is fine. Why not here?"

"C'mon, silly."

"To where?"

"Someplace private."

"This is private enough, what I got in mind."

"Just over here."

They step into the narrow shaft of light. The man's suit is tight, his glossy black hair pulled back from low on his brow. There is a bland cruelty in his eyes.

"You're a hot one, ain't you, baby?" he says.

He roughly opens the woman's white blouse, popping a button as he reaches for a breast. He grabs hold of her rear and squeezes.

"One hot baby."

He leans his mouth into her long pale neck. The woman unbuckles his belt, pulls down his suit pants. His knees are bony, bristly. He takes his hand from her rear, yanks down his own boxers, reaches now under her skirt, growls and laughs at the same time.

With a quick press of her arms, she pushes herself away, leaving him alone in the light, his pants and boxers pooled around his ankles.

"No more teasing, baby. Let's just get to it."

"I can't," she says.

"You can't? Don't act shy now, you tease. Come on, baby, Papa needs to sing."

"Got to go, *baby*."

"Oh no, no you don't. Not till I say you go, understand? Get on your knees, bitch, or I'm going to rip apart your—"

"Hello, Rocco," says Kockroach, taking a step from the shadows.

Rocco Stanzi's head swivels as if slapped. "Blatta?"

"Wait for me in the car."

The woman nods and scampers out of the alley, tucking her blouse in all the while.

"Hey, Blatta, what are you doing? I was just about to get a little action here. Can't you wait until—" Stanzi stops speaking, looks at the girl rushing off. "One of yours?"

Kockroach takes another step forward.

"What, you didn't hear the news? They didn't tell you?" Stanzi grapples for his pants, pulls them up, fiddles unsuccessfully with the belt. "There's a citywide truce. Zwillman's guys and your guys and our guys, all of us, we're on the same side now. Didn't you hear?"

"I heard," says Kockroach.

"Good, yeah. Isn't that something? One day we want to rip each other's guts out and stamp them into the dirt, the next we're bosom buddies. You want a drink or something, to celebrate? No hard feelings about that thing we had, right? That's all past us now. It was only business. But now we gots bigger fish to fry. Moonstone's a bear, he's going to be tough. But together, man, we're going to fry his black ass. And let me tell you, no one's gladder than me to have you on my side. You want a drink? Let me get you a drink. To celebrate our alliance. On me. We're on the same side now, right? We're partners now, right?"

"Right," says Kockroach.

"Good, great." Rocco Stanzi, his belt still undone, his pants held up with one hand, reaches out his other. "Partners?"

Kockroach steps forward, takes Rocco's hand in his own. "Partners," he says. They shake on it, once, twice—and then Kockroach squeezes.

The bones in Rocco Stanzi's hand press against each other, press into each other, grind into each other, grind and twist and split.

As Rocco Stanzi begins to scream Kockroach's free hand dives at Stanzi's throat and clamps hold. The scream is choked off like a stalled engine. Still gripping hand and throat, Kockroach lifts Stanzi in the air.

Stanzi, face now bursting red, swings his arm and feet wildly. He kicks Kockroach in the chest, in the legs, grabs at his eyes. Kockroach pulls Stanzi close, holds him face to face so the flailing limbs lose their leverage. Kockroach's breath washes across Stanzi's purple face. Stanzi's pants drop, binding his ankles together. His flailing grows wilder. Kockroach's smile deepens. The grip on Stanzi's neck tightens. Stanzi's struggle eases. Stanzi's breathing falters, fails.

After, Kockroach slaps the dust off his pant legs. He takes a bag out of his jacket pocket, the brown paper bag with the greasy bottom. From the bag he pulls out a small brick of pastry. He takes a bite. Potato. Kirschner's has the best knishes in the Square, they have them delivered daily from Yonah

Schimmel's on the Lower East Side. He takes another bite and then leans over Rocco Stanzi's body, opens Rocco Stanzi's slack jaw, jams the rest of the knish in Rocco Stanzi's mouth so that it sticks out like a thick beige tongue.

"Nothing personal, pal, just beeswax."

Kockroach puts the bag back in his pocket, wipes his hands on the dead man's shirt, heads back to the car.

Kockroach has a hobby.

It is a very human trait to have a hobby, a pastime with which to while away the hours, and so one might be surprised to learn this of Kockroach. It is hard to imagine him dabbling in watercolors, working with wood, collecting stamps from foreign countries. But Kockroach's hobby is not philately.

Greed and fear, fear and greed. For a cockroach, a perfect hobby would combine the two, obsessively collecting something that also provides protection. Guns would seem then perfect, but Kockroach does not carry a gun and has never fully understood their allure. Oh, the mechanics he understands. Pull a lever and a shard of metal flies out and puts a hole in an enemy at a distance. Marvelously efficient, yes, but the fascination, the glorification is beyond him. Cockroaches don't fight at a distance, they fight up close, claw to claw, mandible to mandible, the desperate hot breath of your adversary pawing across your face. That is how it has always been done from time immemorial. To kill from a distance seems to Kockroach unnatural and, in a way, obscenely human. No, a cockroach wouldn't turn to guns for protection, instead it would want to somehow collect territories, places in which it is safe, holes, crevices to hide. And this indeed is Kockroach's hobby.

He collects real estate.

Kockroach's realtor is a tall mournful man with knobby wrists named Albert Gladden who, before he met Kockroach, managed a few desolate properties scattered along the West Side. Albert owed Big Johnny Callas a debt that was on the books still when Johnny mysteriously disappeared. When Kockroach paid the awkward, mournful Albert Gladden a visit in the dusty office in one of his buildings, the realtor raised his palms and sadly pleaded poverty before proposing a deal: a deserted tenement on Ninety-fourth Street in exchange for the debt.

Kockroach toured his new building, sniffed the ruined plaster, bent his head beneath the leaking roof. In the dining area, his foot stepped through a rotted floorboard. The house smelled of old trash, of dead rats, of animal droppings, of desolation: it smelled wonderful.

Immediately Kockroach wanted more.

Now Albert Gladden works out of an office on a high floor in the Empire State Building, managing the properties of a generically named holding company whose primary shareholder he never reveals and whose empire continues to grow under Gladden's watchful eye. He has a staff of four, including a title man, and each morning finds him carefully perusing the list of property foreclosures. He is still mournful and awkward, Albert Gladden, but now he lives on the East Side, drinks aged Scotch, smokes hand-rolled cigars, is married to a former Rockette with sturdy legs and breasts like huge smothering marshmallows.

As Kockroach drives through the city, he enjoys passing by the properties he owns, run-down brownstones in Harlem, shabby apartment buildings, shabby storefronts, sad sagging hotels like the Murdock, including the Murdock, old industrial buildings, ragged office buildings with long empty halls, a deserted warehouse teetering two blocks off the Square, which Gladden rents to Abagados without ever divulging the name of the true owner. And now, in his inside jacket pocket, Kockroach holds the deed to a large white house in Yonkers that he has just obtained from Cooney. He has a plan for this house, but if this plan of his fails, then he will leave it to his realtor to decide whether to keep it and rent it out or to sell it and use the proceeds to buy something in the city. He leaves everything to Gladden, allows him to buy, rent, sell as he sees fit so long as Kockroach is kept completely informed. Gladden makes his reports in person, at clandestine midnight meetings in deserted alleys so that Kockroach's hobby is kept secret. The only building Albert Gladden is forbidden to sell is the original property on Ninety-fourth Street, sagging, leaking, stripped of all pipe and wire, its front boarded up with plywood, a disaster of a ruin before which the brown Lincoln is now parked.

Istvan taps his fingers on the steering wheel, the woman is asleep alone in the backseat.

Kockroach roams through the dark ruin, stepping around holes in the floorboards, ripping cobwebs from his path, kicking piles of trash, splashing through puddles. The building sags, shifts, strange sounds emanate from the walls, the floors, joists settling, timbers splintering, plaster cracking loose from lathes as if the house is an old living thing falling into senescence. He breathes deep the smell of feces and decay, molder, rot. Home, it smells of home. In this place, of all the places he has been since his molt, he can best remember what he was.

He stops in a stray beam of light floating through the cracked window of the rear door, standing now before a beaten and blackened stove, so worthless with misuse and age it has survived the multiple strippings of the property. Atop the stove sits the photograph Kockroach took from the room where he first awoke with this body. He keeps it in this house for safekeeping. He picks it up, stares at the face that is identical to his and the woman's face beside it. For Kockroach the photograph has become a talisman of both his past and his future. He puts the photograph back upon the stove and stoops down on the filthy wooden floor. He reaches out a hand. From a crevice beneath the stove he sees two strands of brown, waving softly.

He waits.

The strands wave softly, wave, softly wave. And then, slowly, jerkily, with scurries and stops, a lone cockroach emerges and makes its way toward the outstretched hand, stopping just before it, letting its antennae brush the hand's flesh. The cockroach stays there, motionless for a second, for two, before rising slightly on its hind legs. With the tip of his forefinger, Kockroach gently strokes the arthropod's chest. The cockroach sways affectionately into the touch.

Kockroach takes the greasy paper bag from his pocket, reaches inside, pulls out the second Kirschner knish. He twists off a piece, rolls it into a ball, lays it on the floor.

The cockroach approaches carefully, rubs it with its antennae and then mounts the tiny ball, working the greasy piece of starch with its legs, devouring it with its ironlike mandibles and chitinous teeth.

Kockroach twists off another piece, and two more, and ten more, laying them side by side by side.

In the crevice beneath the stove he sees two more softly waving strands, and then two more and then twelve more. One by one the cockroaches emerge, one by one, one by one by one, from under the stove, from a crevice in the corner, through the holes in the wooden floorboards of the dining room, dropping like a battalion of airborne from the ceiling, they stream forward in a great army, scurrying madly now to the feast. The floor itself is alive with their frantic race.

"There is plenty, my brothers," he whispers.

Kockroach twists off more pieces, leaves them in his palm, lets the army swarm over his hand as they battle for the food, swarm so thickly not a speck of flesh is left uncovered. He places the remainder of the pastry on his shoulder and the army drives forward until his hand, his arm, his shoulder and neck, his entire right side is covered with a boiling mass of brown. The feel of them dancing on his flesh, piling one on the other, scurrying around his neck, across his face, nibbling his fingernails, his eyelashes, is lovely, warm, scratchy, familiar, rich, sensuous, luxurious, loving—loving. A connection between word and emotion is suddenly made.

So that is what it means.

"Oh my Lord," says a deep voice at the rear doorway.

Kockroach doesn't startle at the interruption. Without jerking his body or shaking off any of the swarm, he turns his head and smiles at the man in the now-open doorway even as a cockroach dashes from his mouth to his ear.

"My good Lord. Blatta, you are one aberrant son of a bitch, yes you are. Don't be denying it."

"Want to feed my friends?" says Blatta.

"No no no. I spent enough nights with those critters biting at my toes. My bedroom was like a gymnasium when I was growing up. They'd come in, work the light bag, do a few rounds just to keep in shape, then hang in the corner and smoke reefer, snickering at my skinny ass, at the hand-me-downs I was forced to wear. I fed them enough to last me."

The man in the doorway wears a powder blue suit, a powder blue hat. He has a long nose, a small pursed mouth. In one hand he holds a gold-tipped walking stick, the other sports a diamond as big as an eye. His skin is as black as the coal from which the diamond was formed. His name is Moonstone.

"No surprises?" says J. Jackie Moonstone.

"No," says Kockroach.

"They're carving me up like a turkey, Blatta, like it's Thanksgiving already and I'm the only thing in the forest that gobbles. Well, they'll find critters in the forest other than turkeys, won't they? What about Stanzi?"

"Stuffed."

"And they're going to blame Zwillman, like you said?"

"Like I said."

"So everything is smooth, no problems?"

"Nothing I can't handle."

"Like what, for example?"

"Like nothing I can't handle."

"You're holding out on me, Blatta, not a good way to start. Is your boy Pimelia on board?"

"He will be."

"You're sure."

"One way or the other."

"My Lord, you are marvelous, Blatta, yes you are. A couple weeks from now it's just going to be you and me, just you and me on top of the heap."

"And then it's between us."

"No sir, no more fighting. There's more than enough to keep us jazzed and balled the rest of our lives. Whatever split of the other's turf you think is fair is fine with me, just leave me with what I got now and I won't fight it. I know enough not to mess with someone who keeps roaches for pets. We're going to get along like brothers. Here, what you asked for."

Moonstone drops onto the floor a handful of small waxpaper bundles, each tied with a bright red string. A mass of cockroaches sprints from the rest and swarms over the bundles until all that can be seen is a writhing mass of brown.

"Just like you asked for," says Moonstone. "Waxy Red, finest scat in New York City. Pretty soon you're going to have them hooked too. Pretty soon you'll be selling to every roach in the whole damn town."

"How low would I have to be," says Kockroach, "to give poison like that to a cockroach."

Over the rooftops to the east, the first tentacles of dawn reach through the sky like a warning. Istvan is pulling the Lincoln up to the hotel. The woman in the car, awake now, leans her head on Kockroach's shoulder.

"You want me?" she says.

"Not tonight."

"Please, Jerry, let me come up. We haven't been together in ages. I miss you."

"Take her home, Istvan. I won't need the car until the usual time this evening."

"Yes, Mr. Blatta."

"Before then, find Mite and take him wherever he wants to go."

"Yes, Mr. Blatta."

"And then tell me where that is."

"Of course, Mr. Blatta."

Kockroach pats the woman's knee and slips out of the Lincoln. On the way to the entrance, he feels something squirm up his sleeve. A small cockroach climbs out and halts on the cuff, its antennae waving gently. Kockroach lets it climb onto his finger, pets its back, drops it through a grate in the street leading to the sewer, the promised land.

"Good morning, Mr. Blatta," says the doorman in his tall brown hat.

"Busy night, Mr. Blatta?" says the porter standing by the door.

Kockroach slaps green tributes into their hands as he walks through the door into the lobby.

"Your guest is waiting for you, Mr. Blatta," says the desk clerk.

"Very good," says Kockroach.

With a ding of the bell the elevator arrives, white gloves slip out and hold the door as Kockroach steps in.

"Going up, Mr. Blatta?" says the operator.

"To the top," says Kockroach.

13

Was one more player you needs to know about, missy, one more piece what moved across the Square like a deranged knight.

I can see him still, swaggering into some Times Square titty shake. His hat is shiny with grease. His cheap suit is rumpled, like he slept in it two nights running, which maybe he did. His tie is loose, his loose jaw unshaven, his socks smell like old socks.

"Shoot the sherbet to me, Herbert," he says to the barkeep in a voice with more hoarse in it than what's running at Aqueduct. He leans an elbow on the bar and checks out the merchandise. "Gin, straight up. On the house."

"On the house?" says the bartender, whose name is not Herbert and who is new on the Square so he ain't tuned in.

"And put an olive in it."

"Who the hell are you to be getting a drink on the house?"

This Joe he flips up his fedora with his pinkie and stares at the sap for a moment. Then he grabs the barkeep by his bow tie and jerks his fist down till the bartender's forehead it slams smack into the bar. He drags the bleeding face an inch from his own. His breath smells of cheap cigars, of raw onions on street-corner dogs, of wanton unwashed women.

"The name's Fallon, you piece of dick," he says. "Lieutenant Nick Fallon. Vice."

He rose from the mean streets of Hell's Kitchen, and he fell back into them streets afore it was over, but whilst he patrolled the Square, collecting his envelopes and pulling in rubes by the truckload, Fallon was a power. He kept his thumb up everyone's ass, just to be sure of the temperature, and everyone smiled whilst he did it, because he could make things easy for you on the Square, or make them very very hard. And missy, easy was better than hard when it came to Fallon. Manys the poor sap what ended up in the precinct house cage with Lieutenant Nick Fallon's fists asking the questions and the answers already written down afore ever they let slip a word. But he wasn't all hardworking cop, he had a sweet tooth of his own. What else could you expect from a man with vice in his very name?

"You ever have yourself a threesome, Mite?" said Lieutenant Nick Fallon, Vice.

"No, Lieutenant."

"I had one going on last night. Two girls. One of them had legs up to here, the other had Himalayas out to there, and they both still had all their teeth. Fancy that."

"Why you telling me, Lieutenant?"

"I'm telling everyone."

Fallon had yanked me by my collar out to the beach, the thin triangular strip of cement and grate just south of Forty-sixth, and now he was lighting one of his Cuban candles as cars and trucks wheezed by on either side. With the hubbub, the traffic, the backfires and horns, the pall of smoke and noise rising around us, the beach, in the middle of everything, was about the most private place on the Square.

"A threesome's like eating in a chop suey house. And in between, while you're waiting to get hungry again, you don't even have to entertain them, they can entertain themselves. You know how rare it is, a guy looks like me, setting up a threesome with two broads look like that and still got all their teeth."

"I'm guessing raw."

"All their teeth."

"I'm happy for you, Lieutenant."

"Yeah, well don't be. Just as it was getting interesting, a call comes in from my captain. The only bite mark I got on my ass was from his chewing me out, Mite. So I am angry, I am blue, and I want to know what the dick is going on."

"Just the usual, Lieutenant."

"You think it usual for one of Tartelli's boys to end up dead in an alley? You think it usual for the Abagados clan to have a powwow just a few hours before the killing? You think it usual for my captain to suddenly take an interest in what goes on in my territory. You think that's good for any of us? Get smart, Mite. Something's up and I need to know about it. You owe me."

"Hell if I owes you anything."

"Hell you do. Take a gander," he said, spinning around to view the whole of Times Square. "Everyone your eye can spy owes me. I keep it safe, I keep it running, I keep everyone in business. You want they replace me with another Johnny Broderick, the cop who handled the Square before I did?

Johnny Broderick, tapping you on the shoulder with a news-paper wrapped around a lead pipe. He stuffed Legs Diamond headfirst into a garbage can one block down from here, stuffed him into that can and good as finished him off right there. You want another Broderick running the Square?"

When he talked of that Johnny Broderick, something fierce and hard glazed Fallon's bloodshot eyes, and looking at him then, and his thick lips wrapped around that cigar, I saw a touch of froth flit around the corner of his mouth. Just a touch, but it was enough to roil my stomach.

It was going to end up bad, the whole thing, I could see it in his eyes, in the froth at his mouth, the way his hand rolled into a fist for emphasis. It was like a curtain was dropped and I could suddenly see he was made of the same cement and asphalt what we was standing on, what ran from our feets east and west, north and south, off the beach, through the streets, in a great stinking sea of stuff what died at both rivers, made of the same grist as was all the raw matter of the city. He was a cop, but that was a lie, because it made him sound like he was something different from the rest of it when he was the same as everything else of it, all of it, even me, all of it. And his lips they was foaming and his eyes they was glazed and he spun around to make a point and it wasn't no more a cop be-fore me or even a man but a piece of the world what was ani-mated only by Hubert.

I held my stomach and looked down Broadway and tried to blink the sickness away and I did, this time I did, and when I turned back it wasn't this nameless piece of matter facing off

with me no more but a cop, and not just any cop but Lieutenant Nick Fallon, Vice. And I had blinked it away and could go
on like it never happened, play it tough and cool like it never
happened, but it did and I felt it in my bones, along with the
certainty that it was all, the whole thing, going to end up bad.

"So what do you know, Mite?" he said.

"I don't know nothing."

"A midnight meeting at the Acropolis. Every big dick
from Abagados down. I even heard Blatta was there."

"Who?"

"Don't be coy with me, you son of a dick. Start motivating
your mouth. What did you boys talk about?"

"Moussaka."

"Is that a fact? So tell me," elbow in the ribs, ready for the
coded clue, "what was decided?"

"The key is salting the eggplant. Kosher salt works best."

"Kosher salt, huh? Is that why Zwillman he dicked Stanzi?
Not enough *kosher* salt?"

"Zwillman? Is that what happened? I heard Stanzi, he
choked on a knish. That Stanzi, he always liked a good knish."

Fallon looked at me, licked the froth off his lips, filled his
mouth with smoke, blew it in my face. "We got a good thing
going here, Mite. Don't let them ruin it for us."

"Them? Who them?"

"That's the question, isn't it? The coroner says you can't
swallow dick if your throat's crushed, as you could find out
firsthand. I won't let a war break out on my turf unless it's my
war, understand? I find out who is starting up I'll get an army

in here to finish it, understand? I'll be back, and when I do, don't dick with me, Mite. I want answers."

Didn't we all, just then, didn't we all.

What that iceberg it was to the Titanic, the knish sticking out of Rocco Stanzi's mouth, the most famous potato knish in the history of gang warfare, was to our peace. The whole delicate arrangement forged between Abagados and Zwillman and Tartelli, the whole beautiful alliance against J. Jackie Moonstone, was shot to hell. Tartelli, he immediately blamed Zwillman for the Stanzi hit, using as his proof the Yonah Schimmel knish, what was baked in the Lower East Side, Zwillman's territory. And with that accusation Zwillman, slipping into his normal state of apoplectic paranoia, pointed his thick finger at Abagados, what had had his troubles with Stanzi in the past. And Abagados, an old man who had fought too many battles, who had actually lost his fingers as a young Greek soldier in the century afore this one, Abagados struggled with all his powers, political, physical, and persuasive, to bring back the peace. But his efforts were stymied by a series of hit-and-run massacres on the border territories that kept the general uproar uproarious. And nobody knew nothing, nobody, including me, especially me, nobody except those what did, who weren't saying.

"Same as it always was, *Nonos*," I said, alone with Abagados in the back room of the Acropolis. "Everything's the same with him. I been looking like you asked and I ain't found nothing."

"Look harder," said Abagados.

"I don't know what it is I'm looking for."

"Anything that is different, anything that is wrong. Find it and bring me."

"I'm trying."

"Trying? I spit on trying and stamp into dirt. Look at what is happening. Only one man strong enough, treacherous enough, only one man won't let you look him in the eyes."

"He's always been loyal to you, *Nonos*."

"You know why he wears dark glasses? So I can't see into his soul. But when I shake his hand I feel it. It is my talent, I could always feel it. His is cold, hard, ruthless, it is like something dark and small, like something that crawls across your skin in the night. It is why I liked him at the start, a valuable friend he can be. Also a deadly enemy. But so am I, Mickey, so am I."

"I'll keep looking."

"You will find, you will bring me proof of his deceit. And this proof, it bind together once again all the families. And together we will destroy him and dance the dance of wolves on his carcass."

"Add some dip and a swing band and it sounds like a party, Mr. Abagados. But what about me? Blatta and me, we came in together."

"Mickey, my friend, Mickey." He lifted his big mangled hand and slapped the side of my face gently afore clasping his claw onto my cheek. "Find. Bring. They tell me there is no winter in California, just sun. Do you know how to swim?"

"No, *Nonos*."

"You will learn."

"Or die trying?"

He didn't smile, he didn't nothing. Whatever reassurance I was hoping to see in his bitter old eyes, all I saw was a vacancy as dark as Blatta's dark glasses.

So nows you know, missy. Me sitting here, spilling out the whole story for your snitch-sheet exposé, this ain't the first time I betrayed the Boss. Mr. Abagados, what he had wanted that long-ago night at the Acropolis when he rolled me the lemon was for me to spy on Blatta. And I had agreed. Playing Judas, I suppose, is simply my natural role in the Boss's little passion play.

But this I knew with a searing certainty. That thing what happened with Fallon on the beach, that lowering of the curtain and seeing all the city and the fools within it as nothing but the grist of the world? It was happening. Again and again. It was filling me like a fever. It was only a matter of time afore I started spinning and foaming myself. I needed to make something happen, fast. I needed to get on the train west with Celia, fast. I needed to take hold of her love and clutch it like a sword and swing with all my might and separate old Hubert from his head, and I had to do it fast. Because I was losing it, losing it, I was losing it.

"Anything that is different," had said the *Nonos*, "anything that is wrong." I crisscrossed the Square looking for something what didn't make no sense to me, I asked whoever would stand still for the asking, and then the something, it hit me like a punch in the face.

I didn't let Istvan take me. He had been showing up every afternoon at my hotel waiting to whisk me to wherever it was I wanted to whisk, but I didn't want to go where I had to go with him. I let him take me on my rounds and then, with him waiting in the street, it was in the front of Toots's joint, around the big round bar, out through the kitchen, into a taxi afore being let off in the middle of a wide deserted street smelling of blood.

A fog was rolling off the Hudson, a sickly mist. And I walked right into it, turning right then left, crossing a wide cobbled street.

It took me a while to find her, them piers they was one just like the next, hard to tell apart, and telling apart the girls what inhabited them was even harder, each a scabrous spider, clinging precariously to her collapsing web. In the cloaking mist I wrongly approached two strange creatures what grabbed at me like I was a last pitiful hope until I broke away.

But eventually I found the right pier. I stood under the single light and observed a peculiar shadow at the river's edge. An irregular shadow, moving about in slow motion with a steady skritch heard just over the lapping of the water, an inhuman skritch skritch, evidence of some readjustment of finances and fluids.

"Come to check on me, Mite?" she said after half the shadow had scuffled off and she had slipped back into the dim cone of light. "Come to make sure I'm not taking too many coffee breaks?"

"How you doing there, Sylvie?" I said, but I didn't need no answer from her.

She seemed as if she was in the middle of some great fever, bone skinny, shivering and sweating both, her swollen hands shaking at her sides. Her skirt was ragged and filthy, her blouse torn, a long scab darted across her neck. Dirt was streaked on her leg, her forehead, so that she blended into them shadows like a ghost.

"Spend a night here," she said, "in this fog that soaks through to the bone, and see how you hold up. Got a cigarette?"

"Sorry. Gum?"

"Thanks for nothing. What, did Jerry send you to tell me something? Does he even still know I'm alive? Does he care?"

"Sure he does."

"Tell the creep if he wants to send a message he knows where to find me. All right, let me have a stick."

I reached into my pocket, pulled out a Doublemint, watched her unwrap the foil. The boards creaked beneath our feets, some ship offshore, hidden in the fog, belched its horn.

"And this, after all I did for him," she said. "I was the one who spread the word about him to the other girls. I taught him to dance."

"Is that true, Syl?"

"Sure. One night at the Latin Club, after he took over for Johnny. My feet were aching for days after, the way he stepped all over them. I was his first girlfriend in New York, did you know that?"

"That I knew. Don't you remember? I was the one what paid."

"Don't be a silly goose, Mite. I did it for free. It wasn't ever business with him. Oh Jerry, Jerry and me, we had something, don't you remember? We had something real, at least before I got sick. That's the problem, that's why he put me on the piers. But I can't get better out here, it just makes me sicker, the fog, the type of clientele. You don't get the sweet married men from Chicago down here. I told him, let me go back to Pittsburgh and get healthy. I got a sister there, a married sister. I told him, let me go back and I'll return, better than ever."

I reached into my pocket, pulled out my roll, peeled off more than enough. "Here."

"What's this?"

"It's your ticket to Pittsburgh. The Boss, he wants you to go, to get well. But you gots to go now, tonight, run up to the terminal and leave right away while still you can and not say nothing to no one."

"Is that what Jerry wants? He wants me to get well?"

"Sure he does. You always been his favorite, Syl."

"Still?"

"Sure. Go to your sister, she'll take care of you."

She looked at the money for a moment afore grabbing at it and stuffing it under her dress, into the top of her stocking.

"It will be grand back in Pittsburgh," she said. "I was a queen there. You know, my sister, she was always jealous of me. I was the one that had the way with the boys. She didn't invite me to her wedding, afraid I'd steal the groom. Won't it be something when I go back, won't it be a stir. She better hold tight to her man, my sister, that jealous witch, yes she better."

"So tell me something, Sylvie. After what Blatta he done to that Turkish bastard what was supplying Christine, remember her, after that everyone knowed not to supply any flea powder to our girls."

"Course they knew. No one crosses Jerry."

"Not thems that's smart, anyway. So, Sylvie, the question I gots, the question what's suddenly been racking my noggin, is this: Who is it who's been selling to you?"

"What are you talking about? I don't have the least idea what you are talking about."

"Come down off it, Syl. The world can tell you're smacked back just by looking at you."

"Did Jerry say something? Jerry told you, didn't he? And you acting like you don't know, like you don't know when you know everything about everything. What are you playing at, Mite? What's the game?"

I stared at her for a moment, at her reddened nose, her twitching mouth, her eyes narrowing suspiciously at me, and then I knowed, and then I knowed, just like I knowed that she was never going back to Pennsylvania.

"Let me see what the Boss gave you," I said, and she did.

I found him at the Paddock, hard by the Winter Garden, sitting in a back booth in the back room, his hat on and his jaw hanging, a cigar in one hand, a gin in the other, a near-naked broad shimmying in his lap. Lieutenant Nick Fallon, Vice.

"Got a minute, Lieutenant?"

"What does it look like, dick-for-brains?"

"It looks like your head's about to explode."

His smile was wide and scary, near insane, his face was enveloped by smoke, and just then indeed it looked as if he would burst in flames like an earthbound Hindenburg. Fallon was so open in his vices, so damn joyful, that I suppose for him they wasn't vices at all. He didn't feel embarrassed or degraded by them, they was simply worldly pleasures what made life something other than a wait for death. But there was one thing, one need that did embarrass him with its dark power, one secret desire which just then, clever little me, I was beginning to suspect.

Fallon slapped the bare thigh of the girl what was kneeling astride him and she squealed and pinched his cheek and hiked a leg over his lap so as to slide off the seat and leave us alone in the booth. He watched her go with a sweet regret on his ugly mug and then turned that mug on me.

"What's the agenda, Brenda?"

"I've been asking around. I ain't got nothing firm yet."

"And I haven't cracked a little pissant's head yet. You understand what I'm saying?"

"Not yet."

He leaned over and rapped his knuckle into my noggin, loosing a sharp spot of pain. "You are a cute one. You could make some real scratch cruising the Square in a pair a tight jeans and a T-shirt, playing at being a juvenile."

"That ain't my game."

"Mite, you don't know your game."

"I got a question for you, Lieutenant."

"I don't need questions, I got questions up and down my dick. What I need is answers."

Without responding, I reached into my jacket and pulled out the little wax-paper bundle with red thread I got from Sylvie and tossed it onto the middle of the table. It sat there, small and delicate, like a little ornament designed to hang from a Christmas tree.

"I could run you for possession right now," he said slowly.

"I found this on one of our girls. I needs to know who it came from."

"One of your girls? Which one?"

"That don't matter."

"The one you been with at '21,' the one with the bum leg?"

"Shut up, she ain't nothing to do with this, nothing to do with nothing. Leave her out of it."

"She isn't one of your girls?"

"That's what I said. She's pure civilian."

"Not so pure as you might think."

"Don't even start, you scum bastard."

He grabbed my tie, pulled it toward him until I was out of my seat, bent over the table, my face inches from the smoldering tip of his cigar.

"It's Lieutenant Scum Bastard to you, Mite. Don't be forgetting your place."

He let go. I slid back across the table and pooled down to the seat as if my backbone had just been neatly extracted with a filet knife.

"I'll take this," he said, swiping the ornament from the

center of the table, dropping it into his jacket pocket. "This is the part of my job that gives the most satisfaction, taking poison like this off the street."

"I'm sure you'll find a nice home for it."

"Johnny Broderick, that cop I told you about, he was once looking to nab a pimp like you. He got word the sucker was eating dinner in the Automat. Broderick strolled in, took a sugar bowl, whacked the pimp in the head, and then, over his collapsed carcass, he said, 'Case closed.' Johnny Broderick. In his off hours he was Dempsey's bodyguard. They made a movie about him. Edward G. Robinson. Johnny Broderick."

It happened right on cue, Fallon started talking about Johnny Broderick and suddenly the curtain it dropped and everything went nameless and strange on me again. What was this thing sitting across from me? Best I could tell it seemed to be made of cement, with granite lips and asphalt eyes, some great yet jolly creature built with the bones of the earth. And it was talking to me, this thing what had no name and no meaning, talking to me in a voice as deep as the Grand Canyon.

"You keep playing your game, holding out," came the canyon voice out of them gray stone lips, "and I'm going to close the case on you. Time to come clean."

I sat there, trying to blink it away like I done before, but it wouldn't disappear, this thing in front of me. I closed my eyes for a longer time and opened them again, but it was still there, the cement creature with the granite lips and Hubert's voice.

"Suddenly you don't look so good, Mite. You look like you're about to lay a puddle right here on the table. Just keep it the hell away from my suit, it's not even shiny yet."

The cement creature leaned forward, waved a burning tree trunk in the air.

"Go outside and what do you see?" it said. "Sucker bait over every last surface. Signs selling liquor, magazines, movies and televisions, selling sex even, if you can read between the neon. God bless Artcraft. It's the new age, Mite, everything is marketing now. Pretty soon we'll be billboards ourselves, with signs on our hats and shoes."

I closed my eyes to the cement man, just listened to his words, and slowly, gradually, like a lifting fog, the voice lightened and the meanings came clear.

"They call it Waxy Red on the street, or Wacky Red, depending. The thread is the key, the thread is the sign they ask for. Prime quality, expensive as far as horse goes. For junkies who know enough to demand the very best. You can always count on J. Jackie Moonstone to have the fiercest stuff in the city and to know the power of a label."

I opened them suddenly, my eyes, and he was back, Lieutenant Nick Fallon, Vice, no longer cement and stone and asphalt, but a man, a cop with a name and a purpose in life which unbeknownst to him was about to reach a glorious fulfillment.

"Now agitate the gravel," he said, "and don't come back till you have something to tell me about what's going on."

I did as he said, I hustled out of there fast as I could hustle. Time, it was running out on me, it was running out, it was almost gone, and I was almost lost. But I had my answer now. Wasn't I the little detective? I had my answer and I knew where it would lead. Betrayal first, sure. But then west, the golden West.

And in my pocket, to keep up my courage, I had that lemon too, the very symbol of my future, though by now it was bruised, soft and spongy, by now its scent was no longer so sweet but had taken on the bitter aroma of decay.

14 **Within the hard brown** exterior of the Lincoln, wedged in a corner of the backseat, Kockroach feels safer than anywhere else in his new world. As the Lincoln cruises the streets of the city, dodging lane to lane, moving shoulder to shoulder with other cars and trucks, twisting down side streets, turning, stopping, starting, stopping again, as the car transports him through the city in a familiar rhythm, he comes closest to recovering the old sensations: comfort in his skin, purpose, community, the great fear of something coming from above to squash him flat. That is why he sits always in the rear seat's corner, jammed as tight against the door as he can manage, one eye looking out, one eye looking up.

The Lincoln now is double-parked across Broadway from a small, narrow bar called the Paddock. Cars are honking angrily as they stream past but Istvan, in the front seat, doesn't so much as twitch at the hostile sounds. The Paddock is one of Fallon's places, Fallon, whom Kockroach knows to be an enemy.

Kockroach does not have a subtle system of classification. He wants, he fears, those are his twin guiding lights, and when he applies that simple matrix to the humans who surround him, he places them into one of two distinct categories, friend and enemy. A friend is someone who feeds his greed without feeding his fear: Istvan, his prostitutes, Mite—at least Mite before all the questions. An enemy is someone who feeds his fear without feeding his greed: Rocco Stanzi.

Then there are those who feed both his fear and his greed, who supply him with the material things he craves but also nurture the dread that gnaws at his liver with the constant hunger of an arthropod. These others, these in the middle, might give a human some pause, but not Kockroach. They too are enemies, fear is that strongly embedded in the cockroach emotional DNA, enemies to be used as long as possible and then destroyed. Abagados is such an enemy, as is J. Jackie Moonstone, as is Fallon.

Yes, Fallon keeps the Square calm and for a small price allows Kockroach's collections to go unimpeded, but there is something in Fallon that Kockroach doesn't trust, some streak of angry honor that Kockroach believes Fallon will one day turn against him, and so Fallon feeds the fear. And now, from a bartender at the Paddock who is paid to keep tabs on the scum with whom Fallon meets each night, Kockroach has learned that the scum with whom Fallon is meeting this night is Mite.

Mite steps out of the Paddock, hikes up his pants, tilts down his fedora to cover his eyes, looks left and right, slips into the pharmacy next door.

"Pick him up," says Kockroach.

Istvan pulls the Lincoln in front of a green Oldsmobile,

speeds across two lanes, cutting off a Checker cab, makes a fast U-turn, and stops with a squeal and a jerk in front of the drugstore. When Mite exits with a pack of chewing gum, Istvan is outside, holding open the car door. Mite is unwrapping the foil on one of the sticks when he looks up and sees Istvan, the car, the open door. His jaw drops.

Mite takes a hesitant step forward, peers into the car. "What's the word, Boss?"

"The word," says Kockroach from inside, "is Fallon."

"I had a question for Fallon, is all," says Mite, sitting now in the backseat as the brown car cruises north, headed out of the city. "Where are we going?"

Kockroach doesn't answer.

"It was something what was happening with Sylvie. After what you done to the Turk what was doping up Christine, I didn't expect no one would be such a stupid tit-face as to be selling to our girls. But someone was, see, it was obvious with her. So I figured it was good business to find out who. Whoever it was we needed to do something about it, don't you think?"

Kockroach doesn't answer. He is jammed into the corner of the car, staring. He smells something coming from Mite, it smells like cat urine, like the breath of a mouse, it smells like fear. Kockroach lets the silence between them grow until Mite can't help himself from filling it.

"So I went and talked to Sylvie and then to Fallon and this is what I found out. The stuff she's getting, it's coming from up north, from Harlem, from Moonstone. How about them kosher dills? There's no doubtsky aboutsky, Moonstone's the one what's ruined a prime piece of real estate like Sylvie." Mite's head swivels to look outside the car, at the bleak black landscape on either side of the highway. "Where are we going, Jerry?"

Kockroach doesn't answer.

"So you gots to tell me what to do about it. Somehow, Moonstone's slipping it through some tit-face into our territory and taking money out of our pockets. You want I tell what's happening to the *Nonos*?"

Kockroach doesn't answer.

"Where we going, Jerry? I got someplace in the city I got to be. Where you taking me?"

"Did you find out who the tit-face is?" says Kockroach.

"Sure I did," says Mite. "The tit-face is you."

Kockroach doesn't react with surprise, his smile stays broad, his head still, his hands calmly one in the other on his lap.

"Did you tell Fallon?" says Kockroach.

"Nah."

"Did you tell Abagados?"

"Don't needs to, he knows already you're in league with Moonstone without me saying a word. He wants me to prove it is all."

"Can you?"

"Sures I can."

"Will you?"

Mite looks again outside the window, at the unfamiliar landscape passing by. "I suppose you're going to knish me like you done Stanzi."

"That reminds me," says Kockroach. "On the way back, Istvan, we need to stop at Kirschner's."

"Why wasn't it enough what we had?" says Mite. "That's what I don't understand about you getting messed up with Moonstone. We started with nothing, we ended up as kings. Take your cuts, protect your territory, work with Nemo and the *Nonos,* roll in the clover. Why wasn't it enough?"

Kockroach considers Mite's question. One thing Kockroach has learned in his time among the humans is that all humans lie. They lie to get what they want, they lie because they are afraid, they lie to express the very essence of their humanity. Cats prowl, mice devour, cockroaches scurry, humans lie. Kockroach, therefore, had fully expected Mite to lie, he had planned for it, seen the ribbons of possibility float into the future with each expected falsehood. But Mite has turned the tables by telling him the truth. It is why Mite still beats him at the ritual of chess, his maneuvers are always full of surprises. Kockroach considers how to respond, and decides to battle claw with claw. For the first time since the change he will tell Mite the absolute truth about himself and his plans, and he begins with the biggest truth of all.

"I'm hungry," says Kockroach.

"Well, there's the problem right there. You know what you need? You need let me take you out to dinner at Mama Leone's. Seven courses that will split your belly. If the mama don't kill your hunger, nothing will."

"Nothing can. I'm hungry all the time."

"That's sad, really. That's like the saddest thing I ever heard. Don't you want to be happy?"

"Why?"

"Because that's what we all want. The right to happiness, it's in the Constitution or something. Everyone wants to be happy."

"That's not what I want."

"Then what is it you want, big fellow? Tell me. What?"

"Everything."

"Well, that ain't happening. Sometimes you just gots to accept the way things are. I'm small, I'm never going to be big, I accept it. I'm never going to be a swell, I accept it. I'm never going to write one of them thick books, fine. I'm always going to have a boss, I accept it, so it don't matter who it is so long as I get my cuts. You gots to learn to accept things."

"I accept my hunger."

"You should show a little more gratitude to the *Nonos*. He took us in when we had nothing, gave us responsibility, allowed us to rise. He was the one what okayed the move on Big Johnny. He don't deserve what you're doing to him."

"Why should he be the *Nonos*?"

"Because that's the way it is, that's what he is. He's the *Nonos*. Who else but him?"

"Me."

"You? You're not even remotely Greek. That Jerzy thing I made up on the spot. You don't even know what it means to be the *Nonos*."

"Everyone feeds him. I want to be fed."

"Don't we all. But why you? Why not Nemo, what's been around longer than both of us, or Stavros, or even me. Everyone's got to wait their turn to move up. Why the hell do you think you got the right to take over out of turn?"

"The player that knocks over the boss piece wins the ritual."

"And that's going to be you?"

"Sweet pea."

"But we have it cushy as it is. Why you want to risk it all to be top dog?"

"Because I can."

"I suppose that's why you're going to kill me too, because you can. How are you going to do it? You going to crush my throat like you done Stanzi? Or are you going to let Istvan lead me out to one of these deserted woods and put a bullet in my brain. Oh, no answer to that? Well look, I got one request, all right? Two maybe. Two. Don't let it hurt, please. Just don't let it hurt. That's the one I just thought of, but the other, the more important, do me a favor and take care of Celia for me, will you? Will you, Jerry?"

"Sure I will."

"Thanks. You're a pal."

"Palsy."

"Yeah, you son of a bitch."

"Don't you ever think about what the other guy's feeling, Jerry? Don't you ever wonder, when you got the moke's throat in your grip, what's going through his brain and then feel it as if it's going through your own?"

Kockroach pauses a moment. The question puzzles him. Of course he considers the matrix of greed and fear that controls his opponents' actions so that he can plan and plot and gain an advantage. But Mite is asking something different. He tries to remember the most recent moments when he triggered the greatest amount of fear in the humans, Sylvie at the piers, Cooney in his house, Stanzi in the grip of death. In those triumphant moments, did he feel anything that they were feeling, even the least intimation of their emotions?

"No," he says finally.

"Then you're lucky. I does. I can't help it. I looks into their eyes and I feels what they feel."

"I don't understand," says Kockroach.

"Well, yeah, maybe neither does I. This frigging world don't make no sense."

"But it does. Perfectly."

"Go to hell."

"You see what you want and you take it. Others try to take it for themselves. Whoever is stronger wins. What does not make sense?"

"It ain't that easy."

"Sure it is, Mite. It is only you that makes it hard. The world is all beeswax, everything."

"There's more to life than business, Boss."

"Only that something above is ready to squash you flat if you step into the light."

"That's the only part I believe, you ask me. But when you're going after them the way you do, Jesus, I can't help but suffer for them. And when there's the screaming, forget about it. It turns out I don't got the stomach for it. Who would have guessed? It's 'cause I been there, I guess, on the wrong side of the big boy's fist. And when finally I'm on the right side, it's still there, them feelings."

Kockroach wonders if that is a great weakness or a great strength. It could stay an opponent's hand at the crucial moment, but it might also be why Mite still beats him at chess.

"I couldn't take it no more," says Mite. "I had to get out. Them feelings was why I done what I done, if you gotta know. It was never nothing personal. I just saw a way."

"The lemon," says Kockroach.

"Son of a bitch, what don't you know? Where are we going? I got a right to know. Where?"

"Someplace special for you."

"You don't got to be so damn cheery about it. So what do you feel, Jerry? When you got some moke up against the wall and you're there twisting his arm behind his back and he's screaming and the arm is snapping, what do you feel then? What?"

"Hunger."

"Christ, you got it bad, don't you? You got a tapeworm the size of a snake inside your gut. I almost feel sorry for you, you starving son of a bitch. Why don't you just frigging eat me instead of killing me."

"I want to eat the entire city. I want to devour the world."

"You know what, Jerry, all this time I never realized how crazy you are."

"You want to know a secret, Mite? I'm not human."

"Tell me about it."

Istvan slows the car to a stop. "We're here, Mr. Blatta," he says.

Mite's head swivels quickly to look outside. "What is it? Where are we?"

"Get out, Mite," says Kockroach.

"Sure, Jerry. Sure. But can you do me a favor and not let Istvan do it to me? It ought to come from you. Can you do that for me, that little thing?"

"Istvan, stay in the car."

"Sure, Boss."

"Thanks, Jerry, really. You know, when it comes it ought to have the personal touch, don't you think. Most of my life it's been cold, noways reason my death it should be the same."

"Get out, Mite."

Mite nods, opens his car door, steps out. Kockroach steps out the other side. Mite is crouched, as if readying himself to be leaped upon, but when his gaze spins crazily around and he sees where he is he stands straight. They are on a street, a suburban street with thick trees hanging over the curbs and houses on either side. There are lights, streetlights, security lights, cars parked in driveways.

"This ain't no deserted field."

"No," says Kockroach.

"I thought you was sending me straight to hell. Where are we?"

"Yonkers."

"Same difference, then. What are we doing here?"

"Look over there," says Kockroach, pointing. Mite's head twists as he follows the direction until his gaze alights on a large white house on the crest of a hill. A light on the post announces the address and a shallow white picket fence surrounds the front of the property.

"This Cooney's place?"

"It was. Now it's your place. Cooney signed the deed over to me and I'm signing it over to you."

"Me? Why?"

"It's what you want, isn't it? A place out of the city. A plot of grass. A fence."

"Stop that, all right? Just stop it. You know too damn much."

"I don't understand about the fence, it's like putting yourself in a cage."

"I was getting ready to sell you down the river. Why would you do this for me?"

"When I was young, I was left to scuttle for myself. I survived but it was always on my own. I never knew it could be otherwise. And then, after the change, I was a blank in this world."

"What change?"

"You found me and took me to Abagados and taught me chess. Whatever I have become, it is because of you."

"You means you weren't a gangster before this? Is that the change?"

"I was a blank, I did not even know enough to know I was looking for something, but I was. I was looking for you."

"So if I took you to a garage, you would be some crummy car salesman?"

"Want to buy a Buick?"

"Or if I took you to a fire station, you would be saving lives now instead of taking them?"

"I was a blank."

"You was a piece of clay and I was your Old Dudley. Oh God, I really stepped in it, didn't I? I really am damned, ain't I?"

"We are brothers now, Mite. Our possibilities are intertwined. For me it is so foreign a concept, I wouldn't even know it existed if there wasn't a word: *we.* You want a house with a fence, we want the house, and here it is."

"What do you want in return?"

"Loyalty. The loyalty of a brother."

"I never had no brother."

"I've had hundreds, thousands."

"I won't even ask. I won't even frigging ask, you freak. But since you've had so many you needs to clue me in. What does that loyalty-of-a-brother crap mean?"

"It means, Mite, I won't eat you unless I have to."

Istvan stops the big brown car at Kirschner's Delicatessen, double-parking in front of the entrance. "The usual?" says Istvan.

"I'll take care of it," says Kockroach. "Wait here, both of you."

"Get me a pastrami," says Mite. "Funny how thinking you're getting whacked and then not getting whacked it builds an appetite."

Mite and Istvan stay in the car as Kockroach steps out, looks around, heads into the store.

"Look who it is," says the short man behind the counter, his round gray head barely peeking above the white porcelain surface. "Always a treat it is to be seeink you. You want maybe potato or spinach?"

"No knish tonight. They've been hard to swallow lately. Give me two pastramis."

"Don't tell me. On rye, no mustard, no Russian, nothink but meat."

"You got it, sweet pea," says Kockroach before heading to the rear of the store, through a small kitchen, out the swinging back door into an alley. Hunched amidst the Dumpster and cans is a tall man in a beige raincoat, his bony wrists sticking out of the raincoat sleeves.

"I've been waiting," says Albert Gladden, Kockroach's real estate man.

"That's your job," says Kockroach.

"I made the changes you asked for in the deed to the property in Yonkers. As soon as I file the deed, the house becomes his for as long as he lives. Shall I go ahead?"

"Yes. Anything else?"

"An opportunity has arisen. There is a foreclosure on three contiguous brownstones on the East Side. Run-down but worth more than they will get. The price will be high and we'll have to sell some of the Harlem holdings to secure the financing, but I think it's a good trade."

"Do it. Did you bring the keys?"

Gladden hands him a jumble of metal. "This is to the back. Three locks. They think they have the only copies."

Kockroach tosses the keys in his hand, feeling their heft, seeing the dark ribbons of possibility that flow from them. "Is there insurance on the building?" he says.

"Some, but the building itself is not worth as much as the land so the insurance only covers the cost of demolition in case of a fire."

"Get more."

"It doesn't make—"

"Get more," says Kockroach. He grips the keys tight in his palm. "If things go bad, I might need to disappear for a while. I want you to continue as you have so far. But I will be back and I will expect an accounting."

"Of course, Mr. Blatta."

"Do not disappoint me."

"Never, Mr. Blatta."

"How's the wife?"

"She's a whore."

"Lucky you," says Kockroach.

In the alleyway at the side of an old, crumbling warehouse, Kockroach waits as Mite fiddles with the keys. The alley leads around to a loading dock in the back. The warehouse is dark, only a thin strip of light illuminates the side door, where Mite works the keys into the three locks. He has all three keys inserted, but it is hard to tell whether an individual lock is opened or closed. No matter what combination of turns he applies, the door stays tightly locked. Kockroach stands patiently as Mite works.

"What the hell is this place?" says Mite.

"Open the door."

"I'm trying. You got a flashlight?"

"I don't need a flashlight," says Kockroach.

Finally a combination works, the door opens with a shriek to Mite's push. Kockroach steps through the open door and Mite follows. It is cool, clammy, oily and dark. It smells of must, of sulfur. The windows are painted over, the thin light from the alley dies at the doorstep. Kockroach climbs a set of impossibly dark stairs with nary a hesitation, the stairway echoes with Mite's fumbles as he follows.

"Hey, Jerry, what's up?" says Mite. "Turn on a light or something."

Kockroach reaches the top of the stairs and stops. Mite bumps into his back and bounces off.

"Is that you, Jerr?"

"Welcome," says Kockroach.

"Where are we? I can't see a thing. What is this place?"

"Our future."

There is a hiss of light, a flickering flame from a safety match. The diffuse light seems to flow outward slowly, like a fluid, as if Einstein's theory had died at the doorway. With the slow movement of the light, it takes a moment for the scene to compose itself, but it does, it does.

A great space, its far corners still lost in shadow. Piled here and there, front and back, in some insane order are crates, and cartons, green military boxes, stacks of rifles, stacks of bombs. It is an armory, huge and endless, filled with bullets and grenades. Giant guns on tripods, standing like insects ready to march to war. Squat mortars and mortar shells piled haphazardly like bowling pins. Stacks of giant Chinese firecrackers which are not Chinese and not firecrackers.

Kockroach moves the match to his teeth, where a cigarette waits. He lights the cigarette and carelessly tosses away the still-lit match.

"Jesus, Jerry," says Mite as the match lands on the floor, sputters, and dies harmlessly. Darkness returns as slowly as it was erased. "Who owns all this? The frigging army?"

"The *Nonos*."

"The stuff he's collecting?"

"The stuff, yes."

"And you have the key?"

"We have the key."

"It's enough to wipe out the frigging city."

"That's what I'm planning on."

"You're going to blow it up, you're going to level everything?"

"The *Nonos* has set up his pieces. I'm advancing mine. Let's kill all the pawns and see who survives."

"I felt it first time I ever looked in them eyes. You're Hubert, you son of a bitch, ain't you?"

"I am what you have made me," says Kockroach.

Because cockroaches are not religious creatures, they have no theology, none of the glorious jewels of thought that inevitably follow from a simple belief in God. The very concepts of faith, purpose, redemption, grace, life after life, concepts that have warmed and informed the hearts of humans for millennia, have no meaning for a cockroach. But there is one theological concept of which each cockroach does have some understanding, a concept burned into its genetic history and hardwired into its DNA by the crises of the past.

At the end of the Devonian age, 360 million years ago, a great cataclysm occurred. It is unclear whether this cataclysm arose from the sulfurous fire of volcanic eruptions, from the deep freeze of an extended ice age, or from some terrible extraterrestrial impact, but what is clear is that this disaster destroyed a great majority of the newly evolved species on the earth. It was from the shadow of this mass extinction that the first cockroach emerged. Another mass extinction, 248 million years ago, killed up to 95 percent of all marine species, and still another mass extinction, 64 million years ago, caused the destruction of 85 percent of all animal species, including the mighty dinosaur. The cockroach has experienced hellfire from below, ravages from above, the very shifting of the earth, and survived when others, bigger, stronger, smarter, had been blown away as if dust. And through these searing experiences, the order itself has gained firsthand an understanding of one towering idea of Western religion.

For a cockroach it has no name, this cataclysmic destruction, this mass extinction, this tectonic shift in life from which only a cockroach can emerge. It is simply a fact of existence, something of which it is aware, just as it is aware of water and air, of the sound of footsteps, the smell of feces. For the order it has no name and so no word enters Kockroach's mind as he stands among the massive piles of armaments and explosives, but Kockroach knows of it in the blood and the bone and the marrow, knows of it as clearly as if his ancestors had tapped him on the shoulder and explained it all, and in so knowing he understands exactly where now he stands.

And the seventh angel poured out his vial into the air; and there came a great voice out of the temple of heaven, from the throne, saying, It is done. And there were voices, and thunders, and lightnings; and there was a great earthquake, such as was not since men were upon the earth, so mighty an earthquake, and so great.

Armageddon.

15

The train, it shivered as it pulled out of Penn Station, heading west, and I shivered with it. I wasn't alone in that train, they was two of us, and we leaned on each other and had our arms around each another and we whispered pledges of undying fidelity one to the other as the train took us both out from the city and into the great empty West. But stills I shivered.

It wasn't only the late night cold or the effect of the row of martinis I'd swilled. And it wasn't only the new adventure we was embarked upon, just as I had planned, though not as I had planned. I was facing the future, as blank as a white sheet of paper with just one black fact upon it which I could try the rest of my life to erase without succeeding, and that was terrifying, sure it was, but it was interesting too to see the black fact clear for the first time, so it wasn't only that which caused my shivers. It was something else, something I had spied outs the corner of my eye, just a glimpse of a thing, a silhouette against a backdrop of hell, something what would haunt my dreams through the long bland years to come.

After the Boss he showed me that pretty white house in Yonkers with my name on the deed, Celia and me we had ourselves some options. But there wasn't no time to waste. I had been inside the warehouse, had seen the guns and bombs. You see something like that under the thumb of a guy like the Boss, you don't wonder if it will go off, you only wonder when and how far you gots to run to get out from under it. The next night the Boss had planned to meet up with Moonstone's boys at the warehouse, to load a convoy of trucks and take the whole damn arsenal up to Harlem, leaving clues what blamed Tartelli for the theft. It was all coming to a head, the explosion was only hours away.

So I set up the meeting what would decide it all, the fate of my life and Times Square to boot, set it up at our usual place, Jack and Charlie's place with them wooden jockeys standing guard. I bought a new shirt and a new tie and a new pair of roach-stompers with points at the toes, and I ordered the best champagne in the joint because that's what I thought it took. And it was flowing, missy, but then shouldn't it flow on the night what sets you on the direction you'll follow for the rest of your cursed life?

"What's the big surprise, Mite?" asked Celia, sitting next to me at our table, her blue eyes shining in the candlelight, brighter than ever I saw them before, her face more alive, more beautiful, her whole being more vibrant, like she was a different girl altogether, a different girl playing at a different pitch. And tell me if I was a fool to think she had an inkling—the hints I had been giving had not been so subtle, not so subtle at all—and it was the inkling that had brought the flush of life to her cheek.

"You ever been out west?" I said.

"Where, like Montana? Wyoming? The Wild West?"

"I'm talking California."

"California?" Her eyes lit even brighter. "Hollywood?"

"I don't know, anyplace. Just California."

"No, I've never been. Girls from small towns in Ohio get one move. I came to New York."

"You want to go?"

"California? Sure, Mite. Who wouldn't? See some stars, see the Pacific."

"Not for a visit."

"Mite?"

"Call me Mickey, can you do that? Just for the night."

"Sure. Mickey. I didn't know you minded."

"I don't, it's just that some things are changing and maybe others ought change too. I got an opportunity out there. California. I thought I might go for it."

"In Hollywood? In the movies?"

"No, not the movies. I ain't the Bogart type, am I? What would I say, 'Here's looking up at you, sweetheart'? No, not the movies. Agriculture."

Her laughter was lighter than ever I remembered it.

"Mite? Excuse me. Mickey. Mickey? What do you know about agriculture?"

"Things grow, you hire Mexicans to pick the things what grow, trucks take them away and you gets money in return. Seems like an easy racket to me. Hey, don't laugh, I'm serious here. I could do it, why not?"

"Because you're a street kid. You'd be lost on a farm."

"Not a farm. I'm talking trees here. And maybe I don't want to be a street kid no more."

"Oh, Mite, this again? I thought we were going to have fun tonight. I thought you had a surprise."

"I do. I did. So how about it?"

"Mite—Mickey I mean. You know I love you, you know it, but don't be one of those dreary people who can't accept the good that's come into their lives, who have to question the worth of everything. Let's just have fun tonight, let's just be gay. You're on top, in the greatest city of the world. Why would you want to go anyplace else? You should find someone for yourself, spend a night or two dancing at the Stork Club, live it up."

"How about Yonkers, then? I got a line on a place in Yonkers. Nice white house, grass, picket fence, the whole schmear, and just a train ride into the city. A great place for kids."

"Kids?"

"What do you say?"

"What do I say about what?"

"Look." I glanced side to side, lowered my voice. "It's gonna explode, the whole thing down here. It's gonna be ugly and I don't want to have nothing to do with it. I can't take it no more. My suit's so tight it's choking me. I'm getting out."

"You need a vacation."

"It's more than that. I got plans. I got dreams other than this dream. So if I gets what you're telling me, you're thinking Yonkers over California. It's a suit and a tie and a commute to the city instead of long sunny days in the orchard. Fine. What about advertising? Maybe I could snag a job selling toothpaste. Who knows? I got skills I can use in a different way than I'm using them now. And truth be told, I got a feeling he's going to end up on top somehows anyway."

"Mite?"

"Mickey, right?"

"I don't understand what you're talking about."

"California or Yonkers? Take your pick."

"Jesus, Mite—Mickey, I don't know."

"But if you had to choose."

"I suppose anything's better than Yonkers."

"So that's it then."

"What?"

"Look, I got something I need to ask you."

"Sure, Mite. What? Anything."

It was time, I was ready. I had practiced for hours in my room. I had bought the ring from State Jewelers, next to the Loews State, the ring a gaudy diamond on a thin gold band. I stepped out from around the table, took the box out from my jacket pocket. I ignored the look on her face, a puzzled worried look, and slipped to one knee. The box, it opened with a muffled snap. The diamond it truly sparkled in the dark room, sparkled as if lit by a strange inner fire, as if it were the brightest thing in the entire room, in the entire city, as if it had fallen into that box right out from the midnight sky.

And then and there I let slip the words I knew she was hoping for, the words what I was sure would give her everything I supposed she ever could have dreamed.

Late the next day, I climbed to the roof of a building on the West Side, pigeons fluttering about within a wire cage, the birds cooing their sad unrequited songs.

"Shut up," I said as I kicked the coop.

I slipped a block in the jam to keep the door from closing on me and then hopped from one roof to the next till I was across the street from that warehouse. The sun was still out but the fat part of the afternoon had already passed. Night was coming and I wanted my view. I deserved it, I had earned it.

I laid flat on the tar, peeked my head over the shallow lip of the roof, and waited for it all to happen. It was like the whole of the city was a white-suited jazz band and I was the leader with my baton, like Benny Goodman or the Duke. Introducing Mickey Pimelia and his Mighty Mites.

Who the hell said I couldn't be no swell?

The sun set, the light faded, the night turned cold, the sky above grew dark and empty, the stars elbowed out of the heavens by the lights of Times Square just a few blocks off. It was time for the rhythm section to open with a wild dangerous beat, soft yet insistent, thump thump, thump. I raised my baton with a flick of my wrist and the drums started in and it began.

I never saw Blatta show. I thought I'd spy the brown Lincoln but I spied nothing, he must have slid in with Istvan through the alley entrance without so much as giving the street a sniff. But he was there, I could sense it, the way you can sense a bloodsucker landing on your neck even afore the needle nose pricks the skin. And when the trucks started arriving like a bass line plucked note by note, one after the other in a rhythm as steady as the drummer's beat, I knew it for sure. The line of trucks passed the front of the warehouse and then slipped into the alleyway that led to the loading dock at the back. Blatta was there, and now so was J. Jackie

Moonstone and the bulk of his boys, ready to pick Abagados's arsenal clean.

But tonight it wouldn't be so easy, tonight there'd be crashers at the party. Mite had seen to that. Good old Mite, loyal Mite, brother Mite.

It wasn't no surprise to me when, soon as the trucks they slipped down the alley and enough time had passed for the occupants to slip inside, the street it came alive like a sweet serenade of saxophones, blowing one against the other, with a licorice stick dancing riffs around them all. Slowly, quietly, as if in response to my very direction, an army rose from the gutters, as insidiously as if an army of insects, and then another and then a third, lining up on the various sides of the building. Three armies, armed and dangerous, led by three bosses standing now side by side by side right out in front.

Tartelli. Zwillman. Abagados.

Abagados lifted a hand, and like a solo blast from the big trombone, a pane in a warehouse window, it was blasted into shards of light.

"Blatta, you *poutana*," Abagados yelled in a voice shocking strong. "Show you stinking face."

There was silence. Then another window shattered, this time broken from inside the warehouse, and Blatta's voice poured into the street in a starkly inhuman yet hearty yelp. "Hello, *Nonos*."

"Everything in there it is mine," said Abagados.

"Come and get it."

"And how be your new black friend?"

A single shot sounded from the warehouse and dust kicked up at Abagados's feet. Tartelli and Zwillman, along with three of their gunsels, all dived away. Abagados flinched not at all.

"He's swell, *Nonos*," shouted the Boss. "He says hello."

"Before, we would had to hunt you both," said Abagados. "Now there no need."

"I'm always easy to find, *Nonos*. Look to the money, that's where I am."

"I never trust you."

"Trust?" Blatta yelled back. "You humans and your words. Are you ready to fight, *Nonos*?"

"No," said Abagados in a weary voice. "Not fight. In my life I had enough fight." He paused, let his shoulders slump for a moment, and then raised his jaw. "But I ready to kill."

Just then an explosion from inside the warehouse blew out the entire first floor of windows, scattering shards of glass across the street and high in the air, so that small slivers landed atop the far rooftops, even landed atop of me, pricking my exposed skin like sharpened teeth.

Abagados wasn't no doomed Confederate general, there wasn't going to be no valiant charge into the teeth of the enemy's firepower. The boys ringing the warehouse was only there to keep them what was inside from getting out. Earlier that day Nemo had taken a squad into the warehouse, a squad what included me, and set it up just the way he wanted. We took the ammunition out of them boxes, so them big guns they couldn't hurt you unless they was throwed at you. And we wired up the explosives so that a series of fuses lit from outside could start the thing inside to going kaboom. And missy, now them fuses they was lit.

It wasn't going to be a battle, it was going to be murder, pure and simple.

Them fuses they was lit, just like I expected, but they was lit too soon. I looked left, looked right. It was time for the coronets, as if led by Louis Armstrong hisself, with his fanfare entrance and his sweet tone of righteousness. But where was them coronets? I was wondering just that when a second explosion blew another set of glass choppers chewing through the sky.

Where was them coronets?

And then they opened up, as if I had brought them in myself with a swift wave of my baton. Lieutenant Nick Fallon, Vice, and his army of coppers came a-charging. They came a-charging, but not with no chorus of paddy wagons, no ma'am. This wasn't going to be just another raid with all them gunsels down in the street ending with a short pull in the poky afore the mouthpieces showed with piles of cash to spring them like springs. There wasn't no paddy wagons because there wasn't going to be no survivors. Lieutenant Nick Fallon, Vice, sent his army down both sides of the street, two battalions with guns blazing, like a loud blast of brass, shooting away at them boys outside the warehouse, forcing them back, back, back toward the very building they had set to blow.

The entire underworld was going to go up in one great torrent of fire and brimstone to slake the hunger what was burning inside my own damned soul.

It wasn't that she laughed, with me kneeling on the floor before her. I been laughed at near all my life, laughter I can take. It wasn't the laughter, it was the bitterness what was beneath it. Like who did I think I was? Who did I think she was? Did you ever kiss me, Mite? the laughter asked. Did you ever want to kiss me? Do you desire me like a man desires a woman, and don't you think I deserve that? Don't you think me worthy of that? Mite? How dare you, Mite.

I had never felt so small in all my life, smaller even than when them Thomasson twins took their turns with me. I knew what her laughter it was saying, what it was shrieking. And it was while I was still on my knees, and feeling the acid truth of her laughter wash through me, that I decided to follow her and see where she was getting what she couldn't get from me.

And I found out, without a doubt, and threw that moldy old lemon at his door, damn me to hell.

So I told the *Nonos* what I told the *Nonos*. And when I learned what he had in store, to turn that warehouse into a crematorium, I had an even cleverer idea, and so I told Fallon what I told Fallon. He talked about keeping the rackets going, did Lieutenant Nick Fallon, Vice, keeping the status quo so all could take their pleasures and their cuts, but he had hisself his own tidy dream, didn't he? He spilled it to me every time we met, and Hubert showed up laughing every time he spilled it, and it was in Fallon's dream that I spied the means to the ultimate obliteration. For Fallon wanted to be Johnny Broderick but better than Johnny Broderick. Johnny Broderick cleaned up the Square, Fallon was going to clean up the whole stinking town, scrub it fresh in one purifying burn, and in the process earn his own damn movie.

And the world I knew burst into flame. And the smoke billowed. And the heat grew hotter than even I could stand. And the black tar melted against my pants, my suit jacket, my tie. And just at the height of it all, I spotted something across the street, I spotted something, and in a blind fear I tore myself from off the roof, leaped the gap, sprinted back to the open door, raced down the stairs and out, back to the Square.

It was only a few short blocks to Penn Station and the love what was waiting for me on the train, but I had one thing more to do as I made my way out from the Square for the last time, one thing more to do. So I stopped at the Paddock for a drink and then at Benedict's for a drink and then at Kennedy's for a drink, and so Mite is suitably out of his skin and ready, yes he is, for that one thing more to do.

"Hey, Mite," says Tab, what Mite passes on the street, Tab the hustler what was always kidding hisself about who he was. "What happened to your threads, man?"

"Go to hell, you faggot," says Mite.

"I got something just for you, sweetheart."

"Shut up," says Mite. "Shut the hell up, you tit-face queer."

"Hey, baby, I might just be your last chance at heaven."

"You think so, dick-breath?" says Mite. "You really think so?"

"Sure I do."

"Then prove it."

"What? You mean—"

"Shut up and prove it."

And he did, yes, yes he did, and gave me something what I knew for certain only then that Celia never could.

And after, I was on that train heading west, shivering from the cold, from the drinks, from the fire. Shivering from what I had learned about myself from Tab. But shivering most of all from something else, from the thing I had spied afore I had sprinted off that roof.

But leastways I wasn't alone, I couldn't have stood my own damn self if I was alone. We was together now, now and forever. We leaned on each other and held to one another and we whispered pledges of undying fidelity one to the other, Hubert and me, lovers at last.

And Hubert, he was a great teacher, better even than Old Dudley. Old Dudley taught me the way to advance in the world: Behave yourself and eat your spinach and take them mopes for all they was worth. But Hubert, he knew better and showed it to me clear. There is no way, there is no advancement, there is no worth. Everything it is false, everything it is empty. And them things what behave as if it is any different, them things ain't only lies, theys worse than lies. And it isn't good enough to just see them for what they are and let them be, whether the *Nonos* or the Boss or the whole stinking life, no that isn't good enough at all. He lit a hunger in my soul, did Hubert, and there was only one thing what would satisfy it, one delicious thing.

Up on that roof, with the tar melting onto my clothes, I was tasting it. There was a third explosion, and then a fourth, like the sharp final exclamations of my great opus, and it was this fourth explosion what seemed to catch onto something else and blossom wild until the whole building collapsed into the center of a huge flower of fire. And out from the fire billowed a pillar of smoke, gray and thick, and I swear, I swear, it towered so high it fell back down on itself and from the light of the fire I could see the shape of a thick gray mushroom in the sky.

It was biblical, missy, and it devoured everything what was in its orbit, everything and everyone, everything and everyone but one.

A shadow what I swear I saw climb out from the center of the fire and appear to me for just an instant against the surging orange backdrop of flame. A shadow what intruded into my grand finale like the long bass note of an angry tuba. It stood there for an instant, the shadow, staring up as if right at me for just long enough to show me it survived, afore it somehow disappeared. A shadow with broad shoulders and a fedora still in place and a posture so distinctive and jaunty it could only be the shadow of one Joe, one Joe, the same Joe what I followed Celia to after she had laughed me down and set me on my path, the one Joe what was sticking it to her after she done stuck it to me.

Blatta.

And it was that shadow what scared me senseless and sent me running and set me to shivering on the train, with Hubert clutching and smothering me in his long gray arms.

But this I can tell you, missy, this, the strangest thing of all. It was in the outline of that shadow, that jaunty inhuman shadow, and the strange web of emotions it conjured, that lay for me the first intimations that maybe Hubert, he wasn't my one and only, my earthly fate, that somehow the son of a bitch with his deathly death grip could be beaten back.

It was just a matter of doping out how.

16 **Singed and smoldering,** driven relentlessly by fear, Kockroach slithers through the encircling line of police thugs with Thompson machine guns at their hips. He moves stealthily, from shadow to shadow, scuttling as quickly as his leg, burning from some interior fire, allows. When one of Fallon's cops turns in his direction, he slips into darkness and holds deathly still. He is working from deepest instinct, trusting what he had been to lead what he has become to safety.

He is crouching now against the scorching skin of a building across from the blazing warehouse. His hand reaches down to his thigh and feels a warm wetness. He brings his fingers to his mouth and licks them clean with his tongue. Briny, like his evening shrimp. Shrimp. The delicious crackle in his teeth, the sweetness. That, he knows, is now over. All of it is over.

Across the street, his plan to wrest power from the *Nonos* is burning with an intensity that pains the exposed sections of his fragile human flesh. There was a moment when his pieces were in perfect position and the human dream of great power was within his grasp. But now the entire chess board is being devoured by fire. He was betrayed from within, betrayed by Mite.

Mite was up there, on the roof, looking down upon the

destruction. Kockroach gazed up as he made his way out of the blaze and spied him. But it was not a surprise, none of it. He sensed Mite would betray him, always, and knew it for sure when, in the middle of mating, he heard the loud thump on the door. He detached himself from Celia, opened the door to the hallway, saw the remains of the rotting lemon clinging to the wall and wood. And yet, even after seeing the scattered pulp, he continued with his plan. He thought he had enough power to topple the *Nonos* despite Mite's betrayal, but he should have known better. No matter how skillfully he arrays his pieces, Mite always beats him at chess. Maybe there was something in Kockroach that rejected the human dream even as he reached to grab it in his fist.

Kockroach stares at the great conflagration and the burgeoning gray acrid smoke and he feels not bitterness nor anger nor a deep thirst for revenge. It is over. The world he knew and its possibilities are destroyed. He lets the fact of it wash over him and through him until it is part of him.

Deal with it, that is the cockroach way.

He has survived, he will move on, maybe even to molt once more back to his original form. He is through with the gangs, through with the whores, the protection rackets, through with twisting legs and snapping arms, through with humans altogether. The money he has out on the street will stay there and that is the only thing he regrets, along with no more shrimp.

The fear that pushed him out of the burning building and past the police rises up in his throat. It swivels his head, left and right, he searches for a way to escape, left and right. Then he spies something. A hole, in the street, the heavy cover tossed to the side by one of the invading armies. He scans the scene quickly to be sure no one is watching, glances nervously up at the sky, and then dives down into the darkness.

He slops into the slop. The smell is sweet, the darkness a balm, something squeals as it races across his shoe. Kockroach has found the sewers, and like the prodigal son of whom he knows nothing, he has come home.

Chased by fear, Kockroach hobbles through the tunnels, dragging his injured leg behind him. He veers left, hops right, travels straight for a long distance, and then bounds again to the left. He is rushing away from danger and to safety and judges each choice by some instinctive measure which he understands not at all and trusts completely.

When he reaches an obstruction he can't pass he stops, searches for a new route, and finds a long metal ladder climbing to a tiny shaft of light. He clambers up the ladder, places his hands on a metal disk with a single hole letting in the light. A roar reaches through the metal and vibrates into his bones. He stiffens his uninjured leg and pushes upward.

The traffic on Eighth Avenue buzzes ferociously. Taxis and long black cars. A huge gray truck thunders by.

He ignores the traffic, throws the metal lid to the side, lifts his head out of the hole.

A taxi swerves to avoid him, a delivery van sideswipes the taxi. Brakes squeal, a truck blows its horn as it roars right over him. A big black car avoids him by darting to the left before slamming into a parked car.

Accompanied by the sound of traffic snarling angrily around him, the sound of twisting metal and shattering glass, Kockroach climbs out of the hole and stands in the middle of the street. Smoke rises from his suit pants, his hat, smoke rises like an aura of doom from his shoulders.

He looks left, looks right, quickly scurries off the street, through the startled crowd, and disappears.

Kockroach knows now to where he is headed. In the underground sewers, his instincts were leading him to an indeterminate place of safety, but now, as he slides quietly uptown through dark alleys, as he hides in shadows as humans pass, he knows to where he is headed. Something inside of him rises as he comes closer, as he recognizes the neighborhood, the street, as he recognizes the very sheets of plywood sealing up the windows.

He pulls opens the rear door and slides inside his house on Ninety-fourth Street, the one property his real estate man, Albert Gladden, is never permitted to sell.

Once inside, he staggers through the kitchen and falls. The pain and weariness have finally taken him down like a fierce predator leaping onto his back, a panther maybe, black and heavy, or, in his earlier incarnation, a mouse. He drags himself to a corner of the living room, strips off his human clothes, curls up so that three sides of his body are protected.

His leg burns where it is bleeding, his ears ring still from the explosions, his skin throbs red from the heat, his mouth and tongue are raw from smoke, his vision is spotted from the

great balls of fire that blossomed about him. He is in a dangerous state, he knows, his new body is failing him and he has no
idea of what the future will hold. Yet his senses are as over-
stimulated as if he had been antennae fencing with a fleshy
palmetto bug drunk on Sterno. Even as his body burns, and
even as fear shrieks in his ear, he finds himself in the mood to
mate. This is no surprise, really. Kockroach is always in the
mood to mate.

And to a cockroach the crackle of destruction is as seductive as a Barry White sigh.

He awakes with a start at the tiny skritch he feels on his finger. One of his brothers has come to visit.

With his thumb, Kockroach gently rubs the arthropod's
wings. It straightens its legs and lifts its back in response, antennae swaying all the while. A moment later another comes
to be stroked, and then another, and still another until they
swarm over his hand, his arm, his entire body. They are nibbling his nails, gnashing his lashes, crawling in and out of his
ears in search of tasty morsels of wax. They dive beneath his
limbs and massage his skin with their tiny tarsi. Once again
a feeling of connection rises within him, a feeling lovely,
warm, scratchy, familiar, rich, sensuous, luxurious, loving,
and it continues to rise, beyond what he felt before, to almost
overwhelm him.

They are after food, he knows. They are searching for the
delicious balls of knish he has hand-fed them before and he
feels their disappointment, as if it were he himself who was

searching for something marvelous and failing to find it. He has no concern for the scores who have died that night in the warehouse, they are mere humans, but he feels responsible for these dark creatures who are swarming around the wound in his leg, lapping up his blood with the healing touch of their tongues.

And in the middle of the swarm he does feel better, stronger, he does feel revitalized. The world in which he had found himself, the world Mite had led him to, the world of power and death, the world of the *Nonos,* dissolves for him as if he had awakened from a strange dream.

He feels himself revert to a simpler and superior thing.

Kockroach is back on the street, clothed again, haunting the back alleys, the Dumpsters, darting with his limp through the darkness as he searches for food to feed the colony he now supports. The city is no longer a mystery to him, he knows now where to find quickly and safely what he needs. Each night he scours his favorite spots for bits of rotted vegetables, of maggoty meat, of glops of congealed noodles dumped behind chop suey houses. He eats all he can stuff into his throat and brings all he can carry back to his colony.

No more do they move hesitantly in his presence. They rush him as soon as he appears, a great swarm, far more than ever before survived in that house. From the neighboring houses they have come, from the street, from the sewers they have come. They arrive in great heaving armies, racing each madly as they make their dash to the provider. He leaves his special treats and watches as they climb one over the other over the next to devour them. Small white nymphs scurry among the legs of the adults, snapping up the morsels too small for the older ones to bother with. The sight of it fills him with a strange feeling, warm and rich, a feeling that, most strangely of all, has a name.

Satisfaction.

He is living the same way he had lived before ever he met Mite and was led into the dream world from which he escaped. But he is also not living the same way.

He tried to groom himself and his clothes, but that proved unsatisfying. He found the taste and hairs in his teeth to be unpleasant, and he was never as clean as he remembered from the showers. He also missed the fresh feel of the razor scraping his cheeks and jaw. So he has found a bathhouse nearby that is open all night, and a place to buy new clothes after dark, and a barber that cuts his hair and shaves his beard even after midnight. He spends what money that remained in his pockets after the destruction to keep himself clean and his new clothes pressed.

And he understands that this whole provider business is not the way it ever was before, when he was still an arthropod. Cockroaches are not selfless drones, working themselves to death for the common weal. One for one and all for one, is the cockroach motto, so long as you are the one. And yet, Kockroach somehow derives great satisfaction from being the provider.

That word again.

Therein lies the most momentous difference between what

he was before ever he met Mite and what he is now. Not the satisfaction part, the word part.

Before he moved by instinct, reacted without self-consciousness, lived with the empty certainty of a cockroach. But even as he rustles through the night and grabs his food from the Dumpsters and avoids as much contact with the humans as is possible within the dictates of cleanliness, he discovers that words themselves have intruded upon his new life.

He had considered them to be handy things, words, little arrays of strange garbled sound that helped him assuage his fear and feed his greed. He had considered them to simply be tools, which only indicates the depth of the intrusion, because Kockroach had no conception of what was a tool before he learned the word.

Immediately after his escape from the warehouse, lying in the corner of his home, still bleeding, he had been frightened of what the future would hold when, before he was taught the ritual of chess and learned the word future, all his concern was rooted firmly and solely in the present. And then there was that peculiar satisfaction word, a troubling word indeed, because it carries with it a concept so foreign as to be shattering. For when is a cockroach's hunger ever sated, his thirst slaked, his fear eased? For when, simply, is a cockroach ever satisfied?

And it wasn't just that words brought with them strange concepts that had insinuated themselves like a colony of earwigs in his brain. The concepts fed one upon the other, and led to still other concepts in a vertiginous climb of words and ideas that could only be classified as thought.

Thought.

But cockroaches don't think: they do or don't do. When they are still, their sides pushed tightly against the base of a kitchen cabinet, cockroaches are devoid of thought. They are simply waiting for the stimuli to align themselves in such a way that their instincts tell them it is safe again to move forward, to seek out something to mount and devour. Look into the mind of a motionless cockroach and you'll find nothing, a lovely, quiet nothing. Practitioners of the Eastern religions spend their lives training their minds to reach the pure empty state that is first nature to a cockroach. But in fairness to the devout, a cockroach has a natural advantage: no words.

In the human world, even before the destruction, the perverse practice of thought had crept into his mind on hushed little feet. But in the bustle of that world it had all seemed, well, almost natural. Now, among his original species, the flaw is glaring. In the moments between his daytime sleeps and nighttime forays for food and cleanliness, when Kockroach lies naked and awake in his corner, he experiences not that lovely quiet nothing but, instead, the bilious hubbub of words and concepts clashing and climbing in an incessant blabber. In short, he thinks.

He thinks of the future, he thinks of finding satisfactions in the future, he thinks of the tools he'll need to find satisfactions in the future.

He thinks of eating shrimp. He thinks of mating. He thinks of eating shrimp while mating. Of dipping his hands in spicy red sauce and wiping it across a pair of human breasts and lapping it off, lick by lick, while between each delicious lick he eats shrimp.

He thinks of being driven in his big brown Lincoln and surveying his territory and knowing the humans in his territory are under his dominion. He thinks of a human throat in his grip, the feel of blood pulsing beneath the flesh on to which he holds, the hot breath when he brings the victim's face close to his own, the gurgling sound when the throat collapses from the pressure.

He thinks of Celia Singer, her naked body stretched beneath him, above him, away from him even as their genital bond remains ever solid. Her shivering excitement, her blatant need, the way she would place her face wet with tears upon his chest.

He thinks of Mite, but not of his betrayal. He thinks of sitting in the schvitz with Mite, of playing chess with Mite. And he thinks of the conversation they had in the big brown Lincoln as they drove together to see the house in Yonkers, using words like gratitude, feeling, hunger. They had just been words, passed back and forth, tools, but even in the car, Kockroach had known they were more. And he would like now to talk again to Mite about those words and others, words like loyalty and satisfaction. Words like violence and opportunity and power.

This desire to talk, to communicate, is completely foreign to a cockroach and yet it grows ever stronger within him. He knows it is alien, this desire, he knows it is a corruption, and yet it is too strong to deny. Just as words infected him with concepts and concepts infected him with thought, thought infects him with the strange need to talk, to talk in words, to start it all again.

He brings back a great ball of starchy gluck to feed his colony and they swarm over the food and swarm over him, burying him in their writhing brown mass, and it feels still as good as ever it felt, and his genital flap swells and throbs in the middle of it, yes, but it is no longer enough.

He needs to mate, but his molt has made the allure of the female cockroach a vague remembrance and nothing more. He hungers for shrimp, to devour again their crackly briny sweetness. He opens his mouth and a cockroach crawls in and he chews it and swallows and repeats with two more, four more, and it is good, yes, musty and crunchy with a soft gooey interior, yes, but it is not shrimp. And he wants to talk, but his family, his swarm, they have no words, no concepts, no thoughts, and so the talk is painfully one-sided.

He hoped it would be enough, to live as once he had lived and to provide for his flock, he hoped it would be enough, but it is not enough, not anymore, not after being infected with words.

Kockroach needs again to enter the human world.

17

Kockroach moves now through the streets of the city in the bright light of day.

The sun is painful and frightening, even as he keeps his dark glasses on and his hat low, yet he has no choice but to walk among the humans in the daytime. He is no longer afraid of giant predators, and he is no longer afraid that a human will recognize him for what he is and crush him, but that does not mean he is not afraid. Fear and greed, greed and fear, they are always with him, his boon companions. He was in the middle of the explosion. He saw humans flying through the air, humans riddled with bullets, humans torn apart like cockroaches at the many many hands of a millipede. The biggest danger he faces in the human world is to meet up with those who will recognize him and want to finish what he started. So he stays away from the world of his former life, away from Times Square, away from the places in which he had once been known. And, most painfully, he stays away from the night.

Kockroach moves now through the streets of the city in the bright light of day and he is looking for something. He is not sure exactly for what it is he is looking, but he is looking for something and the something has a name, a word Mite had taught him.

Opportunity.

He has thought it through. In his house, in his corner, in the darkness, he has thought it through. What went wrong. Why he continued to the warehouse even after he was certain of Mite's betrayal. From wherein came the destruction. He has thought it through, he could not help but think it through—that is the way of thought he has discovered, it is self-perpetuating and it never shuts up—and the answer he came up with was that violence had guaranteed his failure. Not the violence perpetrated against Kockroach, but the violence Kockroach perpetrated himself.

Two cockroaches chasing after the same female, the same morsel of goop, two cockroaches battle, the stronger wins, the winner mates, the winner eats, it is so simple. And among the humans he discovered that he is the strongest and so it was natural for him to think that anything he saw, any female, any territory, was his to take. But he was wrong.

Human violence is very different from the cleanliness of cockroach violence. There is a battle and one human wins and that should be the end of it, but one battle is never enough. Human violence spirals. And each battle ever after grows in size and intensity as the combatants reach each for their tools. The beaten human comes back with a knife. The stabbed human comes back with a gun. The shot human comes back with a bomb. The bombed human comes back with an army. It continues, back and forth, until one side is utterly vanquished or both sides are utterly destroyed.

That is why Kockroach went to the warehouse even after he was certain that Mite had betrayed him. The fight would spiral into something cataclysmic, it was so destined, it was a human fight, and Kockroach saw no reason to delay the inevitable. He had miscalculated the force arrayed against him, yes, but not the end result. What started with the simple snapping of an arm, with Kockroach winning the battle with the shirtless human who had grabbed Mite by the nose and stepped on a brother cockroach, inevitably led to massive destruction. It is the human way with violence. Cataclysm is cleansing, yes, but surviving the cleansing fire of the warehouse had been mostly a matter of luck. He was lucky once, he couldn't be sure he'd be lucky twice.

And so Kockroach has decided he will have to find a different way to rise again in the human world. And so he is looking for opportunity. He remembers when Mite first gave him the word. "A little business," had said Mite. "Beeswax. Something rich."

Yes, that is what he wants, something rich, a little beeswax, opportunity, that is what he is seeking as he stalks the city's streets.

"You're looking for opportunity, young man?" says the woman behind the desk. She has high gray hair, clear glasses on a chain around her neck, and she looks like she just bit into a mouse.

"You got it, sweet pea."

"Well, we don't wear sunglasses at the bank, or our hats inside, and we don't use words like 'sweet pea.' We maintain a certain decorum. Are you sure this is where you want to work?"

Kockroach looks around. The ceiling is high, men and women behind glass partitions are sorting through money. He wants to be rich again, he wants the green bills to be thick in his wallet and ready to buy food, women, grooming, shrimp. Why would he want to work anyplace else but a bank? "I'm sure."

"Then fill this out." She hands him a sheet of paper. "And don't leave out the references. Three. We do nothing without references."

Kockroach looks at the sheet of paper in his hand, covered with human writing and long blank lines. He looks up at the woman, who is staring at him through those clear glasses.

"I don't read," he says.

"I'm very sorry to hear that," says the woman, without sounding very sorry at all. "But if you don't read, what makes you think you can work at a bank?"

He leans over, tickles her chin. "Because I can count."

Kockroach places the gray tub on the table and starts tossing in the dishes, the silverware, glasses and food. Shards break off as the plates and glasses hit one another from the tossing, but he continues. He is wearing still his suit, his hat, his tie, his dark glasses, but he has now an apron tied around his waist.

"You want opportunity?" had said the man at the register of the restaurant, a short man with a pointed beard. "Why not? This land of opportunity, right?"

"So they say, sweet pea."

"You ever bus?"

"I had a Lincoln."

"Don't be cute. Take apron, take tub, show me something."

Kockroach watched a boy with an apron sweep the remains off a table and, following his example, tied the apron round his back and grabbed a tub and began clearing table after table, giving each a quick swipe with a rag before going to the next. He works fast, with abandon. The clatter and clash of the dishes is lovely, and the smell too. He likes the work, he would do this for free.

A half a sandwich, soggy with spilled coffee, gray with ash, lies on a plate in the tub. He likes his starch soggy. He grabs the sandwich, stuffs it in his mouth.

"What you do?" says the man with the pointed beard, standing now in front of him.

Kockroach looks up at him, bits of sandwich sticking to his grinning lips.

"Get hell out of here. What, you some sort of animal?"

Kockroach drops the tub on the floor, pulls off the apron, wipes his mouth with it, tosses it in the tub.

"As a matter of fact," he says before leaving.

It is harder than he anticipated, this opportunity beeswax.

It seems opportunity is available only to those who can fill out the form that is held in a desk drawer in every building and the form can only be filled out by someone who can read. He needs to learn, he realizes, but who can teach him? He thinks of Mite. If Mite were here, Mite would take care of him, Mite would fill out the form, Mite would teach him how to read. It was Mite after all who had taken him to Abagados where he could find a job without the form. He hadn't realized how difficult it is to navigate the human world without a Mite by his side.

Every attempt to find opportunity fails. The market with all that luscious food, the clothing store, the barbershop, every place is closed to him. He crosses avenues, he hops along streets, he skulks the back alleys, he is looking for something, anything, he is looking for a sign.

And a sign is exactly what he finds.

Through an alley, on a short cobbled street surrounded by the butt ends of huge factory buildings, atop a small building with a ground-floor office, he sees a sign. There are words that Kockroach can't yet read but it is what is above the words that pulls him in. Huge, brown, oval, with six little legs sticking out, two beady eyes, two stubby antennae. It is a giant arthropod, a giant cockroach to be exact, not an accurate rendering, as Kockroach surely knows, but close enough to leave no doubt of what it is.

Kockroach rubs a finger across his teeth, twists his ears.

"Irv," yells the woman at the front counter in a voice that resembles the screeching of a cat with a truck parked on its tail and which Kockroach finds positively lovely. "Is someone here looking for a job."

Her blond hair is piled atop her head like a hornet's nest. She rubs a stick across one of her fingernails. The mounds on her chest are astounding.

"Give him the form," shouts a ragged voice from the back room.

"I gave him the form," screeches again the woman, looking not at Kockroach but at her hand. The stick rubbing back and forth across the nail makes a sound like a cricket. "He says he needs to talk to you."

"I'm busy," the ragged voice shouts back.

"Mr. Brownside is busy," says the woman.

Kockroach leans over the front counter and takes the woman's hand in his own. She tries to tug it away but he holds it fast and brings it to his lips. He licks the middle finger lightly with the dry tip of his tongue.

"What did you go and do that for?"

"I couldn't help myself, sweet pea."

"Well, don't do it again."

He does it again, sees her eyelids flutter. Still holding her hand, he says, "What is your name?"

"Cassandra, with a *C*."

"That's a pretty name. What do you do here, Cassandra, with a *C*.?"

"I'm the receptionist."

"I mean you and Mr. Brownside."

"None a your frigging business. What are you, some sort of gumshoe for his . . . Oh, you don't mean . . . Well, jeez, didn't you see the sign? We're the Brownside Extermination Company. We get rid of bugs."

"Get rid of bugs? How?"

"How do you think? We exterminate them."

"What does that mean?"

"It means you don't want to be no bug around Irv."

"Do you like wine, sweet pea?"

"What does that got to do with exterminating?"

"Let me in to talk to Mr. Brownside and you'll find out."

"What if I don't want no wine?"

"Then we'll drink champagne."

"What if the bubbles set me sneezing?"

"I'll get you a tissue and pour another glass."

"What if I ain't interested?"

He lowers his head, lets his tongue roll out its full ungodly length before gently brushing once again her finger with its tip.

"Irv," she screeches. "Youse got a visitor."

"It ain't so easy as it looks," says Irv Brownside, rumpled and unshaven, big-bellied, big-jawed, wearing a filthy brown coverall. His desk is piled with papers, journals, files, invoices, cans of poison, a thick pastrami sandwich. His work boots sit atop his desk, alongside his feet in their dirty woolen socks. He leans forward, picks up his sandwich, leans back, takes a bite. "You don't just go in and spray. Oh it looks good, you in your uniform with the tank on your back, but when those little buggers they're back that night it's hell to pay. You want to kill 'em, you got to think like 'em. Not just any crack will do. They like it warm, they like it tight, they like it moist."

"Don't we all," says Kockroach.

"What? Oh yeah, right. Good one. You got any exterminating experience?"

"Of course," says Kockroach.

"What kind of pest? Your cockroach, your ant, your wasp,
your termite, what?"

"The human kind."

"What's that? Oh, you're making a joke. You're a funny
guy, huh? Is that why the smile?"

"I always smile."

"I don't like funny guys. Funny guys like to talk instead of
work."

"I like to work."

"You don't seem the type."

"I'm a fool for work."

"Look, if you got no experience, I can't use you. I don't
got time to train. Fill out a form, and if things change, I'll
maybe give you a call."

"No forms."

"Everyone's got to fill out a form. We need your numbers.
The government and all."

"No forms."

"No forms?"

"No numbers."

"What are you, on the lam?"

"Rack of lamb."

"Heh? Oh yeah, again with the funny. So you're talking
something off the books. No taxes, no withholding, none of
that Social Security bullcrap. Cash."

"Perfect."

"And with everything in cash—" he rubs an eyebrow— "you'd be expecting less than minimum, I suppose. Ain't that so?"

"So."

"And you think you can think like them little buggers?"

"I'm sure of it."

Brownside takes a bite of his sandwich, swings his feet from the desk, pushes out of the chair, ambles off into a closet. He brings back a black chest the size of a small suitcase. He opens the chest on the desk. Inside rests an empty cage with a steel frame, wire-mesh sides, a small latched door.

"How many roaches in this city?" he says. "A hundred million or so? Bring me back just fifty and you got the job. Just a measly fifty. It should be the easiest thing in the world, but you got to know where to look. We open at seven. Show me at seven that you know where to look and I'll give you the job."

"No problem."

"Don't be so sure of yourself. Sixteen years in this business I been sending rooks out with that case and not a single one came back with more than twelve. Even pros can't find twenty, nine times out of ten. It's funny how when you don't want them it's all you can find, and when you're looking you can't find a one. Still think you can handle it?"

"Piece of cake," says Kockroach.

Kockroach waits outside the Brownside Extermination offices with the black chest gripped in his hand. He has been waiting since before dawn reached its scaly fingers across the rooftops of the factories backing onto the alley. He didn't want to be late so he arrived while the night was still thick with the imperfect darkness of the city. He waits, but his mind is not empty as before when he waited. Now he waits and, alas, he thinks.

He thinks about how it was before he was given words and about how the thoughts now don't ever stop and leave him be. It doesn't make him better, this curse of thought, of that he is certain, but it does make him different. And why, he wonders, should that difference make a difference?

He thinks about the members of his colony, their hungers, their fears. Cockroaches do whatever they need do to survive. They would eat him if they had the wherewithal to bring him down and teeth sharp enough to chew the meat off his bones. That he is ready to do the same to them is only proof of the continuing purity of his cockroach nature.

But why must he even try to justify his actions to himself when greed and fear were justification enough before? If only the woman in the bank had given him an opportunity, he wouldn't be here, now, beneath this sign, with the case in his hand. That too is something new, along with thought comes what? Regret? He has no doubt about what he is going to do, and yet still he thinks of the reasons why, as if the reasons mattered. This thinking, he thinks, is like a sickness, only you can't squeeze it out with your morning crap.

A boxy brown van drives to the front of the office and shudders to a stop. On the side of the van is an identical sign to that atop the small building, with an identical drawing of an arthropod. Irv Brownside steps out of the van holding a steaming mug and a bag, wipes his mouth, checks his watch.

"You are an eager beaver, ain't you?"

Brownside doesn't wait for a reply. He unlocks the door, steps around the counter and into his office. Kockroach follows.

"Cassie don't come in till eight-thirty," he says when he is seated behind the pile on his desk. He clears a spot in front of him and papers flutter to the floor. He puts down the mug, reaches into the bag, pulls out six donuts, one after the other, lays them on a stack of invoices, licks his finger. "What'd you say your name was again?"

"Blatta. Jerry Blatta."

"What is that? Italian?"

"Greek."

"Son of a bitch. All right. Show me what you got."

Kockroach lays the chest on the floor, unsnaps the latch.

"It ain't so easy, I told you," says Brownside. "Didn't I tell you?"

"You told me," says Kockroach even as he lifts up the small steel cage and unlatches the door.

They fall in a torrent, a waterfall of brown, scurrying madly once they hit the pile, diving beneath the papers, climbing around the canisters of poison, swarming in thick piles over the donuts, hundreds and hundreds, dropping with audible snaps to the floor and dashing to the far walls and crevices.

Brownside jumps back for a second and then raises his gaze from the undulating desktop to Kockroach's face.

"Piece of cake," says Kockroach.

Brownside's unshaven face cracks into a broad smile. He steps forward, swats most of the cockroaches away from one of the donuts, picks it up with two fingers, shakes the rest off, takes a bite. "Help yourself."

Kockroach reaches for a donut himself, shakes it free of arthropods, jams it all at once into his mouth. Vanilla cream oozes through his teeth.

"Welcome aboard," says Brownside. "Let's get you a uniform."

Kockroach stands beside the brown van, outside a tall tenement with cracked windows and weeds sprouting through the brick.

He is wearing a brown coverall zipped to his throat with the crude drawing of a cockroach on the breast, brown gloves, brown boots, a brown baseball cap. His eyes are covered by goggles tinted yellow. Strapped onto his back is a heavy metal tank and in his gloved hands is a metal nozzle shaped like a gun with an extralong barrel. His smile is broad and white and pearly. He looks up at the building rising before him as if he were looking at his hope.

Irv Brownside stands beside him in an identical outfit, though not so well pressed.

"You ready to clean up Tombstone, Jerry?" asks Brownside.

"I'm ready, Irv," says Kockroach. "I've been ready all my life."

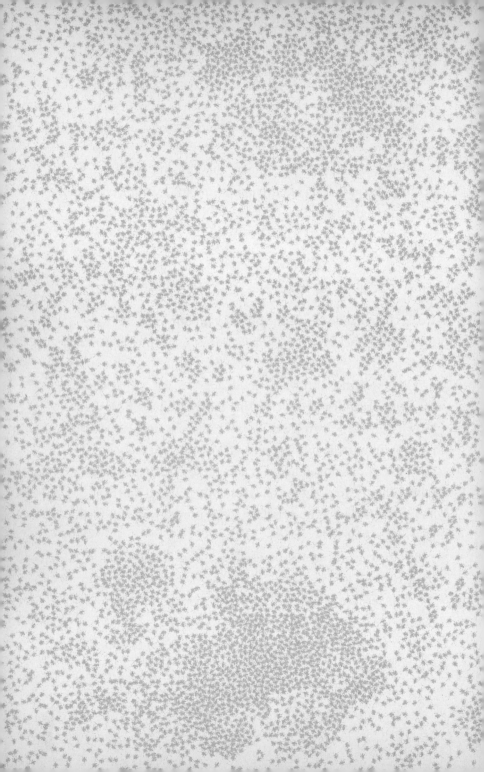

PART THREE

EMPIRE STATE

18

Eight years after, after it all went to hell, eight years after I came back to face the ghosts.

It was Champ what was driving the old '55 Packard over the Georgie W. and he wasn't none too happy about it, no ma'am. Far as he was concerned, he wanted nothing ever more to do with this burg. I knowed that because it's what he tells me while we're stalled in traffic smack in the middle of the bridge.

"I want nothing ever more to do with this burg," he says in his soft voice scarred forever from one too many jolts to the throat. "Look at it there, all towers and lights, leaning forward like a hungry southpaw, just waiting again to knock me on my keister."

"It wasn't the city," I says. "It was Izzy Berg and Fighting Paddy Conaghan what did the knocking."

"They were just the front men, Mick. It was the promoters, the cops, the managers, the cut men, the whole damn city. Slipping that shiv so clean across my brow I didn't feel a thing, ruining me just because I had the local Irish boy in the deep."

"You sure it wasn't a chop to the eye what started you to bleeding?"

"Whatever else I was, Mick, I wasn't a bleeder."

"Excepts for that night. Keep your eyes on the road."

"I hate this city. We've got no call to come to this city. What about we head to the coast?"

"Let me see what I need see, and if it ain't worth our while, then we'll blow."

"We could head out to Santa Cruz, buy a boat. Catch fish for a living."

"What do you know about catching fish?"

"They don't punch back, I know that. And it don't cost nothing to snatch them out of the ocean. It's like gold just floating around, waiting to be hooked and pulled in."

"With all we knows about fishing, we might as well throws a hook into a bathtub."

"I always wanted to own a boat. And what I heard about Santa Cruz, cheap rooms, cheap eats. Man can fish all day, fill his belly at night, and sleep sound in Santa Cruz."

"Things work out like I expect, Champ, we won't need to be watching our dimes no more."

"I miss old Chicago. Best damn hot dogs in the world in old Chicago."

"Well we can't go back to Chicago, now can we?"

"No we can't."

"You took care of that, didn't you?"

"Yes I did."

"Nedick's."

"What say?"

"Nedick's got good dogs. Or I'll take you up to Nathan's on Coney Island. Take my word, there's good dogs in New York."

"Better than Chicago?"

"No, Champ. No place in the world's got better hot dogs than Chicago."

Chicago, city of the big snow, of the cold shoulder, of kielbasa and corrupt aldermen and a rap to the teeth, a punch-drunk city always climbing the ropes for more. After the big blowup I had meant to take the train from New York all the way across to the far ocean, but when it stopped in Chicago, the thought of all them rolling prairies, them palm trees swaying and beaches filled with stuffed bikinis, all of it turned my stomach. I stepped out of the train into the grit of the big city, breathed in the industrial stench, and you know what it smelled like, missy? It smelled like mother's milk, that pure. It smelled like home.

What would I do on a beach, all that sand getting in my Regal shoes, in my fedora, shining up my green suit? What would a guy like me do on a beach, I ask you that?

So I dusted off my suit and stayed, in Chicago. I found a small room with a bed and a sink on the North Side, close enough to the ballyard I could hear the yobs cheering through my window whenever Big Ernie, he parked one on Waveland Avenue, and that's where I stayed to figure it all out between me and Hubert, which is where that lawyer he came in.

"Th-th-thank you for coming to see me, Mr. P-P-Pimelia," he says, sitting at one end of the long conference table, desirous to keep his distance from something so distasteful as the likes of me sitting at the other. "I'm afraid we have some unpleasant b-b-business to which to attend."

His name was McGreevy. He was tall and pale, with a sharp pointy nose. When he spoke his eyelids fell so low you couldn't see the green of his eyes. He wasn't much older than me, but still, with his pale skin, his black vested suit, with his long banker's jacket, he reminded me of the old-money Philadelphia I heard tale of when I was a boy but what I never got a whiff of firsthand, ancient, secret, wealthy, powerful, incestuous, grasping.

"It is your uncle, your dear Uncle R-R-Rufus, third cousin twice removed of your dear departed mother. I am grieved to inf-f-form you your Uncle Rufus has passed away. A tragedy yes. But as in many such tragedies, there is a b-b-benefit to the survivors. Uncle Rufus left a will."

McGreevy, the lawyer, he come along at a low point, that's for sure. It had been four years since I arrived in Chicago and things with Hubert and me hadn't gone so swell, no ma'am. First of all I had run out of money, and the little hustles I had undertaken, the tired scams, the small-time dealing, all of it had proven less than profitable and sent me to the slammer more than once. I was struggling, yes I was, struggling to even make the pitiful rent on my pitiful room. It got so bad I took a job, that's right, a job, bagging groceries, a job. How low had I sunk don't even ask 'cause that will tell you everything. And I was drinking too, and that's not a good thing because I'm not a drinker, never was, could never hold nothing, but I was drinking nightly at the corner tavern to fill the hole.

You see, Hubert, he scoops something out of you and leaves a hole, and you needs to fill it somehow, and I tried, first with the destruction, and then with the drink, and in the end it was with the thoughts that were filling that hole when even the drink it wasn't enough. The destruction that you want to unleash on your enemies and then on the world ends up turning on your own self. That's what the drinking is, another form of destruction to fill the hole, and when that ain't fast enough, then Hubert again starts whispering in your ear and you get faster ideas, and a knife it ain't no longer just a knife and a gun it ain't no longer just a gun and a bottle of pills it's more than a bottle of pills, or maybe less is what I mean, less than anything, an invitation to nothing. And that's where I was when the letter came from McGreevy asking me to meet hisself in the Loop, in the legal offices of some bluenosed firm called Hotchkiss and Tate.

"The will is still in pr-pr-probate, Mr. Pimelia, and pr-pr-probate could last years, decades even. But we are prepared to advance you a sum to tide you over."

"How much of a sum?" I asks.

"A handsome sum, and there will be other payments in the future, so long as you don't in any way c-c-contest the distributions I make to you."

"I should just sit back and takes what you gives and ask no questions."

"Yes, that is exactly what you should do. And you'll need to sign a full agreement to that ef-f-fect, of course."

"And what if I does contest," I says. "And what if I hires my own three-piece suit to make sure I gets all that's coming my way. How do I know I'm not being played for the patsy here? My dear dead Uncle Rufus, I loved the man like a father, I did, and the rest of the family was just ingrates. Maybe I'll decide to muck it up for everyone untils I get maybe even more than my fair share, like old Uncle Rufus would have wanted. What then?"

"Then our b-b-business," he says, "is at an end."

"I noticed your name, McGreevy, it ain't on the door."

"Hotchkiss and Tate is our local counsel."

"So where's your digs?"

"Think c-c-carefully before you decide."

"Tell me this, then. Where did dear old Uncle Rufus kick it for good? Philly? Where should I tell my lawyer to start digging?"

"If you d-d-decide to sign, I can be very helpful in the future. If you need anything, you can simply get in touch with Mr. Tate. If you d-d-decide not to sign, then I won't disturb you further."

"This is screwy. Something it ain't right."

"They say there is a p-p-pot of gold at the end of every rainbow, Mr. Pimelia, but the trick, as in everything in the world, is f-f-finding it."

I signed, course I did. And the payouts they came steady, just as McGreevy promised. And whenever I got the square idea of jumping out for more, it wasn't the paper I signed what stopped me, it was the memory of that bloodless bastard with the stammer telling me about rainbows and pots of gold like he hisself was the leprechaun what could make it all disappear and would, believe you me, of that I had no doubt.

But strangely, McGreevy, that pale bastard, he started me

on filling the hole with something other than the dream of nothing. The money helped, sure, I was done bagging groceries, but it wasn't the money, really, what started me up. No, it was good old Uncle Rufus, who never had I heard word one about in my youth. That someone, somewhere, had thought enough of my mother and me to remember us and want to take care of us, that someone had cared, that did the trick. Funny how much Hubert he hates that.

I had questions, sures I did, but I buried them and went about my life. And with old Uncle Rufus's benediction I began to feel things I hadn't felt in a long time. Connected, is what I mean. I saw a kid in trouble and I was that kid in trouble and I helped him out with a dime or a dollar when I could. I'd look at a Joe struggling with something and I'd feel the strain and lend a hand so I could struggle with him. I wasn't no saint, believe you me, but I was feeling things again.

And then I found Champ. And he filled a hole even Hubert hadn't dug. And Chi-town, when it all slipped into place, became for me a different world where different dreams was dreamed in colors I never knew existed.

But Chicago was dead to us now, both of us, and we couldn't never go back, and so there we was, crossing the Hudson, heading into the Apple, another place that had died to me.

Rate I was going, Santa Cruz would be all I had left.

But first I was coming back to the big town, chasing my ghosts, coming home. Funny, ain't it? I grows up in Philly, spends eight years in the distant wilderness of the Midwest, yet it's New York what I still thought of as home. What did that Joe say, the Joe what wrote all those long sentences that fly around like twittering birds and end up nowheres, didn't he say you can't never go home again? Well, maybe he was right, but there we was, the two of us, driving over the Georgie W., trying to make a liar out of him as I reached out for some shadow barely glimpsed in the midst of an apocalypse. You see, them questions I had buried had risen from the dead and it was time to finds some answers.

"Head south off the bridge," I says. "We'll check out first the Square."

The Square, Times Square, my square, ever the same and yet. And yet.

The signs, sure, still there, brighter than before, but different faces, different products being hustled to the mokes, different names on the movie marquees, half of them with sex in the title or tagline. "Raw Naked Violence." "Sex Without Shame." The whole scene filthier, seedier, sad. The Astor Hotel, the grand old dame of the Square—shuttered up for the wrecking ball. The Latin Quarter—all shot to hell. The Roxy, the frigging Roxy—gone. The life of the place had been chewed off by Sister Time.

I stepped in the Automat, the land of promise for me as a boy, but it too was changed completely. Once an elegant refuge full of promise, a direct link to the grand parade flowing outside its windows, now it was dirty, muted, inhabited by a bunch of low-life bums sitting miserably alone at the tables, no punch or laughter or thrilling sense of possibility.

"What are we doing here?" says Champ.

"I don't know," I says. "But in my life I'll never feel older than I feels right now."

The only moke I recognized at the Automat was, believe it or not, Tony the Tune, still eating his Salisbury steak, still humming away, aged not a day since I left. I went over to ask him where everyone else had disappeared to, but afore I got two words out he blew me off.

"Get away from me, you little scalawag. I got no time to waste on the likes of you."

It was the loveliest thing I heard since we crossed the Hudson.

On the street, I met a hustler with his T-shirt and tight jeans and I asked about Tab, but alls I got was a drugged-out pout and a halfhearted come-on, more pathetic than enticing. The hookers was all strangers too. Not a one of our girls was still on the street. There had always been turnover, sure, that was the nature of the game, but I hadn't noticed how relentless it was whilst I was in the middle of it. But in eight years it must have turned over a couple times or more. Still I took aside what girls I found and asked them some names. Blatta? What's that? Abagados? Who? Fallon? Nothing. Who's in charge now? I asked. A name I never heard of, a name I didn't want to remember.

"You ever hear of Pinnacio?" I says, but not a one a them did.

The legends was all dead.

In the Paddock was a barkeep I never seen before, a broad bus with a bully boy's face who eyed Champ a good long moment afore wising up and giving him a beer.

"Does a copper name of Fallon still come in here?" I asks.

"Who's asking?" he says.

"Just someone what used to work the Square is all."

"Who were you with?"

"Blatta."

"Never heard of him."

"Abagados."

"Never heard of him."

"The extent of what you ain't heard of would float the Hindenburg."

"I got nothing for nobody I never heard of. Get lost."

"Answer his question, Pops," says Champ with that soft ruined voice of his, "and we will."

The barkeep glances again at Champ, takes in his dark face, scarred and mashed, his ears engorged from rabbit punches, his neck thick from all that training, his huge hands laying still and heavy on the bar.

"There's an old wino comes in sometimes, begging for drinks," says the barkeep, talking to me but his eyes all the time on Champ, which was the way of it. "Goes on and on about how he used to be somebody before he starts the shouting and we need to toss him. He says he was a cop and once I heard his name, something like Fallon."

"Where can I find him?" I says.

The barkeep snorts. "Where do you think you find winos like that?"

It didn't take long. I had picked up a new line of work in Chicago. It was all part of that strange feeling I had that I wanted to lend a hand to those what needed it. Not as a charity, that wasn't my way, but in a manner what fit my talents and proclivities and could earn me an almost honest dime. I had done such a job detecting that thing between the Boss and J. Jackie Moonstone, I thought maybe I could actually make a go of the detection racket. So I stripped some leaves off my wad from Uncle Rufus and rented an office, set up a phone, hired a dame with attitude to answer it, and just like that I had my new line.

Mickey Pimelia, P.I., licensed and all.

Fallon wasn't hard to find for a licensed gumshoe. He was holed up in a sad sagging flophouse on the Bowery, a fleabag called the Sunshine. I bought him a sandwich, what kind didn't matter, he probably couldn't taste the difference no more, and a jug of rotgut wine, anything harder he wouldn't be able to stomach, and Champ and me, we walked past the suspicious eyes of the night clerk and climbed the hotel's stairs to pay our respects.

The stench was enough to stagger you, piss and puke and crap like it was rubbed along the walls, the rot of ages. Cockroaches climbed the banisters and clung to the ceiling.

"Go away," was the response to our banging from the other side of the door.

"I'm looking for Fallon," I said, "Lieutenant Nick Fallon, Vice."

Pause. "He's dead."

"I'm an old friend."

"He doesn't have any."

"I got some food and some wine for him."

"Keep it," says the voice, but then we hears the sag of bed-springs and the shuffle of feet and the door it opens.

"Mite," says Nick Fallon when he gets a good look at me out of his rheumy eyes. "You look like dick."

"But you, Lieutenant, you're the goddamn queen of England."

He glances at Champ, back at me, raises his eyebrows, takes the wine out of my hand.

"You don't wants the sandwich?" I says.

"What do you take me for?" he says.

Think of a balloon, all pumped up and proud, its belly sticking out with the authority of the inflated, that was Lieutenant Nick Fallon, Vice, when I knew him when. He was inflated by his position, by his arrogance, by his secret ambition to out-Broderick Johnny Broderick and become a legend hisself. But then the air leaks out as it always leaks out until the balloon is only a ghost of what it was. That was Fallon now, in his ragged suit pants, his filthy undershirt, the sockers with his toes sticking out. He had aged a quarter of a century in the eight years I was away, disheveled hair white beneath the grease, bristly gray beard, skin a haggard sack of wrinkly white rubber hanging off his bones. A deflating balloon with only the final desperate hope that if it drinks enough it will shrink all the way to nothing.

"Oh, Mite, it was something it was, when that warehouse blew into the sky." We weren't so much in a room as in a closet, with only a bed, a locker, and one bare bulb hanging through a chicken-wire ceiling. Fallon was lying on his side on the stinking mattress, gay almost under the influence of the wine, half-empty bottle in his hand, cackling at the grand old times when the Square it was his oyster waiting to be slurped and swallowed. "You should have seen it."

"I seen it all right."

"It lit up the night sky like a second sun."

"I said I seen it."

"The greatest piece of crime fighting ever to hit this town. Wiping out four crime organizations at once. Front page of every tabloid. 'Fallon's War,' they called it. But it wasn't just mine, was it, Mite? Have a drink with me."

"No thanks."

"Old times."

"Get that out of my face."

"Afraid of my little germs?"

"Your germs they the size of small dogs. I can hear them barking."

He smiles, takes another long pull of the wine.

"You find all the bodies?" I ask.

"Most."

"You find Blatta's?"

"I said most."

"But not Blatta's?"

Fallon shrugs. "Gone. Disappeared. Poof. Maybe incinerated, maybe not, who knows? Who could know? Except it wasn't just his body that disappeared."

"Talk to me."

"Where'd you go off to anyways?"

"Fiji."

"Fiji, huh? That where you found Queequeg over there?"

"Watch your mouth."

"Don't be sore, Mite. I just see you found your game after all."

"Talk to me about Blatta."

"Sure, Mite. Don't be so touchy. Was a time you'd eat any crap I'd serve."

"It's a new day, palsy."

"You don't need to tell me. When the Square was still my territory, I kept a file on every hood whose name I even heard whispered. Had a file on you inches thick and a file on your boy Blatta too. There wasn't much there, no one talked about him, it was mostly rumor and a stray piece from a snitch here or a whore there. He was more like a ghost than anything else, with the way you were protecting him. Some in the department even thought he was someone you made up on your own to project some authority. But I had seen him coming out of that hotel of his, heading to his car, I knew he wasn't a ghost. And then, after my victory, he disappeared like the rest of them. No body, but no Blatta either. Case closed, right? File sent to storage and life moves on.

"So one day I'm out of the territory, me and a dame are celebrating, a real special dame, a high-priced hooker doing a pal a favor, which was why I was where I was. This is three or four years after, understand. I'm on the Upper East Side, strange place the Upper East Side, and I was heading down to the El Morocco, and I see this big brown limo slip up the street. The driver has an eye patch and he looks familiar and that's what draws my attention first. And then I notice the back window is open and there's a face looking at me and I'm looking back and son of a bitch if it's not who I think it is."

"Who?"

"Blatta."

"Go on."

"So the next day what I do is send a request to the dead-file room, the morgue, to pull his file and word comes back there isn't a file. How can that be? I made it myself. I send a request to the morgue for yours, since you two were so tight, and yours isn't there either. So I pull the whole Abagados file, the whole thing. My desk is covered with paper, and I go through it page by page, the first time anyone's looked at it since it all went down, but it wasn't the first time anyone's looked at it since it all went down. See, someone else had combed through it with a razor blade and every mention of Blatta or you had been sliced out so neat you wouldn't have known it had ever been there unless you were the guy that put it there in the first place, understand? Far as the department knew, you and Blatta, the two of you never existed."

"Who could do something like that?"

"Someone with the pull of an elephant. It takes pull to get hold of a file from the morgue and take it to a place where you got time to razor it clean. The same kind of pull it takes to haul my ass before the Police Corruption Commission, to get six witnesses to testify to everything I ever done which was hunky and not dory, and then to strip me of my rank, my job, my pension, my life. That kind of pull. Which is how I ended up here, in this lovely abode. Sure you don't want a drink?"

"Revenge for what you did at the warehouse."

"No," said Fallon. "You're not getting it, are you? I didn't end up on Bowery Row because of what I did at the warehouse. I ended up here because I happened to glimpse a face in a window."

"Jesus."

"And if he could do that to me, Mite, for just glimpsing his face, imagine what fun he's going to have with you."

Yonkers in the twilight.

Sounds like a swing-band ballad, don't it? *Yonkers in the twilight, dancing cheek to cheek.* What's the matter, missy, you don't like my chops? As if Louis Armstrong's got a voice of velvet.

We was parked on a hill, Central Avenue down to our left, the Bronx River down to our right, and we was waiting. In front of us sat a lovely white house with a picket fence. Cooney's old house. My old house, except it wasn't really my old house, first because it wasn't really never my house since I never lived there, and second it wasn't my old house, like in something that had passed away long ago, because my name, imagine that, was still on the deed. A life estate, the clerk said, which meant it was mine until I died. But I hadn't paid no taxes on it, had I? And yet the taxes they was paid. And I hadn't been up on the ladder painting that siding, had I? Yet the house it was still all nice and white.

"So who paid them taxes?" I asks the property clerk, a tenner slipped along with the question to grease the wheels of information.

"The reversionary party," he says.

"What the hell does that mean?" I asks.

"The party to whom the property reverts after the death of this Mickey Pimelia listed on the deed."

"And who might that be?" I asks.

"Mickey Pimelia? Never heard of him."

"No, the other thing, the reverberating party."

"Reversionary party. It looks like a corporation."

"Go ahead, holding it in is bad for the kidneys."

"Something called Brownside Enterprises," he says. "In the city. With an address in the Empire State Building."

Can you smell him, missy? Can you? I could, like I was a bloodhound. I was on his trail, I was getting closer, and the blood scent it was coursing through me like a drug. It was only a matter of time afore the Boss and me we was finally, after all these years, once again face to face.

"What are we doing here, Mick?" asked Champ.

"Just want to see who's been living in my house."

"I mean in this city, this state. Didn't you hear what that wino said? He wasn't jiving us, Mick. This Blatta of yours, he ruined that cop just for catching his face. Can't imagine what he's going to do with you once you track him down."

"He's going to give me a hug and wrap a mink round my shoulders."

"Don't you start getting all biblical on me, Mick. Had enough preaching when I was a boy to know life doesn't work out like the stories. Lazarus isn't rising, and those we betray, they don't give us minks."

"You singing the blues, Champ?"

"Who has the right if I don't, Mick, tell me that. Who the hell more than me has the right?"

I first met Champ in an uptown Chicago joint when I was looking for some muscle in the new line I was trying. I asked him to tag along to some West Side motel one night and he came in mighty handy when the mark didn't like me taking that flash picture of him and his secretary tied all in knots. The mark, he lunged, but afore he could get his mitts on the camera, Champ grabbed him by the neck so tight the mark's yard near popped. Then I knew, Champ, he was just what I needed. See, most gumshoes carried a gun, but I never thought guns made much sense. You bring out a cannon and someone's liable to start shooting. I had firsthand experience where that ended, with me on a roof watching the world go mushroom. Hell with that. Champ, he kept things clamped down cool. One look at Champ and even the most pissed-off Joes, they settled into reason.

After that first night, Champ he was by my side whenever I stepped into the night to do any detecting and I was in his corner in the dusty prairie arenas where his title dreams falled and rised and falled again. In Champ I suppose I had found more of the muscle on which I relied account of my size. My fate was ever my fate, by my lonesome I was not near enough, and it was the same in the Midwest as it was in the East, excepting with Champ it was different. First off, with Champ I was in charge, it was my name painted on the door. My name, my license, my line. I was the one making the decisions for once and I liked that, I liked that fine.

And second off, well, yeah it was different all right. It

wasn't like the hard pure thing I felt for Celia. And it wasn't like the desperate empty thing I felt with Hubert, which I got to tell you was a hell of a relief. What with my Uncle Rufus's generosity and the day-to-day details of being a shamus, I just didn't have the time for Hubert no more. No big breakup, like I would expect, just a sort of drifting apart. Funny how love fades, ain't it? And then with Champ, I felt something I hadn't felt before, which finally sent old Hubert packing. It was a little late to be discovering that meat and kidneys had their place, don't you think, but better late than never.

So things was jake, with Uncle Rufus's money and with Champ by my side, things was oh so jake. I had no reason to want to leave Chicago, no reason to heed the faint calls I was hearing from the past. Until, in the middle of a case, I found a kid with a strange welt on his arm and I looked at it closer and it was a burn, perfectly round like the tip of a cheap ten-cent cigar. Champ took care of the cigar smoker, worked him like the heavy bag hanging from the ceiling of the gym, whilst I stood back and watched it all with a satisfaction that was more personal than ever it should have been. But the cigar smoker turned out to be a cop, and the other cops they didn't want to hear about no burns on some skinny waif's arm. So that was it, goodbye Chicago.

"Ever feel, Champ," I said as twilight in Yonkers descended into evening in Yonkers, "like someone's watching over you?"

"Over my shoulder, sure. The cops, waiting for one wrong move to bust me proper."

"Well, someone's been watching over me. You know that money I keep getting from my dead Uncle Rufus?"

"Good old Uncle Rufus."

"I gots the suspicion, Champ, that he ain't dead and he ain't my uncle and his name it ain't Rufus."

"Whoa, Mick, looky there. Is that who we're waiting on?"

I leans forward in the Packard. There are two figures heading down the sidewalk, hand in hand. I can't see their faces, just their silhouettes, heading down the sidewalk and then turning up the little stone path that led to Cooney's house. One is a child, a boy, stocky and thick, his arm raised up to hold the hand of the other. And the other, well the other there was no doubtsky aboutsky. It was that walk, who could ever mistake that walk.

"That's the one," I says.

"You sure you want to be doing this, Mick? No telling what kind of damage you could end up causing."

"The only thing I ever been sure of, Champ, wheresever I go, disaster it follows sure as blood from a wound."

We walked side by side together up the sidewalk, Champ and me, and then we turned into the stone path. This was something I knew I had to do, but even so my step slowed as I approached the house. My house. I had once felt the person inside to be the most important person in my life, someone I believed to be the fulcrum around which my life swayed and tottered. It's not so easy running away from that and not so easy coming back to it again.

"We can turn around now," says Champ. "Let's say we turn around now, fill up the tank, hightail it out of this burg. What about Nogales?"

"You never been to Nogales."

"I heard swell things. You ever have a taco?"

"No, I never had no taco."

"It's jimmy."

"I'm going to ring the bell."

"Do what you got to do, Mick, but I could go for a taco right about now."

"Be on your best behavior," I says as I punch the button. "And smile. We don't wants to scare the kid."

We waits a while, a while longer. I rings again and then the footsteps, the footsteps, and the door opens, and despite my best intentions my heart it takes a leap. It takes a leap, yes it does. It don't matter what we are, the heart it's a strange thing, inexplicable as life itself. It takes a leap and then it settles and I wait as comes first the gasp and then the face in front of me composes itself into a mask of stunned surprise.

"Mite?"

"Hello there, Celia," I says. "It turned out to be Yonkers for you after all, now didn't it?"

19

The night of Mite's reappearance after eight long years, Celia dreamed of the Empire State Building.

In the dream, she hovered over the art deco tower, jaunty and impossibly high, as it danced to the music of some riotous jazz band, twisting its upper-floor windows into a smile, whistling out its piercing crown, snapping to the music with cartoon fingers at the end of stick arms. The shimmying skyscraper, swelling and bopping to the rhythm of the trumpet's Dixieland beat, filled her with joy and fierce longing, emotions so powerful they blistered her heart. And then the skin of granite and glass began to peel away from the top of the tower in one elastic piece, like a sheath being pulled back, and what she saw being revealed was monstrous and dark and she woke with a start.

Well now, thought Celia, catching her breath as she lay next to her husband, Gregory, who snored gently. Not so hard to figure that one out, is it? No need to call in Freud to make sense of that.

"How'd you end up here, in Yonkers?" asked Mite after she invited him and the huge Negro with the scarred face, named Champ, into her house, and spent an awkward time in small talk. Gregory was in a faculty meeting at the college,

Norman was in bed now, and so they were free to talk about old times, as if she and Mite were college chums, with nothing but good memories to bind them.

"We don't own it, we rent it," she said as she poured the bourbon into a glass for Champ. Mite had declined a drink, and maybe she shouldn't have one either, she already felt disoriented from seeing Mite after all these years. But she needed one, she decided, definitely, and she half filled a second glass. "Gregory found the house and brought me here and instantly I loved it. There's some financial arrangement Gregory worked out. Through the college, I think. I don't know how he does it, but he's a genius like that."

"I'll bet he is," said Mite.

"And a small inheritance I received helps," she said as she walked the drink over to Champ, who was sitting next to Mite on the coach.

"That was sure a lucky break," said Mite.

"It was. I love it here," she said, taking a sweet burning sip. "Norman is in third grade now. I walk him to school, just down the road. And there's a small park just the other way, and the neighbors."

"You ever hear from Blatta?"

"Jerry? No, of course not. Didn't you know? You had to know. He died. In the thing. I thought for sure you knew. I was just so happy to hear from that grubby little policeman that you were okay. Mite, tell me what happened. How did you escape?"

"I wasn't in that warehouse when it went down. I was tipped before, you see."

"And Jerry?"

"He wasn't."

"Wasn't what?"

"Tipped."

"Mite? You didn't tell him? Mite? You let him go in there, all the time knowing?" She felt something rise in her, a pain still so fresh it was as if it was only yesterday when the world exploded and a part of her was buried away forever. "Mite?"

"Call me Mickey," he said.

She looked at him, took a swallow from the drink, tried to fight back the emotion, succeeded, because that was what she had become so accomplished at over the last eight years, drinking and fighting back her emotions.

"That was a long time ago," she said finally.

"No it wasn't," said Mite. "I can still smell the smoke."

"Are you sure you don't want anything? Champ, are you hungry? I have cheese and crackers and some grapes. How does that sound?"

"That sounds jimmy, ma'am."

"Good, just give me a minute."

She was headed into the kitchen when Mite said, "He didn't die, Celia."

She stopped without turning. "Who?"

"You knows who. He didn't die."

She spun. "Of course he did."

"It's my house, this house. It's my name on the deed, you can check it for yourself. You didn't get it through no college. He pays the taxes and he made sure you got it for nothing. You had to suspect, ending up in this house, in Yonkers. This was Cooney's house. You remember Cooney, that night in '21'? The mope what gave me this?"

He held up his hand, pointed at the thick gold ring on his finger.

"It can't be," she said.

"And your inheritance. Who was it who died?"

"An old uncle."

"Did you know him?"

"No, actually."

"A lawyer named McGreevy, with his pale skin and stuttering tongue, broke the bad news, didn't he?"

"Stop it."

"You had to have figured he was somehow connected with you getting the inheritance, this house."

"No, Gregory told me—"

"He didn't die in that fire, Celia," said Mite. "He's still alive. He's our Uncle Rufus. And I've found him."

Which was why the dream, and why the next morning, after Celia walked Norman to the school, she found herself calling for a cab so she could catch the commuter line to Grand Central Station. Just to see, she told herself, only that, to see and to prove to herself it was over, all of it, and the life she was living, the family she was raising, was the life and family she was meant for all along.

And now there it was, the Empire State Building, not dancing to some hepcat beat, blessedly, but tall and solid. And yet even as she stood before it and stared upward like a tourist right off the bus, she couldn't help but think of the dark monstrous thing covered by the thin skin of granite and glass and steel. But the monstrosity in her dream wasn't inside the building, she knew, no matter what Freud would have said about it. The dark thing she glimpsed beneath the skin of the building was herself, as she might have been had not everything in her old life gone to a fiery hell.

And yet, like a phoenix, from the ashes she had been reborn into what now she was. Everything her mother had always wanted for her, a husband who supported her, a child whom she adored, a beautiful house with a picket fence, all of it had come into her life. Respectable. That was what she had become, against all odds, and she owed it all to Gregory.

She had gone to him after all of it was over, had gone to him as if just to talk, but all the time hoping that he would save her, and he did, exactly that. Gregory. Without any questions or lectures. The arrogance had somehow been burned out of him in the years after she had sent him packing from the apartment. Gregory. Still the idealist, but more practical than ever she could have imagined. He knew what to do right away. The quick civil ceremony, the new place with room for a nursery, the introductions to the junior faculty at the college. And he did it all without making her feel that he was doing her the greatest favor of her life, even if he actually was. He did it all as if he were doing it out of love, imagine that. It would have been easier if he had turned out like so many of the other professors he worked with, if he drank too much and stomped around like the second coming of Hegel and slept with his young and pretty research assistants, it would have been a relief. Then they would have been even. But he didn't. He was the perfect husband, the perfect father, a more attentive lover than he had ever been before. Gregory. He had made for her a life and she couldn't deny that the affection she held for him had grown deep and strong.

So why was she here, now, on Thirty-fourth Street?

"You ready, Celia?" said Mite, standing beside her, also looking up at the building, captured by his own dark thoughts.

"I don't know," she said, and she didn't, truly, know why she was there. Just to be sure one way or the other, she told herself. Her son deserved that, at least, she told herself. She would only go as far as she needed to find out if it was true, she told herself.

"What if he's not so happy to see us, Mick?" said Champ, who stood like a scarred ebony pillar on the other side of Mite.

"Oh, he'll be happy," said Mite. "He'll be bursting his buttons, he will. It's why he took care of us all these years. He was waiting for us to return."

"You think?" said Celia.

"No doubtsky aboutsky," said Mite.

The very scent of the lower offices of Brownside Enterprises, on the eighty-ninth floor of the Empire State Building, raised the thin black hairs on the back of her neck. The elevator had taken off so fast it was as if a part of her had been left behind in the rise and maybe that was the main cause of her vertigo. But there was also the faint scent of raw animal power that worked on her emotions like a memory. It floated here among the pretty girls with their perfect legs, busily typing at desks arrayed in neatly ordered rows and columns in the middle of

290 • **Tyler Knox**

the floor. It floated among the executives in their suits, bustling in and out of glass-walled offices ringing the floor. And it seemed to flow down the broad staircase that reached grandly from this floor to the next, from this level of worker bees to something high up in the reaches of power.

The buttons of the elevator had gone straight from 89 to 91.

Before the stairs sat a woman in a dark suit, cold and perfect, as if carved from alabaster. There was no typewriter on her desk, just a single flower in a fluted vase and a single phone. Behind her stood a guard with a gun on his hip. The woman at the desk smiled stonily at the three of them as they stepped off the elevator.

"Can I help you?" said the woman at the desk.

"What's upstairs?" said Mite.

"Executive offices."

"That's where we're going."

"Do you have an appointment?"

"No appointment," said Mite.

"Then I'm sorry," she said with a firm smile, "but no one is allowed up without an appointment."

"How abouts you gets us an appointment?" said Mite.

"That is not possible. I am not authorized to make appointments."

"Then why don't you call up on that phone of yours and gets the authorization?" said Mite. "Tell them we're here to see Blatta."

The woman looked at the three of them for a moment and then opened her desk drawer, took out a small book, paged through it. "There is no Mr. Blatta listed, Mr. . . . ."

"Pimelia, but he'll know me as Mite."

"I'm sorry, Mr. Pimelia, but no one is allowed upstairs without an appointment. You'll have to leave. Oscar will show you the elevator."

"Let's go, guys," said the guard, stepping out from around the desk. He was a big man, with the jaw of a moose, but still, after he took a quick glance at Champ, his hand slipped onto the grip of his gun.

Quick as a clap, Champ grabbed the guard's arm with one hand and the holstered gun with the other and lifted the guard slightly into the air so it was impossible for the gun to be drawn.

The guard flailed about for a moment.

"Easy now, Pops," said Champ in his low growl.

Mite stepped toward the desk, sat on its edge, raised the handset of the phone. "About that appointment," he said.

Celia's skin began to itch at the way the woman blanched.

A man came down to get them, a stocky man in a chauffeur's uniform and chauffeur's peaked cap. He walked with a limp, wore a black eye patch over his left eye.

"Well, well, well," said Mite. "Look who it is. I see Uncle Rufus found you too, hey, Istvan?"

It was only then that Celia recognized the man with the eye patch as Jerry's former driver, who eight years before had come with the message from his boss that had started everything.

"Good morning, Mr. Pimelia," said Istvan. "You too, Miss Singer."

"Hello, Istvan," she said softly. "It's Mrs. now."

"Very good."

"Looks like you survived the worst of it, huh, palsy?" said Mite.

"This way, please," said Istvan in a dry voice, before turning toward the stairs and starting up again.

Champ eased the guard down, gently let go of his arm, brushed away the palm mark on his sleeve. Then Mite and Champ, with Celia behind, followed Istvan up the stairs.

The smell grew stronger as they rose, furry, more animal than human, of some great power waiting to be unleashed. The scent flushed through her as if injected straight into her veins. The itch in her skin increased, her heart started kicking beneath her breast.

He was here, she could sense it in every nerve. The presence of Istvan proved it even further. There was no reason to go on, she should turn away, now. And yet she didn't.

They were in a dark imposing space, all wood paneling, with maroon leather chairs like in some fussy old men's club. Istvan led them to a reception desk next to a set of large double doors. The woman behind the desk was pretty, with high blond hair and huge breasts. The nameplate on her desk read: C. Peppers. Behind her was a portrait of a greasy-looking man with an unshaved face and a bemused smile. The bronze plaque under the portrait read: IRVING BROWNSIDE—FOUNDER.

"And how can we help you today?" said C. Peppers, her screech of a voice wildly out of place in the powerful hush of the office.

"We's here to see Blatta," said Mite.

"Whom can I tell them is here and what can I tell them is

the purpose of the visit?" She pronounced purpose like the sea mammal.

"We're not here to see no them, just him. Blatta. The name's Mite. This fellow over here is with me and his name is Champ. We're a team, right? So he sees one, he sees us both. He'll understand, he was once on the other side of that equation. And this here is an old friend of his, Celia, with a *C*."

The woman stopped writing on her pad to eye Celia carefully, her gaze riding down from Celia's face to her waist to the brace on her leg. She seemed relieved to see it and then looked back up with a breath of pity on her face.

So, thought Celia, that's how he has been entertaining himself.

"We just came to wish him Happy New Year is all," said Mite.

"It's May," said the woman with the high hair.

"So maybe we's a little late, but like my momma always said, it's the sentiment what matters."

"My mother wasn't much on sentiment," said the woman. "She preferred diamonds. All right, wait here and I'll see what I can do."

Celia watched as the woman ripped a sheet off her pad, stood, smoothed out her skirt. The blond woman had high heels, and she walked so that she led with her breasts, like a battleship with two great prows. It had been years since Celia felt what she felt as she watched the woman walk to the double doors: envy, bitterness, the strange competitive desire to rip the woman's face off and stuff it down her cleavage.

Whoa, where did that come from?

It was the scent, the dream, the sight of Istvan, the way Champ and Mite abused the woman and her guard on the floor below, it was in the very possibilities that had been raised by Mite's visit. Whatever civilizing had happened to her in the last eight years as a faculty wife and mother in the suburbs had been stripped from her as quick as a snap of the finger. Whose finger? His, of course.

It was time to leave, this was too much for her. Go, she told herself, run away. You have a son, a husband, a family, a life. Run while you can, she told herself, but it was as if the paralysis rose from her leg to overtake the whole of her body as she watched the woman step softly to the large double doors, knock lightly, and push one of them open.

In the moment the door swung wide, Celia caught a glimpse of the room inside. It was large, huge, with a great granite table in the middle and a huddle of men around the table, a strange huddle, like a swarm of insects crowding around something, a huddle of drones dancing and circling and serving the master. And then one of the drones in the huddle lifted his face and stared at the woman in heels and then stared through the doorway at the three of them, stared at her. And in the instant before the door was closed she recognized the face.

Pale skin, pointy nose, lidded green eyes. McGreevy. The lawyer. Her dead uncle's lawyer.

She almost fainted at the sight. The scent, the height of the building, the emotions, everything weakened her. She put a hand on the desk to steady herself and then backed up to one of the chairs and collapsed into it. It was too much, everything was too much. She should never have come, never.

"I should never have come," she said out loud.

"We's just saying hello," said Mite. "Just a hello."

A few moments later the door opened again, that same glimpse of the huddle before it closed behind the woman with the breasts and the high blond hair. She walked over to the three of them. Celia rose unsteadily from the chair.

"Mr. Mite," said the woman in her screetch. "Mr. Champ. I can bring you in now."

"What about me?" said Celia in someone else's voice, a little girl's voice, some strange orphan girl afraid of being left behind.

"Not now," said the woman, "but we may be in touch," as if Celia had just failed her job interview and was being told that, no, they would never be in touch.

Mite gave her a chuck on the arm. "I'll put in the good word for you, Celia," he said, "don't you worry," and then he and Champ and Istvan followed the woman into the room. The door closed solidly behind them all, leaving Celia alone.

20 **Kockroach can feel it** in his bones. Mite is close, closer, Mite will soon be within his grasp.

He sits at the granite table as his employees move in a flurry about him. Before him on the table are papers, files, photographs. He listens to what they tell him, he signs his name where they tell him to sign, he sits quietly while they plot and plan around him. It isn't lost on him that what used to be done by Mite alone now takes dozens. Of course the operation is far bigger, the possibilities of growth in business are endless and Brownside has been growing like a weed from the moment Kockroach sprayed his first building and murdered his first colony. But still he remembers how it was, just him and Mite running the Square together. There were no papers then, no teams of lawyers and bankers and agents. Just money.

Until Mite betrayed him and blew it all into the sky.

But now Kockroach is in the world of business, and business, Kockroach has learned, is all about information. His lines of informants spread throughout the country like great antennae, keeping data flowing from the farthest reaches into his headquarters. And his informants have kept him apprised of Mite's progress.

The lawyer Tate, in Chicago, informed McGreevy of the

problems which forced Mite and his associate, a man named Champ, to flee the city. The girls on the Square informed Istvan of a little man in a green suit asking about a former cop named Fallon and a man named Blatta. The desk clerk at the hotel where Fallon now lives, a hotel bought by Brownside Enterprises as soon as Fallon moved in, informed Albert Gladden of the visit to Fallon's room by the little man in green and his huge friend. The title clerk in Yonkers earned his envelope by informing Gladden the moment anyone asked about the small white house which is owned by one Mickey Pimelia in a life estate.

And now Mite is getting closer, so close Kockroach's ears begin to twitch.

He hears something, just a rustle of a disturbance, but it grabs his attention. As his men continue their work all about him, he leans forward. Footsteps rising up the stairs, stopping at Cassandra's desk, a conversation. The words are muffled but the cadence of one of the voices is shockingly familiar. He is startled at the excitement he feels, like the buzz before mating. Or before squeezing the life out of a human throat.

The door opens, Cassandra enters, closes the door behind her, walks quietly to the table, leans over to whisper in his ear.

"There is a man called Mr. Mite here to see you," she says. "Istvan says you know him."

"Yes," says Kockroach.

"And someone called Mr. Champ."

"Send them in," says Kockroach.

"And a woman called Celia."

Kockroach lets out a gasp that quiets the room.

He had been expecting Mite and his associate, but he had not been expecting Celia. Leave it to Mite to always arrive with a surprise. His head turns left, right, as if he is trapped in a maze and searching for a way out. He spies the wall of windows staring out over the rooftops of the city and imagines himself spreading his wings and flying to safety.

The men surrounding him all stare. McGreevy steps forward.

"Is everything all right, Mr. Blatta?"

"Celia is outside."

"Yes, I saw her. She is with Mr. P-P-Pimelia."

"I don't want her here."

"That's fine, Mr. Blatta," says McGreevy. "Cassandra, send the woman home, please. Tell her that m-m-maybe we'll be in touch in the future."

Cassandra nods and then makes her way out of the room. As she opens the door, Kockroach strains his neck to see outside. Framed in the doorway is a black dress, a heavy shoe. Fear spurts in the back of his throat and he can't help but duck before the door closes.

And then the door opens again.

Mite enters the room with his familiar lively stride, but Kockroach notices immediately that he is not the same Mite. He is older now, there are cracks around the edges of his face now. And he doesn't shift back and forth with an uncontained energy as he did before.

Alongside Mite is a human who is huge and dark and scarred

like an arthropod who has been through the wars. Behind both of them limps Istvan, his hands loose and ready at his sides, his one eye alert. Istvan shuts the door to the conference room and stands in front of it like a sentry. Mite glances back nervously. The huge dark man takes a step forward.

"How you doing there, Boss?" says Mite.

Kockroach, fighting the buzzing in his head, stays seated and stares.

"Long time no see," says Mite. "Looks like you done all right for yourself. What line you in, anyway?"

"Exterminations," says Kockroach.

"So you found your place in the world at last."

"Who's your palsy, Mite?" says Kockroach.

"Oh, I'm sorry. That was rude of me. Boss, this is Champ. He's with me now. Champ, meet my Uncle Rufus."

"It's a pleasure, Pops," says Champ.

"Do you think he can protect you?" says Kockroach.

"Do I need protection, Boss?"

"Everyone leave," says Kockroach. "Everyone but Mite."

The men surrounding Kockroach quickly gather their folders and papers before streaming out a door behind them. McGreevy stands still for a moment, raising his chin and staring down his long pointy nose at Mite before following the crowd and closing the door. On the far side of the room, Istvan opens the door to the reception area, but the big dark man doesn't move.

"It's okay, Champ," says Mite, patting one of the giant man's arms with his hand. "Go on out. Me and the Boss, we got things to talk about."

"Maybe I'll stay," says Champ. "Keep them waters calm."

"I bets they got some premium java in this joint," says Mite. "Go on out with Istvan. Have yourself a jolt. Don't worry yourself about me. The Boss and me are old friends. We just got some unfinished business, is all. Ain't that right, Boss?"

Kockroach, still seated, says nothing.

Istvan holds the door open for Champ, who bobs his head a couple of times as he takes a long look at Kockroach before turning and stepping through the door. Istvan closes the door behind them, leaving Kockroach and Mite alone in the huge conference room.

"What's on your mind, Boss?" says Mite.

Kockroach places his hands on the great granite table, presses himself to standing.

"Can't say you don't got the right to be sore," says Mite.

Slowly Kockroach walks around the table. His hands are still, his head is tilted.

"Here we are again, ain't we, Boss?" says Mite. "Just like on that trip up to Yonkers."

Kockroach closes in on Mite until he is looming over him, staring down through his dark glasses, his smile viciously in place. He can smell the fear, like the urine of a cat.

"How about a game?" says Kockroach.

Kockroach and Mite sit on either side of the granite table. The board is set between them, the pieces are arrayed in their lines of battle.

"You been playing much, Boss?"

"Some," says Kockroach, staring not at the board but at Mite.

"Who with?"

"McGreevy."

"I bet that bastard's got some tricks, he does."

"Your move, Mite."

Mite stares at the board for a long moment and then pushes a pawn. He plays the same as he ever played, with traps and feints, relying on his little pieces to control the board. Mite has a natural affinity for the pawn. His pawn positions used to bedevil Kockroach, but not anymore. With each combination of moves, Mite's lines of defense are swiftly being mauled.

"You've gotten better, Boss."

"I learned the trick."

"What trick?"

"The trick to everything. When you first taught me the ritual of chess, I thought it was all about the pieces on the board. Then I learned the pieces didn't matter."

"What does matter?"

"The human who's moving them. Find what he wants and give it to him, on your terms. That's beeswax. Check."

Mite stares at the board and then pulls his king out of trouble.

"How'd an exterminator end up in the penthouse, Boss, you don't mind me asking?"

"There were just two of us at the start," says Kockroach, "me and Irv, the human who gave me my opportunity in the world of beeswax. A company called us in about a bug problem in their factory. The company made shoes, wingtips. I always liked wingtips. The owners were squeamish about bugs. Imagine that. We murdered their cockroaches, but somehow a nest of rats found their way into the basement."

"Convenient."

"Things happen, Mite. And no matter how hard we tried, we couldn't kill them off. After a few weeks of rats running across their desks, the owners couldn't wait to sell, they even gave us the money to buy the factory. Suddenly we had two companies."

"Clever."

"It's all about information. You'd be surprised how much you can learn in the middle of the night, searching through the nooks of an office building, spraying poison wherever you go. Once I learned to read, the world of information opened up to me."

"You learned to read, Boss? Good for you. Who taught you?"

"Cassandra."

"The one with the melons, what sits outside?"

"She's smarter than she looks."

"God, I hope so."

"Wherever we sprayed, we learned just enough to know what they wanted and then we gave it to them."

"That the other guy's portrait hanging there in the reception room?"

"Irv."

"What happened to him?"

"His wife shot him."

"They tend to do that."

"After the shoe company we bought a funeral parlor. I liked the cars. Then we bought a movie theater. We traded that for a medical company that made needles and probes. By that time I had McGreevy. He got me the government numbers so I could own the stock and put my name on the deeds to my buildings. Now we buy and sell and sell and buy and make more money in a week than we ever saw in a year in the Square. But one company never gets sold."

"What's that?"

"Brownside Extermination. Every now and then I still put on the goggles and the tank. You can never have too much information."

Kockroach moves a bishop.

"I think I'm in trouble here, Boss."

"More than you know," says Kockroach. "The ritual has made me stronger. I can see farther into the future now. And I learned the trick."

"So what is it that I wants?"

"To come home."

"What's the chance of that?"

"Check."

Mite rubs his chin and stares at the board. He blocks Kockroach's attack with his knight.

Kockroach pushes ahead his other bishop.

Mite squirms in his seat as his rook retreats.

Kockroach kills a pawn.

Mite pulls his king farther back.

Kockroach sweeps his queen across the board. "Checkmate."

Mite examines the board for a moment, topples over his king, then sits back and stares at Kockroach.

"You going to kill me now, Boss?"

"No, Mite, I'm going to hire you."

"I need information," says Kockroach.

In the conference room, the chessboard has been removed and replaced with a huge urn of ice and shrimp. The table is littered with shells, Mite's shells. Kockroach still eats his shrimp whole. Kockroach and Mite are leaning back in their chairs, smoking cigars. Kockroach sucks the smoke into his lungs in deep drafts. Mite coughs. The smoke billows about them like the steam in the schvitz.

"Information's good," says Mite.

"It is better than money."

"I don't knows about that."

"Information isn't something you put into a bank, it is what allows you to buy the bank."

"Do you own a bank, Boss?"

"Just a small one," says Kockroach, holding his cigar out in front of him, staring at the glowing tip. "I once looked for opportunity there. A woman sent me home because I couldn't fill out the form."

"What happened to the woman when you bought the place?"

"I promoted her."

"That's funny, Boss. You know, I got myself a new line."

"I heard."

"I can get you information, whatever you need."

"I know you can."

"But I'm with Champ now. You got a job for Champ?"

"What's he to you, Mite?"

"We're a team."

"Mates?"

"You could say that."

"The two of you can live in the house."

"What house?"

"My house. Istvan lives there. Cassandra. Now you and Champ."

"For a time, I suppose."

"So it is settled."

"What about Celia?"

"No," Kockroach says quickly. The same spurt of fear as before. "Not her."

"She's a good girl," says Mite. "She wants to see you. And she's got a kid now."

"I know."

"It wasn't she what betrayed you, Boss. It was all my doing."

"I know that, Mite."

"She just wants to see you."

"I don't work like that."

"Think about it, Boss. All this time she thought you was dead. When she heard you was still breathing she looked like she swallowed a goat."

"No."

"It's your call. But it don't seem fair to me."

"When was I ever fair?"

Mite frowns at his cigar. "Why ain't you wringing my neck right now for what I done?"

"I never expected anything different from you."

"And still you want me on?"

"Brother Mite."

"I'll be square from here in, Boss. I promise."

"Don't bother," says Kockroach. "We are what we are."

Kockroach, alone in the conference room after sending Mite to the house, stares out the wall of windows and thinks. He can't stop himself from thinking. It is the curse of this body.

He stands now high over the city, far higher than even the great smoking face in Times Square. From this vantage the city stretches like a chessboard before him. He can pick out the blocks he owns. That one, and that one, and that one with the tall building there. And the rest he wants to own. The world of business, he has learned, is a marvelous machine for feeding his greed. There are still those who feed his fear. The regulators who paw through his deals. The prosecutors who ask their questions. Fallon, a ruined drunk now but with continuing dreams of rising again to destroy him. It is not a place without fear, the world of business, but those who feed his fear are still without the power to bring him down. The world of business is as close to a perfect spot as a cockroach could ever hope to find.

And yet, it all does not feel the same to him as it once did. Working with Mite, cruising the Square in his brown

Lincoln, feeling the power flow from his very being, the fear, the crush of human flesh in his hands, that had given him a purer satisfaction. And so had the world before that, the daring rushes to feed his greed in his old arthropod body, the stench of the colony, the grit and violence, the life-and-death victory over an adversary.

He misses his old lives.

It is why he took care of Mite all these years, waiting like a patient spider for Mite to come home. And now he has. It is good to have Mite back, like old times, but something is still missing. Mite is back and his colony is growing and the world outside falls building by building under his dominion, but still something is missing. And the something that is missing has a name.

Celia.

He was willing to support her, but he wants nothing else to do with her, ever. The very thought of her fills him with an uneasy dread. She has a child now, a boy, and everything in Kockroach's being screams at him to stay away from a female and her nymph. It is why he reacted with such alarm when he learned Mite had brought Celia here, that she was outside this very room. And what about the boy? Was he here too?

The fear overwhelms him and he lets out a yelp.

The door opens, Istvan steps inside. "Is everything okay, Mr. Blatta?"

"Fine, Istvan," he says without turning from the window. Istvan quietly closes the door again.

Celia.

Kockroach had thought the world of business would give

him less opportunity for sex than the world of prostitutes and violence, but he was wrong. Money, he has learned, draws women like flies to feces. There is a parade of women into his bed, Cassandra of course, and the wives of his business opponents, and the girls Istvan finds for him in the Square, and the writers and the realtors and the ambitious young things. He is gorging on sex as he once gorged on gloop from the Dumpsters in the back alleys. What more could a cockroach want? But something gnaws at him.

Male cockroaches know only sex, they care nothing of the result, have no interest in the act of breeding. Clever as they are, male cockroaches still wonder where all these annoying white nymphs have come from as they go about their business of screwing every female in sight. But Kockroach has begun to imagine Celia's long pale body, and as he imagines it, in the ribbons of possibility that flow from the present to the future, he sees her eyes turn dark and her stomach swell.

And in those moments he can't help but think of the boy.

This is all wrong, this is a corruption of his character. He thinks of all the corruptions he has tolerated so far. The taste for roasted meat, the use of impersonal mass violence, the use of words, the curse of thought and its bastard cousin, regret. He has allowed himself to change so much, is this another change he must abide?

No, this is too much, a connection like this would alter him too fundamentally. This would be worse than thinking, he thinks. He must never allow Celia and her nymph back into his life.

And yet, as he stands before the window to look out at the

world, he can't stop imagining her body, long and pale, supple, her dark hair, her tears and devotion, her stomach swelling to enormous dimensions with his progeny. The image of it touches some strange place in his belly even as it fills him with a familiar desire.

"Istvan," he calls out.

The door opens.

"Mr. Blatta?"

"Send in Cassandra," says Kockroach.

21

Celia moved through the days after her visit to the Empire State Building as if the dancing edifice had been the reality and it was her life that was the dream.

Yonkers felt as if it were deep underwater, slow, cold, colorless, distant. She stopped taking her afternoon walks, she resisted her husband's entreaties to perform the rudimentary duties of the faculty wife, no cocktails at the chairman's house, no dinner parties for the young bucks of the department. Gregory sat her down and told her he was worried that she had become depressed, but she didn't feel depressed, instead she felt detached. Nothing made an impression, the sidewalk beneath her feet, the laugh track on the television, the touch of her husband's hand on her arm. Only the golden flecks in the brown of her son's eyes seemed to burn with life. And it was her son, her lovely Norman, with the chubby limbs and mop of brown hair, that revealed to her the truth.

"Who are we hiding from, Mommy?" he said one afternoon.

"We're not hiding," she said.

"Then why don't we go out anymore?"

"We don't?"

"Not since those two men came. The short one and the big colored one."

"We're not hiding. Do you want to go out now?"

"No."

"Are you sure? Come on, let's go."

"I don't want to. I'm afraid."

"Of what, sweetheart?"

"Who were they, Mommy?"

"Old friends. Just that."

"I think it's good to hide. Sometimes at night I slip under my bed. I like it there for some reason. I feel safe."

"Norman?"

"But who are we hiding from, Mommy?"

Who indeed? Because Norman was right, she was hiding, and she realized now she had been hiding for the last eight years. And it wasn't from that grubby policeman who had given her the business after it all went to hell, and it wasn't from Mite or the other gangsters, and it wasn't from Jerry. She reached out and patted her son's hair and saw again the bright golden flecks in her son's eyes. It was a familiar color, that gold. When she closed her eyes she saw it, a streak of that same golden color, like a flaw running through her soul. It was this that she was hiding from, this part of her, this flaw. It had seemed to shrink in her years in Yonkers, it had blended in. She could almost imagine that it had disappeared, but no more. Now that golden flaw vibrated with color, it glowed as if on fire.

And what was it really? The thrill she felt from her proximity to the raw exercise of power? A sensuality that left her weak and clenched at the same time? A taste for shrimp? A desire for more than that of which she was capable of dreaming? How ridiculously shallow it all was, and yet. Take away the flaw and what was she? A mother, a wife, a daughter, a member of the PTA. Wasn't that just as shallow, to be nothing on her own, someone only defined by the others in her life. The one thing that was truly her own, the one thing that was truly her, was the flaw. And so maybe it wasn't a flaw after all, maybe it was the truest expression of her deepest yearnings.

Maybe what she had been running from all this time was her one true self.

The phone call came four weeks later in the middle of dinner. She had made a meat loaf with ketchup on top, mashed potatoes. She could barely muster enough energy to open the can of green beans. Gregory was talking about the most recent faculty meeting when the phone rang and she knew, immediately, what it was.

She stood, answered it, listened to the message. Then, pausing only long enough to depress the button and get a dial tone, she spun the dial of her phone, called the cab company, gave her address.

"I have to go," she said to her husband.

"Who was it?"

"I have to go," she said simply.

"Where are you going?" said Gregory. "Why? Who was it?" But by then he was talking to her back as she slowly climbed the stairs to the bedroom.

She wasn't up there debating, weighing her options, she wasn't trying to figure out what to do. Instead she pinned up her hair, applied the base to her cheeks, the blush, the eye-lashes, the lipstick. And all the while Gregory was talking to her. He had followed her up the stairs, into the bedroom, had asked, commanded, pleaded, yet she barely heard the words. She put on the long black gown that pushed up her breasts and hugged her hips and hid her leg. She draped her pearls around her neck.

Gregory was demanding an answer, but he would never understand it if it came. It lay in that glimpse through the open doorway, in the huddle of the drones dancing and writhing around a source of great power. Dancing and writhing around him. That was where she belonged, there.

When the horn blared from outside, Gregory stood in the doorway, blocking her path. "I won't let you go," he said. "You're my wife."

"I'm going home," she said.

"This is your home."

"Why didn't you tell me how we got this house?"

"I did tell you. It's from the college."

"He came to you, the lawyer. He made you an offer."

"Celia."

"Tell me the truth for once, Gregory."

"The truth is I love you. And then the lawyer, he showed up at the college and gave us a beautiful house, rent-free. The only condition was that you shouldn't know. What was I supposed to do?"

"You were supposed to tell me. What else did he give you?"

"Nothing, I swear."

"Well, don't fret, dear. I expect you'll be getting something soon."

"It's happening again, isn't it?" he said. "After all I've done, you're doing it to me again."

"I am what I am."

"And what's that, Celia? What kind of woman runs away from her husband and child?"

She looked into his eyes, saw the pain, the fear. The sight filled her with both pity and triumph and the combination gave her a familiar thrill.

"Norman has school tomorrow," she said. "You'll have to take him and pick him up in the afternoon."

"Celia."

"I don't know when I'll be back."

On the way out, she leaned over to kiss her son goodbye. She thought she'd feel a tinge of guilt here, at this moment, but there was none. Was she imagining that the look in his eyes was full of understanding, as if he sensed what was happening, what was driving her, where she was heading, and what it would mean for both of them? Was she imagining that he wished he could go with her?

The address given her over the phone was on the Upper East Side. A large brownstone. It was Istvan, in his chauffeur's uniform, who opened the door. He smiled when he saw her. And behind Istvan stood Champ, wearing a tailored black suit, shiny black shoes.

"Lovely to see you again, Miss Celia," said Champ. "Welcome. I'm sorry that Mickey is out on business, he would love to have been here for you. Are you ready?"

"I think so."

"Upstairs," said Champ. "The door all the way to the right."

"Thank you," she said.

She made her way up the wide stairway, past the old paintings and the paneled walls. The space was bigger than it appeared from outside, three houses had been combined to create a single, glorious mansion, elegant and rich and shiny. The carpet beneath her feet was thick and red, the scent of the place was of polished wood and cigars. At the top of the steps, a long hallway led to the right, with a dark door at the end. She stepped slowly, almost reverently, toward the door, knocked lightly, closed her eyes.

It glowed white hot, her flaw. She could see it now in the darkness beneath her lids, watch it flow like a river of lava, widen, she could feel its heat. And slowly all the steady darkness around it burned away until it was no longer a flaw, until it was all there was in her soul. This, her.

She opened her eyes again and the door was now open and he was now before her. In a brown smoking jacket and ascot, in brown velvet pants and patent leather slippers. His dark glasses were on, his smile was bright. One hand held a cigar, the other was holding something large and pink and doused with thick red sauce. He raised it toward her.

"Shrimp?" he said.

She bowed her head, snapped a bite of crustacean in her teeth, passed him as she made her way into his bedroom.

22   Kockroach is ill at ease.

Possibly it is the outfit he is wearing, a cacophonous clash of stripes and diamonds, a riot of color that makes his skin crawl. Kockroach is only comfortable in brown, he has closets full of suits, racks and racks of them, all in brown. Brown wingtips, brown socks, brown hats, brown ties. Only the shirts are white. But today there is no brown on him, except for the shoes. He must admit he likes the shoes, the way they dig into the carpet, the way they crunch on cement. Yes, the shoes he very much likes, he should wear them all the time, but the rest of the outfit leaves him slightly nauseous.

It was Mite who bought these clothes for him, it was Mite who told him to put them on. "It's what the fat cats will be wearing out there, I'm telling you, Boss," he had said. And Kockroach had gone along. This wasn't pleasure, this was business. So he had put on the colorful socks, the short green pants that buckle below the knee, the yellow shirt, the vest, the hat, not his usual fedora but a slouchy herringbone cap. So maybe it is the clothes that have him ill at ease, but he doesn't think so.

He has felt this before, this unease, and is feeling it now, more and more often. Something has gone astray. For a while, after Mite and Celia came back into his life, he found once again that the simple satisfaction of buying pieces of the city and providing for his colony was enough for him. But Mite and Celia came back years ago and the satisfaction has worn off and now he can't escape the gnawing sensation that something is missing in his life. Which is why he agreed to this meeting. When something is not right in Kockroach's life, he knows what to do. He is a cockroach, he devours.

And today he will devour a company.

"Drive around the side," says Mite, leaning forward from the backseat to get a view.

They are somewhere in the country, everything is green and tidy. The building before them is overly grand, with a tall flagpole in the front. The Stars and Stripes. It is tasty, that flag, like a great cake ready to be eaten. The sight of it stirs his hunger.

Mite isn't wearing the funny colors, the stripes and diamonds, just his normal green suit. And Istvan, driving, is dressed in his normal uniform, and Champ, sitting beside Istvan in the front seat, is dressed in his normal black. Only Kockroach is wearing the ridiculous outfit. He knows in some animal species the strongest male is clad in the gaudiest finery. Maybe that is why Mite had him wear these clothes. So be it, if that is what it takes.

They are meeting today with a man named Gorman. Gorman is the boss of the company Kockroach wants to devour. This is supposed to be just a friendly face-to-face, Mite had

318 • Tyler Knox

told him. Kockroach isn't sure what is friendly about a face-to-face. Business is business, the only question is whose face is going to get chewed off. Gorman started his company from a single dry cleaning store. Now he owns newspapers, magazines, a motorcycle factory. Gorman's cash flow, Mite has said, is like a great green river.

Cash flow. Kockroach has always loved those two words. The sound, the taste. Cash flow. It fizzles on the tongue like champagne.

"Keep going," says Mite.

"The drive ends here," says Istvan. "You want I should drive on the grass?"

"Why not? Let's announce our presence to the swells."

The car lurches as it drives over a curb and then rocks softly across the lawn, coming to a stop beside a closely mowed area with little flags all across its curvy surface. A number of men are bowing down with sticks in their hands, as if praying to the white round fetishes at their feet.

As Kockroach steps out of the car, all the men straighten and stare, their jaws dropping. Kockroach takes a cigar out of his pocket. Mite pulls out a lighter, flicks it alive.

"What do they do here?" says Kockroach, waving at the huge expanse of long green meadows and tall trees.

"It's a golf course," says Mite as he lights the cigar. "It's where Gorman plays golf."

Kockroach rolls his cigar over the flame, sucks in a mouthful of smoke, lets it out slowly as a little man in a suit rushes at the car, waving his arms.

"What's golf?" says Kockroach.

"It's good to finally meet you, Blatta," says the elder Gorman, shaking Kockroach's hand with great enthusiasm. Gorman is one of those humans with a deep chest and a ruddy complexion who squeeze hard when they shake hands. Kockroach has learned not to squeeze back. "I've heard nothing but grand things about Brownside. Our people say your books are shipshape."

"We do our best," says Kockroach.

They are on a flat area overlooking one of the long green meadows. In the distance is a round circle of green with a flag planted in the middle. Gorman is there with his son and two men with green vests who are carrying long bags with metal and wooden implements sticking out of the top. Champ, in his black suit, is carrying the same sort of bag, holding similar implements.

"So what's your number?" says Gorman. "I'm a six. Herman here"—he thumbed at a tall handsome young man with dark wavy hair—"my son, is a scratch."

"Number?" says Kockroach.

"Your handicap."

"Handicap?"

"You don't have a handicap? Where do you play?"

"Play?"

"Golf. Where do you play golf?"

"I don't."

"I was told you played golf," says Gorman, looking now at Mite. "Was I mistaken?"

"He'll do fine, Mr. Gorman," says Mite. "Don't you worry. What say we make a little wager?"

"But he doesn't play," says Gorman.

"That's the beauty of it. He never played before, but I figure he'll pick it up quick. Let's just say he's a natural. No bad habits, right? What about a hundred a hole, against each of you," says Mite. "Even up?"

"Even up, when he's never played before?" says Gorman. "That would be like stealing thirty-six hundred dollars."

"What?" says Mite. "It ain't enough?"

Gorman's son steps up. "Let's not be pikers then," he says, his easy grin showing his even white teeth. "A thousand a hole. Ties carry over."

Kockroach grins back at him. "Sweet pea," he says.

"Herman, stop this," says Gorman. "Mr. Blatta is our guest. This isn't right."

"But of course it is," says Gorman's son. "We're all sporting men here, aren't we?"

"Sure we are, sport," says Kockroach.

"See?"

"You gots a game," says Mite. "Step on up and whack it, why don't you."

As Gorman the younger steps between two large blue balls pressed into the flat ground, Mite sidles up to Kockroach. "Champ used to caddy in New Orleans growing up," says

Mite in a soft whisper. "You listen to Champ and you'll do just fine."

Kockroach watches carefully as Gorman's son takes a stick out of one of the bags, places a little white ball on a small peg of wood in the grass, steps up to the ball, and swings the stick. The little ball sails into the sky and lands far off in the meadow, about two thirds of the way to the green circle in the distance. The young man turns and grins. Gorman sends his ball also into the sky, landing it short of where his son's ball lies.

"Want me to show you how to grip it, Blatta?" says Gorman.

"I can figure it out," says Kockroach.

Champ takes a stick out of the bag, hands it to Kockroach. It is metal, long, with a big blob of wood on the far end. Champ takes a ball, sets it on a small peg in the ground. "Hit it down the middle, Boss," says Champ.

"How far?" says Kockroach.

"See that flag?" says Champ. "That's the target. Right where that flag is, there's a little hole. You want to hit the ball into that hole."

Kockroach steps up, places the wooden blob behind the ball as he saw the two other players do. Swaaaaack. The ball flies as if being chased, rises high, sails long, and then falls far far far beyond the other two balls, before rolling onto the circular green area, stopping just short of the flag in the distance.

"I missed," says Kockroach.

"Well, now you knows to hit it harder for next time," says Mite.

"What do I do now?" says Kockroach.

"You go on up and knock it into the hole," says Champ.

Kockroach looks at Gorman and his son, who are staring at Kockroach with their jaws dropped and something lovely in their eyes.

"You mean I get another chance?" says Kockroach.

"Yes you do, Boss," says Champ, shouldering the bag.

"How sweet is that?" says Kockroach as he tosses the club to Champ and strides off toward his ball, the Gormans staring after him.

Kockroach doesn't understand this thing about humans and their games. The ritual of chess he understands, an exercise in controlling the future, but these other games make no sense to him.

The humans take it so personally, like it is combat, when it is exactly the opposite. Combat between arthropods is a life-and-death affair where everything is on the line, that morsel of food, that attractive female with enlarged glands, leadership of the colony. The beauty of combat is that the stakes are so high. But after the human game is over, everything is the same. And yet humans take it all so seriously. Like this golf. There is a bet, but it is air. A few thousand dollars. The number means nothing to Kockroach, it means even less to the Gormans, who are wealthier. And yet, to watch the Gormans play their game with this paltry amount of money on the line is to watch some awesome weight bear down and crush them. The way their lips press one against the other, the way their knuckles turn white as they grip the sticks, the way their heads drop as Kockroach, on the closely mowed greens, steps up to the ball without the least preparation and smacks it into the hole.

"I've never seen anything like it," says Gorman after Kockroach sends his ball skittering across the green until it drops into the cup. "You've never played before? Really?"

"Really," says Kockroach. "But how hard can it be? It's just a game."

"He hustled us," says Gorman's son as he steps toward Kockroach, the small flat-faced stick still in his hand. The boy's features are twisted in anger, his throat is close enough for Kockroach to grab hold and crush if he so desired. "You're a goddamned sandbagger."

"Herman," says Gorman, "stop it."

"I'm definitely a bastard," says Kockroach, grinning into the boy's face. "And if being a sandbagger's a profitable thing, then I'm that too."

Gorman's son raises his stick into the air like a sword.

Kockroach doesn't flinch.

Champ steps forward, but before he can reach the raised stick, Gorman's son brings the stick down with tremendous force so that its face buries in the soft green ground.

"Herman, enough."

"He cheated us, Dad. Don't you see? You better triple-check his books. He's a swindler."

"You're being rude to our guest."

"Soon enough he'll be an employee," says Gorman's son as he pulls his stick out of the ground and stalks away.

"Pleasant guy, ain't he?" says Mite. "And a good loser, to boot."

"Does this mean the game is over?" says Kockroach.

"I'm afraid so," says Gorman, watching the boy's exit with a pained expression on his face. "And I must apologize for my son's behavior. He's always been quite competitive."

"Aren't we all," says Kockroach, handing his stick to Champ. "So, enough pleasantries. Let's talk business. How much?"

Gorman's gaze snaps back to Kockroach, his face turns impassive. "We haven't gone over all the figures yet, but our accountants have put a preliminary price on the whole of Brownside Enterprises, one I think you'll be pleased with."

"Sweet pea," says Kockroach, "there's been a mistake."

"Excuse me?" says Gorman.

"A mistake. You've made a mistake. You're not buying me," says Kockroach. "I'm buying you."

"I like the shoes," says Kockroach.

He is in the backseat of the car. They are driving away from the golf place, driving toward the big house in the city. "I want to wear them all the time."

"They'll be hell on the wooden floors," says Mite, sitting beside him. "You'll have to get that by Celia."

"But they're my floors."

"So they are," says Mite. "Still, you be the one to tell her. She likes them floors. What do you think of the rest of the outfit?"

"It makes me want to throw up."

"Don't it though? But you was noticed, wasn't you? That Gorman wasn't so happy with the idea of his company getting bought. He near to burst a vein when you told him what you had in mind."

"He'll come around," says Kockroach.

"Don't think so, Boss," says Mite. "Not the way he was acting out there. I think he wants to keep the business for that son of his to take over."

"The sport."

"Yeah. He wants to keep it in the family. They get like that, fathers do. At least some of them. And the son of his has a son of his own to get the company in turn. So it don't look to me like Gorman will be willing to sell, no matter how much we offer."

"He'll sell," says Kockroach. "Get the goods, Mite. Get the goods and we'll convince him."

"How, Boss? I already looked into the guy. There ain't nothing there."

"There's always something."

"I tell you, Boss, I asked around, did the sniffing on my own. Gorman's clean."

"You're looking in the wrong place."

"Where should I be looking?"

"Not at the old man," says Kockroach. "At the sport."

There is a moment of quiet. Kockroach watches as Mite and

Champ glance at each other, and in that moment Kockroach senses that Mite had found something and is holding back. He can feel it in the air, what he felt before, the misty scent that always swirls around Mite like a sour pheromone. Betrayal.

Is that where it comes from, this unease that has once again come over him, is it from Mite? No, nothing there is out of sorts. With Mite there is always a whiff of betrayal in the air. It is part of him, he can't help himself. No, the unease comes from someplace else. For the time he was with Gorman he had lost it, business always puts his mind at ease. But the business now is concluded. After playing the game with the Gormans, he knows it is only a matter of time. They will sell, he saw the weakness in their knocking knees as they tried to roll the ball into the hole. They will sell, willingly, and be ever grateful. And so it is as good as over and Kockroach once again is ill at ease.

He wonders why. It is a puzzle. Something is troubling him. Outside the car window, great fields pass by. The car is deep in the country, the fields are green and stretch on forever and their very greatness is what troubles him.

Business has made him rich, powerful in the world of men. It has allowed him to rise, to support his colony, it has brought Mite back, and Istvan, and Celia, and Norman. But business, he now sees, has its limitations. The more he buys, the more there is to buy. In the ribbons of possibility floating into the future he sees the positions of his pieces on the chessboard advance and then retreat. There are too many other players who all want to be on the same blocks, there is too much money that will never be his. His fear has been greatly eased in the world of business, McGreevy has seen to that, but with the lessening of his fear, his greed has concomitantly grown to monstrous dimensions, whispering, imploring, shouting in his ear that he doesn't have enough, not enough, that he needs more, more, everything.

He gazes outside the window at the passing fields with their rising mounds, their twisting valleys. He wants to stride over those fields, he wants to plow the earth with the spikes hammered through the soles beneath his feet, he wants to spill his seed along the furrows, he wants to make his claim, he wants to mark, control, dominate the entire breadth of the world.

"I like the shoes," he says.

23

I suppose I gots a problem with saying goodbye.

Maybe it's something in my genes. My daddy he wasn't no good at saying so long neither, but at least he would just take a powder. I leans toward the powder keg. Why I can't just get on with it, like other Joes, what shake a hand and are on their ways, is a mystery. Champ, for instance, didn't make no big thing of leaving. It was just, "Goodbye, Mick," two words, a nod, and quick as that he's off in the old Packard for points west.

I ever tell you how I said goodbye to Old Dudley, what first taught me chess and the ways of the world? This was after my mother got swallowed whole by Hubert and I checked out her rainy-day cookie jar and found not a dollar, not a cent, just an IOU signed by, wouldn't you know it, Old Dudley hisself. So we were pulling one of our inside jobs, scouring some house shiny of its jewels and silver and cash, all placed in that white sack of his. And then, just as he's shimmying legs-first back out the window, I slams the frame on his back, locking him in. "Mickey, my boy," he says, that puzzled look on his puss. But the puzzlement it disappears when I takes the sack and starts to bashing his face with it. It was his blood and my tears and so long Dudley. I left him there, trapped like a rat for the cops to find, and used that sack to pay my way to New York. But that's what you get, that's the price of betrayal.

"Goodbye, Mick."

Yeah, and good riddance. Just what I needed, another voice from the chorus singing out my own utter worthlessness.

You want to blame it on something, that soft goodbye? Then blame it on them envelopes, just like the one with Harrington's name you gots your eye on. You been looking at it all this time like it was the holy grail, like it was something powerful and golden, when let me tell you, missy, it is a steaming pile of crap. And how does I knows? Because I'm the rodent what scours them sewers until I finds the tastiest morsels. The lowest rat in the lowest stream of sewage in this whole damn town ain't got nothing on Mite. This is what the Boss has made of me.

"I need information," the Boss told me, all the time knowing I was the one to get it for him. With the new line I had picked up in Chi-town, I could get the goods, I could fill them envelopes. And believe me when I tells you, in the land of money where the Boss now was plying his trade, there was plenty of filling to find.

I thought the Times Square of my young manhood was a place of vice and degeneration, a place where all the lowliest desires could find a few moments of release, but let me tell you this, missy, Times Square never had nothing on the dark and desolate landscape of money. I found thievery and perversion, falsehoods and incest, violence, boorishness, bad breath, and murder. And, worst of all, fools what thought that money it could cleanse the darkest secrets of the soul. And maybe it could have, if I wasn't there with my envelopes. Like I was for a muck-a-muck what faced off against the Boss, name of Nicholas Van Ater.

Van Ater was a society type, loaded to the gills and liked showing it. Short, squat, thick fingers, thick cigars, his black hair slicked back like a cartoon. To see Van Ater was to see a soul swelled fat on money pure. And his wife was so thin, if she turned sideways you could see the bone in her throat. Van Ater had a lien on a property the Boss, he wanted to buy, and Van Ater was leaning a bit too hard. So the Boss, he put me on the case. When it came time for the sit-down with Van Ater, Boss had more than enough information to slap that fat face into submission.

"How'd it go, Boss?" I said when he left out of Van Ater's building with the envelope still in his hand.

"Not so good, Mite."

"You tell him you knows the girl she's only fourteen?"

"He said he likes to reach out to the nation's youth."

"What about the girl afore her, what he beat near to senseless?"

"A lovers' spat."

"And about his wife, the powder up her upturned nose and the tennis instructor what is instructing her plenty with his forehand?"

"He was pleased he was getting value for his money."

"Son of a bitch," I said. "The bastard's shameless."

"I admire that," said the Boss.

"So does I. Want me to spill it all to the press?"

"No," said Blatta. "I sensed there was something else, something you had missed."

"I dug hard, Boss."

"Dig harder. Wipe the smile off his face."

It took me two weeks to find it when it should have taken me two hours. With a society guy like Van Ater, it wasn't enough to find out what sins he committed, sins was why they all had that money in the first place. It had to be something different, something what would make that society hound he had married and the boys at the club take notice. And I found it, sures I did. Because the Boss is right, damn it to hell, it's always there.

"What does that bastard Blatta want now?" says Van Ater. He talks in an affected gangsterese, like he had suckled at the droopy breast of Edward G. Robinson hisself.

I leans back, props my feet on the rim of his huge mahogany desk. "He wants you to mark the lien settled."

"Tell your boss to find some young bear cub he can steamroll," says Van Ater.

"Oh, I thinks you'll do as we wants," I says.

"You know, you're just the size, I'd have fun working you over myself."

"You wouldn't be the first to try, believe me," I says, "I've got a face like a hardball, all stitches and horsehide already."

And then I pulls the envelope out my jacket. I drops my feet, puts the envelope on the desk, pushes it oh so slowly toward his grinning mug.

I watch as he snatches it up, watch as he opens it, takes out the note, unfolds it, watch as the smile is wiped off his fat face just like the Boss, he wanted. Within the week the lien was settled and the property was slipped into the Boss's side pocket. Now Van Ater's one of the Boss's big supporters in the run for the Senate. Funny how it works, isn't it, all from a single name on a folded-up slip of paper?

See, that's how the Boss did business in them days, how he does it still. Because the Boss, he don't strong-arm no more. Now it's all what you know and who you're willing to tell. That's what this envelope is too, a little treat for that son of a bitch Harrington who thinks the open Senate seat is his for the taking, so long as he gets the most votes. Stupid son of a bitch, he don't have the foggiest damn notion of what he got hisself into.

And neither did Champ.

It wasn't like there wasn't no happy times riding along with the Boss. We was a family then, or the closest thing I ever had to one, other than that tight threesome in my boyhood: me, my momma, and Hubert. In the Boss's triple townhouse there lived the Boss and Celia, and Norman, Celia's boy. And there was Istvan, and Cassandra too. And then there was me, the envelope man, and Champ hisself, who from the first day was treated like one of the family. That was the thing about the Boss, he didn't have no hang-ups about color or twisted dispositions. And we couldn't forget the money boys what was always skulking about, McGreevy, looking after all the details, and Albert Gladden, the real estate man, his sad-sack face putting a damper on everything. Not to mention the passel of servants what served us all.

There was one more member I don't want to slight, Glenda,

who moved into the house to nanny the boy and then moved right in on the Boss. Celia was blue in them days, not being able to have no more babies after Norman. And then Glenda shows up, all tall and blond, full of youth and an obvious ambition for the Boss. Celia tried like hell to get Glenda out of that house, but by the time she cottoned to what was going on, Glenda was already under the protection of the Boss, and so no matter how many dishes was throwed, Glenda stayed and Celia just had to learn to live with it.

But then, what's a family without a little family strife.

Look at us there, the family that we was. It's all in the snapshots. Champ and me smoking stogies in Miami. Celia and Norman and the two of us in Hollywood, with our hands on the cement in front of that Chinese Theatre. Norman on the beach, fat and white, standing over a buried Mite, me with my hat still on. Norman in horse pants, getting taller, wider, his smile getting a little too familiar. The whole gang, including McGreevy and Cassandra, Istvan and Glenda and the Boss, on the Strip in Vegas, dressed in our finery, all of us all smiles, excepting of course the way Celia she looks at Glenda as the Boss wraps his arm around Glenda's whippet waist.

It was anything any of us ever could have hoped for, but it wasn't enough for Champ. Not after that last envelope.

It was just another get, nothing big. A fat cat named Gorman had something the Boss wanted to buy, a conglomeration of companies bigger than anything the Boss had bought before. McGreevy worked out a whole new financing arrangement to provide the cash. My job was to get Gorman to sell.

Except the Boss told us right off the key it wasn't Gorman his-self, but the son. And even afore I started looking I knew what I would find. Champ and me, first time we laid eyes on the boy we both of us knew.

And finding proof, what did that take?

Follow the car to the joint west by the Hudson, not far, actually, from the very pier what Sylvie used to work. Wait until the son, he slips out that bar and back to his car with a new pal. Take a few pictures and then slip inside yourself.

Smoke and fancy lights and music what was like a throbbing in your head. A place what was on the other side of the rainbow from where Champ and me we lived our lives. And the ways they dressed, with their feathers and finery, made my green outfit seem pale. Champ and me, we sat at the bar, ordered our drinks, rubbernecked like we was tourists.

"What do you think, Mick?"

"I don't likes it," I said. "It's a damn costume party. When I first came to the Square there wasn't no filly-fallying like this here. When I first came to the Square—"

"I heard it all already," said Champ. "What, are you going to tell me again about Jimmy Slaps?"

"He was an interesting guy, is all. And that's my point. There was a way of doing things then. There was a world to aspire to. But this, this is like giving up. I don't likes it."

"I don't think they care, Mick."

"Shows you what they know. Let's get to work. I'll talk up the barkeep, you start to asking around."

"I don't think so."

I stopped at that, stared at Champ, acted like I didn't know what was up, even though I certainly did. "What do you mean you don't think so?"

"I say we walk out right now and tell the Boss we didn't find a thing."

"Oh, quit your bellyaching. It's business, is all. And it ain't our business the kind of business the Boss plays at."

"But this one is, Mick, can't you see?"

"It ain't no different than Van Ater."

"No, it's not. But I didn't learn about that one till later. You purposely kept that one from me."

"Don't act like some holy shaman. You've been filling them envelopes too."

"But what those fools did is different than what they are."

"Van Ater done plenty."

"But that's not what you put in the envelope."

"I put his name is all."

"His old name."

"That he was passing hisself off as something he never was, acting like there was something to be ashamed of in being the same race as you, that didn't piss you off?"

"Just made me sad for him, Mick. Just that. You don't know what it is."

"Don't tell me I don't know what it is. It's all I ever knowed."

"And now with this boy, it's the same."

"He's a creep."

"He might be that, but that's not what you'll be putting in the envelope, is it? You give what he is to the Boss, you be betraying nothing but yourself."

"Can't say I don't deserve it."

"Maybe not, but you be betraying me too, and I won't be staying around to see that."

"I promised I'd be square with him here on in," I said. "I left him once, I can't leave him again. I don't got no choice."

"Sure you do, Mick."

But did I? Did I ever in the presence of the Boss? Not really. My fate in this world is to latch on to the strong, and no one was ever stronger than the Boss. So, yeah, I handed the envelope with the facts and the photos over to the Boss and he handed it to the Joe what owned the company and, yeah, to keep it quiet from the country club world that his married boy preferred to tango with other boys, Gorman caved. And Champ, well, he was as good as his word.

"Goodbye, Mick."

And goodbye to you, you son of a bitch.

And out of my life went something I never had before and I won't near see again. It's been a year already and still it slays me. Every day. But it was me who said goodbye first, wasn't it? And now I'm saying goodbye again, but not so quietly as Champ.

So here's the envelope what should make the race a one-horse exhibition. Look inside and you'll find everything what Harrington done to make the fortune he's using to buy his seat. All the thieving, all the swindling, an insider stock deal what already has the SEC boys hard just thinking about it. Not to mention the name of his lady friend, with the Spanish eyes and the tits like urns of soft butter, what he keeps in a pad on Park Avenue.

But when betrayal it's in your blood and bones, you end up betraying everyone who ever cared for your soul. So I'm betraying the Boss, too. Without an envelope but with a story of my own. The one I just told. You won't find any of it in the record, McGreevy he scrubbed it clear and created for the Boss an entire background as false as the lifts in my shoes, but write it up just as I told it and you'll be writing up the truth, missy. Pulitzer will be calling, and the Republican Party will soon enough be looking for a new boy to carry its hat into the race. With Champ safe and away in Mexico, I figure it's time to call in my chips.

You don't spend a chunk of your life in a place like Times Square without learning a thing or two. And what I learned was this: People, theys all liars, and the ones they lying to most of all is theyselves. Like Tab, what hustled the men's rooms and back alleys, selling hisself to men, but who insisted all along he wasn't no queer. And Tony the Tune, what was just one fighter away from the big time. And Jimmy Slaps, what was devoting his life to Jesus. And Sylvie, what was going to visit her sister and get herself well. And Old Dudley hisself, what always claimed him bloodying my lip and diddling my yard was done for my own damn good. My own damn good. And even my mother, telling me time and again everything was going to be all right. All of them, every one of them, was just lying to theyselves so they could stand the company for the next couple months or days or hours.

But I'm done with the lying, I'm here to face it all head-on. It wasn't just the last envelope what sent Champ scampering away, it was all them envelopes, taken together. He had seen enough of what I had become in the land of money, the twisted creature you see before you now, without hope or reason, hating everything about his own self, without nothing to hold on to but nothing. Like I was when I set old Times Square on fire. Infected again.

I thought I had finally beaten him away in Chicago, I thought I was free of him for good. But this is what I didn't yet know; in the land of money, Hubert prowls like a god. And in the service of the Boss, once again I was easy prey. But I've stopped fooling myself. There's only one true prescription for the son of a bitch. And I just filled it.

See, the Boss won't be letting me get away with it this time. This time he's going to finish it once and for all. With the end of the story, it's the end of me, too. But no weeping here, it's also my last chance to save myself. I'm looking forward to the fireworks. They'll burn away, finally, the leech on my soul.

So stop the tape and start to typing. Whatever's coming to smite my soul when the story runs is a gift. I'll open my arms to it like it's a lover, tall and black with big teeth and raw scarred flesh and hands like soft leather mitts to wrap you up and keep you safe.

Goodbye, missy. So long.

Kaboom.

24

As Celia Singer sewed the beads on the wedding dress, the delicate teardrops of crystal caught the morning light and sprinkled upon her a rainbow of promise.

Celia was arranging the beads in a pattern across the midriff, above the bunches of pleated silk at the top of the skirt and below the delicate sheet of lace designed to expose the swell of the breasts. It was an intricate and difficult job and Celia wore reading glasses low on her nose to be sure each stitch was exact. She could have had the seamstress do this part—these days she could have someone do everything for her and often did—but she was enjoying the task.

The wedding seemed to be happening around her as if conjured by a spell. It was being planned by planners, catered by caterers, the guest list was being compiled by high-priced political consultants. The ceremony and reception were being covered by the press as if it were the marriage of a prince instead of a politician, which was all part of a political strategy to turn candidate into celebrity. Jerry had hired hired-guns from the publicity departments of Hollywood studios, he had bought space in gossip columns coast to coast. The wedding was simply another leg of the marketing campaign. But it was more than that to Celia, this wedding, and that was why she insisted on sewing the beads herself, stitch by careful stitch.

She couldn't help but remember her mother in the same pose, glasses perched on her nose as she sewed in the parlor. In those days, Celia was always with a book, one Brontë or the other, Balzac, Flaubert, anything that made the librarian sniff. Sometimes, in the evenings, she would look up from the tumescent prose and see her mother sitting quietly, working slowly within the ambit of the lamp, and believe quite earnestly that her mother must be the most boring woman alive. For the whole of her life, she had felt as if she were fleeing the banal priorities her mother had tried to impose upon her. Yet now here she was, having made all her choices, in the same pose as her mother, peering through her reading glasses at the needle, the fabric, the thread.

Her feelings about her mother had changed markedly. Partly it was the conversion that happens to every daughter upon the death of her mother, the bleeding out of anger that accompanies the lowering of the coffin. But it was also a realization that came to her slowly in the past few years. Those long-ago nights in the parlor, her mother wasn't simply sewing on sleeves, embroidering towels, darning socks, knitting scarves, her mother wasn't simply manufacturing objects. She was knitting together the fabric of her family. And that's what Celia felt she was doing now, as she fastened each bead in its proper place. Celia had shed the trappings of religion long ago, and no longer even pretended to the false piety that made life easier among polite folk, but still, this wedding had acquired for her a transcendent significance.

The familiar shuffle across the early morning hush, the familiar creak of the floorboards.

"It is Mr. Pimelia, mum."

"Thank you, Chalmers," said Celia without glancing up. "Send him in please."

"Very good, mum."

She lifted her face to him as he entered the wide formal living room and an unbidden smile brightened her countenance. The same jaunty stride, the same loud suit, the wiseacre's half grin. He was unchanged since the first time she saw him in the Automat, except for the eyes. The desperate hope of the rain-soaked teenage hustler had been replaced by the weary sadness of a short, middle-aged man who had gotten more than he ever could have dreamed in this life and found it wasn't enough. Poor Mite, she thought. It was part of all that desperate wanting, never to be satisfied.

"He's not up yet," said Celia.

"I figured as much," said Mite as he picked an apple out of the bowl, tossed it, snatched it from the air, rubbed it on his sleeve. "But I thought it'd be better to get here early. Don't want him waiting on me, not today."

"I didn't know you two had an appointment."

"Not officially," he said, falling into a chair and biting the apple all in one graceful movement, "but he'll be wanting to see me, I knows that."

"How'd it go yesterday? We were expecting you back."

"It went a little long," said Mite.

She lowered her chin, peered over her glasses. "Everything go as planned?"

"What could go wrong? A piece of birthday cake, it was. Except for the missy, who to tell you the truth wasn't so bright. I had to spell out some things. What, was the Boss asking after me?"

She noticed the worry in his face. Mite never could hide his emotions. It was the one thing she found most annoying in him.

"No," said Celia. "He was busy meeting with the former governor."

"That stuck-up sumbitch?"

"He's been very helpful."

"You gots to watch out for a guy you can't buy, Celia. You can't never trust them. The boy up yet?"

"Already scrubbed and fed and off to school."

Mite glanced at his apple. "Surprised there's still a piece of fruit left. Glenda take care of him?"

"Hardly. She's still in bed."

"With all she's putting away each night, that's no surprise. But that dress is looking jimmy."

"Thank you." She pushed herself out of the chair, held the dress high so that the hem of the skirt barely brushed the floor. "Almost ready."

"Smashing," he said. "The hit of the evening, you ask me. I'd love to see it sashaying down the aisle, I would."

"You will."

"Maybe not, Celia. I might be busy that day."

"Don't be silly. Of course you'll be there. The governor's going to be the best man."

"Rockefeller?"

"Isn't that thrilling?"

"He sure has come up in the world," said Mite. "Rocke-feller, I mean."

She sat down again, bunched the dress on her lap, looked carefully at Mite. That same worry in his face, and something else too. Bitterness? Yes, and also fear. Fear of whom? Whom else?

"Papers arrive?" he said.

"Not yet. Cassandra went out to get them. Can't wait to see the headlines."

"Oh, they'll be something, they will."

"I never much cared for Harrington," said Celia, leaning back in her chair, turning her attention back to the beads. "He doesn't know how to smile. That should be a fundamental re-quirement for being considered human, don't you think?"

"The Boss gots no problem there."

"I guess our friend Mr. Harrington will be smiling even less after this morning."

"He won't be the only one with an itch."

She let out an exaggerated sigh of resignation as she con-tinued to work. "What did you do, Mickey?"

"Only what I should have done afore all this started."

"And what is that?"

"I told the missy everything."

"About what?"

"About the Boss. From the beginning. From when I found him, to the times on Times Square, to the money he was shoveling to the president."

She tried to hide her dismay. Still staring at the dress, she said as calmly as she could manage, "Mickey, you shouldn't have."

"Sures I should. Isn't that what I've become? Isn't that what he's made of me? A teller of tales? And who's got a richer tale to tell, let me ask you, than the Boss?"

She leaned close to the fabric, positioned a bead exactly atop the mark on the pattern. She felt the fear rise in her, unsteadying her hand. There's always something upsetting the balance, turning everything on its head. Just when you make your peace with all you've given up and think all is settled, it starts breaking apart. One more thing to take care of. She took a deep breath before plunging the needle.

"Maybe you shouldn't be here when he finds out," she said.

"Where else would I be?"

"While you're away, I could talk to him. Calm him down."

"I don't wants him calm. If you're gonna sing, you gots to face the music."

She looked up, smiled at him. "You always do, don't you? I'll give you that. This is just like before."

"Before what?"

"Big Johnny Callas. Remember how you stayed around even after you stiffed him his two hundred dollars?"

"That Greek meatball? Yeah, I remembers."

"And then when you came back to Jerry after the explosion. It's the same thing over again."

Mite turned his head away. "Maybe so."

"You know what it was that brought you back? You couldn't leave him. None of us can. But you beat yourself up about it when you should embrace it. You love him. You always have. You love him, we all do, and there's nothing wrong with that."

"Celia, don't be cracked. He's just the Boss is all he is to me, a meal ticket."

"You were true to your heart. You knew where you belonged. Right here with us."

"But not no more, Celia. Not after what I done to his run for the Senate. I thought it was a crap idea from the start. There was no percentage in it, no profit. What was we going to do in a place like Washington, nobbing with the hobs?"

"It will be fabulous," said Celia. "The balls, the intrigue."

"It ain't for me. And now it's done."

"Oh, Mickey, how long have you been with him? And you still don't understand?"

"He won't take it lying down."

"Maybe not," she said. She glanced up at him to be sure he was listening. "Why don't you take a small vacation? Maybe even leave the country. I'll have Cassandra make the arrangements. You can fly to San Diego, catch a bus to Ensenada."

"Ensenada? Why would I go to Ensenada? With the water they got, I'll be crapping out my brains."

She smiled. "And that's a problem how?"

"There ain't nothing for me in Mexico."

"Now who's not facing the music? You can't keep blaming Jerry for what happened, Mickey."

"I'll blame who the hell I want to blame."

"Don't you think it's time you pay him a call?"

"Nope."

"He owns a fishing boat. He takes the tourists out to catch tuna and sea bass."

"I don't care."

"McGreevy set it up for him without him knowing it was set up."

Mite looked up. "You think he doesn't know?"

"I don't know, Mickey. Maybe he does."

"It don't make no difference even so. I ain't going down to Mexico and what's in Mexico ain't got nothing to do with what I done."

"You know what it's called? The boat?"

Before she could tell him, Cassandra entered the living room, striding forward in her heels, clutching a stack of newspapers. "Shocked is what I am," she said in her Bronx screech. "Shocked."

Celia couldn't help but admire the woman who stood before her. Her hair had thinned over the years, but it was still high, her legs were still sturdy. She was older than Celia, and it showed on her face, but she had kept her figure with all its luxuriant curves, and her waist hadn't yet thickened with age as had Celia's.

"Something in the papers?" said Celia calmly.

Mite shrank back into his chair, readying himself for the inevitable.

"Who would have thought," said Cassandra, a sly smile breaking out on her face, "that our nice Mr. Harrington was such a rotten tomato?"

Mite sat up. "Let me see them things," he said, reaching out and snapping his fingers.

"I'm aghast is what I am, aghast," said Cassandra as she tossed the papers in front of him, one by one, their headlines spinning in the air until each landed splat on the floor.

HARRINGTON CAUGHT WITH PARK AVENUE LOVE NEST

SENATE SWINDLE, HARRINGTON'S SORDID ROAD TO RICHES

HARRINGTON UNDER INVESTIGATION BY SEC

HARRINGTON DENIES BEATING WIFE

Mite picked through the papers, staring dumbly at the headlines, before grabbing one and opening it. He paged quickly through, looking for something specific. Finally, he looked up at Celia with an expression of disbelief on his face.

"There ain't nothing in the missy's rag about the Boss," said Mite.

"Of course not," she said.

"I don't understand."

"What did you think, M-M-Mite?" said the pale-faced McGreevy from the doorway. He was in his black-vested suit, he was leaning against the doorframe. "That we'd let you ruin everything?"

"The missy," said Mite with a bite of anger in his voice. "I knowed there was something I didn't like about her."

"Bought and p-p-paid for, before ever we let you get close to her."

"I should have seen it right off," said Mite. "What with all the shrimp. What kind of reporter's got shrimp in her suite?"

"Ours," said McGreevy.

"You bastards set me up."

"They were protecting you," said Celia, her attention back on the dress. She tightened a thread, another bead slipped into place.

"They were protecting the Boss," said Mite.

"Oh, sweetheart," said Celia, "you still don't understand. He doesn't need our protection."

"I'll just tells someone else," said Mite, standing.

"No you won't," said Jerry, now passing McGreevy as he strode into the room.

Behind him, the dour-faced Albert Gladden slunk beside McGreevy, forming a sort of wall of business, barring the door.

Jerry wore his sunglasses, a white silk ascot, a brown silk robe belted tight around his waist. He reached out and patted Cassandra's neck. She bent her head toward his hand like a cat. He leaned over the chair where Celia sat with the wedding dress on her lap and kissed her on the lips. Celia's hands gripped tightly the silk as she felt the rasp of his tongue in her mouth. Like someone was reaching inside and gently squeezing the breath out of her. It was always like that, even after all these years.

"I betrayed you," said Mite. "I told her everything."

"She thought you were insane," said Jerry, still smiling at Celia.

"There was a tape."

"I ate it," said Jerry.

"I owes you, you bastard."

"We owe each other, Mite."

"I'm through."

"No you're not," said Jerry, rising up again and turning toward Mite. "The two of us, we'll never be through."

Celia stared at her men as they went back and forth, Mite and Jerry, and still suffused as she was with the emotions of the kiss, she saw something she had never seen before. But it was now so clear, she didn't understand how she could have missed it. It was in the connection, the rebellion, the unbreakable bond. Their relationship wasn't just boss to employee, or like brother to brother, it was stronger. Jerry had become to Mite like a father. And that explained Mite's twin needs to both please and destroy. And Jerry seemed to understand it too. It was why he always allowed Mite to stray, and why he always took him back. And it was part of what Jerry felt for Istvan too, and McGreevy, and Cassandra, and Norman, and even for herself, in a way that both appalled and thrilled her. He had become as a father to them all.

There was a moment when they stood face to face, Jerry and Mite, father and son, and their future together seemed to tremble.

"Sweet pea," said Jerry as he reached out a hand.

Mite didn't step forward, Mite didn't grasp the hand or hug

the man before him or turn around and bolt. Instead, he looked at the outstretched hand, and then Jerry's face, and then he slipped down again into the chair, as if something had collapsed inside him.

"So it is settled," said Jerry.

"You're a son of a bitch," said Mite.

"I never knew my mother," said Jerry, "so you're probably right. Now, boys. What's the word?"

"Harrington is scrambling to stay alive," said McGreevy. "But our inside sources tell us he got a call this morning from the m-m-mayor. He's being pressed to drop out."

"He'll be gone by the end of the week," said Gladden. "They'll draft Paglia."

"Is that trouble?"

"Paglia is popular in the outer boroughs," said Gladden.

"I'll need you again, Mite," said Jerry.

But Mite didn't respond. Still slumped in the chair, his chin resting on his chest, Mite was lost. The men continued their discussion, walking to the wet bar at the end of the room to plan and plot. Cassandra went into the hallway to answer the ringing phone. Celia held the wedding dress on her lap and waited for Mite. When he looked up, finally, his lips were quivering and it was as if his eyes were focused on some distant shore.

"You never got around to telling me," he said softly.

"The boat's called *Mick's First Mate*," she said.

"Damn," said Mite.

"Should I tell Cassandra to get the tickets?"

"Three words and he's routed again," said Mite, softly, to himself. "It shouldn't be so easy."

"I'll have her get the tickets," said Celia Singer, the soft glow of satisfaction warming her.

This wedding was going to be so special. It was going to be the physical manifestation of everything for which she had ever dreamed, and for which her mother had dreamed too. It was going to create for her, permanently, the family she had always truly wanted. Jerry, yes, and Norman, and Mite too, because he was part of it, surely. And now even Champ would return and join them again. He wouldn't stay on that old boat of his when Mite beckoned him back. This wedding, she knew, was going to be the greatest day of her life. And then, at the edge of her vision, she spotted something swaying in the doorway, all in white.

It was Glenda, in a gauzy white dressing gown, her feet bare, an empty glass in her hand, swaying, as if the slightest of reeds swaying in the wind. Her skin was pale, her blue eyes watery, her lips swollen red. Her beautiful heart-shaped face seemed to float above her narrow shoulders, which in turn seemed disconnected from her thin waist, her slim hips, her long slender legs which showed through the gossamer gown. She looked about the room as if comprehending nothing.

"I don't . . ." she said. "I can't . . ."

"Jerry dear," said Celia, "it's Glenda."

Jerry turned to her, lifted his arms wide. Glenda rose on her toes, staggered slightly to the left.

"Look, Jerry," said Celia, standing now, with the dress in her hands. "Look how exquisite she'll be."

She stepped over to Glenda and lifted the wedding dress so that its shoulders were at Glenda's shoulders, its arms at

Glenda's arms. The pattern of beads traced along Glenda's waist and the hem of the skirt just barely brushed the floor at Glenda's feet. Glenda staggered again, as if under the weight of the garment.

"Lovely," said Jerry. "Just lovely."

Celia was filled with an exultant joy. She leaned forward and kissed Glenda on the forehead. "You'll make the most beautiful, beautiful bride," she said. And she meant every word of it.

25

Kockroach stands at the center of his world. He can feel them all around him, on every side of him, rubbing him and patting him, grabbing him and hugging him. Since his strange molt, it is the closest he has come to feeling, among the humans, the purity of the colony as it huddles and writhes together. There are shouts, shrieks of jubilation, there is a shiver of exultation running through them all. He can smell all of them, each one of them, as they clamber about him. Celia and Glenda, Norman, Cassandra, Champ back from Mexico, Istvan and Gladden, McGreevy and Mite. His colony.

In the distance, the chanting of a name as if it were the name of a god.

Blatta. Blatta. Blatta. Blatta.

The excitement sparks all about him like the burning of a fuse rushing toward some great pile of explosives. The enthusiasm puzzles him, the prize seems so small. To be a senator is to be a barnacle on the rear end of a whale, a parasite along for a pointless ride. Senators are cheaper to buy than buildings. Better to sit on a toilet seat than in the Senate. But every rise needs a first step. In the world of crime, he first was an enforcer. In the world of business, he first was an exterminator. In the world of politics, he first will be a senator.

As he stands in that room behind the stage, surrounded by his colony, he closes his eyes and watches the ribbons of possibility float like writhing snakes into the future. He sees a chessboard of white and brown squares that stretches beyond the city, beyond the country, that spans continents and bridges oceans. His pieces move forward in brutal ranks along columns and diagonals, thwarting attacks, smashing defenses, always advancing. And slowly, magnificently, the chessboard itself begins to change. The white squares shift and darken until the whole board is one huge surface of brown. The brown of his chitin in his earlier life. It will cover the world, he can make it happen.

"It's t-t-time," says McGreevy.

Kockroach knows what to do, as if he were reborn for this moment. The colony parts. He grabs Glenda's hand, steadies her, and then pulls her from behind the curtain and onto the stage. There is more chanting, there are bright lights, there is music. A writhing mass of people stand before him, clapping and jumping and shouting. At the lectern, with his human name emblazoned in red white and blue, Kockroach raises his hands, fingers splayed into twin V's, and quiets the crowd.

"Tonight," he says in a voice that resounds through the ballroom and races across the night sky to the televisions of an entire nation, "tonight is the dawning of a new and glorious era for America."

ACKNOWLEDGMENTS

For their brilliant assistance with, and support for, this novel,
I wish to thank the following:
David Roth-Ey;
Carolyn Marino;
Amy Robbins;
Will Staehle;
Lisa Gallagher;
Michael Morrison;
Wendy Sherman;
Larry Gringlas;
Nate Allen;
My wife; and
My dog.
For any failures of substance, craft, or taste, blame the dog.

My primary entomological reference was an apartment in
the East Village, where I was able to study at close hand the
fauna of New York City. Among a host of other sources used
were *The Compleat Cockroach*, by David George Gordon, a
series of Insect Morphology Posters produced by B. K. Mitch-

ell and J. S. Scott at the University of Alberta, and a quite peculiar paper on the effect of parasitoid wasp venom on cockroach grooming behavior, written by Aviva Weisel-Eichler, Gal Haspel and Frederic Libersat at Ben-Gurion University of the Negev in Israel. Less well known than the cockroach is the common cockroach mite, found within the genus *Pimeliaphilus*, notable for its small size and deficient grammar.

T. Knox

About the author

About the book

Insights,
Interviews
& More . . .

Read on

A Conversation with Tyler Knox

What inspired you to write a "reverse take" on The Metamorphosis?

Kockroach started as one of those ideas that seem to float out of the sky, one after the other like snowflakes only to disappear an instant later upon hitting the ground.

My friend Larry was thinking of writing a book and I threw out some ideas that seemed to fit the books he liked to read, novels like *The Moustache* and *The Joke* and *The Unbearable Lightness of Being*. Writers throw around ideas like football coaches throw around plays or politicians hit up lobbyists for money; it's what we do, compulsively. In the course of the discussion I thought of *The Metamorphosis* and I told Larry he should write a book about a cockroach who woke up as a man and we laughed about that and came up with some other ideas which were considerably less insane. But that night, I started thinking about the idea, working it out. I didn't see it as a book yet, but I saw it as something that might lead to something and so the next day I called Larry and asked him if he was actually going to use the bug idea. He laughed and said no and then I, as politely and as nonchalantly as I

could, asked him if I could have it back and
he graciously agreed and that was how I
swindled Larry out of the idea. He still
hasn't quite forgiven me. I didn't see the
possible novel as a tribute to Kafka—his
work doesn't need my tribute—or as a
parody, but as something springing wholly
new and American from his original
concept.

What is Mite's role in the story?

Early on I realized the book needed a
character other than Kockroach to bring the
story some breadth. During my research,
I learned about the mites that live off
cockroach colonies and that ultimately can
destroy them and from that I had an idea for
a secondary character. I wanted to call him
Mite, but it was such a strange name that I
figured I had to introduce it right off and so I
came up with his first line, "They call
me Mite. You got a problem with that?" And
right there, as soon as I wrote that line, I
thought I might have something that would
be interesting beyond the first ten pages.

*Why did you decide to set the novel in
New York City in the 1950s, the era of
the McCarthy hearings and the Beat
Generation? What was it about the
time period that appealed to you for
Kockroach's transformation?* ▶

Meet Tyler Knox

TYLER KNOX holds
a master of fine
arts degree from
the Iowa Writers'
Workshop. He is a
former resident
of New York City;
Chicago; Iowa City;
Washington, D.C.;
and now lives on the
East Coast with his
wife and their dog.

A Conversation with Tyler Knox *(continued)*

There was something about the surface level of conformity of the time, evidenced by the boxy suits and narrow ties and fedoras—think *The Man in the Gray Flannel Suit*—that appealed to me. It seemed like a perfect place for Kockroach to blend in. But it wasn't all conformity; Ginsberg wrote *Howl* in 1956 and Kerouac published *On the Road* one year later. That tension between the conformity and the rebellion seemed perfect for the interplay between Kockroach and Mite. I also figured if you wanted a metamorphosis to take place in a seedy flophouse off of the Square, the mid-fifties were perfect, a neon fueled time of hustlers and swingers, a last great dip on the dance floor before Times Square fell into the sad and sordid cesspool it became in the sixties. And of course it helped that there were some great photographs and films that helped give me a sense of the place and time, including some photographs I put on the kockroach.com Web site.

In The Metamorphosis, *Kafka never actually states that Gregor Samsa transformed into a cockroach. Why did you decide to make the protagonist of your novel transform from this species, and not another insect or animal?*

66 There was something about the surface level of conformity of [the 1950s], evidenced by the boxy suits and narrow ties and fedoras—think *The Man in the Gray Flannel Suit*—that appealed to me. 99

Everyone just assumes the bug in Kafka's book was a cockroach, so it was an easy misconception to take advantage of. But, more important, I don't think the book would have worked as well with any other creature. Spiders, for example, are patient and clever and build webs and traps, which seems a bit too familiar. Every soap opera is loaded with spiders. And every family has a leech, doesn't it? We've anthropomorphized so many other animals and insects that we see their type all the time, bulls playing football, catlike divas, the loyal sidekick who fulfills the role of a dog. But the natural revulsion we feel for cockroaches allowed me to work from a fairly clean slate as I created Kockroach. And I liked the name.

How would you describe Kockroach?

He's a force of nature, a being outside any traditional notions of morality. Is a tornado evil? Of course not, it just is, and so is Kockroach. In this way he reminds me of some of the girls I dated in the past. In addition he has no prejudice or vanity, no bitterness or deep-seated desire for revenge. He wants and he fears and he lets those two impulses drive him. Let's just say it wasn't as much a stretch as I would have hoped to pop into his head. Just ask Larry. ⌒

> " [Kockroach is] a force of nature, a being outside any traditional notions of morality. "

A Brief Essay on the Genre of *Kockroach*

by Tyler Knox

AS A NOVEL, *Kockroach* fits neatly within the confines of a quite robust genre entitled American Existential Pulp, or AEP. You won't find any conferences on AEP or a pack of tweedy English professors debating its virtues in academic journals because, well, because I made the thing up. Pretty much on the spot. But I still was trying to write within the confines of my made-up genre when I wrote the novel, and I'm not the first.

The great existential works that made me want to become a writer in the first place were books like *The Stranger*, *The Plague*, and *The Myth of Sisyphus* by Camus, *Nausea* and *No Exit* by Sartre, *The Trial* and *The Metamorphosis* by Kafka, *Fear and Trembling* by Kierkegaard, and *The Unbearable Lightness of Being* by Kundera. These books all deal with the conflict between man's desire for order and purpose in a universe inherently disorderly and purposeless. That they often also deal with sex is just a bonus. (Am I the only one who thinks Meursault's girlfriend, Marie Cardona, is way hot?) But as you may notice, all of these works are penned by Europeans, most by

❝ You won't find any conferences on AEP [American Existential Pulp] or a pack of tweedy English professors debating its virtues in academic journals because, well, because I made the thing up. ❞

6

Frenchmen. *Sacre bleu*. Maybe it's something in the foie gras, but the French seem to do existential better than we Americans do.

What Americans do better than anyone is pulp. We started the magazines that defined it—magazines like *Argosy*, *Black Mask*, and *Amazing Stories*—we filled the magazines with murder and mayhem, and we sent those lurid pages all over the world to do their dirty work. Cowboy stories, boxing stories, adventure stories, detective stories, penned by great writers like Raymond Chandler, Robert E. Howard, and H. P. Lovecraft; stories inhabited with classic characters like Tarzan and Philip Marlowe. If you don't think Camus loved pulp then you haven't read *The Stranger* lately, a novel loaded with casual cruelty and casual sex and a cold-blooded murder at high noon. And have you noticed the way the author often seems to be pictured in a trench coat with a cigarette in his lips as if he's channeling Humphrey Bogart playing Sam Spade?

So as an American, I decided that if I was going to get existential—and I sadly admit that I had a hankering to do just that, since I couldn't stop looking around at the world and saying, "What the . . ."—it was probably best to do it in a pulp sort of way, and to do it in stories with American settings and dealing with American issues, like violence and politics and money and sex. (Yes, yes, I know, violence and politics ▶

> " If you don't think Camus loved pulp then you haven't read *The Stranger* lately, a novel loaded with casual cruelty and casual sex and a cold-blooded murder at high noon. "

and money and sex run through the world like the sewers run through Paris, but we do them all our own special way, flavored by an intractable vestige of Puritanism combined with our irritating sense of exceptionality and manifest destiny.) And thankfully, I had a lot of models.

There was often an inherent existential strain in the old pulp stories. *Red Harvest*, by Dashiell Hammett, a classic pulp tale about the efforts of a private eye to clean up a town plagued by crime and violence, seems not so different than a Camus novel about the efforts of the stirring Dr. Rieux to clean up a town plagued by, of all things, the plague. In both novels the hero seems motivated only by the need to fight against disorder, whether or not he can actually prevail. In another great Hammett novel, *The Maltese Falcon*, there is a brilliant bit in chapter 7 about a man named Flitcraft that, with its insight into the human condition, in three and a half pages outdoes the whole of Sartre's *Being and Nothingness*.

This inherent existential strain in the classic hard-boiled detective story was made overt in the seminal postmodern AEP work, Paul Auster's New York trilogy (*City of Glass*, *Ghosts*, and *The Locked Room*), where the detectives and the investigations are turned in on themselves over and again until the only question left is *Who the hell am I?*

> 66 This inherent existential strain in the classic hard-boiled detective story was made overt in the seminal postmodern AEP work, Paul Auster's New York trilogy. 99

The *Washington Post* wrote of the trilogy, "It's as if Kafka had gotten hooked on the gumshoe game." Hmmm. Detective and gangster stories are the perfect AEP vehicles, as seen in books like Jonathan Lethem's *Gun, with Occasional Music*, my favorite of his many astonishing novels, and *Hit Man* by Lawrence Block (you may wonder what he's doing here; read the book and find out).

But it's not just crime stories that fit the genre. Great AEP novels have been written out of the pulp boxing story, such as *Fat City* by Leonard Gardner (maybe the most perfect American novel since *The Great Gatsby*), and *Fight Club* by Chuck Palahniuk (such a brilliant novel that scores of writers have been ruined writing under its influence. The first rule of *Fight Club* is never to try to write like *Fight Club*. The second rule of *Fight Club* is . . .). There are also AEP novels in that tradition of the pulp science fiction story, such as *Freaks' Amour* by Tom De Haven (an overlooked but wonderful book with one of my all-time favorite titles), and the pulp cowboy story, like *Blood Meridian* by Cormac McCarthy. I could cite some AEP adventure stories, but no writer could be more AEP than Robert E. Howard himself. Can't you just imagine Flaubert saying, *Conan le Barbare, c'est moi*? Me neither, but then Flaubert was no existentialist. ▶

A Brief Essay on the Genre of *Kockroach*
(*continued*)

It was in this rich, and, now that I notice it, rather crowded genre, that I was trying to work when I wrote *Kockroach*. I figured the novel would be part fantasy, part detective story, part gangster story, part political pulp (they say all politics is local, I say all politics is pulp) mixed together with questions of how to live within a world where the rules are indecipherable. AEP to its core. And that it included some hot cockroach sex merely sealed its place within the genre. It wouldn't be the first AEP novel, I knew, and it wouldn't be the last.

I have a dream that someday American Existential Pulp will grow and flourish in the stream of American letters. College courses will extol it, whole sections of bookstores will be devoted to it, PhDs in AEP will roll off the line like Buicks, even as politicians bang their desks and denounce AEP as the primary cause of juvenile delinquency in America. But inevitably, in a decade or two, some adjunct professor from a small college in Idaho will create a furor by declaring the death of AEP and be awarded a tenured position at Harvard. And so the dream will seem to end, except at the same moment AEP's funeral bell is being tolled, some kid in Kansas will hold *The Stranger* in one hand and *The Big Sleep* in the other and get an idea for a story. I can't wait to see what she comes up with. ∾

66 That *Kockroach* included some hot cockroach sex merely sealed its place within the genre. 99

Author's Picks
Ten Recommended Works

THE MOST OBVIOUS inspiration for
Kockroach is Kafka's *The Metamorphosis*,
a work of utter brilliance that has
haunted me since the first time I read it in
high school. But I admit to shamelessly
modeling bits and pieces of the book
from a whole host of sources that have
thrilled me over the years. The following
is a list of ten of those works and how
they were important to me in the writing
of the book:

1. ALL THE KING'S MEN (1946), by Robert Penn Warren

This book is known for its portrait of Willie
Stark, a powerful and corrupt populist
politician, but for me its great strength is the
voice of Jack Burden, my favorite narrator
in all of American fiction. Mite doesn't have
the poetics of Jack Burden, but his self-
loathing is a direct descendant of Jack's.

2. THE HUSTLER (1961), by Robert Rossen (director)

Walter Tevis's novel is really good, but I
have to say that this film is the nuts. I love

the scene where Paul Newman comes back
to the hotel room with his thumbs broken,
but the character who really caught my
heart was the lame girlfriend he comes
back to. Piper Laurie plays her as such an
archetypal American figure that she
immediately came to mind as I started
writing Celia. But Celia was also partially
inspired by Hopper's *Automat*.

3. AUTOMAT (1927), a painting by Edward Hopper

Hopper is a painter of spaces, no matter
how many figures are in a Hopper painting
they each are alone, as is the woman in this
painting, a solitary figure drinking her
coffee by the large plate glass window of
the Automat. Is the image familiar? By the
way, if you want to see what a wall of the
Automat looked like, they have one
installed in the ice cream parlor at the
Smithsonian National Museum of
American History in D.C.

4. ON THE ROAD (1957), by Jack Kerouac

On the Road is one of those books that can
be quite dangerous if read at the wrong
time in your life and I am so glad I read it
at the exact wrong time. I always
remembered the scenes of Sal and Carlo

cruising through Times Square with all the hucksters and prostitutes and drug addicts. That's the Times Square I wanted to write about. I even put the two of them in the Automat scene just for the heck of it. A couple other Times Square sources listed below.

5. THE SWEET SMELL OF SUCCESS (1957), by Alexander Mackendrick (director)

This film is a bit melodramatic, but Burt Lancaster's dialogue is a hoot and the movie was filmed in the Times Square of the very era I was writing about. Watching it is like walking through the book. For example, I had heard of Toots Shore's place for years, but the first glimpse I got of its round bar and swanky denizens was in the movie. Tony Curtis is quite good in the film, a hustler as desperate as Mite, but with a prettier face.

6. CITY OF NIGHT (1963), by John Rechy

This brilliant novel, which includes a heartbreaking section about street hustlers in Times Square that was part of the inspiration for Tab, has one of my favorite opening lines: "Later I would think of America as one vast City of Night stretching gaudily from Times

> *Tony Curtis is quite good in [The Sweet Smell of Success], a hustler as desperate as Mite, but with a prettier face.*

Square to Hollywood Boulevard—
jukebox-winking, rock-n-roll moaning:
America at night fusing its dark cities
into the unmistakable shape of
loneliness." I think Rechy must have read
Kerouac at the wrong time too.

7. THE TIMES SQUARE STORY (1998), by Geoffrey O'Brien

A great collection of Times Square
photographs all tied together with some
brilliantly hyperbolic prose.

8. SIN CITY (1994), by Frank Miller

I'd be remiss if I didn't put a comic book
in here. As a reader I started with the
classics, *Robinson Crusoe, The Count of
Monte Cristo, The Complete Sherlock
Holmes,* but I graduated, much to my
mother's disappointment, into comic
books. I loved the speed, the action, the
outlandishness, and have tried to inject
that into my work. Frank Miller wrote
some great Daredevil comics and then
redid Batman in scintillating fashion, but
his Sin City series is the purest
illumination of his rather twisted psyche.
All in the series are a blast, but the first is
the best, with his antihero, Marv, ending
up in the electric chair and damn glad to
be there.

9. RED HARVEST (1929), by Dashiell Hammett

An absolute pulp classic about a lone operative for a national detective agency cleaning up a rotten town by pitting the differing gangs and corrupt police department one against the other until everyone ends up dead. 'Nuff said.

10. LORD JIM (1900), by Joseph Conrad

This might seem way off track, but it is one of the books read by Mite in his early years hanging out in the library, though I took out the reference during my rewrites as I tightened up the Mite sections. Conrad's novel, one of the great adventure yarns of all time, is a strange and marvelous story of redemption in a strange land. The book was on my mind as I wrote of Mite seeking his redemption in the wilds of Times Square. And I have to say, the little bit about the failed guano mining enterprise is one of my favorite parts of any novel I've ever read.

> " [*Lord Jim*] is one of the books read by Mite in his early years hanging out in the library, though I took out the reference during my rewrites as I tightened up the Mite sections. "